RED MANDARIN DRESS

THE INSPECTOR CHEN MYSTERIES

Death of a Red Heroine

A Loyal Character Dancer

When Red is Black

A Case of Two Cities

Red Mandarin Dress

RED MANDARIN DRESS

QIU XIAOLONG

SCEPTRE

First published in the United States of America in 2007 by St Martin's Press
This international edition published in 2007 by Hodder & Stoughton
An Hachette Livre UK company

A Sceptre book

1

A CIP catalogue record for this title is available from the British Library

ISBN 978 0 340 93517 0

Typeset in Adobe Garamond

Printed and bound by Clays Ltd, St Ives plc

Hodder Headline's policy is to use papers that are natural, renewable
and recyclable products and made from wood grown in sustainable forests.
The logging and manufacturing processes are expected to conform to
the environmental regulations of the country of origin.

Hodder & Stoughton Ltd
A division of Hodder Headline
338 Euston Road
London NW1 3BH

To my elder brother, Xiaowei—
but for luck, what happened to him during the
Cultural Revolution could have happened to me.

ACKNOWLEDGMENTS

As with other books, I have a long list of people to thank for their help, among whom, particularly, Lin Huiying, a celebrated mandarin dress designer in Shanghai, for her expert lessons; Patricia Mirrlees, a friend I met twenty years ago in Beijing, for her continuing support after all these years; and Keith Kahla, my editor at St. Martin's Press, for his extraordinary work.

RED MANDARIN DRESS

PROLOGUE

RUNNING ALONG WEST HUAIHAI Road, his breath foggy under the fading stars, Worker Master Huang counted himself as one of the earliest birds in Shanghai. In his mid-seventies, he still ran with vigorous steps. After all, health could be more valuable than anything else, he thought proudly, wiping away the sweat on his forehead. For those sickly Big Bucks, what could all the gold and silver mountains in their backyards possibly mean?

But there was little else for a retired worker like Huang to pride himself on now, in the mid-nineties, as the materialistic transformation was sweeping over the city.

Huang had seen better days. A model worker in the sixties, a Mao Zedong Thought Propaganda Team member during the Cultural Revolution, a neighborhood security in the eighties—in short, a onetime "worker master" of the politically glorious working class in China.

Now he was nobody. A retiree of a nearly bankrupt state-run steel mill, he had a hard time making ends meet on his ever-shrinking pension. Even the title "Worker Master" sounded ironically rusty in the Party newspapers.

"Socialist China gone to capitalist dogs." The refrain from recent doggerel came back to his mind, as if in a counter rhythm to his steps. Everything was changing fast, beyond comprehension.

His jogging was changing too. In the past, running in the starlit solitude, few vehicles visible, he had enjoyed the feeling of the city pulsing along with him. Now at this early hour, he was aware of cars driving around, occasionally honking too, and of a crane cranking in a new construction site one block ahead. It was said to be an upper-class apartment complex for the newly rich.

Not too far away, his old *shikumen*-style house, where he had been living along with a dozen working-class families, was about to be pulled down for a commercial high-rise. Soon the residents were going to be relocated to Pudong, an area that was once farmland east of the Huangpu River. After that there would be no possibility of a morning jog along this familiar street, in the center of the city. Nor could he enjoy a bowl of soy soup served by the Worker and Farmer Eatery around the corner. The steaming hot soup flavored with chopped green onion, dried shrimp, minced fried dough, and purple seaweed—so delicious, yet only five cents. The cheap eatery, once advocated "for its dedication to the working-class people," had disappeared, and now in its place stood a Starbucks coffee shop.

Perhaps he was too old to understand the change. Huang sighed, his steps growing heavy, his eyelids twitching ominously. Near the intersection of Huaihai and Donghu Roads, the sight of the safety island further slowed him down. It had looked like a flower bed in the spring, but now so barren, brown with bare twigs trembling in the wind—bleak, like his mind.

There he glimpsed an alien object, red and white, in the pale ring of the island lamplight—possibly something dropped from a farm truck on its way to the nearby food market. The white part looked like a long lotus root, sticking out of a sack made of what might be old red flags. He had heard stories about farmers putting everything to use, even those five-starred flags. He had also heard that lotus root slices filled with sticky rice had recently become popular in high-end restaurants.

Taking two steps toward the island, he came to a halt, shocked.

What he had taken as a white lotus root turned into a shapely human leg glistening with dewdrops. Nor was it a sack, but a red mandarin dress that encased the body of a young woman, probably in her early twenties. Her face already appeared waxy.

Squatting down, he tried to examine the body. The dress was lifted up, high above her waist, her thighs and groin shining obscenely under the ghastly light. The dress slits torn, several double-fish-shaped bosom buttons unbuttoned, her breast peeping out. Barefoot and bare-legged, she wore nothing under the tight-fitting dress.

He touched the girl's ankle. Cold. No pulse. Her pink-painted toenails still somehow petallike. How long she had been lying there dead? He pulled the dress down over her thighs. The dress itself, sort of a stylish one, seemed inexplicable. Originally worn by the Manchurian, a ruling ethic minority group during the Qing dynasty, hence it became so trendy in the thirties that people took it as the national dress without caring about its ethnic origin. After its disappearance during the Cultural Revolution as a symbol of the bourgeois lifestyle, it had staged a surprising comeback among the rich in recent years. But he had never seen anyone wearing it like that—without panties or shoes.

He spat on the ground three times, a superstitious ritual against the rotten luck.

Who could have chosen to dump a body here in the morning? A sex murder, he concluded.

It occurred to him to report the crime to the police. But it was still too early. There was no public phone service available. Looking around, he saw a light flickering, distantly, across the street. It came from the Shanghai Music Institute. He started shouting for help.

"Murder! Red mandarin dress murder!"

ONE

CHIEF INSPECTOR CHEN CAO, of the Shanghai Police Bureau, was startled out of his dream by an early phone call.

Rubbing his eyes, as he snatched up the receiver, he saw the clock on the nightstand pointing to seven thirty. He had stayed up late last night writing a letter to a friend in Beijing, quoting a Tang dynasty poet, to say what he found difficult to say in his own words. Afterward, he managed to lose himself in a dream of the heartless Tang willows lined along the deserted bank in a light green mist.

"Hello, I am Zhong Baoguo, of the Shanghai Legal System Reform Committee. Is this Comrade Chief Inspector Chen?"

Chen sat up. That particular committee, a new institution under the Shanghai People's Congress, exercised no direct authority over him, but Zhong, higher in the Party cadre rank, had never contacted him before, let alone called him at home. The fragments of the willow-shaded dream were fading quickly.

It could be one of those "politically sensitive" cases, preferably not discussed at the bureau. Chen detected a bitter taste in his mouth.

"Have you heard of the West-Nine-Block housing development case?"

"The West-Nine-Block? Yes, Peng Liangxin's development—one of the best areas in the center of the city. I have read articles about it."

In China's ongoing reform, some of the most unbelievable business opportunities were in housing development. In the past, with all the land controlled by the state, people had depended on the state housing assignment. Chen, too, had been assigned a room through the bureau quota. But in the early nineties, the government started selling land to emerging entrepreneurs. Peng—nicknamed the Number One Shanghai Big Buck—was one of the earliest and most successful developers. Since Party officials determined the land prices and allocation, corruption swarmed around like flies chasing blood. Through his connections, Peng obtained government approval for the West-Nine-Block development project. There, the old buildings had to be pulled down to make way for the new, and Peng drove out the original residents. It did not take long, however, for people to start complaining about the "black holes" in the business operation, and a scandal broke out.

But what could Chen do? Obviously, for a huge project like West-Nine-Block, a number of officials were involved. It could turn into a major case with disastrous political impact. Damage control, he guessed, would probably be the assignment waiting for him.

"Yes, we think you should look into the case. Especially into the attorney, Jia Ming, who represents those residents."

"Jia Ming?" Chen was even more puzzled. He did not know any details about the corruption case. He had heard of Jia as a successful attorney, but why should an attorney be the target? "Is he the attorney who defended the case for Hu Ping, the dissident writer?"

"That's him."

"Director Zhong, I am so sorry. I am afraid I cannot help with your case." He promptly came up with an excuse, instead of saying a straightforward no. "I have just enrolled in a special MA program at Shanghai University. Classical Chinese literature. The first few weeks are for intensive studies—I'll have no time for anything else."

More than merely an improvised excuse, it was something he had contemplated for some time. Technically, he wasn't yet enrolled, but he had made preliminary inquiries at the university about it.

"You are kidding, Comrade Chief Inspector Chen. What about your police work? Classical Chinese literature. Not in the line of your job at all. Are you looking for a new career?"

"Literature used to be my major—English literature. To be a competent investigator in today's society, one has to acquire as much knowledge as possible. This program includes psychology and sociology courses."

"Well, it's desirable to enlarge your knowledge horizon, but I just don't think you have the time in your position."

"It's a sort of special arrangement," Chen said. "Only a few weeks of intensive study—in classrooms like other students, and then nothing but papers. After that, the curriculum will be arranged in a way compatible with my work schedule." It was not exactly true. According to the program brochure he had picked up, the intensive weeks did not have to be now.

"I was hoping I could persuade you. A leading comrade in the city government suggested I talk to you today."

"I'll pay close attention to the case in whatever way possible," Chen said, meaning it as a face-saving comment for Zhong. He did not want Zhong to talk about the "leading comrade," whoever he might be.

"That's great. I'll have the case file sent to you," Zhong said, taking the comment as a concession from the chief inspector.

Afterward, Chen thought in frustration that he should have said no unequivocally.

After hanging up with Zhong, Chen realized he needed to find out as much as he could about the West-Nine-Block case. He immediately started making phone calls, and his gut feeling that this was an investigation to avoid proved to be right.

Peng Liangxin, the real estate developer, had started out as a dumpling peddler, but he displayed extraordinary expertise in building a connection network. He knew when and where to push red envelopes of money into the hands of the Party officials. In return, the Party had helped him push himself into a billionaire in only four or five years. He acquired the West-Nine-Block land with numerous bribes and a business plan for improving conditions for the residents there. Then, with the government document granting him the land, he obtained the necessary bank loans to build the development without having to spend a single penny of his own. He bullied the residents out with little or no compensation. The few resisting families he called "nail families," and he pulled them out forcibly, like nails, by hiring a group of Triad thugs. Several residents were badly beaten in a so-called "demolition campaign." What's more, instead of allowing the original residents to move back in as promised in his development proposal, he started selling the new apartments at a much higher price to buyers from Taiwan and Hong Kong. When people protested, he again enlisted the help of the local Triad, as well as that of the government officials. Several residents were jailed as troublemakers interfering with the development plan of the city. But as more and more people joined the protest, the government felt compelled to step in.

According to one source, Peng got into trouble more or less because of his nickname. There were many rich people in the city, some possibly even richer, but they managed to keep a low profile. Suffering from a swollen head due to his incredibly fast success, he delighted in people calling him the Number One Big Buck in Shanghai. As the gap between the rich and the poor increased, people voiced their frustration with the widespread corruption, and with Peng as a representative of it. As a Chinese proverb says, a bird reaching out its head will be shot.

The situation grew more complicated when the prominent attorney Jia Ming chose to speak for the residents. With his legal expertise, Jia soon uncovered more abuses in the fraudulent business operation, in which not just Peng but also his government associates were deeply involved. The case started to be widely reported, and the city government began to worry about it getting out of control. Peng was put into custody, and an open and fair trial was promised soon.

Chen frowned, picking up another fax page from his machine. The new fax claimed that Internal Security agents had been investigating Jia in secret. If they could find a way to get Jia in trouble, the corruption case would fall apart, but their efforts met with no success.

Chen crumbled the page into a ball and considered himself lucky for having come up with an excuse. At least he could still say he made no commitment because of the special MA program.

And an opportunity did present itself in the special program designed for rising Party cadres, who were supposedly too busy with more important work and were thus allowed to obtain a higher degree in a much shorter period of time.

There was also something else in it for Chen. By all appearances, he had been sailing smoothly in his career. He was one of the youngest chief inspectors on the force and the most likely candidate to succeed Party Secretary Li Guohua as the number one Party official at the Shanghai Police Bureau. Still, such a career had not been his choice, not back in his college years. In spite of his success as a police officer—no less surprising to himself than to others—and despite having several "politically important cases" to his credit, he felt increasingly frustrated with his job. A number of the cases had had results contrary to a cop's expectations.

Confucius says, *There are things a man will do, and things a man will not do*. Only there was no easy guideline for him in such a transitional, topsy-turvy age. The program might enable him, he reflected, to think from a different perspective.

So that morning he decided to visit Professor Bian Longhua of Shanghai University. The program had been an improvised excuse in his talk with Zhong, but it did not have to be so.

On the way there, he bought a *Jinhua* ham wrapped in the special *tung* paper, following a tradition as early as Confucius's time. The sage would not have taken money from his students, but he showed no objection to their gifts, such as hams and chickens. Only the ham proved to be too cumbersome for Chen to carry onto a bus, so he was obliged to call for a bureau car. Waiting in the ham store, he made several more phone calls about the housing development case, and the calls made him even more determined to avoid getting involved.

Little Zhou drove up sooner than Chen expected. A bureau driver who declared himself "Chief Inspector Chen's man," Little Zhou would spread the news of Chen's visit to Bian around. It might be just as well, Chen thought, beginning to mentally rehearse his talk with the professor.

Bian lived in a three-bedroom apartment in a new complex. It was an expensive location, unusual for an intellectual. Bian himself opened the door for Chen. A medium-built man in his mid-seventies, with silver hair shining against a ruddy complexion, Bian looked quite spirited for his age, and for his life experience. A young "rightist" in the fifties, a middle-aged "historical counterrevolutionary" during the Cultural Revolution, and an old "intellectual model" in the nineties, Bian had clung to his literature studies like a life vest all those years.

"This is far from enough to show my respect to you, Professor Bian," Chen said, holding up the ham. He then tried to find a place to put it down, but the new expensive furniture appeared too good for the ham wrapped in the oily *tung* paper.

"Thank you, Chief Inspector Chen," Bian said. "Our dean has talked to me about you. Considering your workload, we have just decided that you don't have to sit in the classroom like other students, but you still have to turn in your papers on time."

"I appreciate the arrangement. Of course I'll hand in papers like other students."

A young woman walked light-footed into the living room. She looked to be in her early thirties, dressed in a black mandarin dress and high-heeled sandals. She relieved Chen of the ham and put it on the coffee table.

"Fengfeng, my most capable daughter," Bian said. "A CEO of an American-Chinese joint venture."

"A most unfilial daughter," she said. "I studied business administration instead of Chinese literature. Thank you for choosing him, Chief Inspector Chen. It's a boost to his ego to have a celebrity student."

"No, it's an honor for me."

"You're doing great on the police force, Chief Inspector Chen. Why do you want to study in the program?" she wanted to know.

"Literature makes nothing happen," the old man joined in with a self-depreciating smile. "She, in contrast, bought the apartment, which was way beyond my means. So we live here—one country with two systems."

One country with two systems—a political catch phrase invented by Comrade Deng Xiaoping to describe socialist mainland China's coexistence with the capitalist Hong Kong after 1997. Here, it described a family whose members earned money from two different systems. Chen understood that people questioned his decision, but he tried not to care too much.

"It's like a road not taken, always so tempting to think about on a snowy night," he said, "and also a boost to one's ego to imagine an alternative career."

"I have to ask a favor of you," she said. "Father has diabetes and high blood pressure. He does not go to school every day. Can you come here to study instead?"

"Sure, if it's convenient for him."

"Don't you remember the line by Gao Shi?" Bian said. " 'Alas, the most useless is a scholar.' Here I am, an old man capable of only 'carving insects' at home."

"Literature is of significance for a thousand autumns," Chen said, quoting a line in response.

"Well, your passion for literature is something. As in a Chinese saying, people with the same sickness pity one another. Of course, you may have to worry about your own kind of 'thirsty illness.' You are a romantic poet, I've heard."

Xiaoke zhi ji—thirsty illness. Chen had heard the term before, in reference to diabetes, which made one thirsty and tired. Bian had a way of talking, making a subtle reference both to his diabetes and to his thirst for literature, but what did that have to do with Chen's being a romantic poet?

When Chen got back into the car waiting for him outside, he caught Little Zhou examining a naked model in a copy of *Playboy* from Hong Kong. The term "thirsty illness" in ancient China, Chen suddenly recalled, might have been a metaphor for a young man's helpless romantic passion.

Then he was not so sure. He could have read the term somewhere but mixed it up with irrelevant associations. Sitting in the car, he found himself thinking like a cop again, searching for an explanation for Professor Bian's usage. He shook his head at his confused reflection in the rearview mirror.

Still, he felt good. The prospect of starting the literature program made the difference.

TWO

DETECTIVE YU GUANGMING, OF the Shanghai Police Bureau, sat brooding in the office—not exactly his, not yet. As the acting head of the special case squad, Yu had the office during Chen's leave.

Few seemed to take Yu seriously, though he had been in effective charge of the squad for longer periods before: weeks when Chen had been too busy, what with his political meetings and his well-paid translations. Still, Yu was seen as stepping in the shadow of Chen.

What troubled Yu was Chen's inexplicable determination to undertake the literature program. It was a decision that had given rise to numerous interpretations at the bureau. According to Liao Guochang, head of the homicide squad, Chen was trying to stay low after having ruffled high feathers, and so was adopting a bookish pose to keep himself out of the limelight for a while. It seemed to Little Zhou that Chen had his eye on a MA or a PhD—something crucial to his future career, for an advanced degree made a huge difference in the new policy of the Party cadre promotion. Commissar Zhang, a semiretired cadre of the older generation, saw Chen's studies in a different light, claiming that Chen planned to study abroad with a *hongyan zhiji*—an appreciating and understanding beauty—who was a US marshal. Like most of the rumors about Chen, no one could prove or disprove it.

Yu was not so sure about any of those views. And there was another possibility he could not rule out: something else might be going on. Chen had asked him about a housing development case without offering any explanation, which was unusual between the chief inspector and Yu.

Yu did not have much time to worry that morning. Party Secretary Li had summoned him to Inspector Liao's office.

Liao was a solidly built man in his early forties, owlish-looking with an aquiline nose and round eyes. He frowned at Yu's entrance.

At the bureau, only a case of extraordinary political significance would go to the special case squad under Chen and Yu. Liao's sour expression implied that another case proved to be too much for Homicide.

"Comrade Detective Yu, you have heard about the red mandarin dress case," Li said, more a statement than a question.

"Yes," Yu responded. "A sensational case."

A week earlier, a girl's body in a red mandarin dress had been found in a flower bed on West Huaihai Road. Because of its proximity to a number of high-end stores, the case had been much reported and was now conveniently nicknamed the red mandarin dress case. The news about it had caused a terrible traffic jam in the area—people hurried over, window-shopping and gossip-shopping, in addition to all the photographers and journalists milling around, information-shopping.

Newspapers went wild with theories. No murderer would have dumped a body in such a dress, at such a location, without some reason. One reporter saw it pointing to someone at the Shanghai Music Institute, located across the street opposite the flower bed. One deemed it a political case, a protest against the reversal of values in socialist China, for the mandarin dress, once condemned as a sign of capitalistic decadence, had become popular again. A tabloid magazine went further, speculating that the murder had been orchestrated by a fashion industry tycoon. Ironically, one result of the media coverage was that several stores immediately displayed new lines of mandarin dresses in their windows.

Yu had noticed the mystifying aspects of the case. According to the initial forensic report, bruises on her arms and legs indicated that the victim could have been sexually assaulted before death of suffocation, but no trace of semen was found on or in the body, and the body had been washed after her death. She had nothing on underneath the dress, which was in contradiction to the common dress code. Then the location itself was so public that few would have chosen to dump a body there.

In one of the bureau's initial theories, the murderer, having committed the crime, put clothes on her for the purpose of transporting, but in a hurry, he either forgot to put on her panties and bra, or did not think it necessary. The dress could have been the same one she had worn before the fatal encounter. The location might have no significance: the criminal could have been reckless and simply dumped her body at his first opportunity.

Yu did not give too much credit to the random-act theory, but it was not a case assigned to his special case squad. He knew better than to cook in other people's kitchens.

"So sensational," Yu repeated, feeling obliged to speak again, since neither Li nor Liao made a response. "The very location of it."

Still no response. Li started panting, his eye bags hanging heavier in the ominous silence. A man in his late fifties, Li had extraordinary eye bags and thick gray brows.

"Any breakthrough?" Yu said, turning to Liao.

"Breakthrough?" Li growled. "A second body in a red mandarin dress was found this morning."

"Another victim! Where?"

"In front of the Newspaper Windows by the number one gate of the People's Park—on Nanjing Road."

"That's outrageous—in the center of the city," Yu said. The Newspaper Windows were a row of glass-covered newspaper cases along the park wall, and a large number of readers gathered there most of the time. "A deliberate challenge."

"We have compared the two victims," Liao said. "There are a number of similarities. Particularly the mandarin dress. The identical material and style."

"Now the newspapers are having a carnival," Li observed as a stack of the papers was being delivered to the office.

Yu picked up *Liberation Daily*, which featured a color picture of a young girl in a red mandarin dress lying under the Newspaper Windows.

"The first serial sex murder in Shanghai," Liao said, reading aloud. " 'Red mandarin dress' has now become a household word. Speculations spread like wildfire. The city shivers in anticipation—"

"The journalists are crazy," Li cut him off short. "Precipitating an avalanche of articles and pictures, as if nothing else mattered in our city."

Li's frustration was understandable. Shanghai had been known for its government efficiency and, among other things, its low crime rate. Not that serial murders had never happened in Shanghai before, but because of the effective media control, they had never been reported. Such a case could have implied that the city police were incompetent, an implication that government-funded papers were anxious to avoid. In the mid-nineties, however, newspapers were now responsible for their own bottom lines: the journalists had to grab sensational news, and media control no longer worked out so well.

"Nowadays, with all the western mysteries in bookstores or on TV—some of them translated by our Chief Inspector Chen," Liao said, "people start playing Sherlock Holmes in their columns. Look at *Wenhui*. It's predicting the date of the next strike. 'Another body in a red mandarin dress by next Friday.' "

"That's common knowledge," Yu said. "A serial killer strikes at regular intervals. If uncaught, he may continue throughout the course of his life. Chen has translated something about a serial killer. I think we should talk to him—"

"Damn the serial killer!" Li appeared exasperated by the term. "Have you talked to your boss? I bet not. He's too busy writing his literature paper."

The relationship between Chen and Li had not been good, Yu knew, so he refrained from responding.

"Don't worry," Liao commented sarcastically. "Even without Butcher Zhang, people will still have pork on the table."

"These murders are a slap in the face to the police bureau. 'I've done it again, cops!' " Li went on heatedly. "The class enemy is trying to sabotage the great progress in our reform, damaging the social stability by causing panic among the people. So let us focus on those with deep-rooted hatred for our government."

Li's logic was still echoing that little red book of Chairman Mao, and according to that logic, Yu reflected, anybody could be a so-called class enemy. The Party Secretary was known for formulating political theories about homicide investigations. The number one Party boss sort of fancied himself the number one criminal investigator too.

"The perpetrator must have a place to commit the crime first—most likely his home," Liao said. "His neighbors could have noticed something."

"Yes, contact all the neighborhood committees, especially those close to the two locations. As Chairman Mao says, we have to rely on the people. Now, in order to solve the case as quickly as possible," Li concluded with all the official seriousness in his voice, "Inspector Liao and Detective Yu, you are going to head a special team."

It was only after the Party Secretary left the office that the two cops were able to discuss the case in earnest.

"I know so little about the case," Yu started, "practically nothing about the first victim."

"This is the file about the first one." Liao produced a bulging folder. "At the moment, we are still gathering the information about the second."

Yu picked up an enlarged picture of the first body. The victim's face partially covered by her black hair, she showed a good figure, her curves accentuated by the tight-fitting dress.

"Judging from the bruise on her arms and legs," Liao said, "she could have suffered some sort of sexual assault. But there is no sign of any semen or secretion in her vagina, and the medical people have ruled out condom-use as the reason. There was no condom lubrication found there, either. Whatever he did to her, he afterward put the dress back on her rigid body roughly and in a hurry. Which explains the torn slits and loose buttons."

"But we can be pretty sure that the red mandarin dress was not hers," Yu said, "since the second victim was found in an identical dress."

"No, the dress was not hers."

Yu examined the torn slits and loose buttons in the picture. If someone had indeed gone to the trouble of arranging for an expensive, fashionable dress beforehand, then why had he dressed the body in such a reckless way—and on both occasions?

"On the second victim, is the dress also torn in its slits?"

"I see what you are getting at," Liao said grumpily, nodding.

"When did you establish the identity of the first victim?"

"Not until three or four days after the body was found. Tian Mo, twenty-three. People called her Jasmine. She worked at the Seagull Hotel, which is near the intersection of Guangxi and Jingling Roads. She lived with her paralyzed father. According to her neighbors and colleagues, she was a nice, hard-working girl. She didn't have a boyfriend, and none of the people who knew her believed that she had had any enemies, either."

"It appears that the murderer dumped her body from a car."

"That's too obvious."

"What about a taxi driver or a private car owner?"

"Taxi drivers work in a shift rotation of twelve hours. After the second victim was reported, we immediately checked those working on both of the two nights. Less than twenty fit into the time frames, and every one of them has receipt tabs for at least one of the nights. Now, how would a taxi driver between fares have time to murder her, wash her—probably in a private bathroom—and put her into the mandarin dress?" Liao shook his head before moving on. "The private car is a possibility. The number of them has been increasing dramatically in the last few years, with all the Big Bucks in business and Big Bugs in the Party. But we don't have the resources to knock on their doors, one after another, throughout the city, even if our Party Secretary turns on the green light."

"What do you make of the locations, then?"

"For the first one," Liao said, producing a picture with the traffic light visible at the intersection in the background, "the murderer had to step out of the car to place the body. A high risk. In the area, traffic is practically nonstop. The number 26 trolley bus stops running only after two thirty, and then it starts again around four. Besides, there are occasional cars passing by, and late-working students moving in and out of the institute across the street."

"Do you think that the place the body was dumped has a specific meaning in connection to the music institute, as those journalists claim?" Yu said.

"We looked into that. Jasmine never studied at the institute. She was fond of music, like most young girls, humming a song or two occasionally, but nothing more than that. Nor did her family have anything to do with the school. Since the second victim was dumped at a different location, I don't see any point in taking the newspaper crap about the music institute seriously."

"Li may have a point here. The two locations both being very public, the criminal could be bent on making a statement," Yu said. "You must have already contacted all the nearby neighborhood committees."

"You bet, but the queries focused on one type of criminal—sex offenders with previous records. Nothing so far. The second body came up only this morning."

"Tell me what you know about the second one."

"The body was discovered by a *Wenhui* boy who came to replace the newspapers there. He pulled down the mandarin dress over her bare thighs and covered her face with newspapers, then he called the newspaper office instead of us. When we got to the scene, a large number of people had been gathered around there for quite a while, having possibly turned the body over and over. So any examination of the scene was practically meaningless."

"Has the forensic report come out?"

"No, not yet. Only an initial report done on the scene. Again, death by suffocation. The victim seemed to have suffered no sexual assault, but like the first one, she had nothing whatsoever on underneath the mandarin dress." Liao produced more pictures on the desk. "No trace of semen, with vaginal, oral, and anal swabs taken. The latent-print people have done their job too, and they did not see even a single stray hair on the body."

"Any copycat possibility?"

"We have examined the two dresses. The same material with an imprinted design on it, and the same style too. No copycat could have known or reproduced all those details."

"What else have you done for the second?"

"A notice with her picture has been sent out. Phone calls have been coming in, offering a number of possible leads. The bureau machine is clunking into high gear."

"Whether Li likes the term *serial murderer* or not," Yu said, "there's no ruling out the possibility. In a week, we might find ourselves with a third body in a mandarin dress."

"Politically, Shanghai cannot acknowledge a serial killer. That's why Li brought in your special case squad."

"In case it is a serial killer," Yu said, aware of the long rivalry between the homicide and the special case squads, "we need to establish a profile."

"Well, the dresses are very expensive, so he probably is rich. He has a car. He most likely lives by himself: he could not have done all of this without a place of his own—an apartment, or an independent villa. Certainly not in a single room in a *shikumen* house with twenty other families squeezed together—there is no way to quietly move the bodies in the midst of all those neighbors."

"That's true," Yu said, nodding. "He is also a loner, and a pervert too. The victims were stripped naked, but there's no standard sexual assault. He's a psycho who gets his mental release from the ritualistic killing, leaving the red mandarin dress as his signature."

"A psychopath with his mental release?" Liao exclaimed. "Come on, Detective Yu. You sound just like those mysteries your boss translates. Full of psychological mumbo-jumbo, but with nothing we can grasp."

"But from that sort of a psychological file we may move on to learn other things about him," Yu said. "I think I read about it in a book he translated, but it was quite a long time ago."

"Well, my file is far more practical, material rather than otherwise, and it is effective in narrowing down our suspect range. At least, we don't have to worry about those who don't meet these material conditions."

"What about the red mandarin dress?" Yu said, avoiding for the moment a confrontation with Liao.

"I thought about putting up a reward for information, but Li vetoed the idea, worrying about rampant speculation—"

Their talk was interrupted by the entrance of Hong, a young graduate from Shanghai Police Academy who worked as an assistant to Liao. She was a handsome girl with a sweet smile that showed white teeth. Her boyfriend was said to be a dentist who had studied abroad.

"Well, I'll start looking into the folders," Yu said, standing up. As he walked out, he found himself thinking that Hong bore a slight resemblance to the first victim.

THREE

CHIEF INSPECTOR CHEN WAS on his way to the Shanghai Library.

That morning, he chose to walk along Nanjing Road, his pace leisurely as he thought about a possible topic for his first literature paper.

Near Fujian Road, he stopped at a new construction site and lit a cigarette. Looking ahead into the crowd of new stores and signs, he still recognized a couple of old stores, though these were thoroughly redecorated, as if having undergone plastic surgery.

The Shanghai First department store, once the most popular in the city, appeared shabby, almost depressed in contrast to the new buildings. He had worked on a homicide case in the store. At the time, the decline of the store was not foreseeable to the victim, a national model worker who had been worried about her own fading political status. Now, the state-run store, instead of representing reliability and respectability, was known for its poor "socialist service and quality." The change was symbolic: capitalism was now recognized as superior.

In the store window, a slender model—a foreign one—stretched herself in an amorous gesture, staring out at Chen, who pulled himself back from wandering thoughts.

An idea for his first paper had come from his talk with Bian, from one particular phrase: *thirsty illness.* He had looked up the term in dictionaries at home; none of them supported the way Bian had used it. While *thirsty* might be used as a general metaphor for yearning, *thirsty illness* referred only to diabetes. So he planned to spend the morning looking through reference books in the library. Perhaps he could get something out of it—maybe an evolution of semiotics—for the paper.

The pinnacle of the library came into view, shimmering over the corner of Huangpi Road. The library, too, was said to be moving soon. Where would the new site be, he wondered, pushing open the revolving door.

On the second floor, he handed over a list of books to Susu, a pretty, young librarian behind the desk. She flashed him a smile that brought out two vivacious dimples, and started checking for the books.

He had just installed himself in the reading room overlooking the People's Park and opened the first book when his cell phone rang. He pushed the button. No one spoke. Possibly a wrong number. He turned the phone off.

The term *thirsty illness* first appeared in "The Story of Xiangru and Wenjun," originally in a biographical sketch in Sima Qian's *Shiji.* The library edition of *Shiji* was a fully annotated one, so he could be quite sure of its meaning. The story began at the very beginning, narrating how Xiangru and Wenjun fell in love through music.

He sang the lines at a grand banquet in the mansion of Zhuo Wangsun, a rich merchant at Lingqiong. Zhuo Wangsun's beautiful daughter was in the adjoining chamber, where she stole a glance at Xiangru. She proved to be one who truly understood the music. So she made up her mind to elope with him that night. They became husband and wife and lived together happily ever after. . . .

The story mentioned the term *thirsty illness,* but only once.

Xiangru stammered, but he was an excellent writer. He suffered from thirsty illness (xiaoke ji). *Since he married into the Zhuo family, he was rich. He did not commit himself to an official career. . . .*

The sketch then moved on to Xiangru's literary career and did not touch on the subject of his thirsty illness again. Given the seminal significance of *Shiji,* the story came to be retold in a number of literary versions, proving to be archetypal in its influence on the late genre of scholar-beauty romance.

Chen then started checking through anthologies and collections. One of the earliest literary versions of the love story appeared in *Xijing Zaji,* a collection of anecdotes and stories.

When Sima Xiangru returned to Chengdu with Zhuo Wenjun, he was poverty-stricken. He pawned his sushuang *feather coat to Yang Chang and bought wine for her. She threw her arm round his neck and burst into tears. "I have always lived in affluence. Now we have to pawn your clothes for wine!" After much discussion, they set about selling wine in Chengdu. Wearing no more than short pants, Xiangru himself washed the utensils. He did so to embarrass Zhuo Wangsun. Wangsun was overwhelmed by shame and provided handsomely for Wenjun, thus making her rich.*

Wenjun was a beauty. Her eyebrows were as delicate as the mountains seen from a distance; her face as charming as a lotus flower; her skin was as soft as frozen cream. She had been widowed at the age of seventeen. She was loose in her ways. So impressed by Xiangru's talent, she trespassed the grounds of rites.

Xiangru had previously suffered from thirsty illness. When he went back to Chengdu, he became so enamored of Wenjun's beauty that he had a relapse of the illness. Therefore he wrote the rhapsody "Beauty" to satirize himself. However, he could not mend his way and finally died of the illness. Wenjun wrote an elegy for him, which is extant today.

In the *Xijing Zaji* version, Chen observed, the term *thirsty illness* appeared in a context quite different from the *Shiji's*. Instead of beginning from the beginning, the later tale started with the plight of the couple on their return to Chengdu, leaving out the romantic part and highlighting their materialistic motives. Xiangru was portrayed as a mercenary conspirator, and Wenjun, though a beauty, was a woman of suspect morals.

A substantial difference came in the semantics of *thirsty illness*: here, it was an illness caused by love. Xiangru was aware of the cause and effect, trying to satirize himself out of it, but to no avail. He died of his passion for Wenjun.

So here the meaning of *thirsty illness* was close to Bian's—a consequence of romantic passion. That was what Bian jokingly meant by the romantic poet's "kind of thirsty illness."

Chen opened *Ocean of Words*, the largest Chinese dictionary, in which *thirsty illness* clearly meant diabetes. "It is so named because the patient feels thirsty, hungry, urinates a lot, and looks emaciated." A medical term carrying no other association whatsoever—exactly the same as its use in *Shiji*.

He pulled over other reference books, thinking about the superstitious beliefs about sexual love in ancient China. As far as he could remember, the Taoist opposed sexual love—or, to be more exact, ejaculation—on the grounds that it deprived a man of his essence.

Whatever the philosophical or superstitious influence, an association between love and death appeared on the thematic horizon of the literary version. The romance thus contained within itself an "other," which decried the romantic theme.

Also, the later version's Wenjun appeared as a frivolous and sinister woman. Chen copied in his notebook a sentence: "So impressed by Xiangru's talent, she trespassed the grounds of rites." He underlined the word *rites,* thinking of a Confucian quotation, "Do all things in accordance to the rites."

But what could have been the rites regarding people falling in love?

He went to request more books. Susu said that it could take some time to get them because of the staff's lunch break. So he decided to go out for lunch. It was a warm afternoon for that time of the year.

People's Park was close by, in which there was an inexpensive but nice canteen. Many years ago, his mother had taken him there. It took him a while to find it, but he finally did. He ordered a plastic box of fried rice, slices of beef in oyster sauce with green onion, plus a fish ball soup in a paper bowl. The same beef recipe, he hoped, as he had enjoyed in the company of his mother.

He also looked for a bottle of *Zhengguanghe* lemon water, but he saw only a variety of American brands: Coca Cola—*Delicious, Enjoyable*; Pepsi—*Hundreds of Things Enjoyable*; Sprite—*Snow Pure*; 7-Up—*Seven Happiness*; Mountain Dew—*Excited Wave*. At least the translations of the drinks were not so Americanized, he contemplated in wry amusement.

His cell phone started ringing again. It was Overseas Chinese Lu, his middle school buddy, now the owner of Moscow Suburb, a swank restaurant known for its Russian cuisine and Russian girls.

"Where are you, buddy?"

"In People's Park, enjoying a box lunch. I have this week off for my Chinese literature paper."

"You must be joking—a Chinese literature paper in the midst of your soaring career?" Lu exclaimed. "If you are really going to quit the police force, come and be my partner, as I've said hundreds of times. Indeed, customers will come pouring in because of your connections."

But Chen knew better. His connections came from his position. Once out of that position, most of his "friends" would evaporate into thin air. He would probably never go to work with Lu, so he saw no point in discussing it.

"Come to Moscow Suburb," Lu went on. "I have all my Russian waitresses wearing mandarin dresses. It's a weird sight. Westerners look out of joint in mandarin dresses. Still, so mysterious, so exciting, so delicious that customers practically devour them alive."

"The exotic flavor, I bet."

For an entrepreneur like Lu, it was natural to seize any opportunity to make money without worrying about aesthetics, or ethics.

"Whatever flavor, the plastic box lunch in the park is definitely not edible. A disgrace to a renowned and refined gourmet like you. You have to come—"

"I will, Lu," Chen said, cutting Lu short, "but I have to go back to the library now. Someone's waiting for me."

The box lunch was waiting, to be exact. It would soon get cold.

Before he opened the plastic box, however, his phone shrilled yet again. He should have turned it off during the break. It was Hong, the young cop in the homicide squad who worked as Liao's assistant.

"This is a surprise, Hong."

"Sorry, Chief Inspector Chen, I got your cell phone number from Detective Yu. I tried your home first, but no success."

"You don't have to say sorry for that."

"I have to report a case to you."

"But I'm on vacation, Hong."

"It's important. Both Party Secretary Li and Inspector Liao told me to contact you."

"Well," he said. A lot of things could have turned into important grains in Li's political mill. As for Liao, his request that Hong call Chen was possibly no more than a deferential gesture.

"Where are you, Chief Inspector Chen? I can come over immediately."

It could be another sensitive case, something not convenient to discuss on the phone. But, if so, then it wasn't for the library, either.

"Come to People's Park, Hong. Close to the entrance of the number three gate."

"You're enjoying your vacation. People's Park. What a coincidence!"

"What do you mean?"

"A second body in a red mandarin dress was found early this morning. In front of the Newspaper Windows close to the number one gate of the park." She added, "Oh, Detective Yu has joined the special investigation too."

"A serial murder!" Chen recalled having seen a crowd there earlier, though he hadn't paid any particular attention. It wasn't an unusual scene for the Newspaper Windows.

"That's what I'm calling about. They wanted me to be the one to contact you because they said that Chief Inspector Chen would not say no to a young girl."

The request could not have come at a worse time—for his paper. Still, he had to do something. It was the first serial murder case for the city, for the bureau. At the very least, he had to make a gesture of concern.

"Bring me the information you've gathered, Hong. I'll take a look in the evening."

"I'm on my way."

The lunch box remained untouched, now totally cold. He threw it into the trash can. He rose and moved toward the gate in question, trying to imagine the scene earlier.

The Newspaper Windows were located at the intersection of Nanjing and Xizhuang Roads, an area that permitted no parking along the curb. Any car parked there would get immediate attention, and the police patrol went on all night.

The murderer must have planned it carefully, Chen reflected.

There was a large crowd of people there, but the area around the Newspaper Windows was not taped off. He didn't see any cops moving around, either.

He caught the sight of a young girl walking over in a white overcoat, like a pear blossom in the morning light. A far-fetched metaphor, for it was still early winter. She was not Hong.

Several old people stood in front of the Newspaper Windows, reading, talking, as usual. To his surprise, the newspaper section that drew the most readers was that of the stock market. "The Bull Is Crazy," the headline read in bold.

FOUR

DETECTIVE YU CAME HOME later than usual.

Peiqin was washing her hair in a plastic basin on a folding table near the common sink, in the common kitchen area shared by the five families on the first floor. He slowed to a stop by her side. Looking up with her hair covered in soap bubbles, she motioned to him to move into their room.

In the room, the table held a platter of rice cakes fried with shredded pork and pickled cabbage. He'd had a couple of steamed buns earlier, so he thought he might have a cake later as a nighttime snack. Their son Qinqin was studying late at school, as usual, preparing for the college entrance examination.

Yu felt exhausted at the sight of their bed, with the dragon-and-phoenix-embroidered cotton padded quilt already spread out, the soft white pillow set against the headboard. Without taking off his shoes, he dumped himself across the quilt. After two or three minutes he sat up again, and leaning against the hard headboard, produced a cigarette. Peiqin would not come in for a while, he guessed, and he needed to think.

Smoking, he found his thoughts still stuck, as though in a pail of frozen glue. So he tried to review the work already done on the mandarin dress murders.

The whole bureau had been bubbling like a pot of boiling water. Theories were advanced. Cases were quoted. Arguments were pushed. Everybody appeared well-informed on the case.

Party Secretary Li's insistence on the "reliance-on-people approach" hadn't worked. The neighborhood committees accosted a large number of people seen in the vicinity and asked them to provide alibis, but that hadn't led to anything. That was no surprise.

In the sixties and seventies, the committees had been an effective government watchdog because of the housing conditions and the ration-coupon system. When a dozen families lived together in a *shikumen* house, sharing one kitchen and yard, neighbors watched one another, and because the food and grocery ration coupons were distributed by the neighborhood committees, the committees' power over residents was enormous. But with the improvement in housing conditions and abolishment of the ration coupons, committees no longer found it easy to monitor a resident's life. They could still be somewhat effective in the remaining old neighborhoods of ramshackle overcrowded *shikumen* houses, but this killer apparently lived in a different environment, enjoying both space and privacy. In the mid-nineties, a neighborhood cadre could no longer so easily barge into a family's life as during the years of Mao's class struggle.

Inspector Liao's revision was of little help. While his material profile narrowed the range of suspects, none of those with previous history of sex crimes met all of Liao's specified conditions. Most of them were poor, just two or three lived by themselves, and only one, a taxi driver, had access to a car.

Their research into the red mandarin dress also failed to go anywhere. They sent out a notice to all the factories and workshops that made mandarin dresses, requesting any related information, but so far they had received nothing about that particular dress.

With each passing day, the possibility of another victim loomed closer.

Yu was gazing through a smoke ring from his cigarette, as if flying invisible darts, when he heard Peiqin pouring water down the kitchen sink. He ground out the cigarette and put the ashtray away.

He didn't need her to start harping on his smoking tonight. He wanted to discuss the case with her. She had helped with his previous investigations—in her way. This time, she at least could tell him more about the dress. Like other Shanghai women, she liked shopping, though she was mostly confined to window-shopping.

Peiqin poked her head into the room.

"You look beat, Yu. Why not turn in for an early night? I'll dry my hair quick and join you in a minute."

He undressed, climbed into bed, and shivered under the chilly quilt, but it did not take long for him to feel warm and comfortable, expecting her.

She hurried in, treading barefoot on the wooden floor. Lifting the quilt, she slid in beside him, her feet touching his, still cold.

"Would you like a hot water bottle, Peiqin?"

"No, I have you." She clung closer against him. "When Qinqin goes to college, there'll be only two of us here, an empty old nest."

"You don't have to worry," he said, noticing a single white hair at her temple. He took the opportunity to lead the talk in the direction planned. "You still look so young and handsome."

"You don't have to flatter me like that."

"I saw a mandarin dress in a store window today. It would become you nicely, I believe. Have you worn one before?"

"Come on, Yu. Have you ever seen me wearing a mandarin dress? In our middle school days, such a garment was out of the question, decadent and bourgeois and whatnot. Then we both went to the godforsaken army farm in Yunnan, wearing the same imitation army uniform for ten years. When we came back, we didn't even have a proper wardrobe for ourselves under your father's roof. You have never paid any proper attention to me, husband."

"Now with a room for ourselves, I can try to do better in the future."

"But why are you suddenly paying attention to a mandarin dress? Oh, I know. Another case of yours. The red mandarin dress case, I've heard of it."

"Surely you know something about the dress. Maybe you examined one in a store."

"Once or twice, perhaps, but I never go into any of those fancy stores. Do you think a mandarin dress would fit me—a middle-aged woman working in a shabby restaurant?"

"Why not?" Yu said, his hand tracing the familiar curves on her body.

"No, don't sweet-talk like your chief inspector. It's not a dress for a working woman. Not for me, in that *tingsijian* office smeared all over with wok fumes and coal soot. I saw a long article about mandarin dresses in a fashion magazine. Why the style has suddenly become so popular again, I can't figure out. But tell me about your case."

So he summed up what he and his colleagues had done, focusing more or less on the failure of routine police procedure.

At the end of his summary, she said quietly, "Have you discussed it with Chen?"

"We talked on the phone yesterday. He's on vacation, working on a literature paper with a so-called deconstructive approach. About the case, he just mumbled several psychological terms, probably from his mystery translations."

"Chen can be like that," she said. "If the murderer is a nut, it can be really difficult, since he acts out of a logic comprehensible only to himself."

He waited for her to go on, but she didn't seem to be concentrating on the discussion.

"What about your chief inspector's literature program?" she asked, changing the subject unexpectedly. "Do you think he's going for a career change?"

"He's unpredictable," Yu said. "I don't know."

"He may be facing a midlife crisis—too much work and stress, and no one there for him back at home. Is he still seeing that young girl, White Cloud?"

"No, I don't think so. He's never talked to me about her."

"But the girl had a crush on him."

"How do you know?"

"The way she helped take care of his mother during his delegation trip."

"Well, that Big Buck could have paid her."

"No, she did a lot of things she didn't have to just for the sake of money," she said. "The old woman likes her a lot too. A college student, clever and presentable. In the old woman's eyes, she must be a good choice. And he is a very dutiful son."

"That he is. He keeps talking to me about his not having provided better care for his mother, about his having let her down by not following in the academic footsteps of his father and by not having had a family of his own."

"When he called in yesterday, we talked a little. He explained that his decision to enroll in the special program was partially made for her. In spite of her deteriorating health, she's still worried about him. He thought that, if he could do little to change his bachelor status, then at least an MA degree might comfort the old woman a bit."

"According to a fortune-teller, he has no peach-blossom luck," Yu said, sighing. "Like in a Chinese proverb, one with good luck in their career may have none in love."

"Come on. He's had his share of peach-blossom luck. Like his HCC girlfriend in Beijing. Things just didn't work out. Still, White Cloud could be the one."

"I'm not surprised about her crush, but I don't think it will happen. There are so many rivals watching over him. What happens when they find out about her K girl background?"

"She might have worked as a karaoke girl, but a number of college students work at jobs like that today. It shouldn't matter much, as long as she didn't go all the way, and I don't think she did," Peiqin said. "What matters is whether she will make him a good wife. Clever, young, and practical, she may be a good match for your bookish boss. It's not just his rivals that matter, though. I don't know if he himself is capable of disassociating her from her K girl experience."

"You are so perceptive, my wife."

"It's time for him to settle down with a family. He cannot remain single forever. It's not good for *his* health either. And I don't just mean somebody taking care of him at home."

"Now you are talking like his mother, Peiqin."

"As his partner, you have to help him."

"You are right, but at the moment, I wish he could help me."

"Oh, the red mandarin dress case. Sorry about the digression," she said. "That case is urgent. You have to stop the perpetrator before he kills again. So what's your direction?"

"We don't have a workable direction," he said. "And it's the first case for me as acting head of the squad. I don't think Liao is going to get anywhere with his routine focus. So I think I have to try something different."

"You saw a mandarin dress in a store—not for me, for your case," she said with a smile. "Perhaps more than one store. What did the clerks tell you?"

"Liao and I both visited boutiques specializing in the dress, as well as high-end department stores which carry them, but none of them carried such an old-fashioned mandarin dress. According to the store clerks, no store in the city would stock anything close to it. The specific style is too old. At least ten years old. In the mid-nineties, a mandarin dress usually comes with higher thigh-revealing slits and more sensual curves. It's sleeveless and sometimes backless too, not at all like the ones on the victims."

"Do you have a picture of the mandarin dress with you?"

"Yes," Yu said, taking several photographs out of the folder on the nightstand.

"The dress may be worth further study," she said thoughtfully, examining the pictures closely. "Also, there might have been something about the first victim which sent the murderer over the edge."

"I've thought about that too," Yu said. "Before his first psychopathic action, before he turned into a nut, his initial attack—the one on Jasmine—could have been triggered by something in her, something still comprehensible to us."

As always, the discussion with Peiqin helped. Especially with regard to Jasmine. Yu had talked to Liao about it, but Liao insisted that his squad had already done a thorough job checking on her background and that there would be no point in repeating the effort. Lying beside Peiqin, however, Yu decided he would reexamine her file the next day.

Stretching himself under the quilt, his feet touched hers again. Slightly sweaty, he reached to caress her hair, his hand gradually moving down.

"Qinqin may come back soon," she said, sitting up. "I'll warm the cake in the microwave for you. You have not had your dinner yet, and we both have to get up early tomorrow."

He was disappointed. But he *would* have to go into the bureau for an early morning teleconference tomorrow, and he *was* tired.

FIVE

DETECTIVE YU WAS AT his office early the next morning.

Sitting behind his desk, he steadily drummed his middle finger knuckle on the desktop, as if counting the efforts made by the cops. Dozens of political lectures delivered by Party Secretary Li; the crime scenes photographed and studied hundreds of times; thousands of tips from the public registered and followed up on; the meager material from the victims examined time and time again by the forensic laboratory; two more computers installed for their group; numerous known sexual deviants checked and double-checked; several detained and questioned about their activities during the time of the first and second murders. . . .

For all their work, there was little progress made in the investigation, but a considerable number of theories and speculations kept popping up both in and outside of the bureau.

Little Zhou, the bureau driver who had just started taking an evening police course, barged into Yu's office.

"What do we find in common between the two cases, Detective

Yu?" Little Zhou started dramatically. "The red mandarin dress. A dress known for its Manchurian origin in the Qing dynasty. What else? Bare feet. Both victims had no stockings or shoes on. Now, a woman may appear sexy walking barefoot in a bathrobe, but in a mandarin dress she has to wear pantyhose and high heels. It's the basic dress code. Otherwise she simply makes a laughingstock of herself."

"That's true," Yu said, nodding. "Go on."

"The murderer was able to afford the expensive mandarin dress and had the time to put her body into the dress. Why would he have left off her stockings and shoes?"

"So what do you think?" Yu asked, beginning to be intrigued by the would-be detective's argument.

"I was watching a TV series last night, *Emperor Qianlong Visiting South of the Yangtze River*. One of the gifted and romantic emperors in the Qing dynasty. There are different versions about his real parentage, possibly Han instead of Manchurian, you know—"

"Come on," Yu said, cutting him short. "Don't try to talk like a Suzhou opera singer."

"Now, what set the Manchurian apart from the Han ethnic group? The Manchurian women did not bind their feet, and were able to walk barefoot. But the Han women in the Qing dynasty, though their bound feet received erotic comparison to three-inch-long golden lotuses, could hardly walk at all, let alone go barefoot. And the mandarin dress, of course, was only for a Manchurian woman—at least at the time."

"Do you mean that the combination of the mandarin dress and bare feet delivers a message?"

"Yes. We have to take into consideration the obscene pose too. So it's a message against Manchurian culture."

"Little Zhou, you have watched too many of those shows about conspiracies of Han against Manchurian, or the schemes of Manchurian against Han. Before the Revolution of 1911, such a message might have made sense, since a large number of the Han people were against the Manchurian emperor. But nowadays it's a myth found only on TV."

"There're so many TV shows nowadays about great Manchurian emperors and their beautiful and clever concubines. Some people might think it necessary to send the message again."

"Let me tell you something, Little Zhou. Manchurians have disappeared—assimilated into the Hans. Last month a friend of mine for many years turned out to be a Manchurian. Why? Only because a good position requesting a minority ethnic background came along, did he reveal his Manchurian heritage. Sure enough, he got the job. But for all those years, he was never aware of any ethnic difference in himself. His family had changed their Manchurian surname to a Han surname."

"But how do you explain the exquisite dress and bare feet—of both victims?"

"One possible scenario is that the criminal was victimized by a woman dressed just like that."

"In such a dress," Little Zhou said, "with the torn slits and loose buttons. How could a victimizer—not a victim—have appeared like that?"

Little Zhou was not alone in putting forth wild theories.

In the routine meeting in Party Secretary Li's office that morning, Inspector Liao tried to modify his focus and his approach.

"Apart from what we have already discussed, the criminal must have a garage. In Shanghai, only about a hundred or so families have their own private garages," Liao declared. "We could start checking them one by one."

But Li was against it. "What are you going to do—knock on one door after another without a warrant? No. Such an approach would cause more panic."

The private-garage owners were going to be either well-connected Big Bucks or high-ranking Party cadres, Yu observed. Liao's suggestion amounted to swatting a fly on the forehead of a tiger, and it was a matter of course that Li opposed.

After the meeting, Yu decided to take a trip to Jasmine's neighborhood without mentioning it to Liao. There was something about her that made the effort worthwhile, Yu convinced himself, as he walked out of the bureau. Also, there were some differences between her and the second victim that couldn't be dismissed. The fact that she showed bruises on her body, which was subsequently washed, suggested a possible sexual assault and then an effort to cover it up. In contrast, the second victim, a more easily picked-up target for a sex murderer, showed no traces of sex before her death. Nor was her body washed afterward.

Shortly before noon, he arrived at the street Jasmine had lived in: a long and shabby lane on Shantou Road, seemingly forgotten by the reform. It was close to the Old City area.

It turned out to be almost like a visit back to his old neighborhood. At the lane entrance, he saw several wooden chamber pots airing with contented grins in the midst of the chorus of two women's sweeping with their bamboo brooms, a scene still fresh in his memory.

The neighborhood committee was located at the end of the lane. Uncle Fong, the head of the committee, received Yu in a tiny office and poured a cup of tea for him.

"She was a good girl," Uncle Fong started, shaking his head, "in spite of all the problems at home."

"Tell me about her problems at home," Yu said, having heard of some of them, but Liao's version was not detailed.

"Retribution. Nothing but retribution. Her old man deserves it, but it's not fair for her."

"Can you be more specific here, Uncle Fong?"

"Well, her father, Tian, was somebody during the Cultural Revolution, and he had his fall afterward. Fired, jailed, and paralyzed. So he became a terrible burden for her."

"What did he do during the Cultural Revolution?"

"He was one of the Worker Rebels, wearing an armband, bullying and beating people. Then he became a member of a Mao Zedong Thought Worker Propaganda Team sent to a school. Really powerful and swashbuckling at the time, you know."

Yu knew. The Mao Zedong Thought Worker Propaganda Teams—sometimes shortened as "Mao Teams"—were a product of the Cultural

Revolution. At the beginning of the movement, Mao had rallied young students in the name of the Red Guards to take back power from his rivals in the Party, but the Red Guards soon went out of control, posing a threat to Mao's own power base. So he declared that the workers themselves should play the leading role in the Cultural Revolution, and he sent Mao Teams to schools as unchallengeable forces, crushing the students and teachers. A teacher at Yu's middle school had been beaten into a cripple by a Mao Team member.

"So he was punished," Uncle Fong said. "But there were millions of rebels like him in those years. It's just his luck to be chosen as an example. Sentenced to two or three years in prison. What karma!"

"Jasmine was still quite young?"

"Yes, she was only four or five then. She lived with her mother for a couple of years and then, after her mother's death, she moved back. Tian never took good care of her, and five or six years ago, he became paralyzed," Uncle Fong said, taking a long thoughtful drink of his tea. "She, on the other hand, took good care of him. It wasn't easy, and she had to save every penny. He didn't have a pension or medical insurance. She never had a boyfriend because of him."

"Because of the old man? How come?"

"She did not want to leave him alone. Any prospective suitor would have had to take over the burden. And few were interested in doing that."

"Very few indeed," Yu said, nodding. "Didn't she have any friends in the lane?"

"No, not really. She did not mix with girls of her own age. Too busy working and taking care of things at home. She had to work at other odd jobs, I believe." Uncle Fong added, putting down the teacup, "Let me take you there, so you may see for yourself."

Uncle Fong led Yu to an old *shikumen* house in the midsection of the lane, pushing open a door directly into a room that looked to have been partitioned out of the original courtyard. It was an all-purpose room with a disorderly bed in the center, a ladder to an attic of later construction, an unlit coal briquette stove close to the bed, an ancient chamber pot practically uncovered, and hardly any other furniture. For the last few years, this small room must have been the world for Tian, who now sprawled face-up on the bed.

Jasmine might have had reasons not to stay at home much, Yu realized, nodding at her father.

"This is Tian," Uncle Fong said, pointing. The man looked as emaciated as a skeleton, except for his eyes, which followed the visitors around the room. "Tian, this is Comrade Detective Yu of the Shanghai Police Bureau."

Tian hissed something indistinct in response.

"She alone understood his words," Uncle Fong commented. "I don't know who will come to help now. It's no longer the age of Comrade Lei Feng and no one wants to follow the selfless communist model."

Yu wondered if Tian's mind was clear enough to grasp what they were talking about. Perhaps better if not. Better a total blank page than to mourn the death of his daughter and face his own inevitable end. Whatever he had done during the Cultural Revolution, the retribution was enough.

Yu pulled the ladder over and climbed up cautiously.

"Yes, that's where she lived." Uncle Fong remained standing on the floor, looking up. The climb was too difficult for him.

It was not even an attic. Just a "second floor," added in a makeshift way over Tian's bed, which occupied most of the first floor. A grown-up girl, she had to have some space for herself. Yu was unable to stand erect up there, his head touching the ceiling. Nor was there a single window. In the darkness, it took him a minute or two to find a lamp switch, which he turned on. No bed, only a mattress. Beside it squatted a plastic spittoon—possibly her chamber pot. There was also an unpainted wooden box. He opened the lid to see some clothes inside, most of them cheap and old-fashioned.

It seemed pointless to stay any longer. He climbed down to the side of the bed, raising no questions. How could Fong know anything about the case?

Yu said good-bye to Uncle Fong and left the lane, feeling depressed by the visit.

If a girl, in her flowering age, had chosen to live like that, she wouldn't likely have been an easy target for a sex murderer or triggered a serial killing.

Instead of going back to the bureau, Yu went to the hotel where Jasmine had worked, which was located in the Old City area. The Seagull wasn't a fancy hotel, but because of its convenient location and reasonable price, it had become a "hot choice for budget travelers." In the crowded lobby, Yu saw a group of foreign students carrying huge knapsacks. The front desk manager appeared professional in his scarlet uniform, speaking fluent English to them. He stammered, however, at the police badge Yu produced. He led Yu into an office, closing the door after them.

"Whatever we talk about here, please don't let any media people know about the hotel's connection to the red mandarin dress murders. Or our business will go down the drain. People are superstitious and they won't stay in a hotel where they think someone has met a violent death."

"I understand," Yu said. "Now tell me what you know about her."

"A good girl, hard-working, easy to get along with. We're all shocked by her death. If anything, perhaps she worked too hard."

"I've talked to her neighborhood committee. They also told me she worked really hard, and she did not stay much at home. Do you know anything about a possible second job of hers?"

"That I don't know. She worked overtime here, for which we paid her time and a half. She worked for housekeeping in the morning and helped at the hotel canteen. She worked extra nights too. She had to pay her father's medical bills. Ours is a hotel capable of housing foreign tourists, so we would rather have trusted employees working here. Our general manager gave her as many hours as she pleased. People like a young pretty girl."

"People like a young pretty girl—what do you mean?"

"Don't get me wrong. We do not tolerate any improper service here. A girl of her age could have chosen to work somewhere else—say, a nightclub—for far more money, but she stayed here, working longer hours."

"Do you know anything about her personal life? For instance, did she have a boyfriend?"

"I don't know," the manager said, stammering again. "That's her private life. She worked hard, as I've said, and she did not talk much to her colleagues here."

"Is it possible that there was anything between her and someone staying at the hotel?"

"Comrade Detective Yu, ours is not a high-end hotel. And the people staying here are no Big Bucks. They come for a convenient location at a reasonable price, not for . . . companionship."

"We have to ask all sorts of questions, Comrade Manager," Yu said. "Here is my card. If you can think of anything else, please contact me."

The visit to the hotel yielded little new information. If anything, it only confirmed his impression that a girl like Jasmine probably wouldn't have set off a lust killer who happened to cross her path, either by the grubby lane or at the shabby hotel.

SIX

PEIQIN, TOO, HAD BEEN giving a lot of thought to the mandarin dress case.

Not just because there were so many puzzling things about it, but also because it was Yu's first case as acting squad head.

As before, she drew a line for herself between what she could and could not do. She didn't have the resources available to the cops, nor the time and energy. So she chose the red mandarin dress as an entrance point.

As an accountant, Peiqin didn't have to work at her office in the restaurant from nine to five every day. So on the way to the restaurant, she stepped into a boutique tailor shop. It wasn't known for its mandarin dresses, but she was acquainted with an old tailor there. She explained the purpose of her visit and showed him an enlarged picture of the dress.

"Judging from its long sleeves and low slits, it's quite old-fashioned, possibly a style from the early sixties," the white-haired-and-browed tailor said, adjusting the glasses along the ridge of his angular nose. "I doubt it's mass-produced nowadays. Look at the craftsmanship. The double-fish-shaped cloth buttons. It probably takes a day to make them."

"Do you think it was made in the sixties?"

"I cannot tell that from a picture. Altogether, I've only made about half a dozen of them. I am no expert, but if a customer gave me the material and the design, I think I could do the job."

"One more question: do you know any other store that could have made it?"

"Quite a number of them. In addition, there are private tailors who work at the customer's home. No stores for them, you know."

So there was another problem. Many private tailors worked like that, moving from one customer family to another. The cops were incapable of investigating all the possibilities.

Leaving the store, Peiqin decided to go to the Shanghai Library. If she was going to help, she had to proceed in a way different than the cops.

In the library, she spent about an hour checking through the catalogue and requested a pile of books and magazines.

It was already past ten when she climbed up into her office at Four Seas Restaurant, carrying a plastic bag of books in her arms. Manager Hua Shan wasn't there that morning. He had been out for two days, starting his own company, though he still kept his job at Four Seas.

In spite of its good location, the state-run restaurant was having a hard time. Between socialism and capitalism, as the new saying went, falls a shadow of difference—that between the people working for themselves and the people working for the state. The restaurant had suffered losses for months. Hence, there were talks about introducing management responsibility: the restaurant would remain state-run in name, but the new manager would be responsible for its profit or losses.

In the midst of a chorus of ladles clanking and clattering on the woks downstairs, she made an effort to focus on the books in the tiny office above the restaurant kitchen.

What she had told Yu was true. She knew little about the dress. In her school days, she had seen it only in movies. And then in a Cultural Revolution–era photograph of Wang Guangmei, the "ex-first lady" of China, who was forced to display herself in public wearing a torn scarlet mandarin dress and a chunk of white Ping-Pong balls in imitation of oversized pearls—both the dress and jewelry serving as evidence of her decadent bourgeois lifestyle.

Looking at the materials spread out on the desk, Peiqin was at a loss. She leafed through one book after another until a black and white picture caught her eye: a picture of Ailing, a Shanghai novelist rediscovered in the nineties, wearing a florid mandarin dress in the thirties. In a recent TV show, Peiqin recalled, a young girl strolled musingly along Huanghe Road, as if stepping about on the clouds of fashionable nostalgia, and pointed at a building behind her. "Perhaps it is here, from this quaint building, Ailing would walk out, blossoming in a mandarin dress she herself had designed. What a romantic city!"

A self-proclaimed fashion critic, Ailing had drawn a series of sketches of Shanghai-style clothing, which was reprinted at the end of the book. But Peiqin became more interested in the personal story of Ailing. Ailing started publishing early and became well-known for her stories about Shanghai. She endured a heartbreaking marriage with a talented womanizer, who later made a small fortune by writing about their ill-starred marriage. After 1949, she went to the United States, where she married an aged, impoverished American writer. As in a Tang dynasty poem, "Everything turns out sad for a poor couple." The biographer diagnosed her marriage as self-deconstructive. After the death of her second husband, she shut herself up in her apartment in San Francisco, where she died alone. No one was aware of it until several days later.

Peiqin read the tragic story, hoping to gain insight from a historical perspective into the popularity of the mandarin dress. By the end of two hours' reading, however, she had learned little. If anything, her research only confirmed her earlier impression that it was a dress for well-to-do or well-educated women. For someone like Ailing, but not for a working woman like Peiqin. Tapping on the book, she absentmindedly noticed a tiny hole in her black wool sock.

She was intrigued by the biographer's analysis on the "self-deconstructive" tendency of Ailing. Chen, too, was engaged in a so-called deconstructive project, she had heard. She wondered what the term meant.

There was a knock on the door. She looked up to see Chef Pan standing in the doorway, carrying an earthen pot in his hands.

"A special pot for you," he said.

"Thank you." She did not have the time to clear away the books displaying an array of mandarin dress pictures.

"What are you reading, Peiqin?"

"I'm trying to make a dress for myself. So I'm comparing designs."

"You are really a capable woman, Peiqin," he said, putting the pot on the desk. "And I've been meaning to mention something to you. We've been losing money for almost half a year. The socialist system has gone to the dogs and people are talking about the new management system."

Peiqin took the lid off the pot and smiled. "Wow, wonderful," she said. "The food, I mean." It was the chef's special: the carp head covered in red pepper on a bed of white garlic at the bottom.

"The pot keeps things warm for a long time. It's still very hot," Pan went on, rubbing his hands. "A middle class is rising fast in China. They come to a restaurant for something special, not for homely dishes they can cook themselves. So we need to change too. How about you taking over the management? I'll back you up. Socialist or capitalist, this restaurant is ours."

"Thank you, Pan. I'll think about it," she said, "but I may not be qualified for the job."

"Do think about it, Peiqin," he said, backing toward the door. "We never know what we can do until we try."

Helping herself to a spoonful of the soup, she thought to herself that she might indeed be able to do a better job for the restaurant—or at least a more conscientious job than the current management was doing. But what about her family? Qinqin was studying hard for the college entrance examination. For his future, a first-class college was a must. Yu, too, had reached a critical stage in his career. She had to take care of things at home.

After lunch, she found it hard to concentrate on the books again. Downstairs, a squabble seemed to be breaking out in the kitchen. Hua called in, saying that he wouldn't be coming in that day. Peiqin had another idea about the red mandarin dress, so she decided to take the afternoon off.

She might be able to learn something about it from the movies. The dress could have some specific meaning that she was not aware of in her lusterless daily life. She walked out, heading toward a DVD store on Sichuan Road. The afternoon had turned cold. She wrapped herself more tightly in the cotton-padded army jacket, one of the few remainders from her army farm days in Yunnan. Ironically, the imitation army jacket, too, seemed to be getting popular again.

The store was huge, with thousands of VCDs and DVDs displayed in various sections. To her amazement, she saw quite a few new movies that had not been officially released.

"So how can there be DVDs so quickly?" she asked the storeowner, who was also a customer at her restaurant.

"Easy. Someone sneaks into a preview with a camcorder," he said with a broad grin. "We guarantee the quality. You can return the DVD for a full refund."

She thanked him and looked around. In the section of Western classics, she came upon a movie entitled *Random Harvest*, adapted from the novel by James Hilton. It was the first English novel Chen had read in Bund Park, Yu had told her. The Chinese version had a fascinating title: *A Pair of Mandarin Ducks' Dream Re-dreamed.* In classical Chinese poetry, a pair of Mandarin ducks stood for inseparable lovers. So this must be a love story. She put the movie into her shopping basket.

In the domestic section, she picked up *A Nurse's Diary*, a movie made in the fifties. She remembered having seen a poster of the young nurse wearing a mandarin dress. Another love story, judging from the glamorous DVD cover. She also chose *Golden Lock*, a Hong Kong movie based on a novel by Ailing.

But she failed to find a documentary movie about the dress, nor any movie with a title directly connected to it.

The moment she got back home, she turned on the DVD player. There were still a couple of hours before she had to worry about dinner. She took off her shoes and socks, stretched herself out on the sofa, and covered her feet with a cushion.

She watched *Random Harvest* for only ten minutes. Too old-fashioned Hollywood for her. What would Chen think about the movie, she wondered.

A Nurse's Diary was a different story: it was about a group of young people dedicated to building a new socialist China. By today's standards, it didn't come close to being a romantic story. The young nurse was too busy making the revolution to have many romantic thoughts. In fact, romantic affairs were far from encouraged at the time. The movie appealed to Peiqin, however, particularly for the idealistic theme song: " 'Little swallow, little swallow, / you come back here every year. / Can you tell me why?' / The little swallow replies, / 'The Spring is most beautiful here,' . . ."

The most beautiful "here" in the song, she contemplated, must refer to somewhere along the northwest borders, still impoverished, undeveloped, forsaken. No one would ever think of going there today.

"The Spring is most beautiful here." On the screen, the slender nurse, played by the actress Linfeng, was humming the song, her face lit up with the passion of the socialist revolution. Years later, Linfeng emigrated to Tokyo, where she was said to be running a Chinese vegetarian restaurant. There she sang the song occasionally for overseas Chinese customers, her figure out of shape and too much makeup on her face. Of course, it would be naïve to expect an actress to keep playing such a role—or showing such a figure—all her life.

As it turned out, in the movie the dress was worn by the nurse's mother, a middle-aged lady of the upper class in the old society, still resistant to the socialist revolution. But Peiqin was not exactly disappointed. As in her initial impression, mandarin dresses—in movies and in life—were mostly for those women moving about in fashionable upper-class.

As she was about to watch *Golden Lock*, her glance fell on a book she had brought home. The white-haired author looked strangely like her late father. She read the short biographical information beneath the picture on the cover. "Shen Wenchang, a well-known poet before 1949, and after 1949, an internationally known expert on the history of Chinese clothing."

She opened the book, but it touched on the mandarin dress in only two short paragraphs. In the notes at the back of the book, she did not find a single scholar dealing exclusively with the mandarin dress. So perhaps the best she could get would be a paragraph here and there.

The old man must be in his eighties. She put down the book, gazing at the picture. If only she could consult an expert like him, she thought wistfully.

Around dinnertime, the phone rang. It was Chen, who expressed regret upon learning that Yu was still at work.

"Yu's been so busy the last few days that he often comes back late. Don't worry about him," she said. "How is your paper going?"

"Slowly but steadily. I am so sorry about the timing, but it may be the last chance to try my hand at something different," Chen said. "How are things with you?"

"Not that busy. I'm just reading some books. Everybody is talking about the red mandarin dress, so I thought I might learn something about it."

"You are trying to help again, Peiqin. Have you found anything interesting?"

"Nothing yet. I've just started reading a book on the history of Chinese clothing. The author used to be a poet too."

"Shen Wenchang?"

"Do you know him?"

"Yes. A great scholar. There's a new documentary movie about him."

"I haven't seen that movie. Oh, I bought a DVD, *Random Harvest*, from the novel you like. Yu told me about your days in the park."

"Thank you, Peiqin. It's so thoughtful of you. I can't wait to watch it." Chen added, "When Yu gets home, tell him to call me—oh, and to bring the movie over to me at his convenience."

SEVEN

CHEN WOKE UP DISORIENTED, as if still floundering in a sea of thoughts.

With the second body found in the center of the city, with the media clamoring like cicadas in the early summer, he had to do something to help. He owed that to Yu. And to Hong too, who had kept him updated with the latest developments, smiling a radiant smile in spite of Liao's grouchiness.

Having reviewed all the measures taken by his colleagues, however, Chen concluded he could hardly do any more than they, at least not as an "outside consultant." He was still too much engaged with his paper. Running an investigation could be like writing a paper; ideas come with undivided concentration.

A bitter taste returned to his mouth. Brushing his teeth vigorously, he was struck with an idea—Peiqin's idea. He happened to know Shen, the authority on the history of Chinese clothing.

Shen had been a poet in the forties, writing in a then-fashionable Imagist style. After 1949, he was assigned a job at the Shanghai Museum, where he denounced his earlier poetry as decadent and threw himself into the study of ancient Chinese clothing. Probably a neck-saving choice in the deteriorating political climate of the mid-fifties. As in *Tao De Jing*, misfortune leads to fortune. Because of his abrupt disappearance from the literary scene, the young Red Guards in the mid-sixties failed to recognize him as a "bourgeois poet," and he was spared the humiliations and persecutions. In the eighties, he reemerged with a multivolume work on the history of ancient Chinese clothing, which was translated into several foreign languages, and he became an "internationally known authority." The literary scene was busy with new voices and faces and few remembered him as a poet anymore.

Chen would not have remembered him either but for a meeting with a British sinologist who raved about Shen's earlier literary work. Chen was impressed by a short poem about Shen's early days:

> *Pregnant, happy / for the coming baby / who'll be able to be / a Shanghainese, his wife's touching / the blue veins streaking / her breasts, like—//the mountain ranges / against the pale clouds the day / he left, his grandmother / stumbling after him / in her bound feet, putting / a chunk of the soil /in his hand, saying, / "It—(a mutilated earthworm / wriggled out of the lump)—will / bring you back."*

As an executive member of the Writers' Association, Chen took it upon himself to arrange for a reprint of Shen's collection. It was not an easy job. The old man was nervous about poetry, like a man once bitten by a snake, and the publisher, hesitant about possible financial loss, was like a man in fear of a snake. Still, the collection came out and was caught up in the city's collective nostalgia. People were pleased to rediscover a poetic witness of those golden years before the revolution. A young critic pointed out that the American Imagist poets were indebted to classical Chinese poetry and that Shen, labeled an Imagist, was actually restoring the ancient tradition. The article appealed to a group of "new nationalists," and the collection sold fairly well.

Chen took out his address book and dialed Shen's number.

"A gentleman's request I cannot refuse," Shen agreed, quoting from Confucius. "But I have to take a look at the mandarin dress."

"No problem. I'm not in the bureau today, but you can talk to Detective Yu, or to Inspector Liao. Either of them will show you the dress."

He then informed Yu of Shen's visit. As Chen expected, Yu was pleased with the unexpected help, promising to show the dress to the historian. At the end of their call, Chen added, "Oh, it's so thoughtful of Peiqin—she had the copy of *Random Harvest* specially delivered to me. I've been looking for that movie for a long time."

"Yes, she's been watching a lot of DVDs, trying to find clues there."

"Anything new?"

"No, nothing so far, but the DVDs might give her a break from her job."

"You're right about that," Chen said, though he didn't really think so. It was like his reading for the last two weeks. Once he took it seriously—as something he had to do, something with a purpose—it gave him no break.

Before he could leave for the library to continue his work, there was another special delivery to his home. It was a package of new information about Jia Ming from Director Zhong.

Mostly it was speculation about Jia's motive for making trouble for the government. Jia and his entire family had suffered during the Cultural Revolution; Jia ultimately lost his parents. He had become a lawyer in the early eighties, when such a career choice was uncommon. During the sixties and seventies, attorneys were hardly existent or relevant in China. Lawyers, like stocks, were considered part and parcel of capitalist society: hypocritical and for the rich. Major cases were determined or predetermined by the Party authorities, all in the name of the proletarian dictatorships. Liu Shaoqi, chairman of the People's Republic of China, had been thrown in jail without a trial, and there he died alone, without a notice sent to his family for years. Jia had deliberately chosen to become an attorney at a time when it was far from a popular profession: he had planned to make trouble for the government from the beginning.

Because of his early entry into the field, he was quickly successful. As a legal system was advocated and recognized as part of China's reform, he became well known for his defense of a dissident writer. He made such a brilliant defense that the judge appeared tongue-tied several times, which people caught on TV and applauded. The "new" legal practice gathered steam, and law offices sprung up like bamboo shoots after a sudden spring rain.

But Jia was different from the others. He didn't take on only profitable cases. Partially because of his inheritance from his family after the Cultural Revolution, he didn't have to work for the sake of money. From time to time, he would take on controversial cases, which put him on a blacklist composed by the city government, even before he took over the West-Nine-Block housing development case.

Chen decided not to read any more. During his college years, he, too, had been put on a blacklist, by groundless political interpretations of his modernist poetry.

It was past ten when Chen arrived at the library. Susu, the librarian with enchanting dimples, brought him a cup of fresh coffee, strong and refreshing.

Still, his mind started wandering. Perhaps he was more drawn to the murder case than to the love stories, a realization that did not exactly surprise him.

Only after the second cup of coffee did he manage to settle down to another tale selected for his paper, "The Story of Yingying."

The Tang dynasty *cuanqi* story was composed by Yuan Zhen, a well-known poet and statesman. According to subsequent studies, the narrative was largely autobiographical. In the year 800, Yuan traveled to Puzhou, where he met a girl named Yingying. They fell in love. Yuan then went to the capital, where he married a girl of the Wei family instead. Eventually, Yuan wrote a story based on the Puzhou episode.

Chen turned to the story with interest. In it, a scholar named Zhang traveled to the Temple of Universal Salvation, where Mrs. Cui was staying with her daughter Yingying on their way to Zhang'an. As the troops nearby rose up in mutiny, Zhang obtained help from his friend to provide much-needed security for the people in the temple. Out of gratitude, Mrs. Cui invited Zhang to a banquet, during which he met Yingying and fell in love with her, though she rebuked his advances with Confucian moralist lectures. One night, however, in a dramatic turn, she came to his western-wing room, offering herself to him. Soon afterward, he left for the civil service examination in the capital, where he received a letter from her. Part of the letter read:

When I offered myself to you in your bed, you took me with the kindest passion. I was so ignorant as to believe that I could depend on you ever after. How could I have realized that having succumbed to the attraction of a gentleman like you without following the proper marriage rites, there was no chance of serving you openly as a wife in the future? To the end of my days that will be an everlasting regret—I could do nothing but to stifle my sighs and be silent. If you, out of the greatest kindness, would condescend to grant the fulfillment of my secret wish, though in death I would be happy as in life. But if, as a man of the world, you curtail your feeling, sacrifice the lesser for the sake of the more important, and regard the affair as shameful, so that our solemn vow can be dispensed with, still my true love will not vanish, and in the breeze and dew it will follow the ground you walk on, even as my body decays, dissolves. . . .

Yuan's scholar-protagonist then showed the letter to his friends before he deserted Yingying with a surprising moralistic argument, which came at the end of the story:

It is a general rule that those Heaven-endowed beauties invariably either ruin themselves or ruin others. If this Cui girl were to meet someone with great wealth and position, she would use the favor she gains to come in cloud and rain, or dragon and monster—I cannot imagine what she might turn into. Of old, King Yin of the Shang and King You of the Zhou were brought low by such women; in spite of the size of their kingdoms and the extent of their power, their armies were destroyed, their people butchered, and to the present day their names are objects of ridicule. I have no inner virtue to withstand this evil influence. That is why I have resolutely suppressed my love.

At that point in the narrative, the author—posing as Zhang's close friend in the text—stepped in to endorse Zhang's behavior in his own words.

Zhang's contemporaries for the most part commended him as one who had done well to rectify his mistake. I have often mentioned this among friends so that, forewarned, they might avoid making such a mistake, or if they already did, that they might not get totally lost.

Zhang's decision, Chen observed, came as a volte-face, severing at one stroke the romantic theme. The character's argument amounted to an assertion that a woman, if irresistibly charming, should be disposed of as an "evil influence," for she will "ruin" the man close to her like a "monster."

Chen thought that a better self-defense could have been made. The self-justifying rhetoric about Yingying's being a monster seemed to Chen nothing but brazen hypocrisy—a poor excuse for Zhang's having seduced her and then deserted her, making the story fascinating and confounding. It invited speculation about its inconsistencies: romantic passion, for example, was commended in the first part of the story and condemned in the second.

But for the purpose of his paper, the story's similarities to the other tales he'd read was beginning to suggest a topic for his project. "The

Story of Yingying," like "The Story of Xiangru and Wenjun," effected a deconstructive turn in the narration of the romance. The Han-dynasty story attributed the hero's death of thirsty illness to the heroine, who, implicitly evil in her sexual insatiability, depleted and eventually destroyed him. In the Tang-dynasty story, the hero averted his destruction by accusing the heroine of being a monster who ruins people close to her. In both stories, the romantic theme was eventually denounced.

Chen was reminded, unexpectedly, of something in the red mandarin dress case: the killer's ambivalence or contradiction. The murderer stripped and killed the victims, but he put their bodies in expensive, elegant dresses.

It was an elusive parallel, fading from his thoughts before he could fully articulate it. So he tried to refocus himself on the books, exploring the background of Yuan further. In literary criticism, the biographical approach sometimes contributed to one's understanding of a difficult text.

But what about the criminal investigation? With the perpetrator's identity unknown, biographical analysis seemed out of the question, and the meaning of the contradictory clues seemed indecipherable.

Again he found his mind stuck, torn between the two projects, which further confused and confounded him.

Around one o'clock, Shen called him at the library.

"Any discovery, Shen?"

"It's a long story, Chief Inspector Chen," Shen said. "I'd better tell you in person, I think. I can show you some pictures."

"Great. Let me buy you lunch. How about Five Fragrance Resort? It's a restaurant across the street from the library."

EIGHT

AS CHEN STEPPED INTO the restaurant, a waiter who had known him for years greeted him warmly.

"You haven't come here in a long time, Chen. What would you like to have today?"

"Whatever you recommend, but not too much. Only for two people."

"How about the Chef's Special Combination for two?"

"Great. And a pot of strong green tea, please."

While waiting, Chen tried to think about his paper again. Perhaps it was not enough to analyze only one or two stories. If he succeeded in proving the thematic contradiction as something common in classical love stories, it might be an original, worthy project. So he had to choose one or two more stories. He wrote that down in his notebook.

Closing the notebook, he looked up to see Shen shuffle into the restaurant, leaning on a bamboo stick topped with a dragon head. A white-haired and browed man in his early eighties, Shen looked spirited, wearing a cotton-padded traditional Tang costume and black cloth shoes. Chen rose and helped the old man to the table.

As it turned out, Shen hadn't had a pleasant experience at the bureau. Detective Yu had hurried out for something urgent; Inspector Liao received Shen instead. Liao, declaring that he had already consulted several old tailors, showed little interest in Shen.

There might be another reason, Chen suspected, for Liao's manner. Shen's coming to the bureau at Chen's request could have rubbed Liao the wrong way. It wasn't necessary, however, to explain the bureau politics to the elderly scholar.

"Don't worry about Liao. He can occasionally be as stubborn as a mule, and as stupid too," Chen said, pouring a cup of tea for Shen as the waiter started serving cold dishes. "Please give me an introduction into the history of the mandarin dress. I am all ears."

Shen, helping himself to a spoon of white jade tofu flavored with green onion and sesame oil and nodding in approval, started. "Now, why is it called mandarin dress? There are a number of theories about it. For one, the Manchurians, both male and female, wore gowns of bright colors. It is also said that in the early period of the Qing dynasty, the Manchurians divided their people into eight groups, or *qi*, each sporting a flag of a special color and design. *Qi* is the same as in *Qipao*—mandarin dress, you know. It was not until the twenties and thirties, however, that the dress suddenly turned into a nationwide hit, shedding its ethnic suggestion. It then enjoyed great popularity until the beginning of the Cultural Revolution. In the mid-eighties, it was reembraced, and now it's internationally popular. Hollywood stars wear mandarin dresses to the Oscar ceremonies. People believe that it hugs a woman's body subtly, bringing out her curves like no other dress. . . ."

It was a long introduction but Chen listened with great interest. The mandarin dress being an unmistakable signature of the murderer, a cop couldn't be too knowledgeable about it.

"About the mandarin dress Liao showed me: it was made years earlier, probably more than ten years ago," Shen said, producing several pictures, "based on the color of the thread—already yellow with time. When you consider the material, the special damask with its exquisite print pattern, it possibly goes back even earlier. The sixties, I would say. The same with the tiny steel press buttons. Tailors only used them during that time period or earlier. Since the early eighties, they've used plastic zippers instead, which are more comfortable and tighter fitting. The style of the dress also belongs to that period. Look at the whole-piece sleeves. Fashionable people now prefer separate-piece sleeves, which bring out the curves more eloquently. They are also much easier to make—"

Shen's lecture was interrupted by the arrival of their main dishes. Among them, there was a glass bowl containing live shrimp immersed in white liquor. The drunken shrimp were still jumping, though less and less energetically.

"A fashionable dish," Shen said, "sort of rediscovered too."

For a man his age, Shen showed quite a good appetite. He chop-sticked a twitching shrimp into his mouth and Chen followed suit. The shrimp tasted slightly sweet, but he didn't like the slippery sensation on his tongue.

"Now I have to say a word about its tailoring," Shen went on, puckering his lips. "A hundred percent handmade. Only an old, experienced Ningbo tailor could have produced such a dress. It took at least a week to finish. Today you may see a mandarin dress displayed in a high-end store, shiny and splendid with a staggering price tag, but the quality is just a joke. All machine made and not at all comparable to the one Liao showed me."

"So it was made at least ten years ago, and the material and the style date back even earlier—the sixties or fifties," Chen said, writing it down in his notebook. "In other words, the criminal had to special order material from an earlier period, and then custom-tailor it in a special way."

"That's beyond me," Shen said. "But there's something else in the way the victim wore the dress. The essence of mandarin dress aesthetics is subtle suggestiveness. The dress slits, for instance, reveal a woman's legs, but not too much. A partial glimpse of her thighs could stir up the imagination most effectively."

"So it's like classical Chinese poetry," Chen cut in. "Imagination rises out of what the poet does not say, or not directly."

"Exactly. You know the difference. For example, a tall, buxom American star may wear a so-called modified mandarin dress, backless and extremely short in the skirt part. I, for one, would have lost all my sense of imagination at the sight of her bare back covered with speckles, and her legs and thighs shaven like mammoth tusks."

"You are still so good with your Imagist touch, Master Shen."

"To put it in another way, it is a dress that allows the wearer's inner grace to shine through. Sensual, subtle, svelte. It's not a costume that becomes everyone."

"Yes, there is quite a lot of knowledge in that," Chen echoed.

"The length of the side slits is another point of subtlety. For a woman of a good family, the slits are usually modest, suggesting her refined sense of decorum. Strictly speaking, when wearing a mandarin dress, a woman walks with small steps, without showing any dramatic body movement. A fashionable girl, however, may have to have higher slits for dancing or strutting around. As for a girl in the entertainment business, she would choose one with the highest slits possible, showing her legs and thighs seductively, and sometimes her buttocks too. It's sort of the mandarin dress semiotics. In the thirties, a potential customer on Fourth Street would have approached her."

"Yes, the dress etiquette speaks," Chen said, swallowing another live shrimp without chewing it—a throat-scratching mistake with a terrible aftertaste. Fourth Street was an area where prostitutes had congregated before 1949.

"Also, an elegant lady wears stockings and high heels to match her dress, though not necessarily so formal at home. But look at the picture—no bra, no panties, no shoes, and the dress is rolled up high above her groin. Whoever did this murdered the dress too." Shen paused for a moment before going on. "She's a sex victim, I understand, but this dress is too old and rare to have been acquired by accident. Also, it is a fairly conservative dress—a woman doesn't have sex in it. It doesn't make sense."

"A lot of things in this case don't make sense," Chen said, clearing his throat.

"I don't know about the case, Chief Inspector Chen," Shen said in confusion. "I know only about the dress."

"Thank you, Shen. Your expertise has surely thrown light into the investigation."

Chen did not say, however, that it also raised more questions than it resolved. The mandarin dress, if as old as Shen thought, was not popular when it was made. Whoever made it, made it against the fashion of the time. That suggested a possible cause embedded deeper in history, which only led to more questions.

Shen was picking up the last live shrimp with his chopsticks when Chen's cell phone shrilled. Shen was startled, and the shrimp fell back into the bowl, splashing, jumping high as if having escaped its fate.

The phone call was from a *Wenhui* reporter, who wanted to find out Chen's theory on the red mandarin dress case.

"Sorry, I can't give you any theory. I'm on leave, working on my literature paper."

The instant he hung up the phone, he regretted having made the statement. It was true, but it could cause speculation.

"Really?" Shen wanted to know, rising slowly. " 'The most useless is a scholar,' like me, but there may not be too many capable cops, like you."

Chen rose to support him on their way out without making a comment.

Near the exit, there were a couple of large glass tanks containing live shrimp and fish, all of them enjoying a leisurely swim, unaware that their fate might change with the next customer's order.

NINE

OUTSIDE OF THE RESTAURANT, Shen moved slowly to the curb, then lowered himself into a taxi, his body doubled like a shrimp.

Waving at the taxi, Chen chided himself for the image. Shen was an original poet and an original scholar. Perhaps his academic success came from his Imagist poetics. He didn't see a dress merely as a piece of clothing but as an image with meanings and associations.

An organic image full of life in itself, which may speak more than pages of words.

Chen recalled one such image of clothing in *Random Harvest*, the novel he'd read many years ago, in Bund Park. It was an image from the heroine's first appearance—"a little fur hat, like a fez." It was symbolic in the text because the protagonist's niece also wore a fur hat like a fez on another occasion. A subtle suggestion, as Chen interpreted it, about something similar between the two. When he had read it the first time, *fez* was an English word he didn't know. So he looked it up in a dictionary, which defined it as a "red felt headdress, shaped like an inverted flowerpot."

With his sentimental partiality, it would be hard for a movie to do justice to the original, and he tried not to expect too much from the one Peiqin had sent him. Still, he couldn't help being disappointed. The film was in black and white and such a headdress didn't stand out at all.

But what about the red mandarin dress as an image?

He stood transfixed by the question, still waving his hand at the street with the taxi long out of sight.

A good image may have a specific meaning to the author, and to the readers too. In Shen's poem, passion for his home came out vividly in the "mutilated earthworm." On the other hand, a bad image may be so specific to the writer that it is incomprehensible to the readers.

The murderer was no author, who worried about his readers' comprehension. The more puzzling to others, the more satisfactory to himself, and the more successful his performance.

Chen suddenly became aware of something vibrating in his pant pocket. The cell phone. This time, the caller's ID showed Party Secretary Li.

"I want you to cut short your leave. Don't worry about your paper, Comrade Chief Inspector Chen. The murderer must be found before he strikes again. You don't need me to tell you that."

"I'm paying close attention to the case, Party Secretary Li."

That much was true, though Chen didn't acknowledge his effort on the side. He had a feeling that the murderer was not only highly intelligent but also well-connected. For once, Chen had the advantage of staying behind the scene, and he wanted to keep it.

"The city government is concerned about the case. A leading comrade has mentioned your name again this morning."

"I know. I'll discuss it with Detective Yu."

"So come back to the bureau this afternoon."

"This afternoon. . . ." He was not pleased with Li's ordering him around, nor ready to go back. "You may not know that I've been looking into the West-Nine-Block housing development case. Director Zhong of the Shanghai Legal System Reform Committee wants me to—"

"So your Chinese literature paper is only an excuse," Li snapped. "You could have told me earlier."

Another imprudent slip. Chen had assumed that the excuse would put Li off for the moment, but he forgot that Li's not knowing about Chen's involvement was too much a loss of face for the Party boss.

"No, it's not an excuse. I mean the paper. I do have to turn in the paper on time. As for the housing development case, you may have heard of its political sensitivity. As yet, I have done nothing about it—there was nothing to report."

Indeed, a power struggle was being staged at the very top, Chen had learned, in the Forbidden City. Now that several high-ranking Shanghai cadres were implicated in the scandal, someone in Beijing wanted to exploit it for ulterior motives.

"You are too big a clay image for our small temple, Chief Inspector Chen."

"No, you don't have to say that, Secretary Li. I'm going to discuss the red mandarin dress case with Detective Yu. I give you my word."

So instead of going back to the library after finishing his talk with Li, Chen called Yu.

"Sorry, Chief. I had to run out this morning. I missed Mr. Shen."

"Don't worry about that. We just had lunch together and Shen gave me quite a lecture about the mandarin dress."

"Where are you?"

"Close to the Shanghai Library."

"Do you have some time this afternoon? I'd like to talk."

"Yes, so would I."

"Great. Where shall we meet?"

"Well—" It was not practical to discuss a murder case in the library. Looking around, Chen saw a pottery bar around the corner with only a young couple sitting inside.

"What about the pottery bar on the corner of Fengyang Road, opposite the library?"

"Oh, it's so fashionable, the pottery bar. I'll be there in twenty minutes."

Chen walked into the bar, which had an L-shaped interior. The long side wasn't that different from a café, and the short side was like a workshop with large desks, piles of clay, and a stove on the end. A customer could try his hand at pottery while enjoying a cup of coffee. Perhaps because of the time of the day, there were only the two young people in the workshop and Chen alone in the café section. The price could have been another reason. A cup of coffee here cost much more than at an ordinary café.

As he took a sip at the hot coffee, the sight of the young lovers bending over their project brought to mind a scene from a Hollywood movie, and then an image in a classical Chinese *ci* by a thirteenth-century woman poet, Guan Daoshen.

You and I are so crazy / about each other, / as if lost in the potter's fire./ Out of a chunk /of clay, shape a you, / shape a me. Crush us / both into clay again, mix / it with water, reshape / a you, reshape a me. / So, I have you in my body, and you have me in yours too.

In the workshop, the girl started smearing the boy's face with her clay-covered hand, her laughter sounding like silver bells, though Chen failed to make out the endearments whispered between the two. A touching image, just like in the poem. He contented himself with black coffee, attempting to digest the information from Shen.

He thought about Shen's Imagist approach to the mandarin dress. It was possible that the dress's meaning was not exclusive to the "author," but that meaning was difficult for the cops to figure out because the dress had been made in accordance to a model, or an original image, such a long time ago.

Peiqin had been searching movies for something like an archetype.

Perhaps he could do more than she in that aspect. Not because of his abilities but because of his connections.

He took out his address book, looking for the number of Chairman Wang of the Chinese Writers' Association, who also served as the First Associate Party Secretary of the Chinese Artists' Association, whose members including fashion designers, photographers, and directors. Not too long ago, Chen had helped Wang in his way.

"Have you heard or read about the red mandarin case in Shanghai, Chairman Wang?" Chen said directly as soon as the long-distance call got through.

"Yes, I read about it here in a Beijing newspaper."

"I have a favor to ask of you. Supposing the dress is an image some people may have seen, can you try to gather information about it from your members? Send a fax of the mandarin dress to the branch offices all over the country. Any information will help."

"I'll contact all the people I know, Chief Inspector Chen, but who has not seen a mandarin dress or two, in pictures or in movies or in real life? It's neither here nor there."

"There are three things unusual about the dress. First, as you may have read in the newspaper, the red mandarin dress is of high quality and craftsmanship, but in a old fashion, possibly from the fifties or sixties. Secondly, the woman wearing the mandarin dress was barefoot, and finally, she had a possible connection to a flower bed or a park."

"That may narrow down the range," Wang said. "I'll have my secretary contact every provincial branch, but I can't promise you anything."

"I really appreciate your help, Chairman Wang. You are going out of your way for me, I know."

"You would do the same for me," Wang said, "like last time."

Not like last time, Chen groaned. That was a real headache, even thinking about it.

Closing the phone, he was about to light a cigarette when he saw Yu enter the bar, walking in big strides.

"A quiet place, Chief," Yu said, seeing they were the only ones in the café section.

"Any new developments?" Chen asked, pushing the menu toward his partner. "Anything from the neighborhood committees?"

"No, nothing substantial or useful."

A waitress came over to their table, eyeing the two curiously. Stiff in his cotton-padded uniform, his hair rumpled and his shoes dust-covered, Yu cut a contrasting figure to Chen, who looked more like a regular customer at such a café, in his black blazer and khaki pants, a leather briefcase beside him. The young lovers in the pottery section were standing up to leave, a decision possibly prompted by the arrival of a cop.

"Tea," Yu said to the waitress before turning to Chen. "I still can't drink coffee, boss."

"I am not too surprised about the neighborhood committees," Chen said after the withdrawal of the waitress. "If the murderer could have succeeded in dumping two bodies at those locations without being seen, it wouldn't be realistic to expect that his neighbors saw anything either."

"Liao thinks that he must have a garage, but Li is against searching each and every garage in the city."

"No, I don't think the murderer has to have a garage."

"Oh, the identity of the second victim has been established. Qiao Chunyan. An eating girl. Usually at a restaurant called Ming River."

"One of the three-accompanying girls?"

"Yes, that's how she lived, and how she died too."

Yu did not have to elaborate. The three-accompanying girls—the girl who accompanied customers in eating, in singing, and in dancing—was a new profession and a new term in the Chinese language. Sex business was still officially banned, but people managed to carry on under all kinds of guises. So the "three-accompanying" business flourished. There was no law against girls eating, singing, and dancing with customers. As for the possible service afterward, the city authorities acquiesced, with one eye open and one eye closed. The girls had to face occupational hazards, of course, including a sex killer.

"So they both worked at low-end jobs," Chen said.

"That suggests a new direction for Liao. He thinks the killer might have a grudge against those girls. That's how he started the serial killing," Yu said. "But I don't see a real connection between the two. For the second, there was a possibility of her falling into the killer's hands because of her job. For the first victim, however, it's a different story."

"Yes, you've done a thorough job on her."

"A hotel attendant is not a three-accompanying girl. From what I've gathered, she was a decent, hard-working girl. She helped at her hotel canteen too, but it's too small for Big Bucks or eating girls. If she were an unscrupulous gold digger, she wouldn't have chosen to work at a small hotel."

"I think you're right," Chen said. "So what do you think is the connection between the two?"

"Here is a list of what the two have in common," Yu said, producing a page torn from a pad. "Liao has checked most of the points."

"Let's go through the list," Chen said, taking the page.

1. *Young, pretty girls in their early twenties, unmarried, not highly educated, of poor family background, working at low-end jobs, possibly engaged in some indecent business.*
2. *Each in a red mandarin dress. Torn in the side slits, several bosom buttons unbuttoned, thigh-and-breast-revealing, erotic or obscene in the effect, though the dress appeared exquisite and conservative in style. No underwear or bra, either, in contradiction to the common mandarin dress code.*
3. *Bare feet, Qiao with red-painted toenails, Jasmine's unpainted.*
4. *Neither of them was sexually assaulted. While the first body showed bruises possibly from resistance, no trace of penetration or ejaculation was found. As for the second, no bruises suggesting sexual violence. The first body was washed, but not the second body.*
5. *Public locations. Highly difficult and dangerous to dump the bodies unseen.*

"Have you got any new pictures that tell us more about who they were and how they lived?"

"Yes, mostly Qiao's pictures. She had a passion for them."

"Let's take a look at them."

Yu arranged the photographs in a line on the table.

Chen studied them, like a man examining possible dates suggested by a matchmaker. It might be sheer coincidence, he noted, that each of the girls had a picture taken at the People's Square, in the summer. Jasmine wore a white cotton summer dress, and Qiao had on a yellow tank top and jeans. Chen put the two pictures side by side. Jasmine appeared to be the slimmer of the two, and possibly taller as well.

"Do you notice the difference in their build, Yu?" he said, gazing at the pictures.

Yu nodded without speaking.

Chen placed two pictures taken at the crime scenes underneath the two taken at the People's Square.

"According to Shen, a good mandarin dress has to be customer-tailored, tight-fitting, so it brings out all the curves. Look at the two-crime-scene pictures. In both, the dress really clings to the body. We should check the dress sizes. See if the two are slightly different."

"I'll check." Yu added, "But if it is so—"

"It means that he has a supply of expensive, vintage mandarin dresses—identical in color, material, and design, but in different sizes for him to choose from."

"He could have made them for someone he loved or hated," Yu said, "but why in different sizes?"

"That puzzles me," Chen said. It was yet another contradiction, like in those love stories he had been analyzing.

"What else has Shen told you?"

Chen recounted his discussion with the elderly scholar.

"In the light of Shen's analysis," Chen said, "the murderer could have had these made in the eighties, after a particular fashion from even earlier, and kept them in a closet all these years until the first strike two weeks ago."

"Why the long wait?"

"I don't know, but that may explain your failure to find any clues about the mandarin dress. It's such a long time ago. In the early eighties, the mandarin dress was not yet back in fashion, so no mass production. They were possibly made by an individual tailor, who could have since passed away, retired, or moved back to the countryside."

"Yes, that's what Peiqin thinks," Yu said. "But if they are from the sixties or seventies—during the Cultural Revolution—I doubt anyone would have chosen to wear them in those years. Peiqin recalls only one example from then—the photograph of Wang Guangmei being mass-criticized in a torn mandarin dress."

"It was like the scarlet letter. Peiqin is right," Chen said. "Are there any new theories in the bureau?"

"Liao still holds on to his material profile. And I've told you about Little Zhou's, haven't I? The elaborate theory about an anti-Manchurian message. He is still hawking it around."

"That theory isn't credible. Still, it pushes for an organic interpretation of the contradictions. In the city of Shanghai, for one thing, it is out of the question for a woman in an elegant mandarin dress to walk around barefoot. Such a contradiction can be part of the ritual meaningful to the sex criminal."

"But whatever contradiction we are talking about," Yu said, "I don't think the first victim is the type of three-accompanying girl Liao has in mind."

"What's Liao's theory on the relationship between the red mandarin dress and the sex business?"

"As it seems to Liao, a three-accompanying girl in a mandarin dress might have dumped and deceived the killer. So he justifies his action by putting each of his victims in such a dress."

"But that does not account for the exquisite craftsmanship and conservative style of the dress. I don't think a three-accompanying girl could have afforded to wear a dress like that. And since the killer went to such trouble for the dress, I don't think he thought of his victims as trash."

"So what's your take on the dress, Chief?"

"The dress might have been part of the psychological ritual or sexual fantasy with a special meaning for the murderer."

"Then how can we know what it's supposed to mean, if he is such a nut?"

"Liao's material profile may help, but for a serial killer, we also need to have a psychological profile."

"I mentioned your translation of psychological thrillers to Li, but he wouldn't listen to me."

"In Li's logic, serial killing can occur only in Western capitalist societies, not in socialist China."

"I have read some mysteries, but I haven't made any systemic study of them. I wonder how a psychological approach could help the present case."

"Here in China? I don't know. In the West, psychoanalysis being a common practice, things can be different. Those with psychological problems might have medical records somewhere. Doctors may perform a psychological evaluation of the suspect. Or cops may have had special training. In my college years, I never took a psychology course. Just read a couple of articles on psychoanalysis for the sake of my literature papers. As for the theories and practices in mystery novels, you can't take them seriously."

"Still, tell me about the psychological approaches in those books. Like Liao's method, it may help narrow down the range."

"Well," Chen said, "let me try to recall some points. We'll examine them in the context of our red mandarin dress case."

"I am all ears, Chief."

"Now, the identity of the second victim suggests something frequently read in those books. A goal-oriented serial killer characterized with an obsessive-compulsive mindset. He has deep-rooted psychosexual problems, psychotic, but not delusional. He is obsessed with the desire to rid the world of the people classified in his mind as undesirable and unworthy. The three-accompanying girls can be so categorized. The goal is to deal a crushing blow to the sex industry, and the victims also happen to be the most vulnerable, easy to pick up. When such a murderer is finally apprehended, he usually turns out to be an upstanding citizen fitting with Liao's material profile."

"So there may be something in Liao's focus," Yu said, nodding.

The waitress came back to their table with a tray of desert samples. Chen ordered a wedge of lemon pie for himself, but Yu chose a steamed bun of barbecued pork. The bar was a mixture of East and West, at least in its desert tray.

"Now, believe it or not," Chen resumed, "the sex killers in those mysteries are often impotent. They experience a mental orgasm without a physical ejaculation. So the medical examiner may not find semen in the victim."

"Yes, our forensic people have already excluded the possibility of the assailant being a condom user. No condom lubrication left on the victims. So the killer does fit that profile so far. With both victims stripped, yet not raped, he could be a psycho like that." Yu added thoughtfully, "In one of the books you translated, it has something to do with sexual abuse in his childhood. He grows up all twisted. Impotent."

"According to Freud, the importance of one's childhood experience can never be exaggerated. In most cases, such a killer has experienced some sort of sexual abuse that influenced his behavior."

"But how can it help our work?" Yu said. "In China, no one talks about childhood sexual abuse. Admitting it is worse than abuse itself. The very concept of face."

"Yes, it's a taboo, cultural as well as political. Too much face loss," Chen said, wondering if there was such a term as *face loss* in Western psychology. "In recent years, it has become quite popular for people there to talk about their traumatic childhood, but it is still unimaginable in China. Also, some childhood traumatic experience here may be taken for granted—in a Shanghai family, with three generations squeezed in the same room, exposure to parental sex, for instance, can be a matter of course. No one talks about it."

"Yes, it reminds me of a story from my old neighborhood. A young bridegroom could not consummate because of the creaking sound of his bed, which would be audible to his parents staying at the other end of the room partitioned by a bamboo screen. In his childhood, he had heard his parents' creaking bed, and he didn't talk to anybody about it. But he didn't turn into a killer. After two or three years, he moved into a new room, and all his problems were solved."

"But if he had consulted a doctor, he could have gotten immediate help."

"Well, I happen to know him, so I can guess at some cause of his problem. But we have no clue at all as to the identity of the murderer."

"We do know that he kills his victims and disposes of the bodies in basically the same manner. And that he won't stop until he is apprehended."

"How does that help us, Chief?"

"If we aren't sure how he picks his victims, I think we may at least assume that he'll probably dump a new body in another public location. And on Thursday night. And that's where and when we have to heighten our patrolling activities."

"But in a city like Shanghai, we can't put our people in every possible corner."

"If we are shorthanded, the neighborhood committees aren't. There are quite a lot of people being laid off nowadays. Not to mention all the retired workers. So we could pay them ten or fifteen Yuan for just one night, Thursday night. Keep them walking about all the time, and checking every suspicious car, possibly with a man and an unconscious woman inside, especially when it pulls up or parks at those public locations."

"Yes, that's something we can do," Yu said. "I'll go back and discuss with Liao. He may be grumpy about you, but he'll take a good suggestion."

"No, keep me out of it," Chen said, draining his coffee. "I have to finish the paper in time. I have promised Professor Bian."

TEN

ALONE IN HIS OFFICE, Detective Yu tried to size up the situation. It was worse than hopeless, he admitted to himself. Worse with the certainty of another killing in three days, and with his inability to do anything about it.

Since early morning, he had been overwhelmed by a deluge of reports and statements. The telephone kept ringing, somehow like the funeral bell in a half-forgotten movie. After only a few hours' sleep last night, having skipped breakfast for a teleconference with a Beijing forensic expert, he began sweating in his cotton-padded uniform. Like the other cops in their group, he already felt jaded in the morning, brewing another cup of extra-strong tea—a cup half full of tea leaves.

Liao seemed discouraged, no longer talking about the profile or the garage. Nor about his sex business scenario, which had been vetoed by Li. The sex industry in the city was an open secret, but no one was supposed to talk about it, especially not in connection with a sensational serial murder case.

As for the psychological approach expounded by Chen, Yu didn't even mention it in the bureau. He didn't think anyone would take it seriously. Psychological studies would help only after the criminal was caught, but not when he remained unknown and at large. Still, Yu recommended heightening security with the help of the neighborhood committee on Thursday night. For once, Li agreed readily.

Yu was preparing to make a second cup of tea, putting another pinch of oolong tea leaves into the old cup, when the phone rang again.

"May I speak to Detective Yu Guangming?" It was an unfamiliar voice, possibly that of a middle-aged woman.

"This is he. Speaking."

"My name is Yaqin. I worked with Jasmine. You came to our hotel the other day. I saw you talking to the front desk manager."

"Yes, I did."

"Is the reward for information about Jasmine still available?"

"Yes, two thousand Yuan, if it leads to a breakthrough."

"Jasmine had a boyfriend. She met him several months ago. He stays at our hotel when he comes back from the United States. He's a regular customer here."

"That may be something," Yu said. "Can you give me more details, Yaqin?"

"His name is Weng. He's not that rich, or he wouldn't stay at our hotel, but he has bucks, at least enough so that he's capable of staying here for months at a time. And he has a green card, which is enough for many a Shanghai girl to have hooked up fast and furious. Anyway, they hit it off. People have seen them dining outside, her hand grasped in his."

"Have you seen them together?"

"No, but I saw her sneaking into his room late one afternoon, about a month ago. It was not during her shift that day." She added, "He was a realistic choice for the girl. He's about fifteen years older, but he could have taken her to the United States."

"Have you noticed anything suspicious about him?"

"Well, nothing that I am sure of. His family is still in Shanghai, but he chooses to stay at a hotel. Why? That's beyond me. No one knows what kind of work he does, nor where his money comes from. The cost of a hotel for three or four months is a sizable sum."

"I talked to your manager the other day. He didn't say anything about Weng or about his relationship with Jasmine."

"He may not know," she said. "Besides, the hotel business has been affected by her murder. There may be no interest in drawing more public attention like that."

"Is Weng at the hotel right now?"

"He came in from the States this morning. He has been shut up in the room ever since."

"I'll come over immediately. If he comes out, tell him not to leave the hotel." Yu said, "Are you sure he was in the United States for the last two weeks?"

"When she died, he wasn't here, but I'm not sure where he was. And he arrived with all his luggage this morning."

"Can you check his passport? Particularly the date of his latest entrance."

"That should be easy. He leaves his passport in a safety box here. I'll check it out for you." She added, "But I don't want to be seen talking to or passing information to a cop."

"No problem. I understand. I won't come in uniform."

Forty-five minutes later, Yu arrived at the hotel lobby dressed in a gray jacket Peiqin had bought him. No one seemed to recognize him. He soon saw Yaqin, a short woman wearing her hair in an old-fashioned knot, though probably only in her mid-forties. She sneaked him a photocopy of the passport. It showed that Weng left via Guangzhou the day Jasmine was murdered and came back only this morning. Weng would have hardly had the time for the first crime. Definitely not for the second.

"Thank you, Yaqin," he said. "Is Weng still here?"

"Room 307," Yaqin said in a whisper.

"I'll call you later," he said in a low voice. "So we can meet away from the hotel."

She nodded, picking up a full ashtray from the lobby table like a conscientious hotel employee.

He stepped into an old elevator, which bobbed him up to the third floor. Following the narrow corridor to the end, he knocked on a brown door marked 307.

The door creaked open. The man inside appeared to be in his early forties, his hair uncombed, his eyes red, slightly swollen. Yu recognized him as Weng, though his passport picture looked younger. It was evident that Weng had not changed since his arrival, his clothes rumpled, encompassing his stout body like an overstuffed duffle bag. Yu produced his badge and came straight to the point.

"You must know why I am here. So tell me about your relationship with Jasmine, Mr. Weng."

"You are moving fast, Comrade Detective Yu. I've just come back this morning, and you already have me as a suspect."

"No, I don't. As you may not know, there's been another victim here while you were in the States. You don't have to worry about being a suspect, but what you tell me will help our work. You want to avenge her death, don't you?"

"Yes, I'll tell you what I know," Weng said, letting Yu into the room. "So where shall I start?"

"Let's start when you met—but no, let's go to the very beginning. Tell me first about your trips back to Shanghai," Yu said, taking out a mini recorder. "It's just our routine procedure."

"Well, I left Shanghai to continue my studies in the United States about seven or eight years ago. I got my PhD in anthropology there, but I couldn't find a job. Finally I started working for an American company as their special buyer in China. With no factory or workshop, the company designs the products in the US, has them manufactured here, and then sells them for a good profit all over the world. Sometimes they simply buy wholesale at the Yiwu Small Product Market and put their own labels on them. They hired me because I speak several Chinese dialects and am capable of negotiating and bargaining in the countryside. So I fly back and forth regularly, with Shanghai as my base. After all, it's my home city, and it's convenient for me to go anywhere from here—"

"Hold on a minute, Weng. You still have your family here, why don't you stay at home?"

"My parents had only a room of sixteen square meters, in which my elder brother still lives with his wife and two kids, all huddled up together. I can't squeeze back into that one single room. My brother might not say anything, but his wife would grumble nonstop. The company pays all the expenses for my business trips. Why should I save money for them?"

"I see," Yu said. "So you met her during your stay in the hotel."

"I met her about half a year ago, in an elevator incident. The ancient elevator stopped moving between the fifth and sixth floor. We were trapped inside, just two of us, facing each other and the possibility of its crashing down the next instant. All of a sudden, I felt her so closely. In her hotel shirt, skirt, barefoot in plastic slippers, carrying a pail of soap water. At a flowerlike age, she looked too good to be at such a menial job. Then the light went out too. She grasped my hand in panic. After the longest five minutes in my life, the elevator started moving again. In the light, which came back like soft water, she looked so pure and charming. I asked her to have a cup of tea with me in the canteen—to relieve the shock in an old convention. She declined, saying that it was against the hotel policy. The next morning I happened to see her again in the lobby. She looked worn out, having just finished the night shift. I followed her out and invited her to a restaurant across the street. She agreed. That's how things began to develop."

"What kind of a girl did you find her?"

"A really nice girl. There are not too many left like her nowadays. Not materialistic at all. She could have earned much more at a nightclub, but she would rather earn her honest money at the hotel. I don't think she took me as a Big Buck. She knew better. And she was so devoted to her sick, paralyzed father too. An extraordinarily filial daughter!"

"Yes, I've heard that. Have you visited her home?"

"No, she didn't like the idea. She wanted to keep our relationship a secret."

"Because you were staying at the hotel?"

"You could say that."

"But you went out a lot with her. People would have discovered your relationship sooner or later."

"Maybe, but we didn't go out that much. I was busy, flying here and there, and she had to take care of her father."

"Now a different question. Did she ever wear a red mandarin dress in your presence?"

"No. She was not a fashion butterfly. I tried to buy some new clothing for her, but she invariably said no. She had a pajama top made from her mother's fifteen years ago. No, she did not—" Weng broke off, as if overwhelmed in memories. "The Old Heaven is blind. A girl like her should not have suffered such a string of bad luck, and such an end—"

The room phone started ringing. Weng snatched it up as if he had been expecting it.

"Oh, Mr. Newman, about that deal—hold on," Weng turned around, covering the phone with his hand. "Sorry, it's an international call. Can we talk another time?"

"That's okay," Yu said, pulling out a business card and adding the cell phone number the bureau had temporarily given him. "You can call me anytime."

The visit hadn't yielded much, but at least he could rule out two possibilities. First, Weng was excluded as a suspect, and more importantly, Jasmine was not an easy-pick-up target engaged in sex business, contrary to Liao's suspicions.

Still, he felt he might have missed something in the interview. Though what it was, he couldn't figure out.

ELEVEN

AGAIN, PEIQIN WAS TRYING to help in her way.

She attempted to gather background information about Qiao, the eating girl. Since Peiqin herself worked in a restaurant, she had no trouble getting people to talk about those girls. Chef Pan turned out to be knowledgeable on the subject.

"Oh, three-accompanying girls—singing, dancing, eating," Pan started with great gusto over a dish of peanuts flavored with Daitiao seaweed. "Another characteristic of China's brand of socialism. Socialism still has to provide a cover for everything, like a sign of a sheep's head, behind which dog or cat meat is selling like crazy. The Party authorities keep saying that there's no prostitution here, black words on white paper, so there appeared the gray area of three-accompanying girls."

"You've worked at high-end restaurants," Peiqin said, pouring him a cup of ginseng tea, a gift from Chief Inspector Chen, "and you surely know a lot."

"Confucius says, 'Enjoyment of delicacy and sex is of human nature.'

In the unprecedented economic reform led by Comrade Deng Xiaoping, what industry has scored the most incredible expansion? The entertainment industry. All the new and fancy restaurants and nightclubs, where Big Bucks and Party cadres are spending money like water. So eating girls appeared as a matter of course."

"But how does an eating girl make her money?"

"For a Big Buck rolling obscenely in money, the company of an attractive girl adds a finishing touch to a perfect night, her nestling against him at the table, putting the delicacies on his plate. It boosts enormously his feeling of power and success, a sensual candle flickering between them. Actually, there are high requirements for the profession. She has to be pretty, and clever too, capable of convincing a Big Buck that he is getting his money's worth with her company. For her, it's a free dinner, plus a huge bonus. Through her choice of expensive wine and delicacies, the bill can be staggering, from which ten percent goes to her, not to mention the tip. In addition, she may strike a clandestine deal on the table, or under the table. What happens afterward does not concern the restaurant. So all in all, it's a sizable income for her."

"You have observed well, Pan."

"Eating girls won't come to a shabby place like ours, but they bring profit to a restaurant. We will have to change too."

"Thank you so much," Peiqin said, though slightly disappointed with the general introduction. For her purpose, she needed to know something more concrete.

The tidbits about three-accompanying girls from her other colleagues were also secondhand, vague, unreliable with their embellishments. After all, none of them had any real experience.

So Peiqin went one step further. Through her connections, she succeeded in obtaining help from Ming River, the particular restaurant where Qiao had served for the last year. The restaurant manager, Four-eyed Zhang, suggested to Peiqin that she should talk to Rong—a "big sister."

"Rong, the eldest among the girls, is in her mid-thirties, a big sister with longer experiences, more connections, and more importantly, a list of those regular customers requesting the service. And she's well-read in her way, too, especially about Chinese culinary history, which makes her popular among old customers," Zhang said. "Some of them will call ahead for eating girls, and she helps to make arrangements. As for new customers, it's not always easy to approach them, and her experience can be invaluable. Rong is also said to have befriended Qiao."

"That would be the perfect one for me. Thank you so much, Manager Zhang."

"But you have to get her to talk. She's quite a character."

So she phoned Rong. Peiqin introduced herself as a would-be writer. Having learned from Zhang about Rong's knowledge of Chinese cuisine, she invited Rong out to lunch at Autumn Pavilion, a restaurant known for its fresh seafood. Zhang must have known Rong well as she agreed readily.

Rong stepped into Autumn Pavilion in a white jacket and jeans. A tall, slender woman, with no makeup or jewelry, she was not easily recognizable as an eating girl. Choosing a table in a quiet corner, Peiqin explained what she needed—in addition to an introduction to China's culinary tradition, she would like to learn something about Qiao, so she might be able to write a short story about it. It was not too difficult for Peiqin to play a would-be writer, filling her speech with popular quotes, but she wondered if Rong really believed her.

"It's interesting," Rong said. "Not too many people want to be writers nowadays. You crawl on the paper for months, and all the money you make can hardly buy a meal."

"I know. But I've been working in a restaurant for more than ten years. I have to do something different besides caring about three meals a day."

"You may be right about that. Now, we are sort of colleagues, so you don't have to order like those Big Bucks," Rong said in a crispy voice, picking up the menus. "Slices of lotus roots filled sticky rice, home-grown chicken immersed in Shaoxin yellow wine, live bass strewn with ginger and onion slices. These should be enough."

"What about the appetizers?"

"Let's have a couple of deep-fried oysters. I'm going to Ming River tonight, you know. We are here to talk."

"Great," Peiqin said, glad that Rong knew better than to be an eating girl in her company. "Now, how long have you known Qiao?"

"Not too long. From the time she came to work at Ming River. That's about a year ago, I think."

"According to Zhang, you kindly befriended her. So you know a lot about her."

"No, I don't. In our business, people usually don't ask and don't answer. She was young and inexperienced, that's why I gave her a suggestion or two. Now that she's dead, I don't think I should tell—even if I knew something."

"Whatever you tell me goes only into the background of my story. No real names will be given. I give you my word, Rong."

"So it does not have to be about her?"

"No, not necessarily." Peiqin understood her reservation, for people could sell the information about Qiao to a tabloid magazine. "Zhang knows me well. Otherwise he would not have given your name to me. It's just for my fictional story."

"Well, here's a fictional story," Rong said, draining her cup in one gulp and holding a golden-fried oyster in her fingers, "but with real background information about the profession. I won't give the girl's name. For a story, you don't have to take it too seriously."

It was smart of Rong, whose insistance on its being fictional meant she was not responsible for whatever she was going to say.

"She was born in the early seventies," Rong started, nibbling at the fried oyster. "The maxim that 'beauty is not edible' was a favorite one for her parents. On the wall above her cradle was a poster of Chairman Mao's 'iron girl,' tall and robust, muscles hard like iron. Indeed, when people have a hard time feeding themselves, beauty is like a picture of cake. In her elementary school, she drew a magnificent restaurant as her dream home, which she didn't step in until she was fifteen.

"Her beauty blossomed in the mid-eighties. While her parents' maxim might no longer be universally true, it still applied to her. In an age of connections, it took much more than looks to become a model or a star. She had no connections. For a girl from an ordinary worker family, a state-run factory job was considered an ideal 'iron bowl.' So upon high school graduation, she started working in a textile mill, a job made available through her mother's early retirement.

"There, her beauty meant nothing. She worked three shifts, dragged her tired feet around the shuttles, back and forth, like a fly circling the same spot. Back home, she kicked off her shoes and clasped her callused soles. Outside the window, the willow shoots barren in the autumn wind, she knew one thing for a fact: a textile worker grows old quickly. *Soon, the spring splendor fades / from the flower. There's no stopping / the chill rain, or the shrill wind.*

"But that was also the period when things started changing. Deng Xiaoping was launching China's reform. She started to have dreams unimaginable to her parents. Looking through fashion magazines, she couldn't help feeling left out. In the descriptions of the neighborhood matchmakers, she made the clothes beautiful, rather than the other way round.

"So she came to a decision. She would make the most of her youth. An elaborate plan evolved out of Shanghai dating conventions. Young people would customarily dine out on their first one or two dates. The expense varied in proportion to his wallet or to her glamour. As in a proverb, a beauty's smile is worth a thousand pieces of gold, especially at the early stages of a possible romantic relationship. The man would be generous with his money like a Sichuan chef with his black pepper. Once the relationship grew more stable, a Shanghai girl would urge her lover to save for their joint future. Occasionally, they might still go out to a good yet inexpensive place, like Nanxiang Soup Bun in the Old City God's Temple Market, where they would spend two hours contentedly standing in a long line, waiting for their turn to savor the celebrated buns. It was only for a short period, she concluded, that a working-class girl like her might enjoy herself.

"Her mother was worried about her showing no sign of settling down. 'I'm not ready yet,' she said to her mother, 'for a life with my family squeezing in a room of nine square meters, the baby crying, the wok smoking, the diaper dripping, and the walls peeling like irrecoverable dreams. No, I'm not looking forward to it. I will marry, eventually, like anybody else, but let me first enjoy life a bit.'

"And she enjoyed herself by trying those dates out in restaurants, insisting on expensive food and wine in the company of each man. The bill cut like a sharp knife, but if he winced, it was his problem. She kept her relationship with each man short and sweet. Well, short, though not that sweet when he could no longer afford her company. She had oyster sauce beef in Xingya Restaurant, roast Beijing duck in Yanyun Pavilion, baked crab meat with cheese in Red House, sugar silk apple in Kaifu Hotel, sea cucumber with shrimp ovary in Shanghai Old House, and so on and on.

"Her fifth date, allegedly with a wealthy uncle in Hong Kong, proved capable of taking her to one restaurant after another. At the end of two months, however, he, too, failed to show up in front of the Cathay Hotel. She was a little disappointed, but the next week, she met her sixth date in Spicy and Hot Pot, enjoying slices of lamb, beef, eel, shrimp, and all other delicacies imaginable, in a boiling pot of chicken broth between them. 'The spring bamboo shoot looks so shapely,' she said, picking one with her chopsticks. 'So do your fingers,' he said fatuously, holding her other hand. She did not withdraw it. After all, he spent so much for the meals. The following month, she met her seventh date in Yangzhou Pavilion, billing and cooing over a turtle steamed with ice sugar and ham, a celebrated special known for its supposed boost to sexual energy. She smiled, putting a piece of turtle meat onto his plate, and another into her mouth.

"Before long, she had a problem in the circle she had been moving. Those men introduced to her by her neighbors or colleagues were of similar social levels. None of them could really meet her expectations. One of them sold blood, it was said, before making the last appointment with her at Red Earth Restaurant.

" 'It's not my fault,' she defended herself. 'They don't have to hang on like that. Why are those restaurants so expensive? The quality. Why me? My beauty. I eat out not just for the taste in the mouth. In a factory, in front of a machine, I am like a screw, fixed there, lusterless, lifeless. In a high-end restaurant, I am a human being, a real woman being served and pampered.'

"With high-end hotels and restaurants appearing like bamboo shoots after a spring rain, and with young beautiful girls hanging around them like wild weeds—three-accompanying girls—she soon made another decision. She was attractive, and knowledgeable about food too, and as an eating girl, her company at the dinner table was desirable. Also, she might be able to meet, at one of those Big Buck dinners, her future 'gold-turtle' husband instead of waiting for matchmakers to introduce to her another man incapable of paying the bill for her.

"It turned out to be quite a profitable profession. Choosing ten-year-old Huadiao wine, or the chef's secret specials, such as dragon fighting tiger—with cat and snake meat in a pot, you know—or abalone with shark fin, she would get a sizable bonus. If the customer wanted some additional service, it was discussable. Soon she began to 'turn adrift with the waves and currents.'

"One night, after a light meal with a Japanese customer, she followed him out to a five-star hotel, where she enjoyed for the first time the room service of sushi and saki. To oblige him, she changed into a Japanese kimono, kneeling on a soft cushion until she was rigid like cracked plastic lotus flower. After three cups of saki, however, she began feeling as if burgeoning out like a real night flower, fragrant with the knowledge that the meal cost thousands of Yuan. Later on, he had her take a shower, lie on the rug, and spread wasabi on her bare toes. He took them one by one into his mouth, sucked it like a baby, and declared it more delicious than the salmon sushi. He then moved to spread the green mustard on the other parts of her body while she giggled and gasped under his ticklish touch. He swore by his mother's name that the 'female body banquet' was based on a time-honored Japanese gourmet tradition. Drunk, she missed the details of the 'sensual feast.' The next morning, when he offered her money, she declined. Her grandfather had been killed in the anti-Japanese war, she suddenly recalled. Instead, she took hotel restaurant vouchers equal to the amount.

"Walking out of the five-star hotel, she still felt like she was treading on the clouds and rain of the last night, when she was pushed into a police car. At the time, it was illegal to sleep with a foreigner. She was released after three days because she had no previous record, nor was any Japanese Yuan found on her. Still, it was a huge humiliation and a 'political mistake.' She tried to hold her head high, though, showing the room service menu and vouchers to her colleagues.

"That happened at a time when the city textile industry was already in trouble. Shanghai, once an industrial center, was turning into a financial center. While the new skyscrapers outlined the skies, the old factories were shut down. The factory director seized the opportunity to fire her with one comment, 'She ate herself out.'

"So she turned into a full-time eating girl."

After a short spell of silence, Rong took a deliberate sip at the wine, which was glittering in the cut glass like a lost dream. She recited a few lines from a poem.

"The memories of the rouge-colored tears, / of the night amid cup . . . / When will all that happen again? / Life is long in sadness / like water flowing and flowing east."

The lines sounded familiar. Apparently, Rong came to the end of her narrative. Peiqin was disappointed. It was more about the metamorphosis of a girl into an eating girl. She also wondered whether it was somewhat autobiographical, studying the expression on the narrator's face.

The waiter brought over a large fish platter in hurried steps. It was perhaps the last course.

"Look at the fish," Rong said, raising her chopsticks. "Its eyes are still rolling."

The bass, covered in brown sauce, appeared nicely cooked with its tail fried golden. The waiter helped with a long spoon, coming up with a white filet. The meat was tenderly done, but the fish's eyes seemed to be still blinking.

"There is a special recipe for the fish. You stuff ice cubes in the mouth of the live fish, fry it in a large wok keeping its eyes out of the sizzling oil, take it out in less than a minute, and pour special sauce all over it on a platter. Every step has to be precise and quick. Then serve it hot. That's why the waiter was trotting out of the kitchen."

So Rong proved her expertise in culinary knowledge, and Peiqin had a recipe that might also go into a story, but that was not what she really wanted to learn.

"Thank you so much, Rong. It is a good story," Peiqin said, trying to redirect their talk. "But I am still shocked about Qiao. How could a girl like her have come to such a tragic end?"

"You never know what a customer can turn out to be," Rong said, looking Peiqin in the eye. "We are not talking about Qiao, are we?"

"No. I am just using her as an example."

"What happened to Qiao is beyond me. Something like that has never happened."

"Could she have made enemies because of her service?"

"No, not that I know of. In fact, of the three-accompanying girls, an eating girl is the least likely to get into trouble," Rong said. "Not like in a karaoke club, where the fee for a private room can be a huge ripoff. A lot of things are not listed, and you don't know the expense until they hand you the bill. Here, all the prices are printed on the menu. You lose no face if you say you don't like a particular dish. I have suggested a house special called live monkey brain, for instance, to god knows how many customers, but none of them ordered it. No hard feelings against them. It's too cruel, with a chef sawing off the monkey's shaven scalp, and ladling out the brains in front of the dinners, and the monkey squealing and struggling in pain all the time—"

"Now back to Qiao," Peiqin cut in. "Were you with her the night she disappeared?"

"No. She should have come that night, but she didn't."

"Could she have gone to another restaurant instead?"

"No, I don't think so. Competition is fierce everywhere. Among the girls too. Most of them make a point of going to one particular restaurant, and in a more or less organized way. To be frank, that's how I have helped occasionally. Things can be complicated. A girl has to deal with the restaurant owner and waiters for the profit-sharing; with the local business management bureau for a business license; with the gangsters for so-called protection; and with the cops too, who may make things difficult for her. So if she turned up in a new place all by herself, she could be driven out by the waiters or gangsters, if not by other girls. It's their territory. She could get into other trouble too."

"So you don't think she fell prey to the murderer during the service."

"No, not in our restaurant."

"Another question, Rong. Did she have a boyfriend?"

"No, she did not. It's not easy for a girl here to keep a steady relationship. What would he think—as a man? She has to lie to him about her profession, and the game never lasts long. Once he finds out, everything is finished—because of his wounded male ego."

"Did she talk to you about her future plans?"

"She said she was saving for a flower shop, she had no plans to be an eating girl forever." Rong added, "Before she had her flower business, she said she wouldn't think about other things."

"So what do you think of the case?"

"A murderer might have met her in the restaurant, got her phone number, and asked her out days later. On the other hand, she might also have met her fate in a way unrelated to her service."

"That's true."

"You are not a cop, are you, Peiqin?"

"No, I am not," Peiqin said. "I have worked at the Four Seas since my return from Yunnan. Our state-run restaurant has suffered losses and our chef suggests that we should run it like a high-end restaurant with fashionable services. You may be able to give us advice."

That was a true statement. Rong might help too. Not necessarily in the aspect of three-accompanying girls—an aspect Peiqin didn't want to envision yet.

"Now that we are talking about it, Peiqin," Rong said, "there might have been one thing—about Qiao, I mean. Three or four days before that fatal night, a customer came to Ming River, alone. He didn't look like one who would require a girl, so I didn't pay any attention to him. He contacted a waiter, requesting a girl's company. Qiao went over to him. Nothing happened that evening."

"Can you give a description of that man?"

"If I remember him at all, it's because he didn't look like those upstarts. A gentleman, I would say. Medium height. Oh, one more thing, perhaps. He wore a pair of amber-colored glasses. Not exactly sunglasses. Still, it's rare for people to wear that kind of glasses in the winter."

"Did Qiao tell you anything afterward?"

"No. She worked late. She had another old customer that night."

"Did she have a cell phone?"

"No, not that I know of. Nor is there a phone at home. If I had to contact her for something, I called her neighbor on the third floor. Not too many people knew that number," Rong said, rising with a smile. "I think it's time for me to start preparing for the evening. I may put on a mandarin dress too. It's hot."

TWELVE

EARLY IN THE MORNING, a pile of newspapers was special-delivered from the police bureau to Chen's home, along with the latest case reports and tapes of Yu's interviews.

Instead of opening the collection of Song and Ming stories, as he had planned the night before, Chen started looking through the material prepared by Yu, wrapping himself in a robe and reclining against the headboard.

There was a cup of tea on the table, left over from last night, cold, almost black. People are not supposed to drink last night's tea. But he did.

Shortly afterward, a second package was delivered to him. A package of books from the Shanghai Library, most of them on psychology.

In his college years, Chen had dabbled in the subject—particularly in Freud and Jung—for literary criticism. To his relief, he found himself still responding to those psychological terms. *Collective unconscious,* for one, jumped out at him. There could have been something like a collective unconscious, he realized, behind the deconstructive turn in those love stories.

Or behind the deconstructive message—if he could so term it—in the red mandarin dress case too?

For many years after 1949, psychological problems had not been acknowledged in socialist China. People were supposed to have no problems, psychological or otherwise, as long as they followed the teachings of Chairman Mao. If they admitted to having trouble, they had to reform their minds through hard labor. Psychology was practically declared a bogus science. Psychoanalysis didn't exist as a practice. Nor was it sensible for people to go to an analyst—if one was available at all—since talking about their problems could become evidence of serious "political crime." In recent years, psychology had been gradually reintroduced and somewhat rehabilitated, but most people remained wary of it. Psychological problems still could easily turn into political problems.

As a result, a psychological approach was considered unorthodox in the police bureau. Detective Yu, too, was full of reservations about it, believing that a psychological explanation might be helpful at the conclusion of a case, but not in the middle of the investigation.

Chen started reading Yu's reports in earnest.

Yu had a hard time with Liao. Apart from the long rivalry between the two squads, Liao didn't approve of Yu's focus on Jasmine. Liao declared that the homicide squad had done everything possible in that direction. The killer was a nut, killing at random, and it would be a waste of time to look for a rational explanation.

But in a *go* chess game, an experienced player is capable of instinctively grasping an opportunity on the chessboard. One small white or black piece, in a marginal position, hardly of any significance in itself, can contain the possibility of turning the table. Yu was good with his hunches on a *go* chessboard. And in his investigations too.

After the first interview with Weng in the hotel, Yu had continued exploring along that direction. He checked Weng's records elsewhere, including at the airport. There was nothing wrong with the entry date, but Yu had an unexpected discovery in Weng's custom declaration. On the slip, Weng had checked the "married" box on his marriage status. That necessitated a second interview.

Chen put the second interview tape into the cassette player, skipping the preliminary part, going to where Yu questioned Weng about his relation with Jasmine in the context of his marital status.

WENG: When I first met her, I was still married, but already separated from my wife. I was just waiting for the divorce to be final. Jasmine knew that too, though perhaps not at first.

YU: Was she upset with the discovery?

WENG: I think so, but she was also relieved.

YU: Why?

WENG: I tried to start up an antique business of my own. With my anthropology background, I thought I could do much better than those quack dealers, especially with a huge market in China nowadays. So I wanted her to move to the States, where she might help run a store. I looked into the possibility of putting her father up at a nursing home here. But she was not too anxious to leave, worrying about him. In fact, everything could have been taken care of in a couple of weeks. It's just her luck. She was really cursed!

YU: You've mentioned her bad luck. Can you give me some examples?

WENG: A lot of ill-fated things happened to her. So inexplicable. Not to mention what happened to her father—

YU: Well, let's start with her father. So we'll have a complete story, starting with her childhood.

WENG: Tian was a Worker Rebel during the Cultural Revolution. Not a nice gentleman, to be sure. He was punished—sentenced to two to three years. He deserved that, but after his release, horrible luck dogged him like his shadow.

YU: Karma, as his neighbors have put it.

WENG: Karma, perhaps, but there were so many Red Guards and Worker Rebels in those years. Who was really punished? Tian alone, as far as I know. His divorce, his loss of his job, his years in prison, his failure in the restaurant business, and finally his paralysis. . . .

YU: Slow down, Weng. Details.

WENG: After the Cultural Revolution, his wife received anonymous phone calls about his affairs with other women. That was the last straw for their marriage. She divorced him. Surely not a model husband, but his affairs were never proven, and no one knew who made the phone calls. Then his factory came under pressure from above and he was fired and sentenced too. What happened to his ex-wife then was even more unbelievable. Divorced, only in her early thirties, she started dating another man. Soon, pictures of her sleeping with him appeared. In the early eighties, it was a huge scandal and she committed suicide. Jasmine moved back in with Tian. He borrowed money to start a small restaurant, but in less than a month, several customers suffered food poisoning there. They sued him with the help of an attorney, and Tian went bankrupt.

YU: That's strange. At that time, few would have sued for something like that.

WENG: Do you know how he was paralyzed?

YU: A stroke, right?

WENG: He was so desperate that he tried to reverse his luck on a mahjong table. And he was caught by the neighborhood cop the second time he sat down at the table. A heavy fine and a lecture. He suffered a stroke right there and then.

LIAO: Karma indeed. Now, what about Jasmine's bad luck?

WENG: It was hard for a little girl, but she turned out to be a good student. On the day of the college entrance examination, however, she was knocked down by a bike. Not badly hurt, she told the biker not to worry, but he insisted on having her checked at a hospital. When everything was finished, she had missed the examination.

YU: It was an accident. A responsible biker could have done that.

WENG: Perhaps. But what about her first job?

YU: What about it?

WENG: She couldn't afford to wait for the examination the next year. So she started working as a salesgirl for an insurance company. Not a bad job, with a sizable bonus for her. Insurance was then new in the city. During her third or fourth month on the job, however, someone sent a letter to her boss, complaining about her "promiscuous lifestyle and shameless tricks" in selling policies. Her boss didn't want the company's image affected by a scandal and fired her.

YU: Well, that's the version from her perspective.

WENG: There's no point in making up things like that. I never raised a question about her past.

YU: Did she herself make any comment about her bad luck?

WENG: She seemed to have always lived in the shadow of it. So she came to believe that she was born under an unlucky star. She applied for other jobs, but she had no success until she came to this shabby hotel, taking a dead-end job.

YU: How did she come to tell you all this?

WENG: She suffered from a sort of inferiority complex. When we first started going out, and I talked about our future, she could hardly believe the change in her life. But for the incident in the elevator, she would never have agreed to go out with me. She was a little superstitious, taking the incident as a sign. With so much bad luck in her young life, you understand.

YU: One more question: when did you plan to marry her?

WENG: We did not have an exact date, but we agreed that it should be as soon as possible—after the divorce. . . .

Chen fast-forwarded the tape toward the end, but Yu didn't make any comments, as he had sometimes did. There were no comments on the written report, either.

Chen rose to make a cup of coffee. A cold morning. Outside the window, a yellow leaf finally tore itself from the twig, trembling, as in a story he had read a long time ago.

He moved back to bed, putting the coffee mug on the nightstand, tapping his finger on the cassette player.

Chen could see Yu tapping his finger on a *go* chessboard, grappling with a possible opening, not exactly identified—not yet.

It was Weng's statement about Jasmine's curse.

While Tian deserved the punishment, most of the people like Tian remained unpunished after the Cultural Revolution, with Chairman Mao's portrait still hanging on the Tiananmen Gate. As a Chinese proverb goes, to kill a monkey is to scare the chickens, and Tian happened to be the monkey, that was perhaps just his luck.

But what about Jasmine? The bike incident might have been an accident. The anonymous letters, however, went too far. She was only seventeen or eighteen. How could anyone have hated her that much?

The cell phone rang, breaking into the gloomy thoughtful morning.

"Let's have brunch at the Old City God's Temple Market," White Cloud said, her voice sounding close by. "You like the mini soup bun there, I know."

Probably a good idea to take a break. Talk with her might help—about the paper, and about the case too.

"There are several boutiques selling mandarin dresses there," she went on before he responded. "Quite a variety of them—not good quality, but fashionable, and some of them nostalgically fashionable."

That clinched it for him.

"Let's meet at Nanxiang Soup Bun Restaurant."

It was for the sake of the investigation, he told himself. She might serve as a fashion consultant in a field study, though he was slightly uneasy about it.

Was it because of something he had been studying for the paper—a femme fatale? There seemed to be a weird echo from the story he had just read. According to one critic, Yingying, in "The Story of Yingying," was actually someone of dubious background, like a K girl in today's society.

Chen started dressing for brunch.

About twenty minutes later, he found himself walking in under the familiar entrance arch of the Old City God's Temple Market.

For most Shanghainese, the temple represented not so much of an attraction in itself, but simply a name for the surrounding market of local snacks and products—originally booths and stalls for the temple festivals. For Chen, the attraction came from those eateries, whose offerings were inexpensive yet unique in their flavors, such as chicken and duck blood soup, soup buns in small steamers, radish-shred cakes, shrimp and meat dumplings, beef soup noodles, fried tofu and vermicelli. . . . All these he had liked so much, in the days when society was still an egalitarian one, in which everyone made little money and enjoyed simple meals.

Things were also changing here. There was a new tall building rising behind the Yu Garden, which had originally been the back garden of the Shanghai mayor in the late Qing dynasty and was built in the traditional southern architecture style of ancient pavilions and grottos. In Chen's childhood, his parents, unable to afford the trip to Suzhou and Hangzhou, had taken their son to the garden instead.

Moving past the garden, he stepped up onto the Nine Turn Bridge—allegedly with nine turns so that the evil spirits wouldn't be able to find their way around. An old couple stood on the bridge, throwing breadcrumbs to the invisible golden carps in the pond and nodding at him. It was too cold for the fish to come to the surface, but the old couple remained standing there, waiting. The last turn of the bridge brought him to the Nanxiang Soup Bun Restaurant.

The first floor of the restaurant appeared little changed: a long line of customers waited outside for their turn to get in, watching through the large kitchen window, the never-boring scene of the kitchen assistants picking out the crab meat deftly on a long wooden table and mixing it with minced pork meat. He took the winding stairs up to the second floor, which was quite crowded in spite of the double price charged there. So he climbed up another flight of steps to the third floor, which charged three times as much for the same soup buns. The table and chairs were of imitation mahogany, not too comfortable, but there weren't too many people there. He took a seat overlooking the lake.

As a waiter came to pour him a cup of tea, White Cloud walked up the staircase, tall and slender in a white imitation-fur overcoat and high heels. Helping her take off the overcoat, he saw her wearing a modified backless pink mandarin dress. The dress fit her well, accentuating her curves. Once more he was reminded of that famous Confucian statement, *A woman makes herself beautiful for the man who appreciates her.*

"You are floating over like a morning cloud," he commented before ordering four steamers of soup buns stuffed with minced crab and pork meat. The waiter took the order from him, stealing a look at her.

"Your appetite is good today," she said, placing on the table a pink silk purse that matched the color of her dress.

"*A beauty is so delicious that people want to devour,*" he said, quoting Confucius.

"You are being romantic." She tore open a small packet with an alcohol-seaked cotton ball that she carried in her purse, wiped his chopsticks first, and then hers. Nanxiang was one of the few old Shanghai restaurants that still resisted using disposable chopsticks.

"Nostalgic, perhaps," he said, immersing the ginger slices into saucers of vinegar. One of the saucers was cracked, just like in the old days, as on that afternoon with his cousin Peishan.

In the early seventies, Peishan had been one of the first educated youths to "go to the countryside for reeducation by the poor and lower-middle-class peasants." Before leaving Shanghai, Peishan took Chen to this restaurant, which, like other restaurants at the time, was supposed to serve only working-class people "in the Party's glorious tradition of hard working and simple living." Culinary enjoyment was denounced as a decadent bourgeois extravagancy. People were supposed to eat simply for the sake of making revolution. A number of high-end restaurants were closed. Nanxiang Soup Bun survived as a lucky exception owing to its incredibly cheap price: a bamboo steamer for only twenty-four cents, affordable by any working-class standard. That afternoon, Peishan and Chen patiently waited no less than three hours for their turn. Consequently they gave a huge order: four bamboo steamers for each of them, after the long wait and Peisan's sentimental comment, "When, when can I come back to Shanghai—to the delicious soup buns?"

Cousin Peishan did not come back. In the far, far away countryside, he suffered a nervous breakdown and jumped into a dry well. He might have starved to death there.

Twenty years has passed like a dream.
What a surprise I am still here, today!

Chen chose not to tell White Cloud of this episode from the Cultural Revolution, which was not fashionably nostalgic. A young girl of another generation, she probably wouldn't understand.

But the soup buns appeared and tasted the same, fresh, steaming hot in the golden bamboo steamers, rich in the combined flavor of the land and river, with the scarlet crab oval so tantalizing in the afternoon light. The soup inside the bun came bursting out at the touch of his lips, the taste so familiarly delicious.

"According to a gourmet book, the soup in the bun comes from the pork skin jelly mixing with the stuffing. In a steamer over the stove, the jelly turns into hot liquid. You have to bite carefully, or the soup will splash out, scalding your tongue."

"You have told me about it," she said, smiling, nipping gingerly before she sucked the soup.

"Oh, you brought a bag of them to me during the New World project."

"It was a pleasure to serve as your little secretary."

"I have to ask you another favor today," he said. "You are a computer pro, I know. Can you do an Internet search for me?"

"Of course. If you want, I can also bring Mrs. Gu's laptop back to you."

"No, I don't think I have the time," he said. "You must have heard of the red mandarin dress case. Can you do a search on the dress—a comprehensive search, about the history, the evolution, and the style during different periods? Anything directly or indirectly related to such a dress—not just currently, but also in the sixties or fifties."

"No problem," she said, "but what do you mean by anything directly or indirectly related?"

"I wish I could tell you more specifically, but let's say any movie or book that has a mandarin dress as an important part of it, or somebody known for it, either wearing or making it, any relevant comments or criticism about it, and of course any mandarin dress bearing a resemblance to the one in question. And I may need you to run a couple of errands for me too."

"Whatever you want, Chief."

"Don't worry about the expense. A portion of the chief inspector fund hasn't been spent this year. If I don't use it up soon, the bureau will cut the fund next year."

"So you are not going to quit, Chief Inspector Chen."

"Well—" He cut himself short, the soup spurting out of the thin-skinned bun despite his caution. She was perceptive, handing over a pink paper napkin to him. It was not too bad to be a chief inspector, after all, to have a "little secretary" sitting beside, like an understanding flower.

At the end of the meal, she asked the waiter for a receipt as Chen was producing his wallet.

"Don't worry," he said. "Let me buy this meal for you. No need to ask for government reimbursement."

"I know, but it's for the government's benefit."

The waiter gave her something like two receipts, one for fifty Yuan, and another for a hundred.

"The city's tax income has increased more than two hundred percent last month, because of the newly invented official receipt with a lottery number on it," she said, scratching the receipt with a coin. "Look! You bring me luck."

"What?"

"Ten Yuan. Look at the lottery number printed on each receipt."

"That's a novel idea."

"Capitalism in China is like nowhere else in the world. Nothing but money matters here. In restaurants, people didn't ask for the receipt except for 'socialist expense,' so most restaurants reported losses. With the lottery practice, everybody is asking for receipts. It's said that one family won twenty thousand."

Chen also scratched a receipt. No luck, but no disappointment, with her hair touching his face over the number on the receipt.

They then walked out to the oriental clothing boutiques scattered in the back area of the market. A sort of niche business created for foreign tourists, the small stores displayed an impressive array of mandarin dresses in their windows. Taking his arm, she led him into one of them.

"The dress you are investigating is old-fashioned, not like any of these you may see here," she said, examining around. "He is perverse, humiliating the victim in such a dress."

"Oh, you mean the murderer? Elaborate for me."

"He wants to display her as an object of his sexual fantasy. The graceful mandarin dress, elegant yet erotic with the torn slits and loose buttons. I have seen several pictures in newspapers."

"You're talking like a cop," he said. At this moment, everybody in the city seemed eager to be a cop, but she had a point. "Surely you know a lot about the fashion."

"I have two or three mandarin dresses. Occasionally, I have to put one on in haste, but I have never ripped the slits."

"He might have put the dress on her after her death—her body rigid, and her limbs uncooperative."

"Even in that scenario, the ragged, torn slits don't make sense. Whatever way you put it on, you won't damage it like that," she said, turning to him. "Would you like to do an experiment—on me?"

"An experiment, how?"

"That's easy," she said, scooping a scarlet mandarin dress from the hanger and dragging him into the fitting room. Closing the door, she handed the dress to him. "Put it on me as roughly as possible."

Kicking off her shoes, she was peeling off her dress, and in less than a minute, she was standing in her white panties, wearing a lace bra.

It was only for his work, he told himself. Drawing in a breath, he found himself in a clumsy attempt to put the dress on her.

She held herself still and rigid—like a lifeless victim—against his rough hands. No expression on her face, hardly any flex in her muscle, her limbs unresponsive, yet her nipples visibly hardened. She blushed as he yanked the dress down on her.

No matter how hard or violently he tried to pull the dress down, the slits were not damaged.

And he noticed her lips trembling, losing color. There was no heat in the fitting room. It was hard for her to play a half-naked, lifeless model for long.

But she had already confirmed her point. The slits must have been deliberately torn. And that was an important fact.

He insisted on paying for the dress. "Don't take it off, White Cloud. It looks wonderful on you."

"You don't have to do that. It's for your work," she said, producing a small camera. "Take a picture of me in it."

He did, having her stand in front of the boutique store. And then he put her coat over the dress.

"Thank you," she said wistfully. "I have to go to school now."

Afterward he decided to walk back, alone, at least for a while.

It required strenuous effort to expel the image of her body struggling in and out of the mandarin dress. The image got juxtaposed with another, of her standing naked in a private room of the Dynasty karaoke club, in the company of other men.

He was disappointed with himself. She had done that for his police work, but he kept thinking of her as a K girl, imagining things about her, in a mandarin dress or not.

And that excited him.

He thought about the stories of women being trouble and monsters. *Subjectivity exists only to the extent of its being subject to the discourses*—an idea from a book of postmodernist criticism he had picked up in his effort to deconstruct those classical love stories.

Perhaps the stories had read him.

THIRTEEN

ANOTHER BODY IN A red mandarin dress was discovered early Friday morning.

The body was found at another public location—by a shrub grove on the Bund, close to the intersection of Jiujiang and Zhongshan Roads.

Around five that morning, Nanhua, a retired teacher, was heading to a small square called Tai Chi Corner on the upraised bank near the intersection. As he was about to climb up the stone steps, he saw the body lying underneath the bank, partially concealed by the grove. He started shouting for help and people gathered around. Reporters hurried over from their offices nearby. It was only after they had all taken pictures, from various angles, that one of them thought to report the body to the police bureau.

When Yu and his colleagues arrived, the scene looked much like a farmer's market in the morning, noisy and chaotic, full of people making comments and comparisons, as if bargaining with peddlers.

It wasn't just an area with people and traffic moving through it all night long, but it was one of those "most sensitive areas" with heightened patrol activities by the police as well as the neighborhood committees. That the murderer had left the body there spoke for itself. It was a more defiant message than before.

The murderer must have thrown the body out of a moving car. It was out of the question for him to pose the body like before. That accounted for the different posture of the third girl.

She was lying on her back with one arm thrown over her head, wearing an identical mandarin dress with torn slits and loose buttons. The left leg was bent and the knee drawn up high, revealing her pubic hair, black against her pale thighs. She looked to be in her early twenties, though with plenty of makeup on her face.

"That bastard," Yu cursed through his clenched teeth as he squatted down by the body, pulling on his gloves.

Like the first two victims, death appeared to be the result of asphyxia. For the time of death, he roughly estimated it at three or four hours earlier, judging by the loss of the pinkish color in her fingernails and toenails. Aside from the fact that she had nothing under the dress, there were no outward signs of sexual abuse. No semen visible around the genitals, thighs, or in the pubic hair; no blood, dirt, or skin under her nails. Her legs and arms were unbruised, without lacerations or bite marks.

The police were busy gathering up whatever was discoverable at the crime scene, cigarette butts, stray buttons, scrap paper. With the scene already so damaged, Yu didn't think their efforts would yield anything useful.

But he saw a light-colored fiber on the sole of her left foot. Possibly from her socks, or she could have picked it up while walking barefoot somewhere. He removed it and put it in a plastic envelope.

He stood up. A chilly wind was blowing from the river in a squealing gust. The big clock atop the Custom House started striking. The same melody, never lost in the change of times, reverberated against the gray sky, oblivious of the irreversible loss of a young girl in the morning.

He knew he had to go back to the bureau, leaving his colleagues to work the scene.

The Shanghai Police Bureau, too, seemed to be shuddering in the cold morning wind. Even the retired-and-rehired doorman, Comrade Old Liang, stood there shaking his head at Yu, like a helpless plant frostbitten overnight.

Phone calls started pouring in from the city government, from the media, from the public. Everyone was talking about a serial killer at large, a murderer brazenly defiant of the city police.

The knowledge that all this had happened twice before and that it was likely to happen again was a staggering blow to the police force. Three victims in three weeks and, given that they had made no progress in their investigation, quite possibly another one at the end of another week.

Yu's colleagues were going all out, extending the search into every possible corner. The technical division was reexamining the scene of the crime, a temporary hotline was receiving tips from the public, every radio patrol car was on the watch.

A picture of the victim was faxed and posted everywhere. There was no point covering it up, and no attempt was made. Far more graphic pictures were being printed in the newspapers along with lurid descriptions. The news was spreading like wildfire, threatening to consume the city.

Grinding out his fourth cigarette in the morning, Yu looked up to see Liao striding into his office with the initial medical report. It confirmed strangulation as the cause of death. Lividity and rigor were also consistent with Yu's estimated time of death. Like the second victim, there were no indications that the girl had sex before her death.

Since the second victim was a three-accompanying girl, Liao suggested that they try to identify the new victim by focusing on the entertainment business. It was consistent with his new focus, and Yu agreed.

Sure enough, around eleven o'clock, her identity was established. She was Tang Xiumei, a singing girl, more commonly known as a K girl, at the Music Box Karaoke Center. The manager, alert after the earlier cases, recognized her from the faxed picture.

"What did I tell you?" Liao said, waving a fax page in his hand.

What a K girl did in a private K room was open knowledge in the city. If a Big Buck took a fancy to her, he could demand services other than singing, and outside of the karaoke room, too, by paying for the so-called "company hour." No club would say no. Tang's coworkers said that she hadn't shown up at the club that evening. But that wasn't uncommon for her.

According to the manager, Tang didn't come to work last night or the night before. What a girl chose to do on her own time was beyond the club's control or knowledge. The manager's statement, along with the testimony of several other girls, ruled out the possibility that the murderer picked her up in the club Thursday night.

Inquiries about the customers she'd met for the previous few nights led nowhere; the regular customers had solid alibis for that night, and none of the new ones had left their name or address.

Yu contacted Tang's neighborhood committee. Liu Yunfei, the head of the committee as well as a neighbor of Tang's in the same building, answered the phone.

"What can I say about those girls? Materialistic from head to foot. Tang had a favorite saying: to work well is not so important as to marry well. So she went to work in a K club, hoping that she could meet and marry a Big Buck."

"Did you notice anything suspicious about her in the last few days?"

"She hardly talked to anybody in the neighborhood. If she wasn't ashamed for herself, we were ashamed for her."

"Did her neighbors notice anything on Thursday?"

"Well, she left a bit earlier, according to Auntie Xiong, who lives on the same floor. Around three. Normally she did not leave until around dinnertime. That's her shift. Of course, we didn't really know about her work schedule."

"So she stayed at home all day?"

"Not exactly. She could be busy with so many things. But when she left for her shift, she was dressed like a vamp. Always in her pantyhose and high heels. So we knew."

"Can you write me a report?" Yu said. "Include whatever you and your neighbors know about Tang."

Yu made some more calls, talking to her neighbors and coworkers. After more than an hour on the phone, he learned practically nothing beyond the initial details he had gotten from Liu.

Shortly afterward, a three-page report came in through the fax machine. It was from Liu and contained everything he had learned from the neighborhood. It was fairly detailed, considering the short notice.

Tang had lost her mother quite young. When her father was laid off, she, still a high school student, became a K girl with a government-issued license. Her father, too ashamed to continue living in the lane, went back to his old home in Subei. So she lived alone and occasionally brought people home. The committee was well aware of it, but unlike in the years of class struggle, the neighborhood cadres couldn't go barging into her room without something like a warrant. Fortunately, most of her clients preferred to go to a hotel instead of her small room in the squalid lane.

She had no phone at home, nor a cell phone, since both were still too expensive for her. Occasionally she used the public phone service at the lane entrance, but she had a beeper with text messaging, which she used a lot.

Yu checked with the beeper company. The response came back fast. There was no activity on Thursday night.

As Yu finished reading the report, another emergency meeting was called at the bureau.

"Look at the headline. 'Shanghai in crisis,' " Party Secretary Li said, his face livid, his words stumbling out in rage. "Our bureau is a laughingstock."

Neither Yu nor Liao had an immediate response. The headline might be an exaggeration, but the bureau was in a crisis.

"Third! On the Bund!" Li went on. "Have you found anything?"

Yu and Lao were pulling hard at their cigarettes, shrouding the office in smoke. Hong looked flushed, with a hand pressed against her mouth for fear of coughing out loud.

"The investigation must take a new direction," Liao said. "Two of the three victims were in the entertainment business—the sex business. Both the second and the third were easy targets at a restaurant or a karaoke bar. Most of those girls wouldn't tell their families about their activities, so clues about their disappearance would be hard to find. More importantly, such a girl usually believes she is going out with a customer and goes to a secluded area to perform her job. They wouldn't have resisted until it was too late."

"What about Jasmine?" Yu said.

"She worked at a hotel," Liao said, "but he could have easily picked her up. In fact, her boyfriend met her like that. That's why I've been pushing for a different focus."

"What's your point?" Li said.

"The motive is evident. Hatred against those girls. He could have paid a terrible price because of someone in the business—a sexually transmitted disease, for instance—and wants revenge. That's why he stripped those victims without having sex with them."

"What about the red mandarin dress?" Li asked again.

"He makes a point of dressing his victims like the one who gave him the sexual disease. A sort of symbolism."

"But there could be different revenge scenarios," Yu said. "A woman he loved, let's say, dumped him for another. In his mind, she's no better than a prostitute."

"But that explains his choice of locations too. Inspector Liao's theory, I mean," Hong cut in. "A protest against the booming sex industry in the city. He must blame not only those girls, but the city government as well, I believe, for allowing it to take place."

"Leave our government out of it, Hong," Li said. "Whatever scenarios or theories we come up with, the killing will continue. And what are we going to do to stop the killer?"

A short spell of silence ensued in the office.

With the entertainment industry increasingly prosperous in the city, it wouldn't be difficult at all for him to find new victims. And it was out of the question, everyone in the room knew, to shut down the business.

"I suggest we check the hospitals," Liao said. "They keep all records of all sexually transmitted disease."

"It's too much of a long shot," Li said. "Before you could go through all the records, he'll strike again. We only have one week's time, Inspector Liao. Besides, even in your scenario, he could have sought medical help secretly."

"Most sex murderers are sexually impotent," Yu said. "According to Chen, the murder is a sort of mental orgasm. So the theory of sexually transmitted disease may not hold."

"Liao has a point," Hong said more resolutely. "Out of the three victims, two were engaged in some sort of sex services. That at least suggests a pattern. Often, the victims fit a certain stereotype, which plays an important role in the killer's sexual fantasies. He may or may not have been hurt by one of these three-accompanying girls, but it is evident that he has a grudge against them."

"So what's your proposal?" Li demanded.

"I would like to make a suggestion based on Liao's analysis. If he is going to strike again, it's probably among those girls. Let's set up a decoy for him."

"There are so many karaoke clubs, nightclubs, and restaurants in the city," Yu said. "How could you tell from which one he'll pick his next victim?"

"I don't think he would repeat himself."

"Please explain." Li appeared to be interested.

"After Jasmine, one was an eating girl, one was a singing girl—out of the three-accompanying girls. The next one, logically, would have to be a dancing girl. People are all creatures of habit," Hong said. "So he locates his victims by frequenting those entertainment spots of the city. They are easy targets, as you just said. But more importantly, he is a man given to symbolism. The red mandarin dress may be just part of it. So he will most likely choose a dancing girl as the next victim in his elaborate scheme."

"But to set up a decoy for him may just be like waiting for a rabbit to knock itself out on an old tree, as the proverb goes," Yu said. "And he is far more dangerous than a rabbit. I talked to Chen; he believes such a psychopath is capable of anything."

"Do you have a better idea?" Li turned to Yu, almost fiercely. "Or does your Chief Inspector Chen?"

"Perhaps the bureau is too small of a temple for someone like Chen," Liao joined in.

Yu, surprised by the animosity demonstrated by both Li and Liao, made no response.

No one made any further objection to Hong's proposal. No one had a better idea, as Li had put it. So Hong was going to a dance club that afternoon.

Afterward, Yu considered it necessary to contact Chen. After the headline "Shanghai in Crisis," he didn't think that Chen would keep burying his head among books.

As he picked up the phone, he thought he knew how to guarantee Chen's full attention.

"I have to talk to you now, Chief. Let's meet in front of Bund Park."

"Why Bund Park?"

"The third red mandarin dress victim was found there this morning, close to the Tai Chi Corner on the Bund, just a stone's throw from the park."

"What—the third one was found on the Bund?"

"You'll read about it in the newspapers—perhaps along with a reader's letter, asking, 'What is our Chief Inspector Chen doing?' "

"I'm on my way, Yu."

FOURTEEN

TWENTY MINUTES LATER, YU arrived at the Bund again.

Checking around, he chose a green bench that faced the park. Sitting there, he could see down into the shrub grove where he had examined the body earlier. A crowd was still lingering there. The shrub grove looked somewhat like the flower bed where the first victim was found, but that might just be a coincidence. He didn't believe the murderer could have chosen the places to dump the bodies for that reason.

With the heavy traffic along Zhong Road, it wasn't practical to cordon off the area. There wasn't any yellow crime scene tape there, which would have attracted even more people. Nor was it necessary. Any evidence at the scene was long gone.

It wasn't long before he saw Chen emerging out of the throng, climbing up the flight of steps. A man taller than most of the people around him, Chen wore a trench coat and was carrying a briefcase. He had a pair of tortoise-rimmed, amber-lensed glasses that accentuated his broad forehead. Perhaps Chen didn't want people to recognize him, what with reporters still at the scene, looking around for familiar faces. Chen came to a halt as he reached the top step and took off his glasses. Then he spotted Yu and came over.

Chen took a seat beside Yu.

"What do you think of the location?" Yu asked.

"An act of deliberate defiance. Any clues?"

"No. Like the previous two victims, there was no evidence at the scene."

"No sexual assault on the victim?"

"No. None that I could see, but she was also naked under the red mandarin dress."

"What about her identity?"

"A singing girl. Identifying the victim was quicker this time," Yu said, thinking it unnecessary to elaborate. "She was a K girl."

"Another one in the entertainment business."

"Yes, so Liao really wants to focus on that angle," Yu said. "He sees a motive as well as a pattern—hatred against girls in the sex business. It fits in with your analysis of the killer as a psychopath, including the red mandarin dress."

"The red mandarin dress must be significant. No question about that. Victimology analysis, through which you explore a possible relationship between the victim and the murderer, helps too. But the first victim doesn't fit, does she?"

"I raised the same question."

"Another thing that's beyond me," Chen said, standing up and casting a glance toward the shrub grove. "He took a deliberate risk in dumping the body on the Bund, knowing that traffic and people go by here all night long."

"It was an act of vanity, I suspect. To show his defiance, and to taunt and torment the police. As you said, a serial killer has his signature—unique ways to commit a crime, like placing the body in a public location. Irrational, but it makes sense to his irrational mind."

"I've got a strange feeling, Yu. Not that he is so cocky, but that he is so desperate—"

"What do you mean, Chief?"

"He is desperately sick. An end to all this may not be unacceptable—a death impulse or whatever," Chen said, but he declined to explain further. "What are you going to do now?"

"Hong is going to set herself up as a decoy, posing as a dancing girl."

"A decoy is a good tactic, if you're certain of the murderer's pattern. A dancing girl makes sense, but it may not yield results in a week. A lot depends on the circumstances. Besides, it can be dangerous for the decoy."

"Yes, I'm concerned. She is a young cop."

"If she insists on doing it, then assign an officer to protect her, to always remain in her company."

"I'll talk to Liao about it."

"Also, try to keep her assignment as a decoy a secret."

"Within the bureau?"

"Not in your group, naturally, but from everyone else. The criminal may be well connected," Chen said, frowning. "For instance, consider his choice of the Bund last night. He could have learned about the neighborhood committee patrol. The Bund happens to be one of the few public places—perhaps the only one—that was barely covered by such patrols. It's all government and business buildings along Zhongshan Road, and there is no residential neighborhood committee nearby. The police patrol alone was not enough to cover the area."

"It could just be a coincidence."

"For once, Party Secretary Li may have a point. The murderer's choice of the Bund makes the message a political one, but I doubt it's a call for action against three-accompanying girls. Rather, it's a secret, strange message, full of contradictions. The contradictions may serve, however, as a point of entry for us, just like symptoms for a psychoanalyst." Chen added, "Incidentally, I've adopted a similar approach for my literature paper."

"Really!" Yu said. "Your paper must be an interesting one, but first tell me about the contradictions in the case."

"Let me start by telling you about my paper, briefly," Chen said. "I've read a few classical romance stories, and I've been confused by their contradicting messages. This reminded me of something in the red mandarin dress."

"Or vice versa," Yu said grumpily. That was just like his bookish boss. They had three murder victims, and the chief inspector actually wanted to discuss his literature paper.

"In psychoanalysis, a patient may have problems or contradictions beyond his own comprehension, and an analyst is supposed to find the cause embedded within the subconscious. I tried to focus on the contradictions in this case too, especially with regards to the red mandarin dress. So I have put together a list."

"Now you have another list."

Chen ignored him. "To begin with, the contradiction between the graceful dress and the obscene pose."

"I think we discussed that last time. He could have been hurt by someone wearing such a dress," Yu said. "And, according to Liao, by a girl in the sex business."

"That leads to another contradiction relevant to Liao's theory," Chen said. "The dress is too conservative for a three-accompanying girl. Too old-fashioned. According to Mr. Shen, it was probably made more than ten years ago, and made in a style that dates back even further. There was no entertaining business at that time, nor three-accompanying girls."

"No, I don't think there was."

"Then there is all the attention to the details of the dress. It's not a dress likely to be affordable for a three-accompanying girl. The dress is exquisite, made with high-quality craftsmanship."

"Yes, Mr. Shen has mentioned that."

"And then the torn slits on the dress. White Cloud did an experiment for me."

"So you have her working as your assistant," Yu said, remembering what Peiqin said about the possible relationship of the two. "What experiment?"

"Well, she knows much more about the dress than I do. She demonstrated that there's no way that the slits could be torn accidentally, no matter how roughly the dress is put on. In other words, the criminal must have deliberately torn them. With no sexual assault, no penetration or ejaculation, why would he insist on such an appearance? There must be a reason for it."

"You mean it's not for the sake of misleading us, but a reason understandable only to himself?"

"Possibly not even understandable to himself. More like a ritual. Only with the victim in the mandarin dress, with all the details observed, like torn slits, bare feet, loose bosom buttons, and the obscene pose, of course, does the ritual become complete. For him, only part of the kick is physiological. The other part may come from the ritualistic behavior that accompanies acts of sexual perversion. Again, not unlike those romantic stories, the contradictions may hardly be comprehensible to the author. So why?"

"Why?" Yu echoed, noticing another group of people swarming around the shrub grove. There was also a TV station car pulling up nearby, causing a temporary traffic jam. "I haven't studied psychology, but I know a patient has to sit and talk in front of a doctor. In our case, with no clues as to the identity of the criminal, how and what can we analyze?"

It was an issue Yu had raised last time, and Chen hadn't been able to give him a real answer.

"Well, by analyzing those contradictions, we may still come to know something."

"Really, Chief!"

"To begin with, the style and material for the dress probably came from the sixties. Possibly the early sixties, but not after the outbreak of the Cultural Revolution in 1966. Based on Mr. Shen's opinion, we may assume it's a conservative style for a married woman in her thirties. If this original mandarin dress wearer were alive today, she would be in her mid-sixties or seventies."

"So you are now talking about the original mandarin dress wearer thirty years ago?" Yu asked.

"Doesn't Liao also believe that the case is related to the original mandarin dress wearer? For me, it's just another wearer, of different social status and age than Liao assumed. And following that, it leads to the man connected to her. Let's assume for the moment that he was the same age. If so, now he would be in his sixties or possibly seventies."

"Yes?" Yu said in exasperated confusion. "How does all that come into your picture?"

"Now for our serial murderer. Three victims in three weeks, the bodies dumped at three public locations. Do you think an old man could have been up to the task? Just now I stood by the shrub grove for several minutes. Not once could a car have slowed down or pulled up there without other cars behind it honking like mad. So if he pushed the body out while driving, most likely he would have been seen by the cars behind him, even at night. He must have driven around several times, I believe, before he would have been able to pull it off."

"That's true. To dispose of the bodies like that, one would have to be really quick and agile."

"So the murderer has to be no older than a middle-aged man. But if so, the one connected to the original mandarin dress wearer was, at the time, only a boy."

"That doesn't make sense."

"That's another contradiction, to be sure, but again in these psychological studies, there's something called Oedipus complex."

"Oedipus complex?" Yu repeated.

"A son's subconscious sexual desire for his mother."

"What? That's supposed to help us find a boy who grew into a middle-aged man who is capable of committing three murder cases in three weeks?" Yu said without trying to conceal the satire in his tone. "That's totally beyond me."

Yu had never heard of the so-called Oedipus complex. Absurd as it might sound, however, it was not unlike the chief inspector, who was known for his unorthodox ways.

"No, I don't think it's too likely, either," Chen said in an unperturbed way, "but according to the theory, he's probably a middle-aged man with a traumatic experience in his childhood, possibly during the

Cultural Revolution. And he must have had conflicting feelings toward the woman who wore the original mandarin dress."

"That's a novel theory indeed," Yu exclaimed. "So after waiting twenty years, his passion for his mother suddenly drove him into a frenzied killing streak."

"It's not my theory, Yu," Chen said. "Still, it explains some of the contradictions."

Yu regretted his satirical comment to his boss. After all, Chen had been thinking hard about the case, checking through his books. Still, his approach appeared to be too psychological, too academic.

"Oh, some people are talking about your vacation during the investigation," Yu said, changing the subject.

"Let them complain. Just tell them I'm too busy with my paper."

"But even Old Hunter says that you could put your paper aside for a short while."

"That's exactly what I am going to do, but we don't have to tell the others."

A young couple came over. After looking around for several minutes, they chose to sit on the bench, beside the two cops. This wasn't unusual on the Bund. While there were more and more places for young people in the city, the Bund was still the number-one spot. There were all the colorful vessels sailing in the background and the romantic memories of the city still vibrant in the impressive neocolonial buildings. Besides, it was free. So lovers would take any available seat on the Bund. That made it impossible, however, for Chen and Yu to continue their discussion of the murders.

"So are you going to push ahead with your theory?" Yu said, rising.

"It's just a theory in books," Chen said. "In fact, your focus on the possible triggering factor in Jasmine's murder may be the right direction. But we may have to move back further in history."

Yu didn't know how much further they could move back. Still, there was no telling what surprises his boss would come up with.

FIFTEEN

ON TUESDAY MORNING, CHEN woke up still exhausted, as if he hadn't slept at all. There was also the suggestion of a nagging headache. He started rubbing his temples.

He had spent the weekend working on the red mandarin dress case, pushing along several fronts.

He'd phoned a friend in the United States, asking for her help with a background checkup of Weng. With her connections, she soon obtained the required information. What Weng had told Yu was basically true. He had been a special buyer for an American company. The divorce proceedings with his wife had hit no snag and should be finalized in a month or two. In fact, his wife was looking forward to it, as she had a new boyfriend.

He'd contacted Xiong, the city government cadre who had spoken to Tian's factory about his actions during the Cultural Revolution. Xiong said that he'd done so because of an anonymous letter he'd received about Tian's atrocities. According to Xiong, he didn't try to put any pressure on the factory. Once somebody in Xiong's position had spoken, however, it was a matter of course that other people would do everything possible to comply. That spelled the doom for Tian. An anonymous letter was smart, though not necessarily suspicious, as it allowed the author to "kill with somebody else's knife." Xiong had no idea at all who had written the letter.

Chen also researched the mandarin-dress-related mass-criticism during the early part of the Cultural Revolution. Like Peiqin, he recalled the image of Wang Guangmei being mass-criticized and humiliated in a mandarin dress. Thinking that others could have suffered like that as well, he had a computer search done by White Cloud and then, also with the help of White Cloud, he got in touch with Yang, a movie star who had been mass-criticized in a mandarin dress. There were some minor differences in details, though. As far as Yang remembered, it was a white dress, and she wasn't barefoot. Instead, she had on worn-out shoes, which symbolized a bourgeois promiscuous lifestyle. Yang offered one more detail that differed. Her dress slits had been cut up to the waist, revealing her panties, and it had been done by the Red Guards with a pair of scissors. The murder victims' slits, in contrast, seemed to have been torn, as in a struggle. He immediately checked with Yu, who confirmed his impression. With the first victim, the dress could have been torn in rage by the perpetrator, and for the second and third, possibly in an effort to produce similarity among the victims. Whatever the interpretation, the suggestion of sexual violence was unmistakable.

On Monday, he talked to Ding Jiashan, the attorney who represented the diners in the food poisoning case against Tian. According to Ding, there was something suspicious about the whole thing. It was a case few attorneys would be interested in. The attorney's fees would almost certainly be higher than what the clients would recover from such a small restaurant, but the diners seemed to be so determined that they were willing to pay his fee up front. And they were prepared too. They had the receipt from the restaurant, they had the record from the hospital, and their stories supported one another. So, on their behalf, the attorney complained to the business bureau first, which fined Tian heavily and closed the restaurant for violations. The diners seemed to be happy with the initial result but, a few days later, when he tried to contact them about the next step, they had canceled their phones. The attorney wasn't even sure that they had given him their real names.

This further confirmed the scenario that somebody had been after Tian. But that wasn't necessarily a lead in the red mandarin dress case.

In the meantime, he read through the material prepared by Yu and Hong. Hong had not called in during the weekend, though. She must have been busy with her decoy assignment.

He also experimented further with focusing on the contradictions in the case, which seemed only to lead to more contradictions.

By Tuesday, however, he had again arrived at the conclusion that he could hardly do any better than his colleagues, in spite of the fact that he had been going all out, concentrating on the serial murder case.

Just as he was about to brew a second pot of coffee in frustration, Professor Bian called and asked about his progress with the paper.

"I've been working on it," Chen said.

"Do you think you can turn it in with others?" Bian asked. "It's a promising paper."

"Yes, I'll turn the paper in on time."

After he hung up, he became worried. He had a longstanding habit of setting deadlines for himself, as he needed the extra pressure to complete a project, such as a poem or a mystery translation. This time was different. He was already under too much pressure. Since all of his efforts in the investigation seemed to be going nowhere, with not even the suggestion of a possible breakthrough anytime soon, he decided he might as well try to finish his paper first. In the past, he'd found himself coming up with new ideas about a project after temporarily putting it on the shelf. The working of the subconscious, perhaps.

It was no longer possible for him to focus while at home, however. Phone calls kept coming in, and unplugging the phone line didn't help. Now that there were three victims in the case, his cell phone number had become suddenly known to many, including the media. Even at the library, he was recognized by a couple of people who then peppered him with questions about the murder case. Last night, a *Wenhui* journalist had come knocking at his door, carrying a package of barbecued pork and a bottle of Shaoxin wine, eager to discuss her theories with him over the feast—almost like a passionate female character stepping out of one of those romantic stories.

He decided to go to the Starbucks Café on Sichuan Road.

Starbucks, along with McDonald's and Kentucky Fried Chicken, had mushroomed in the city. The café was regarded as a cultivated resort for the elite, and the atmosphere there was supposedly quiet and peaceful. At the café, where he was nobody, he could have an undisturbed morning and concentrate on the paper.

Choosing a corner table, he took out his books. He had gathered five or six stories, but three might be enough for the paper. The third one, "Artisan Cui and His Ghost Wife," was originally narrated by Song dynasty professional storytellers in marketplaces or tea houses where old people sat talking loudly, cracking watermelon seeds, playing mahjong, and spitting to their hearts' content.

Sipping at his coffee, he started reading. In the tale, Xiuxiu, a pretty girl in Lin'an, was purchased as an embroidery maid by Prince Xian'an, the military leader of three commanderies. In his household worked a young jade carver named Cui, who gained the prince's favor for having carved a marvelous jade Avalokitesvara for the emperor. So the prince promised to marry Xiuxiu to Cui in the future. One night, fleeing from a fire at the prince's mansion, Xiuxiu suggested to Cui that, instead of waiting, they become husband and wife there and then. So that night, the two left for Tanzhou as a couple. After a year, they ran into Guo, a guard for the prince. Guo reported the whereabouts of the fugitives to the prince, who had them brought back. At the local court, Cui was punished and banished to Jiankang. Xiuxiu overtook him on the way there, telling him that after getting her punishment in the back garden, she was set free. As it happened, the imperial jade Avalokitesvara needed repairing, so the

Cuis moved back to the capital, where they again ran across Guo. Once more the prince sent for Xiuxiu, but when the sedan chair supposedly carrying her arrived, there was no one inside. Guo then got a severe beating for his false information. Next, Cui, too, was brought to the prince, at which point Cui learned that Xiuxiu had been beaten to death in the back garden. So it was Xiuxiu's ghost who had been with him all this time. When Cui returned home, he begged her to spare him, but she took away his life so he could keep her company in the next world.

As with earlier stories, Chen soon detected suspicious ambiguities in the text. An implied critique was discernable even in an alternative title of the story: "A Curse in Life and Death for Attendant Cui." There was no mistaking the message about Xiuxiu being a curse. Cui was doomed because she, in the name of love, never let him get away—doomed to the loss of his position, the punishment at court, and eventually the loss of his life. Xiuxiu embodied the contradiction: a pretty girl who loves Cui with a courageous passion rarely seen in classical Chinese literature also deliberately destroys Cui with her own hands. Attraction and repulsion were like two sides of a coin.

For the merging of the two sides, Chen found an explanation in the contemporary generic classification. The story belonged to the category of *yanfen/linggaui. Yanfen* referred to tales of beautiful women in amorous affairs and *linggui*, to tales of women identified as demons and ghosts.

There was a similar term in western literature—*femme fatale.*

In "Artisan Cui and His Ghost Wife," Xiuxiu was exactly such a curse. Chen took out a pen to underline the paragraphs at the end of the story.

Cui returned home in a depression. He stepped into his room only to see his wife sitting on the bed. Cui Ning said, "Please spare me, my wife."

"I was beaten to death by the prince because of you and was buried in the back garden," Xiuxiu said. "How I hate that Private Guo for

talking so much! I have finally avenged myself—the prince has beaten him fifty times on the back with a stick. Now that everybody knows me as a ghost, I cannot stay here anymore."

With that, she sprang up and grabbed Cui Ning with both hands. He screamed and fell to the ground.

At that moment, there happened to be something falling to the floor in the café. Chen turned to see a girl slipping from a bar stool. She had overreached to kiss a young man across the bar, her foot stretching to the floor for balance, and her high-heeled sandal flew off into a corner.

The café was not as quiet as expected. Customers came pouring in, most of them young, fashionable, and spirited. One brought in a laptop and started playing a game, her fingers pecking and chirping like noisy sparrows on a spring morning. Several had cell phones in their hands, talking as if there were no one else in the world.

Chen ordered another cup of coffee.

How could Xiuxiu bear to take away Cui's life? Chen turned back a few pages, to the part about Cui and Xiuxiu running into each other on the night of the fire.

"Do you remember the night when we were enjoying the moon on the terrace?" Xiuxiu said to Cui Ning. "I was betrothed to you and you just kept on thanking the prince. Do you remember or not?"

Cui Ning clasped his hands and could only respond with "Yah."

"That night, all the people were congratulating you, saying 'What a wonderful couple!' How come you've forgotten all about it?"

Cui Ning again could only respond with "Yah."

"Rather than continuing to wait, why don't we become husband and wife tonight? What do you think?"

"How would I dare?"

"You dare not? What if I shout and ruin your reputation? You can never explain why you brought me home. I shall report you to the prince tomorrow."

Chen was now beginning to see Xiuxiu "seducing" Cui. Cunning and calculating, she actually dragged Cui into it.

There were still questions left unanswered in the story, but Chen believed he had found something in common with the other stories. He would be able to wrap up the paper, even though it was not as ambitious a project as he had hoped.

Draining the coffee, he flipped open his phone. There were quite a few messages, including one from White Cloud. He called her back first. She reported to him like a cop, about the lack of progress in her computer research, but toward the end, she made a suggestion like a "little secretary."

"Give yourself a break, Chief. Go to a nightclub. There you can experience the environment of the victims firsthand, and get to relax a little too. And you can always have my company, you know. You have too much on your mind and I'm worried. Your nerves won't stand the strain."

Whether that was intended as a hint, he didn't know. As an ex–singing girl herself, though, she knew about the business, and it might be helpful to the investigation.

"Thank you, White Cloud. That might be a good idea, after I finish my paper in a couple of days."

He then made a phone call to Professor Bian, who was at home, picking up on the first ring.

"How is your paper coming, Chief Inspector Chen?"

"I've been working on another story," Chen said. "Do you think an analysis of three stories will be enough for the paper?"

"Yes, three should be enough."

"They share a common movement: each of them contains something that contradicts the love theme generally taken for granted, with the heroine unexpectedly turning into a demon or a disaster. The turns come through a tiny detail: a medical term, an ambiguous poem, or a phrase thrown in at random. Once those are examined closely, the romantic motif undergoes a dramatic reversal."

"You have an original point. But you have to prove what's behind it, I think."

"What's behind it?" Chen said, echoing Bian's comment. No coincidences, just as in police work. Or as in psychoanalysis. There had to be an explanation for it. "You're right, Professor Bian."

"The stories were written during different dynasties, and the writers came from different social backgrounds—"

"So you mean something that is always there behind the scenes, going on through the different dynasties, whether those writers were aware of it or not."

"If you want to see it that way. Something deep within the Chinese culture. So your project may not be an easy one."

"I'll think about it. Thank you so much, Professor Bian."

Indeed, that was thought-provoking. As Chen put down the phone, the first thought that came to him was about Confucianism, the ruling ideology for two thousand years in China, something hardly ever challenged until the beginning of the twentieth century.

However, Confucius said nothing about romantic love, as far as Chen could recall.

But he still felt excited, as if standing on the threshold of a breakthrough. He had borrowed several Confucian canons, which he hadn't had the time to read. Now he should be able to work out a conclusion for the paper. Ideas came crowding into his mind when the phone rang again. It was Director Zhong.

"I've been looking for you all morning, Chief Inspector Chen."

"Sorry, I'd forgotten to turn my phone on," Chen said. "Anything new in the housing development case?"

"The trial date has been moved up to about two weeks from now. It was a decision made in Beijing."

"Why such a hurry?"

"A longer night has more nightmares. No one wants the case to drag on. Peng is to be punished anyway, so why delay? People will see that the Party authorities are on their side."

"That's good," Chen said. But it was just another case in which politics dictated the outcome of a trial. "So we don't have to worry anymore."

"Well, Jia has been pushing hard. He declares that Peng is not alone in the scandal. What is wrong with this attorney? Peng may be acquainted with some people in the city government, but being acquainted doesn't necessarily lead to corruption. Have you found anything out about him?"

"Not anything special," Chen said. True, he had been too busy with his own things to delve deeply, but it was also true that no one had said anything special to him about Jia. "But I'll keep checking."

When he closed the phone, Chen had already lost his earlier train of thought about the paper. Another cup of coffee failed to help.

He looked up at the clock on the wall, feeling sick.

SIXTEEN

EARLY THE NEXT MORNING, Chen woke up with a terrible headache.

He made a pot of strong coffee and gulped down two cups for breakfast—nothing else. His headache did not improve.

No ideas came to him for the paper or for the case.

But another special delivery came from the police bureau, including a report from Hong about her decoy activities as a dancing girl.

So he brewed a second pot. He also devoured a handful of Korean ginseng pills with the coffee and smoked a cigarette.

Shortly afterward, he felt sick and shaky and broke into a cold sweat.

He was seized by an overwhelming impulse to do irrational things—to kick the wall, to howl like an owl, to smash, to shout the politically blasphemous.

Sweating, stuffing a fist into his mouth like battling a toothache, he hurried to lock the door before swallowing a couple of sleeping pills and slumping across the bed.

He awoke later to find himself a scared scarecrow. A nervous breakdown, he thought, recalling T. S. Eliot's collapse in Switzerland. He was shaken by the realization.

What if an irrational compulsion gripped him again? Fortunately he was at home now, but there was no telling where he'd be the next time. It would be a disaster if he were caught going crazy like that in public.

He searched through the medicine cabinet without finding anything else, imagining himself the hollow man in Eliot's poem.

Around nine, when White Cloud called, making a routine report about her computer search, he had hardly the strength to talk.

"Don't move," she said with genuine worry in her voice. "I'm on my way."

Half an hour later, she arrived and, to his surprise, she came with Gu, her former employer, the chairman of the New World Corporation. Gu carried a large plastic bag of Chinese herbal supplements.

Ever since they had met in another homicide case, the resourceful entrepreneur had proclaimed himself a friend of the chief inspector. A connection like Chen could be valuable to his business, but Gu had also helped Chen in his way.

"You need a vacation, Chief Inspector Chen," Gu declared. "A vacation at the Ting Mount and Lake Vacation Village. You are going there today. I'll make the arrangements."

Gu had invested in a number of properties, including the well-known vacation village along the border between Shanghai and Zhejiang Province.

It was a tempting suggestion. For the last few days, Chen had been worn out by the pressure from the housing development case, from the mandarin dress case, from the politics inside and outside the bureau, and in addition to all that, from the paper deconstructing classical love stories. A short vacation might help.

"Thank you, Mr. Gu," he said. "I owe you one."

"What is a friend for, Chief?" Gu said, "I'll send a car for you."

"I could also serve as your health secretary there," White Cloud said with a knowing smile. "You definitely need a break."

"Thank you for everything, White Cloud. I think I just need a couple of days for myself. But if there is anything you can do for me, I'll contact you."

"Make yourself available for him whenever he needs, White Cloud," Gu said. "Let me know."

White Cloud had previously worked as a singing girl for Gu, and then later for Chen as a "little secretary" paid by Gu. That was probably all there was to it—Gu wasn't suggesting anything improper.

After the arrangements were made, Gu and White Cloud left. Chen started packing. For a quick recovery, he knew he'd better forget about all his worries and responsibilities while on vacation. Still, if he felt better there, he might try to finish his paper. So he decided to carry with him a couple of Confucian classics for the conclusion of the paper. This was probably his last chance, he thought, to strive for a different "self-realization." It would be too easy for him to turn back into Chief Inspector Chen.

He put a packet of sleeping pills in his wallet, hiding them beneath the picture of White Cloud wearing that mandarin dress in the Old City God's Temple Market. It would look natural for him to check a girl's picture occasionally. But he needed to reassure himself that the tranquilizers were there, available through her smile.

He was not going to carry the cell phone with him, or his vacation would come to nothing. He should be able not to be a chief inspector for a couple of days. Besides, he couldn't do anything as a cop right now. His psychological approach was going nowhere.

When the car Gu had sent for him honked its horn under his window, however, he stuffed in his bags the folders containing the case files, almost mechanically.

In the Mercedes, Chen borrowed a phone from the driver to call his mother, saying that he would be out of the city for a few days. She must have taken it for one of those mysterious assignments, and she did not even ask him where he was going.

Afterward, he contacted White Cloud, asking her to call his mother from time to time, insisting that she reveal his whereabouts to no one.

Ahead, the fleeing clouds revealed the lines of the distant hills.

SEVENTEEN

IN THE LATE AFTERNOON, Chen arrived at the vacation village.

It turned out to be a large complex consisting of a hotel-like main building and a number of villas and cabins, along with a swimming pool, sauna rooms, tennis courts, and a golf course. All of them appeared embosomed in the hills, against a large lake shimmering at the back.

He saw no point in checking into a villa, which, as a special guest of Gu, the manager offered to him. Chen chose instead a suite in the main building. The manager presented him with a booklet of coupons.

"The coupons are for your meals and services. You don't have to pay for anything. General Manager Pei will have a special dinner for you tonight—a *bu* feast, not in herbs, but in delicacies."

"A *bu* feast!" Chen said, amused.

Bu defied translation. It could mean, among other things, a special herb and food nutritional boost to the body, a concept embedded in

Chinese medical theories, particularly in terms of the yin/yang system. But how such a banquet would work, Chen had no idea. He guessed it must have been Gu's suggestion.

The suite assigned to him consisted of a living room, a bedroom, and a spacious walk-in closet. Chen took out the books and put them on a long desk by the window, which looked out onto the hills wrapped in the winter clouds.

He wasn't going to open those books today, he reminded himself.

Instead he took a long, hot shower. Afterward, reclining on the sofa, he fell asleep in spite of himself.

When he awoke, it was almost dinnertime. Perhaps it was a belated effect of the extra dose of sleeping pills. Or perhaps he had already begun unwinding in the vacation village.

The restaurant was at the east end of the complex. It boasted a magnificent, Chinese-styled façade with two golden lions squatting at each side of the vermilion-painted gate. Waitresses in red jackets with shining black lapels bowed to him at the entrance. A hostess led him through a huge dining hall and into a private room partitioned with frosted glass.

At a large banquet table, General Manager Pei, a stout man with a pair of big black-rimmed glasses and an amiable expression, was waiting for him with several other executives, including the front desk manager he had met earlier. Every one of them started paying Chen compliments, as if they had known him for years.

"Mr. Gu keeps raving about your great achievements, Master Chen. It takes so much energy and essence to produce masterpieces like yours. So we think that a *bu* dinner may help a little."

Chen wondered how he had become a "master," but he was grateful to Gu for not revealing his identity as a police officer and for arranging all of this.

As a starter, a waiter brought a huge platter called Buddha's Head. It had but a slight resemblance to a human head—it was carved out of a white gourd, steamed in a bamboo steamer covered with a huge green lotus leaf.

"A special dish." Pei was all smiles, giving the go-ahead signal to the waiter holding a long bamboo knife.

Chen watched the waiter saw a piece off of the "skull" with the knife, put the chopsticks into the "brains," and come up with a fried sparrow—inside a grilled quail—inside a braised pigeon.

"So many brains in one head," one of the executives chuckled.

"It's Buddha," Chen said, smiling. "No wonder."

"All the essences mix together to produce an extraordinary brain boost," another manager added, "for intellectuals who constantly cudgel their brains out."

"A perfect balance of yin and yang," still another said, "from a variety of fowls."

Chen had heard of theories regarding dietary correspondence between humans and other species. His mother used to cook pork brains for his benefit, but here it was far more elaborate than he had expected.

Then came a lake turtle, steamed with crystal sugar, yellow wine, ginger, scallion, and a few slices of *Jinhua* ham.

"As we all know, turtle is good for yin, but all you can get at the market are farm-raised, fed with hormones and antibiotics. Ours is different. It comes directly from the lake," Pei said emphatically, sipping at his wine. "People have erroneous notions about yin/yang. In the winter, they devour red meat, such as lamb, dog, and deer, but that's not dialectical—"

"Supposedly a boost to yang, so it's good in the cold winter, I've heard," Chen said, intrigued by Pei's lecture, which sounded quite philosophical, "but I've never learned about the dialectical part."

"For some people, with the yang in their system already pathologically high, the red meat choices could be harmful. In a case like that, the turtle actually contributes to the balance," Pei said, looking flushed more from Chen's response than from the wine. "Now another common mistake is that people believe sex leads to the depletion of yin and is therefore dangerous. They forget that hard work also consumes yin."

"Really!" Chen said, thinking of the "thirsty illness" he had been analyzing for his paper. "That's quite profound."

"Our dinner is a perfectly balanced one. Good for both yin and yang. Confucius says, you cannot be too selective with your food. What does that mean? Surely it is not just about the taste. For a sage like Confucius, it goes much deeper. Food must be a real boost, so that you will make a great achievement for your country."

Whether or not it was copied from those classic books solely for business purposes, it was true that Confucian echoes still resounded in Chinese daily life.

Pei proved to be eloquent on more than theories. The banquet continued on with one surprise after another. The gigantic-fish-head soup enriched by American ginseng; Hajia—special Guangxi lizards, fresh instead of dried and processed as commonly seen in herb shops—stewed with white tree ears; and swallow-nest congee strewn with scarlet Gouji.

"Oh, the swallow nest," Pei exclaimed, raising a ladle. "To make their nests on cliffs, swallows have to take whatever they can pick up and mix it with their saliva—the essence of life."

The swallow nest was a time-honored *bu* product. The dainty bowl of sweet congee reminded him of a passage in *Dream of the Red Chamber*, in which a delicate girl's swallow-nest breakfast costs more than a farmer's food for a whole year.

"But how can the swallow saliva be so special?" Chen asked again.

"From time to time people feel dry in their mouths, lacking saliva, especially after the cloud and rain, you know," Pei said with a warm smile. "That's a symptom of insufficient yin."

"Yes, thirsty illness," Chen said. But people could feel thirsty for all kinds of reasons, he reflected, not necessarily because of the clouds and rain.

To Chen's surprise, what appeared next on the banquet table was a bowl of fatty pork braised in soy sauce. A homely dish, in sharp contrast to all the extravagances.

"Chairman Mao's special," Pei said, reading the question in Chen's eyes. "On the eve of a crucial battle during the second civil war, Mao declared, 'My brain is worn out, I need soy-sauce-braised fatty pork to boost it up.' In those years, it was not always easy to serve meat on the table, but for Mao, the Central Party Committee managed to provide a bowl of fatty pork every day. Sure enough, Mao led the People's Liberation Army from one victory to another. So how could Mao be wrong?"

"No, Mao could never be wrong," Chen echoed, finding that the pork tasted quite good.

The climax of the banquet came in—a caged monkey with its head sticking out, its skull shaven, and its limbs fixed. A waiter put the cage down for them to inspect, holding a steel knife and a small brass ladle, smiling, and waiting for the signal. Chen had heard of the special course before. The monkey's skull was to be sawed off, so the diners could enjoy the live brain, so fresh and bloody.

But Chen was suddenly unnerved, sweating, almost like he had been that morning. Perhaps he hadn't recovered yet.

"What's wrong, Master Chen?" Pei inquired.

"I am fine, Manager Pei," Chen said, wiping the sweat on his forehead with a napkin. "The pork is so good, reminding me of what my mother cooked for me in my childhood. She is a devoted Buddhist. So I would like to make a proposal on her behalf. Please release the monkey. In the Buddhist belief, it's called *fangsheng*—release a life."

"*Fangsheng*—" Pei was not prepared for it at all, but he was quick coming around. "Yes, Master Chen is a filial son. So we will do what he wants."

The others agreed. The waiter carried out the cage, promising to release the monkey into the hills. Chen thanked him, though wondering whether the waiter would keep his word.

Pei was such a warm, gracious host that soon Chen forgot all about the monkey episode. Outside the window, the evening spread out like a scroll of a traditional Chinese landscape, presenting a winter panorama against the distant horizon. At this altitude, the light remained longer. The peaks had never appeared more fantastic, as if sporting their beauty as a last plea to remain in the glow of the day.

He was warmed with a sense of well-being, holding a cup. The *bu* banquet worked, if only psychologically.

When he got back to his room later that night, he felt almost like a recharged battery in a TV commercial.

He also felt relaxed. Reclining against the soft-cushioned headboard, he indulged in a wave of pleasant drowsiness. In the city, he had had trouble falling asleep. But he didn't have to worry tonight. Could that be because of the dinner? The boost to yin, or to yang, to which his body had already responded.

In the midst of his wandering thoughts, he fell asleep.

And he slept on. He must have woken up a couple of times, but with the curtains shutting out the daylight, with no city traffic noise coming from below, and with a feeling of laziness enveloping him, he didn't get up. He wasn't hungry. He didn't even check the clock on the nightstand. It was a rare, inexplicable experience, but good for his recovery, he thought.

He fell asleep again, losing track of time.

EIGHTEEN

OUT OF THE BLUE, the Shanghai Police Bureau got a tip.

The tip—if that it was—came in the *Shanghai Evening News*. To be exact, in a classified ad clipped from the newspaper and mailed to the bureau, in an envelope addressed to Inspector Liao:

LET'S GET THROUGH the three-accompanying. After the singing and eating, it's time for dancing. As for the place, which is better than at the Joy Gate? The usual time, you know.—Wenge Hongqi

---

It could have been a humorous message among friends. But the message, when addressed and delivered to Liao, turned sinister.

"It's not a tip," Liao said, frowning.

Among the red mandarin dress victims, one was an eating girl, and another, a singing girl, so the next should be, as Hong had suggested, a dancing girl.

"The usual time" sounded even more urgent. Thursday night, or early Friday morning.

"Wenge Hongqi" was evidently not a real name. It could be interpreted as "red flag in the Cultural Revolution"—an unlikely nickname for anyone in the nineties.

"Red flag in the Cultural Revolution," Yu said. "Sounds like the name of a rebel organization from those years."

"Hold on," Liao said. "*Hongqi* also sounds the same as the first two syllables in *hongqipao*—red mandarin dress."

Liao lost no time getting in touch with the newspaper. The editor maintained that he hadn't seen anything improper with the ad. It had been paid for in cash and delivered to the editorial office through "quick delivery," one of the newest services in the city, which anyone could start up with a bike or a motorcar, and possibly without a license. There was no way of tracking down the quick-delivery company. The man who wrote the ad left no address or phone number. It was not required in the case of cash payment.

It was an unmistakable message from the murderer. An unbearable challenge too.

He was going on with his killing, in spite of all the police efforts. Furthermore, he told the cops when it would happen, and where too.

Soon information about the Joy Gate came in. The dance hall was in a six-story building located on Huashan Road, close to Nanjing Road. It had a proud history—in the glittering thirties, the rich and fashionable from all over the city flocked to its dance floor. After 1949, however, social dance had been banned as an attribute of a bourgeois and decadent lifestyle. The building was turned into a movie theater; as such it survived the Cultural Revolution, during which the name of the Joy Gate was nearly forgotten but for one incident. Its huge neon sign of dancing English letters, long unlit and broken, fell and killed a pedestrian walking underneath. The incident was then declared as symbolic of the end of an age. In the early nineties, however, Joy Gate was rediscovered in the collective nostalgia of the city. A Taiwan businessman launched a large-scale renovation of the building's bygone glories, keeping everything the same as it was in the thirties. Time-yellowed posters and decoration were unearthed, old band members reengaged, rusty lighting fixtures and chandeliers refurbished, and the dancing girls, young and pretty, came back, wearing mandarin dresses.

In short, business was booming there again. In the Shanghai tourist guidebooks, the Joy Gate was one of the must-see attractions.

Yu and Liao looked at each other. There was no choice left to them. Hong had been working the case as a decoy—and now the perfect situation for it had arisen.

Yu still had his reservations about the decoy approach. But his colleagues had pressed for it. As the Chinese proverb went, when one was desperately sick, one would seek help from any quack. So Hong had been visiting one nightclub after another, dressed like a butterfly, flipping, flashing, flirting. A considerable number of clients had approached her, according to her reports, but none of them proved to be really suspicious. In order not to alarm the real one, she had to humor them all until the last minute. Her reports didn't mention, understandably, how much she had to put up with from those lecherous customers.

Now the situation was different.

"He is a devilish one," Yu said simply.

"She's been with us for about two years. Well-trained in the academy and with us," Liao murmured, as if trying to pump confidence into his voice before dialing Hong's extension. "A clever, capable girl."

Though Yu didn't know Hong that well, he thought highly of her. Sharp, down to earth, and dedicated to her job. That was quite a lot to say about a young cop. The homicide squad had come under too much pressure, and Liao's decision was understandable.

"This could also be a fake move," Yu said. "If we put our people at the Joy Gate, he may strike somewhere else."

Liao nodded without responding immediately, as Party Secretary Li was striding into the office, panting, and declaring in a strident voice, "That's too much. You have to stop him. Our whole bureau is behind you. Tell me how many people you need, and you will have them."

Hong, too, came into the office. She took a seat opposite, her hands crossed in her lap. She was outfitted like a "girl," in a dress with thin straps and high slits. She didn't use any makeup, her face clear and serene in the morning light.

"I want you to understand that this is voluntary," Liao started, pushing the newspaper clipping across the desk. "Unlike what you've been doing, this is not an assignment. You can say no. Still, you are the one best qualified for the job."

She took a look at the clipping, pushed the hair off her forehead, and nodded, her black bangs swinging softly over her arched eyebrows.

"If you go to the Joy Gate tonight," Liao went on, "we'll be there too. You just let us know the moment he approaches you."

"How can I tell if it's him? Those men all play pretty much the same tricks with a girl."

"I don't think he'll try to do anything to you inside the club. He has to get you outside. Once he makes such a move, we'll stop him. We will be prepared for any possible situation."

But there was only half a day to get ready, Yu thought. The cops couldn't really prepare for anything. Perhaps Hong alone had no problem with her role—thanks to her earlier decoy experience.

"Let's do it," Li said. "I'll stay in the office tonight. You keep me informed throughout."

So they were going to the Joy Gate. Hong took a taxi home to change for the night. Yu and Liao took a minivan with "Heating and Cooling Service" painted on one side, which would serve as a field office. Several cops would soon join them there.

Since the murderer might be connected with people at the Joy Gate, they decided to walk in without revealing their identity and look around like ordinary visitors.

According to a colorful brochure Yu picked up at the entrance, the first three floors of the building were exclusively for dancing, consisting of ballrooms of different sizes and services in terms of "male and female dancing partners," all at different prices too. In addition to the entrance ticket, there was a so-called fee system that charged by the unit, equivalent to per dance, from 25 to 50 Yuan. That, of course, did not include the tip.

"In addition to those 'professional dancing partners,'" Liao said, "there are also 'dancing girls,' who make money not through dancing but mainly through their service afterward."

It was in the early afternoon, so only the first floor was open for business. The ballroom was lined with tables on both sides and had a stage at the other end. A singer in a florid mandarin dress was performing with a small band. The neon lights produced a nostalgic mirage of money-drunk and gold-charmed dreams. Most of the dancers were middle-aged, and the dancing girls were not too young, either.

"It's a relatively cheap time period," Liao said, studying the price list on the brochure.

The people here now would dance until seven. For the evening, the balls would be on the second and the third floors. On the third floor, a group of Russian girls were scheduled to perform onstage that night, so most of the customers would be there enjoying the show. The cops needed only to focus on the second floor. The fourth and fifth floors consisted of hotel rooms.

"Who would want to stay in a hotel room here with the earsplitting music and noise coming up all night?" Yu said.

"Well, it's in a good location," Liao said. "Some of the guests may come down to dance, and bring a girl up to their rooms afterward."

Both the ballroom and the hotel guests had to come in and out the front entrance on Huashan Road. There was a video camera already installed over the front entrance so they didn't have to worry about putting up one there.

When they moved back into the service van, Hong and several officers joined them. They made plans for what they were going to do that evening.

Hong would go into the second floor ballroom, wearing a pink mandarin dress and carrying a mini cell phone specially programmed. If she touched one button, the cops outside would be on high alert, and another button, the cops outside would rush in. She had practiced *Shaolin* martial arts at the police academy so she should be able to cope with an unexpected situation, at least long enough to contact her colleagues in time. She was also supposed to call them at regular intervals, though she preferred not to, lest people find it suspicious.

Sergeant Qi would go in with her, pretending to be a customer who did not know her. He would stay in the ballroom at all times, in constant contact with the other officers, and with the dual responsibility of covering her and looking out for anything suspicious.

They also had two cops stationed outside the ballroom on the second floor. They would take turns sitting on the sofa close to the entrance, like a customer taking a break there. Their responsibility was to watch for Hong's exit, either in the company of someone, or alone.

That evening, the third floor was hardly a possibility. It was inconceivable that the murderer would approach a Russian girl who couldn't speak Chinese, and who was onstage too. At Li's insistence, however, they also had a plainclothes officer on the third floor.

Finally, they put several more people around the building entrance on Huashan Road. One was disguised as a newspaper man selling the evening newspaper, another as a flower girl, and still another, a photographer soliciting tourists for instant pictures there.

Yu and Liao stayed in the van outside the Joy Gate, each listening with a headset, waiting, like two toy soldiers, motionless, imagining all the disaster scenarios.

The first half hour passed uneventfully. Still too early, Yu guessed, looking out at the Joy Gate. To his surprise, he saw a young mother kneeling on the sidewalk close to the entrance of the dancehall, shivering in her threadbare clothes, her hair disheveled, holding a seven- or eight-month-old baby in her arms, kowtowing on a written statement spread out on the pavement. Beside the mother and her baby was a broken bowl containing several coins. People went in and out of the Joy Gate without looking at them. Not one of them threw down any money.

The city was breaking into two, one for the rich, and one for the poor. A tip for a dance could have kept the woman and her baby fed and sheltered for a day. Yu thought about stepping out with some coins in his hand, but a patroller came over and drove the woman away.

Sergeant Qi kept reporting from inside, "Everything is fine." Yu could also hear Qi whistling, occasionally, like a pro, with the music rising and falling in the background. "When Are You Coming Again, My Dear," a melody Yu recognized as one of the most popular ones in the thirties.

Hong contacted them only once, "I've had several invitations."

Outside the van, the lights gradually turned on and more customers went into the Joy Gate in high spirits. In the thirties, Shanghai had been called a "nightless city."

Around eight forty-five, there came a period of silence. About twenty minutes. Liao checked with Qi, who explained it as a false alarm. Seven or eight minutes ago, Qi lost sight of Hong in the ballroom. He started looking around and saw her sitting with a drink in a recess of the small bar. As he also had to watch the whole scene, he sat himself at a table where he could watch both the bar and the ballroom.

"Don't worry," Qi said. "I am keeping everything in sight."

Then came another short period of silence. Yu lit a cigarette for Liao and then another for himself. Li called them, the third time in the evening. The Party Secretary didn't try to conceal his uneasiness.

After ten minutes or so, Qi called them, reporting in a panic-stricken voice that the woman in the bar, though in a mandarin dress too, turned out not to be Hong.

Yu dialed her cell phone, but she didn't pick up. The noise inside could be too loud for her to hear it ring. Liao tried as well, two or three times more. Still no response. Liao then talked to those stationed outside the building. They reported no sign of her exit, either, declaring they would not have missed her in her pink mandarin dress.

Yu contacted the sentry outside the ballroom. They sort of assured him, saying neither of them had seen her exit. So she must still be inside. Yu ordered the two stationed outside the ballroom to move in and join Qi.

In the meantime, Liao hurried to the camera surveillance room, where a cop was with the building security man.

In less than five minutes, however, Yu saw Liao walking out again, shaking his head in confusion. There was no sign of Hong on the videotape recording of the activities at the front entrance.

But the people in the ballroom called too, reporting that they had looked into every corner. Hong seemed to have evaporated.

Something terrible must have happened.

About thirty-five minutes had passed since Qi had first noticed her absence.

Yu ordered an instant blockade of the building entrance. It wasn't the time for them to worry about the public's reaction. Liao called for emergency reinforcements before announcing evacuation of the ballroom.

The cops rushed up and checked each and every person leaving the ballroom, but Hong was not among them.

When the ballroom was finally empty, like a deserted battlefield strewn with cups and bottles, cosmetics on the floor, there was still no sign of her.

"Where could she be?" Qi said miserably.

The answer was loud and clear in everyone's mind.

"How the devil could he have slipped out," Liao said, "together with Hong?"

"Here," Qi exclaimed, pointing to a door in a cubicle inside the bar. The door was hardly visible to the people in the ballroom unless moving in behind the bar.

Yu hurried over and pushed open the door, which led out to a corridor. He saw a side elevator in the corridor around the corner.

"He must have taken her out the side door, to the elevator, and then out of the gate—" Liao said in a husky voice, "but no, not yet, or they should have been seen and stopped by our people."

"That's impossible—" Yu said, but he was seized by a premonition. "Damn. Check all the hotel rooms."

The front desk produced a list in no time. There were thirty-two rooms registered for the night. Following the list, the cops started pounding on the doors. At the third door, they got no response from inside. According to the list, it was registered for single occupancy just for the day. The waiter took out the key and opened the door into the room.

It was the cops' worst fear. They found no one in the room, only Hong's clothes scattered about on the floor. The pink mandarin dress, bra, and panties. In a corner, the high-heeled shoes anchored the ominous silence of the room.

She must have been abducted into the room, where the murderer stripped her like the others, put the red mandarin dress on her, and carried her out.

Again they reviewed the videotape. This time, they noticed something they had seen, but not suspected earlier. A man in a hotel uniform helped another one walking out in a hurry. Both of them were in identical hotel uniforms and hats. The man looked to be in his mid-thirties or early forties. With his hat pulled low, plus a pair of amber-colored glasses, the video didn't catch a clear shot of his face. The other one appeared to be female, with a wisp of black hair escaping the hat, perhaps sick, leaning heavily on the first one's shoulder.

The hotel manager hurried over, declaring that the two in the videotape were not hotel employees.

So the murderer had registered with a fake identity, forced Hong into the room, where he changed her clothes and walked her out. Judging from the tape, she was already nearly unconscious. She must have been overcome without the time to alert her colleagues. Once outside the Joy Gate, he moved her into a car parked nearby or hailed a taxi. The plainclothesman stationed outside, however, didn't remember having seen two hotel people getting into a car.

The neighborhood committees and taxi companies were immediately contacted for information about two people in hotel uniforms, one of them probably unconscious.

Party Secretary Li was swearing on the phones, screaming, striding back and forth like an ant crawling desperately on a hot wok. In spite of his earlier opposition, he ordered citywide surveillance of the families with private garages, for which the police again enlisted help from all the neighborhood committees.

From the time recorded on the tape, it was now only about twenty-five minutes after their exit from the Joy Gate. The cops might still be able to intercept the criminal before he reached his secret den or catch him at the moment when he was entering the garage. They believed that he still had to put the red mandarin dress on her.

The hotel manager called. A waitress reported that a middle-aged man had approached her, asking whether there was a new girl that night, but she could barely give a description of the customer, except that he wore gold-rimmed spectacles with amber-colored lenses. Since he sat at a table, she couldn't tell his height.

A neighborhood committee cadre also contacted them. Earlier in the evening, in a shabby side street one block north of the Joy Gate, he had seen a white car—a luxurious model, though he could not tell what brand—parked there. It wasn't common for such a car to park on that street.

But for the cops, all these tips were of little use at the moment.

Time weighed on them, heavier by minute, the more unbearable because they had no information whatsoever, in spite of the fact that the entire city police machine was grinding on.

Finally, around one a.m., a call came from a patrol officer near the Lianyi cemetery in the Hongqiao suburb.

The cemetery had been deserted for years. In a recent security report to the bureau, it had turned into a hot spot for grave robbers, and the district police station sent a patrol there from time to time.

About an hour before, one of the grave robbers stumbled upon something totally unexpected. The body of a young female in a red mandarin dress. Like others in his profession, he was superstitious, so he screamed and scurried and was caught by the patroller. The mention of the red mandarin dress was enough to put the officer on the alert, so he called at once.

Liao had hardly started the van when a second call came in from the patrolling cop.

"A hotel uniform was also found there, not too far from the body, and a hotel hat too." The patroller added, "Come quick. The grave robber has fainted. He believes he has seen a ghost."

NINETEEN

FRIDAY MORNING CHEN FINALLY woke up refreshed and reinvigorated.

He wondered how he could have slept like that for almost two days. It could have been due to the fabulous *bu* dinner. Some special herb with a miraculous effect. Manager Pei had real medical knowledge; he must have diagnosed Chen's problem from Gu's description and arranged for the particular *bu* dinner Chen needed. In traditional Chinese medical theory, Chen recalled vaguely, certain herbs could bring out the symptoms, so the body would adjust itself accordingly. Chen had overworked himself, so the special dinner enabled him to sleep soundly, making up for all those years of lost rest. Now yin and yang or other elements in his body would move in harmony again. Whatever the Chinese medical theory and practice, Chen hadn't felt so good in a long time.

But he was slightly disturbed too. He'd had a weird dream shortly before dawn. He was sitting in an exotic garden, watching a young woman perform a striptease, dancing, singing like a siren, when he was suddenly seized with a fit of inexplicable abhorrence. He grabbed her, trying to strangle her in the flower bed. Struggling against him, the woman was no other than White Cloud, her dress turning into the red mandarin dress against the green grass.

The red mandarin dress case was still on his mind, but the appearance of White Cloud in the dream bothered him, not to mention his own behavior. Perhaps it was because of his experience in the Old City God's Temple Market. Or perhaps it was the *bu* feast—such an unusual boost to yin or yang that he was aroused. Still, it might be a good sign. He had recovered enough to dream like a young man.

He decided not to think about it. It was not a morning for dream interpretation. He thought about the case in Shanghai again. It was Friday, he realized. Chen was tempted to call Yu, but he thought the better of it. Once he did so, his vacation here would be, for all practical purposes, finished, though he felt it had only started. He hadn't even walked around the village a single time. Nor had he done anything about his paper yet.

He called White Cloud instead. She hadn't read or heard anything new about the case, and she urged him to enjoy his vacation. She had visited his mother, who was getting along fine at home, so he didn't have to worry.

Looking out of the window, he thought that he might take a stroll along the lake.

It was a bit cold outside and the lake looked rather deserted this time of the year. There was only one old angler sitting on the waterfront, wrapped up in a worn-out army overcoat. The bamboo basket beside him was empty. He seemed to be lost in meditation, or in a pose of meditation.

Chen walked on without disturbing him.

Chen looked up at the mountains silhouetted against the horizon. There seemed to be a cascade murmuring, not too far away. Looking back, he glimpsed, now at distance, a faint flickering light in the hand of the old man.

Against the woods and hills, the tiny light gleamed and was gone. A rustle of the pines swept through. A long deep sigh of the wind. He was strangely saddened. Then he turned onto a slippery trail, which wound between clumps of larches and ferns. He had to move slowly. It must have rained while he slept. Soon he reached a long carpet of pine needles, which muffled his footsteps. Then the trail widened unexpectedly, leading him to a local market.

The market was already alive at this hour, and most of the people there were tourists looking for souvenirs. He spent several minutes making his way through the crowd, when he came to a stop at a booth displaying afterworld money, a superstitious product not commonly seen in Shanghai.

"Dongzhi is approaching," the peddler said warmly, folding the silver paper into a *yuanbao*-shaped silver ingot. In the Chinese afterworld, the main currency seemed to still be the silver ingot. "Folks need money to buy winter clothes there."

On an impulse, Chen purchased a bunch of the afterworld money. He didn't believe in it, but his mother did, burning it now and then for the benefit of his late father, particularly during such festivals as Dongzhi or Qingming.

Back in his hotel room, he picked up the books he'd brought and went to the indoor swimming pool.

The pool room had a wall set in one-way glass, so the swimmers could enjoy the warm, luxurious privacy while looking out to the view of the lake and hills in the winter. After a vigorous swim, he sat in a reclining chair at poolside and started reading.

Perhaps because of his English studies at Bund Park, he'd developed the ability to read and concentrate while outside. At that time, there was the ever-changing background of the Bund to distract him. Here, in addition to the view outside, he was enjoying the sight of young girls frolicking in the pool, their luscious bodies flashing in the blue water whenever he looked up from the ancient Confucian classics. It was ironic, for Confucius says, "A gentleman should not look if not in accordance to the rites."

In accordance to the rites or not, the background made the reading less boring for him. His late father having been a neo-Confucian scholar, and Confucian maxims still part of Chinese daily life, as at the *bu* banquet, "Confucius says" wasn't unfamiliar to him. But he had never systematically studied Confucianism, which had been banished from the classroom during his school years. He wished he had talked more to his father, whose early death had cut short the older man's plan to instill the tradition into his son.

Chen took out his notebook. Some of his earlier research notes seemed related to Confucian rites. For Confucius, rites are everywhere and ever present. As long as people behave in accordance with the ancient rites, everything will be right, as they had supposedly been in the golden old times. While there appeared to be so many rites regarding so many things, Chen had never learned or heard about any regarding romantic love.

That morning, checking through the books he had carried there, he failed to find anything. Confucian masters neglected romantic passion, as if it were nonexistent.

Then Chen extended his search to marriage—*hunli* literally meant marriage rites in Chinese. Sure enough, he found several paragraphs on the marriage rites, though not a single word touching on passion among young people. To the contrary, young people were not supposed to meet before the wedding, let alone have feelings for each other. Marriage was to be arranged entirely by the parents.

In the *Book of Rites*, one of the Confucian canons, there was a straightforward statement on the nature of marriage.

[The rites of] marriage exist to make a happy connection between two [families of different] names, with a view, in its retrospective character, to secure the services in the ancestral temple, and in its prospective character, to secure the continuance of the family line. Therefore the gentleman sets great store by it. . . .

The marriage rites consist of six consecutive ritual steps, which are the matchmaker's visit, inquiries about the girl's name and birth date, a horoscope for the couple, betrothal gifts, choosing a marriage date, and the bridegroom's welcoming the bride home on the day of the wedding.

Throughout these activities, Chen read, the man and woman did not have a chance to meet until the very day of their wedding. Marriage, conducted in the name of the parents, for the sake of continuing the family line, had nothing to do with romantic love.

In his copy of the *Mencius*, Chen underlined a passage condemning young people who fall in love and act for themselves in disregard of an arranged marriage.

When a son is born, what is desired for him is that he may have a wife; when a daughter is born, what is desired for her is that she may have a husband. This feeling of the parents is possessed by all men. If the young people, without waiting for the order of their parents and the arrangement of the go-betweens, shall bore holes to steal a sight of each other or climb over the wall to be with each other, then their parents and all other people will despise them.

What the philosopher Mencius described as hole-boring and wall-climbing, Chen knew, became standard metaphors for rendezvous between young lovers.

Closing the book, he tried to sort out what he had just read. In a family-centered social structure, arranged marriage was in its interest, for romantic love could transfer the center of affection, loyalty, and authority from the parents.

"Excuse me, may I sit here?"

"Oh," he said, looking up to see a young woman, pulling over a recliner to his side. "Yes, please."

She stretched herself out on the recliner beside him. An attractive woman in her early thirties, she had clear features with a straight mouth, her hair framing her face in delicate curls. Over her swimming suit, she wore a white wrapper or sari of light material, probably a white caftan, which floated around her long legs. She also had a book in her hand.

"It's so lovely to read here." She crossed her legs and lit a cigarette.

He was not in the mood for talk, but he didn't see it as a bad thing to have a pretty woman reading alongside him. He smiled without saying anything.

"I saw you at the restaurant a couple of days ago," she said. "What a banquet!"

"Sorry, I don't remember seeing you there."

"I was sitting outside at a table in the dining hall, looking in through the windows. Everybody was busy making toasts to you there. You must be a successful man."

"No, not really."

"A Big Buck?"

Again he smiled. She wouldn't have believed him to be a cop—alone, trying to finish a literature paper. Nor was there any point in revealing his identity here.

But what could be hers? An attractive woman all by herself in an expensive vacation village. He checked himself from thinking like an investigator. A nameless tourist on vacation, he was under no obligation to pry into other people's lives.

"What are you reading?" she asked.

"A Confucian classic," he said.

"That's interesting," she said, casting a glance toward the young girls in the pool. "Reading Confucius by the poolside."

He was aware of the subtle irony in her comment. Confucius was right about one thing: *I have never seen one who likes studies as much as beauties.*

She, too, started reading her book, her hair jet-black in the sunlight, her eyes shining with "autumn waves"—possibly an expression from those love stories. He felt her closeness, noticing her unshaven armpit as she stretched one arm behind her head. She wore a bangle of a red silk string, which accentuated her shapely ankle. And he remembered some lines about a man's mind digressing at the sight of a woman's legs, white and bare, but in the sunlight, with a down of light black hair.

He chided himself and began questioning the necessity of the vacation. The scary experience he had had at home was perhaps an attack of coffee sickness. He might have been too panicky. Now he felt his normal self again. So why go on with the vacation here? A serial murderer was at large in Shanghai, but he was reading by the poolside, in a vacation village hundreds of miles away, thinking of amorous poetic images.

At least he should try to make some progress on the paper. So he opened his notebook and started to put something down for the conclusion.

In traditional Chinese society, the institution of arranged marriage implied hostility toward romantic love. But then how did there come to be all these love stories? Though he had analyzed only three, there were a large number of them. The publication and circulation of them, against the social norm of arranged marriage, should have been impossible—

An interruption arrived in the form of a waiter who recognized Chen as the "distinguished guest" at the banquet dining room and came over with a bottle of wine in an ice bucket.

Perhaps it was part of the routine service here, Chen thought, saying, "Sorry, I don't have the coupon with me."

"Don't worry, sir," the waiter said, putting the bucket on a small table beside his recliner. "It's on the village."

Chen gestured him to pour out a glass for the woman on the recliner next to him first.

"You're somebody," she said, taking a small sip, nodding her approval, before she set the glass back on the table.

"*A lone stranger, far away from home*," he said, quoting a line from a Tang dynasty poem.

"Well, my other half went away for a business meeting," she said, leaning over the table toward him, accentuating the swell of her breasts. "So I am left here, all by myself. *The tide always keeps / its word to come. / Had I known that, / I would have married a young tide-rider*."

It was a quote from another Tang poem, the first half of which read: *How many times / I have been let down / by this busy merchant of Qutang / since I married him!* A surprisingly clever and self-deprecating quote, which implied that her husband was a busy and callous one, and she was lonely here.

"But a tide-riding young man couldn't afford to bring you to a luxurious vacation village."

"How true, and how sad. My name is Sansan. I teach women's studies at Shanghai Teachers College."

"My name is Chen Cao. A part-time student at Shanghai University."

"I like traveling. So I should consider myself lucky to have a husband capable of affording the vacation package. By the way, are you so interested in an academic career?"

"Well, I don't know," he said. "You just quoted a line concerning the woman's status in the Tang dynasty. At the time, she might not have had much choice for herself. Do you think her problem was a result of her arranged marriage?"

"A problem of an arranged marriage? No, I think that's too simplistic an explanation. My parents had an arranged marriage. A most happy one, as far as I know," she said, taking another drink. "But think about the divorce rate today among young couples who have pledged their love by mountains and seas."

"That's some statement from a scholar on women's studies!" he said. "The Confucian classics talk about nothing but arranged marriage. So I wonder how the Chinese people lived for two thousand years without talking about romantic love."

"Well, the world is in your interpretation. If you believe it—I mean the interpretation that parents understand and always work in the best interest of the young people—you then live accordingly. Just like today: if you believe a materialistic basis is essential to any superstructure—with romantic love as a decorative vase on the mantelpiece—then you won't be surprised by all the personal ads seeking millionaires in our newspapers."

"This is indeed a Chinese brand of socialism."

"You can say that again. Do you believe that love is something that has always been there, from time immemorial?" she said cynically. "According to Denis de Rougemont's *Love in the Western World*, romantic love didn't exist until it was invented by the French troubadours."

He felt shaken, sitting there inhaling the scent of her hair. For the last few years, with one case after another on his hands, he hadn't had much time for reading, while she like so many others had been reading things he hadn't even heard of. *Seven days up in the mountains, thousands of years down in the world.* Perhaps it was already too late for him to dream of another career.

"So are you reading Confucian classics for a project on arranged marriage?" she asked.

"I have been reading a number of classical love stories, and there is one aspect they have in common. Inevitably, the heroines seem to be demonized in one way or another, and the love theme is thus deconstructed." He added, "You're a scholar in the field. Can you enlighten me on it?"

"I like your choice of terms. Demonization of women and the deconstruction of love," she said. "Long ago Lu Xun said something on that point. Chinese people always put the blame on women. The Shang dynasty collapsed because of the Imperial Concubine Da; King Fucha lost himself, as well as his kingdom, through the beautiful Xishi; Minster Dong Zhu fell prey to the charms of Diaochan. The list could be much longer. Even today, we all blame the Cultural Revolution on Madam Mao, though everyone is aware of the fact that without Mao, Madam Mao would have been nothing but a B-movie actress."

"But that's not something one finds only in China," Chen said. "In the West, there is a similar concept—the femme fatale. And stories of vampires too, you know."

"Good point. But have you noticed one difference? There are male as well as female vampires. Can you think of anything similar here? Besides, the femme fatale isn't the most common image of women in the mainstream of Western thought, not the most important one in the dominant or official discourse."

"That's true. Arranged marriage was definitely an inherent part of Confucianism. So do you think that the stories in question became distorted under the influence of those dominant ideologies?"

"And those lovely women cannot but be crushed—in one way or another. It cannot be helped."

"Cannot be helped—" he echoed as he thought of the case again.

Perhaps an author was somehow like a serial killer, who couldn't control himself. According to postmodernist criticism, people are spoken by the discourse, rather than the other way around. Once a particular discourse takes control, or, as in a Chinese expression, once the devil takes over the heart, it's the devil that acts, in spite of the man himself. In Freudian theory, the man's actions are dictated by something in the subconscious, or the collective unconscious. It would be easy to write the murderer off as a nut, but it would be hard, yet important, to discover what discursive system was dictating him to do the killing. And how that system had been formed for him—

"For instance, in *Plum Blossom in Golden Vase*," Sansan went on, taking his preoccupation as being induced by her words, "Ximenqin has to die because he has too much sex with women, ending with a final image of his semen gushing nonstop into Pan Jinlian, the shameless slut who literally sucks him dry."

"Yes, I remember that."

"And in another novel, *Flesh Cushion*, the hero has to castrate himself in the end because he can't resist the sexual attraction of women."

Apparently her work focused on the unfair representation of women. The talk was a lucky random harvest for his paper, for it indirectly supported his thesis.

"Yes, I can think of several common expressions that support the idea," he said. "*Hongyan huoshui*, disastrous water of beauty, and *meiren shexie*, a snake and a spider of a pretty woman."

He was encouraged by this train of thought. Indeed, it could prove to be something that hadn't been previously explored. Not specifically, anyway. An original paper, as Professor Bian had put it.

"The expressions speak for themselves," she said, then she changed the subject. "You quoted a line from Wang Wei. A lone stranger. So you have traveled to write your paper here?"

"Well, the paper is part of it." He added, "I was sort of stressed out, so I thought a vacation would do me good."

With that, their conversation drifted toward other topics.

"When the only criteria for a man's value is in terms of his money, how long can an individual hope to hide himself in something like Tang dynasty poetry? For a romantic morning, perhaps. That's how my moneymaking husband can be so important to me." She added, "Don't be so hard on yourself. Repression won't do you any good."

It was a comment he hadn't expected. It was almost a Freudian echo, and he was slightly uneasy about her. Not because there was something cynical about her or because she was a feminist. His glance fell on the bangle of red silk string and silver bells around her shapely ankle.

Taking a deep breath, he dispelled the confusing ideas. He was not a scholar, perhaps not meant to be. Nor a Big Buck having his fling at a luxurious hotel—not the man in her imagination.

He was but a police officer, incognito, on a vacation paid for by someone else.

He noticed the pool beginning to empty. Perhaps it was time for it to close.

"There will be a ball here this evening. Will you be attending?" Her voice came soft in the afternoon sunlight.

"I would love to go," he said, "but I may have to make several phone calls."

Was that a professional excuse or was he really a busy businessman, like her husband?

"We're staying in the same building, I think. My room number is 122. Thank you for the wine," she said. "See you again soon."

"Bye."

He watched her leave, her long hair swaying across her back. At the turn of the path, she looked back and waved her hand lightly.

"Bye," he said one more time, and then audible only to himself, "Have fun tonight."

TWENTY

IT WAS THE WORST blow Yu had suffered in his career as a policeman.

After a sleepless night first at the cemetery, then the bureau, he rubbed his bloodshot eyes and decided to go again to the Joy Gate, where a young colleague of his had been abducted and murdered while he was stationed outside, entrusted with the duty of protecting her. He could think of nothing else.

At the Joy Gate, the police were still searching and re-searching all the rooms, hoping against hope that they might find some undiscovered evidence left behind. He didn't think joining them would be of any help.

He went to the front desk and asked for a list of regular customers. The criminal must be familiar with the building to be capable of having made such a plan. At his insistence, the day manager produced a printout.

"It really doesn't mean any—anything," the manager stammered, swallowing hard. "They are just good, regular customers."

"Good customers, I see," Yu said. "How regular?"

"The basic fee is not expensive, but with drinks and tips, it could be easy to spend five or six hundred Yuan an evening. A regular customer comes at least once a week."

"Has any of the regulars stayed in the hotel above?"

"The hotel is not so fancy. Not too many care to stay here, what with the noise all night long. Nor is it always a good idea, either. People make assumptions about what a customer and a dancing girl are up to in a room upstairs. So many would rather go to another place."

"That makes sense," Yu said, nodding.

It was a list of names, addresses, and phone numbers. Some of them also indicated their profession or preferences. It was possibly a PR list.

"When we have special events," the manager explained, "we like to notify them."

He would make calls to some of the people on the list, Yu thought. Then one of the names seemed to jump out at him. Jia Ming, his profession indicated as a lawyer. It was a name Yu remembered. Chen had asked him to check into him with regard to a high-profile housing development case.

It was strange that Jia, a well-known lawyer, busy with a controversial case, would have the time to be a regular customer here.

"Can you tell me something about this man?"

"Jia Ming," the manager said with an apologetic smile, "I am afraid I cannot tell you much. He's not that regular."

"What do you mean?"

"Most of the people on the list are Big Bucks. They come here to 'burn money,' squandering it on girls and services. Jia comes, but he pays only for an entrance ticket, sits in a corner, watching over a cup of coffee, seldom dancing, and never asking anybody out. He's here just once or twice a month."

"Then why is he on your list?"

"We wouldn't have noticed him but for a phone call from the city government several months ago. Someone wanted us to report on any of his improper behavior here. But he didn't do anything out of line—we've never seen him taking out a girl—and we reported truthfully. A strange request, you may say, but we always cooperate with the authorities."

So the authorities had been following Jia, trying to find something against him in an effort to wreck the housing development case. Jia's visits here might not mean anything. Intellectuals could be eccentric. Chief Inspector Chen, for me, still met with an ex–singing girl.

Yu grew upset at the thought of his partner. Since Wednesday, he'd repeatedly tried to contact Chen, but without any success. Last night Yu marked his call "urgent," requesting an immediate call back, but still no response. Early this morning, he had Little Zhou drive over to Chen's place, but no one was there.

How could the chief inspector have disappeared at this particular juncture?

Yu decided to revisit the cemetery. He didn't really think he would find something new there. Still, in the daylight, he might be able to see more.

The cemetery was taped off as a crime scene. In the distance, a mud-covered hut stood silhouetted against the rugged hills. No one seemed to be caring for the place. He moved to the spot where they had found her body. He lit a cigarette against the chilly wind, shivering, as if going through the nightmare again. The image would be with him forever: she had been lying with the top part of her body half hidden by the tall wild weeds. Her legs, wide apart, were stretched out on the damp ground. Her skin appeared slightly bluish, with her black hair falling across her cheek. She was barefoot, and dressed in a mandarin dress that slipped up her waist, leaving her thighs bare. . . .

A lone crow was circling overhead, crying, homeless in the winter.

In the bureau, there were wild theories about the location. Unlike the places where the first three victims were dumped, the cemetery was far from the center of the city. Party Secretary Li declared that the criminal had dropped the body there because of police pressure. Little Zhou incorporated a Qing dynasty ghost story into his earlier theory.

Yu didn't believe either of them, but he didn't have a convincing theory of his own.

To his surprise, he saw a boy coming over to him carrying a bag of newspapers, shouting, "Special edition! Red mandarin dress victim found in the cemetery here!" Giving him a handful of coins, Yu grabbed several of them.

It turned out that the man who patrolled the cemetery was a superstitious and garrulous man. While he had lost no time informing the police, he was also spreading the news around. The mention of the red mandarin dress was like a loud siren cracking the night sky, and people shivered.

As Yu dreaded, the newspapers were full of the latest victim in the red mandarin dress case. These reporters hadn't yet discovered her identity, but some of them had already sensed something unusual about the commotion at the Joy Gate last night. One reporter even hinted at a connection between the dance hall and the cemetery.

In the newspapers, Yu read a number of superstitious interpretations about the latest twist in the case.

Wenhui, for instance, had a special report titled "Lianyi Cemetery!" Narrated from the collective perspective of local residents, the reporter launched into a lurid, superstitious interpretation.

> *It used to be an expensive cemetery in the fifties and sixties, well-maintained and well-guarded. It was regarded as a propitious site with the dragon-shaped hill in the background, in accordance to a popular belief that a burial ground with such excellent feng shui would bring good luck to the offspring. At that time, only the wealthy Shanghainese could obtain a resting place here, lying at peace in expensive coffins, surrounded with luxurious clothes, quilts, silver and gold jewelry—supposedly for their benefit in the underworld.*
>
> *In spite of its feng shui, the cemetery bore the brunt of the Cultural Revolution like anywhere else. The practice of burial in a coffin was declared feudalistic, and overnight most of the people buried here*

became "black" in their class status. To denounce the "black spirits and monsters," the Red Guards had their tombs demolished and their bodies dug out, as in a Beijing opera, "to be whipped three hundred times." Some coffins were opened to search for so-called criminal evidence as part and parcel of the Campaign of Sweeping

Away the Four Olds—old ideas, old culture, old customs, and old habits. The cemetery was practically destroyed.

After the Cultural Revolution, the political statuses of some of the dead were rehabilitated, but not their tombs. Their families were too brokenhearted to come back there for ancestral worship services. Some families removed the existing remains, if any, to other places. So the cemetery lay in ruins, with stray dogs sulking around, digging up white bones from time to time. Some local residents reported scenes of ghosts walking around at night, but according to a police report, the rumors originally started among the superstitious grave robbers.

That gave an insightful property developer an excuse. No longer a cemetery in use, nor a good image for the city, the land might well be used for new commercial construction. The developer bought the cemetery from the city government, planning to convert it into a golf course.

In spite of all the new science and technology of our time, people can still be superstitious. The commercial transformation of a cemetery was considered an unpardonable disturbance of the dead. Some old residents nearby were worried that the dead would rise to haunt the living. To reassure them, the developer lit tons of firecrackers and had a feng shui master write an article saying that after the disaster of the Cultural Revolution, the feng shui was restored, and with a new subway to be built nearby, "the energy of the dragon" would make the area really valuable.

Now the body in the red mandarin dress found in the cemetery has reminded people of all the superstitious stories. As an old scholar of local history argues that the red mandarin dress murder has originated from the disturbed cemetery. Several months earlier, people saw a woman in a red mandarin dress walking in the midst of the tombs at night. According to his research, there was a movie star so attired buried there, though he chose not to reveal her identity. She was terribly wronged in life, and even more terribly after death—with her body tossed out of the coffin, and her red mandarin dress stripped by a group of Red Guards. That's why the dead appears in an old-fashioned mandarin dress.

It was a long article, and Yu didn't have the patience to go through any more of it. It was potentially an additional headache to the bureau and the city government. As long as the case remained unsolved, wild stories would keep coming out.

But to an extent it was understandable. Even for a cop like him, the case took on something of a supernatural dimension. In spite of all the police effort, a criminal had ruthlessly murdered four young women with his elaborate "signature." He seemed invisible as a ghost, especially at the Joy Gate, where every step involved enormous risk. His exit through the side door, for instance, where the bar girl could have moved back at any moment and seen him. And his escape in a hotel uniform, with an unconscious Hong supported in his arms, could have been easily suspected and stopped by hotel workers. Still, he pulled it off.

Yu opened another newspaper, *Oriental Morning*, which was very critical of the bureau. "Last night the police were at the Joy Gate—in an alleged raid against three-accompanying girls—while on the same night, another red mandarin dress victim appeared, far away, in a cemetery."

It was perhaps only a matter of time, Yu thought, before the reporters found out the identity of the latest victim. Reading the article, Yu got a phone call from the bureau lab technician.

"About the fiber you found between the third victim's toes," the technician said. "The fiber is wool. Possibly from her socks. Scarlet wool socks, I think."

"Thank you," Yu said. That wasn't too surprising. Peiqin, too, wore a pair of wool socks. It was a cold winter, and there was no heat at the shabby restaurant where she worked. But as he turned off the cell phone, Yu remembered something else. According to the description given by the eating girl's neighbor, she went out that day in a dress with pantyhose and high heels. Then how come the wool socks?

"Hi, Detective Yu."

Yu looked up to see Duan Ping, a *Wenhui* reporter who had once interviewed Chief Inspector Chen at the bureau.

"Have you read it?" Duan said, pointing at the Lianyi Cemetery article in the newspaper in Yu's hand.

"It's unbelievable."

"It is the vicissitude of things in this world, and in the underworld too," Duan said. "These days Chairman Mao cannot lie in peace in his crystal coffin."

"Don't bring Mao into your tall stories."

"It is a tall story, like it or not. This time, this place—why? People believe it is because the root of the trouble lies here. They believe that the ghosts are out for revenge, that the murders are the retribution of the supernatural. Who else could have committed the crimes, dumped the bodies in those places, and have gotten away? It's totally beyond me. Do you have any clue, Detective Yu?"

"That's nothing but superstitious crap. Those atrocities happened during the Cultural Revolution. If there were really ghosts seeking revenge, they could have done so more than twenty years ago. Why the long wait?"

"Now that's something you don't understand. With the star of Mao still high and bright in the sky at the time, these ghosts wouldn't have dared to come out and make trouble. But with Mao gone, it's their turn," Duan said. "There's also a new interpretation, which I learned only twenty minutes ago. According to it, the red mandarin dress victims are all daughters of those Red Guards."

So some people were taking the story to a more collective level. Instead of one unhappy woman buried in the cemetery, as maintained by that old scholar of local history, now it was all the ghosts of the disturbed cemetery, taking revenge on the daughters of their persecutors during the Cultural Revolution.

"These interpretations are totally unfounded," Yu said.

"Let me ask you a question, Detective Yu. Does the name Wenge Hongqi mean anything to you?"

"What do you mean?"

"Did you notice a highly unusual ad in the *Shanghai Evening News*? It was put there under that name. If you think about the other red mandarin dress victims—one a singing girl, the other an eating girl, the message in the ad makes sense," Duan said. "The Red Guard group that 'made revolution' to the cemetery was called Wenggehongqi. The connection is obvious. These interpretations are not so unfounded."

"It's wild speculation and nothing but coincidence," Yu said emphatically, though he didn't believe in coincidence. "How did you notice that ad?"

"There is no wall that does not let wind get through. Your people checked with the *Shanghai Evening News*, and we share the same office building. I believe the murders are a call for attention to the atrocities in the Cultural Revolution, particularly against a woman in a red mandarin dress. Is your interest in the ad part of your investigation?"

"Come on. There were a large number of Red Guard organizations with names like that. I really have to warn you, Duan. You have to take responsibility for such wild stories."

"That's nonsense, Comrade Detective Yu. If the case isn't solved, more and more stories will come out. Several colleagues of mine are coming now, I think," Duan said, pointing to a minivan that was pulling up to the cemetery entrance. "By the way, how is it that Chief Inspector Chen is not here with you today? Please say hi to him from me."

With more reporters swarming over, Yu knew he had to leave. Hurrying toward the cemetery exit, he called Chen's mother.

"It's so nice of you to call, Detective Yu, but I'm fine. You don't have to worry," she said, as if she had been expecting his call.

"I've been looking for Chen, Auntie. Do you know where he is?"

"You don't know where he is? Oh, I am so surprised. Two or three days ago he called me, saying that he was going away for something important. Out of Shanghai, I believe. I thought he must have told you about it. What has happened?"

"No, nothing. He must have left in a hurry. Don't worry, Auntie. He'll contact me."

"Call me when you hear from him," she said, obviously concerned. She, too, apparently felt that, unless something unusual had happened, her son wouldn't have kept Yu out of it.

"I will," Yu said. He recalled Chen's having seemed different of late. Too much stress, as Peiqin saw it, but Yu didn't really think so. Who wasn't under stress?

"Oh, White Cloud called me yesterday," she said, murmuring as if to herself. "She said everything is fine with him."

"Yes, he must have phoned her," Yu said. "I'll call you later."

But Yu had more immediate things to worry about. Party Secretary Li called him, demanding, "You are going to take care of the press conference today."

"I have never done it before, Party Secretary Li."

"Come on, Chief Inspector Chen has done it many times. You've surely learned the necessary tactics from him." Li added, "By the way, where on the earth has he been?"

"I've just left a message for him," Yu said evasively. "He'll call back soon."

On the way back to the bureau, he got White Cloud's phone number from Peiqin.

It was not so enviable to be Chen's partner, Yu thought.

TWENTY-ONE

IN A TAXI THAT was literally crawling through the traffic of Shanghai, Chen sat devastated by the news of Hong's death.

Wednesday morning. A week earlier, he had been sitting in a car bound for the vacation village, worrying about his nervous breakdown; now he was heading back, sweating over the latest development in the serial murder case. So many things had happened in Shanghai, while all the time—or most of the time—he had slept on like an idiot and mused about love stories from thousands of years ago.

He shivered at the thought of the afterworld money he had bought at the local market Friday morning. He wasn't a superstitious man, but he was unnerved at the coincidence.

It wasn't until Yu succeeded in contacting White Cloud that she became aware of the desperateness of the situation. Still, she had been too concerned about Chen's health to deliver the message to him instantly. She wasn't a cop, and she was not to blame for it. After learning of his recovery at the vacation village that morning, she told him the news about the Joy Gate. He at once cut short his vacation and boarded the first long-distance bus to Shanghai, without even saying good-bye to his host.

Sitting in the car, his thoughts revolved around Hong. He hadn't known much about her until their contact on the red mandarin dress case.

Hong was said to have a surgeon boyfriend at a Japan-China Friendship Hospital who had urged her to quit. He insisted that her income wasn't worth all his worrying about her. But she happened to believe in her job. At a Chinese New Year Party in the bureau, she read a poem about being a "people's cop." Not much of a poem, but it was passionate about a young officer patrolling the city. One of its refrains read, Chen remembered, *The sun is new every day.*

Not for her, not today.

He would never regain his peace of mind, he knew, looking out onto the traffic snarl along Yan'an Road, if he failed to avenge her.

He opened his briefcase for the folder on the red mandarin dress case. While at the vacation village, he managed not to touch it. But now as he took out the folder, to his astonishment, he saw his cell phone lying under it. Turned off, of course, but lying there all the time. Before he had left for vacation, he had decided not to carry it, he remembered clearly. How the phone had gotten into the briefcase, he had no recollection. There might be something in Freud's argument about forgetting, but he decided not to worry about Freud.

Checking through his phone messages he found that, in addition to the detailed messages left by Yu, Li and several senior officers had also called, repeatedly, urging him back to work. Even Old Hunter began fidgeting about his absence, leaving a message to the effect. A young cop had laid down her life in an effort to trap a serial murderer who struck out in defiance of the whole police force. It was a crisis beyond any that the bureau had experienced before.

What's more, they weren't able to openly investigate. As in the Chinese proverb, they had to swallow the knocked-out tooth without spitting out the blood. Any public knowledge of the identity of the latest victim—killed in a messed-up decoy attempt—would not only spell the worst humiliation for the police but also send new waves of panic through the public.

Although the identity of the victim still "remained unknown," no one in the bureau believed that it would remain so for long. According to a message left by Yu, reporters were already suspicious. For the moment, Yu and his colleagues had even more serious worries. What would happen this week? No one had any doubt about it now. And no one believed that they could stop the killer in less than two days.

Chen looked at his watch. It was close to ten. He decided not to go to the bureau or even, for the moment, to contact Yu.

There was one thing in particular about the case that alarmed him. The devilish masterstroke—the whole Joy Gate episode, from the newspaper ad to the backdoor exit—could very possibly have been planned by the murderer from the first day of Hong's work as a decoy. Everything had been arranged too perfectly. The more Chen thought about it, the more he suspected that the ad in the newspaper hadn't come out of the blue. More likely, it was a countertrap set with the use of inside information.

So whatever Chen was going to do, he would keep the bureau out of it. People talked about the chief inspector having lost himself in his literature paper, or having lost his guts in the serial murder case. Let them talk like that. He would continue to stay in the background.

"Sorry, I've changed my mind," he said to the driver. "Let's go to the Joy Gate instead."

"Joy Gate? The cops raided it last week."

It was perhaps a well-meant caution. In his trench coat, with his bag and briefcase, Chen looked like a tourist interested in the must-see attraction of the city.

"Yes, the Joy Gate."

He would do whatever was possible because he felt responsible for her death, more than anyone else in the bureau. If it weren't for his vacation, he could have led the investigation and prevented her from going to the Joy Gate, or at least stayed with the cops outside.

He took out the copy of *Oriental Morning* he had bought at the bus terminal. The newspaper had a picture of her lying spread-eagled in the cemetery, in a torn red mandarin dress, against the ruined tombstones. Underneath the picture was a couplet, "The apparition of her in a red mandarin dress, / Petals on a wet, black bough."

It read like a parody of an Imagist poem, but was poetry relevant at a moment when innocent people were dying, one after another?

Finally emerging out of the traffic congestion, the car came in sight of the refurbished art deco facade of the Joy Gate.

It might not be the time yet for regular customers to start arriving. There were only two or three people taking pictures in front of the building. Possibly journalists or plainclothes cops. He walked on in, keeping his head low. A middle-aged man sitting at the front desk didn't even look at him.

His colleagues would have combed the place already. He didn't expect to find anything new. Still, he wanted to step inside, as if to establish a bond between the living and the dead.

Moving up the marble staircase, he saw posters of 1930s movie stars on the walls. Each of them had danced here, leaving behind stories or pictures that echoed through the passage of time.

On the second floor, he thought he caught sight of a familiar face in the hall. So he turned aside, climbing up into a small balcony with a dark alcove behind. There he stood for several minutes, looking down at the now empty ballroom where Hong had danced like a radiant cloud. He murmured her name.

Several workers were arranging the tables and chairs for the night. The business would go on, as usual. He decided to leave.

As he stepped out of the Joy Gate, he saw, not too far away, a magnificent Buddhist temple with its glazed tiles and tilted eaves shimmering in the sunlight. It was Jin'an Monastery, allegedly built hundreds of years earlier, and lately redecorated. In his childhood, his parents had taken him there for ancestral worship services, sometimes renting a partitioned room, bringing in a variety of special snack offerings, and engaging monks for scripture-chanting.

On an impulse, he purchased a ticket and entered the temple he hadn't visited in years.

The front courtyard appeared to have changed little, though it was covered with new cobbles. He strolled on like a pilgrim, sorting through his fragmented childhood memories—the miniature room with shining religious instruments, the monks with their large floating sleeves, the vegetarian meal in imitation of various fish and meat, the flight from the imagined ghosts along the corridors, the scripture–chanting sounding like mosquitoes on a summer night.

He felt slightly dizzy again, as if searching along a long dark corridor, expecting something ahead, but he wasn't sure what. Sure enough, he saw a row of west-wing rooms still lining the wall. In the small rooms, people were sitting or kowtowing, their traditional offerings set out between burning candles. A file of monks moved in, beating fish-shaped wooden instruments and performing their religious service against the vanity of this mundane world. However, the resemblance to his childhood memory ended there.

A young monk strode out toward him, wearing a pair of gold-rimmed glasses and holding a cell phone. He greeted Chen with a look of expectation shining behind his light-sensitive glasses.

"Welcome to the temple, sir. Donate as much as you please, and your name will last forever here. We keep every offering in the computer's record. Take a look at the billboard."

Chen saw a donation billboard presenting an impressive picture of a tall gold Buddha, reaching out his hand, as if urging believers to donate. For the amount of one thousand Yuan, the donor could have his name engraved as a benefactor on a marble plaque, and for a hundred, his name would be stored in the electronic record. Next to the billboard was an office with its door ajar, showing several computers that guaranteed the proper management of the donations for the gold Buddha image.

Taking out a hundred Yuan bill, he inserted it into the donation box without signing his name in the register book.

"Oh, here is my card. In the future, you can send checks too," the young monk said pleasantly. "A lot of people are burning incense at the burner over there. It really works."

Chen took the card and headed to the huge bronze incense burner in the center of the temple courtyard. There he saw people putting afterworld paper money as well as incense into the burner.

An old woman was pouring in a bag of afterworld paper money, each piece already folded into the shape of a silver ingot. He had had no time for the job of folding, so he simply threw his bunch of silver paper into the burner. Slowly, it started burning with a somber flame, but its ashes swirled up high in a breath of wind, like a dancing figure, before vanishing out of sight.

"A sign," the old woman murmured in an awe-stricken voice, alluding to the belief that the spirits take away the money in a sudden wind. "You don't have to worry about her clothing in the winter."

How could the old woman know that the offering was for a woman? He did it for Hong, thinking of her in that silk red mandarin dress.

Chen didn't believe in the afterlife. Like a lot of Chinese, he simply felt a sort of comfort following some religious conventions. Somewhere, somehow, something possibly existed beyond human knowledge. Confucius says, "A gentleman doesn't talk about spirits." According to the sage, a gentleman has so many things to do in this world that there is no point worrying about the other world not known for sure. Still, Chen saw no harm in lighting a candle, holding incense, burning some afterworld money. Perhaps it could lead to a sort of communication with the dead.

He bought a bunch of tall incense and lit it, like others. He prayed that Buddha would guide him in his effort to catch the murderer, so that Hong would rest in peace.

As if that were not enough, he made a pledge, holding the incense: if he succeeded in catching the criminal, he would be a cop all his life, forgetting about all the other plans or ambitions he had for himself. A conscientious cop, contented.

Afterward, he moved to the back of the temple, where he climbed a flight of stone steps to a high-raised courtyard. Leaning against the white stone railing, he tried to think, gazing at the ancient eaves of the temple against all the postmodern skyscrapers.

He became aware of another monk coming toward him. It was an old monk with a weather-beaten face and a deeply lined forehead, carrying a long string of black beads in his hands, his steps barely audible on the stone.

"You look worried, sir."

"Yes, Master," Chen said, hoping that it wasn't about making another donation. "I'm an ordinary man, lost in the mundane world of the red dust, so I am burdened with worries like a snail carrying its shell."

"The snail may appear so because you think so. There is nothing but appearance."

"You have put it so well, Master," Chen said reverentially, for the old monk struck him as erudite. He recalled stories of sudden enlightenment in ancient temples. This could be an opportunity for his investigation. "Buddhists talk about seeing through—through the vanity of things in the world. I am trying hard, but I just can't."

"You are no ordinary man, that much I can see. Have you read the poem about the sudden enlightenment of Liuzhu?"

"I have read it, but it was such a long time ago. A metaphor about the bronze mirror, right?"

"Yes and no," the old monk said. "When the elderly abbot was going to name a successor, he decided to test his disciples. The number one candidate came up with a poem. 'My body is like a Bodhi tree, / my heart, a bronze mirror, / which I keep wiping, / so there's no dust left.' Not a bad one, you may say. But the dark horse, Huineng, a house-cleaning monk, proved to be the wiser in his poem: 'Bodhi is no tree, / and mirror is no heart. / There's nothing there. / How comes the dust?' "

"Yes, that's the story. Huineng was surely more thorough, and he succeeded."

"Nothing but appearance. The tree, the mirror, yourself, or the world."

"But we are still living in the world, Master."

"While you still have a lot of things to do, you may not be able to see beyond that world so quickly. An ancient proverb says, Discard your knife and turn yourself immediately into a Buddha. It's a proverb because it is by no means easy."

"You are absolutely right. It's just that I am so dumb."

"No, it's not easy to reach enlightenment. But you can try to clear your mind of all the disturbing thoughts—for a short while. You have to move ahead step by step."

"Thank you so much, Master."

"It's our lot that we should meet here today," the old monk said, pressing his palms together in a gesture of departing. "So why thank me? Good-bye. We will meet again if it's so destined."

According to Buddhism, everything happens through a sort of karma—a drink of water, a peck by a bird, or a meeting with an old monk, all of which must come out of what has happened earlier, and all of which leads in turn to something else.

So why not try, as the old monk suggested, to forget all the thoughts he had already had about the case and see it from a fresh perspective?

He remained standing by the railing, closing his eyes to empty his mind. He did not succeed at first. Perhaps people perceive only within the framework of preconceived ideas or images. No one lives in a vacuum.

So he took a deep breath, concentrating his mind on the *dantian*, a tiny spot above his navel. It was a technique he had learned in his Bund Park days. Gradually his energy seemed to start moving in harmony with the singular milieu of the temple.

All of a sudden, the image of the red mandarin dress came to him.

It appeared, however, in a way he hadn't experienced before. He seemed to be seeing it *then and there*—in the sixties, against a background of red flags of the Socialist Education Movement, and himself wearing a Red Scarf, shouting revolutionary slogans with the "revolutionary masses." It came to him that such a mandarin dress, whether in a movie or in real life, could have been controversial at the time, even though conservative by today's standards.

He took out his cell phone and called Chairman Wang of the Chinese Writers Association. Wang didn't pick up, so he left a message, emphasizing that, in addition to what they had already discussed, the image of the red mandarin dress could have been controversial in the early sixties.

Encouraged, Chen tried to repeat his experiment, but nothing came of it. He further modified it by lowering himself to the courtyard, where he sat in a lotus position with his legs crossed, reviewing the case from the very beginning—not like a cop, but like a man whose mind was not clogged by police training. Still nothing, though his mind seemed to obtain an intense clarity. He took a case folder out of the briefcase and began reading there, like a monk, as the temple bell began tolling.

Turning over a page, he lit upon something. Jasmine's bad luck. Buddhists talk about retribution. "Retribution comes, but in time." In a sort of secular Buddhist version, Chinese believe that people are punished or rewarded for what they do in this life—or even in the previous life.

Tian's horrible luck might be so accounted for. It was too much, however, with Jasmine. Chen didn't believe in punishment for a previous life. Nor did he see it as coincidence—that both father and daughter had such bad luck.

He thought of a novel he had read in his middle school years: *The Count of Monte Cristo.* Behind a series of inexplicable disasters was the mastermind Monte Cristo, working for his relentless revenge.

Was this possible in the case of Jasmine?

With her, and with her father too. A Mao Team member in those years, Tian could have persecuted or hurt someone who later carried out his or her revenge. If so, the style as well as the material of the dress would be accounted for.

But why the long wait—if done out of revenge for something that happened during the Cultural Revolution?

And what about the other girls?

He didn't have immediate answers. Still, the last question let him see the difference between Jasmine and the other girls in a new light.

Those girls might not have been related to Jasmine at all.

The sound of the bell came again in the wind. He shivered with a vague possibility.

It was time for him to go to the bureau. He would talk to Detective Yu, whose frustration with his unannounced vacation was evident in the messages left on his phone. Whether he would be able to make a satisfactory explanation to his partner, he didn't know. It didn't seem a good idea to talk about his nervous breakdown, not even to Yu.

At the temple exit, he got a call from Chairman Wang in response to his message.

"Sorry I didn't pick up in time, Chief Inspector Chen. I was in the bathroom, but I got your message about the possible controversy. It reminded me of something. Xiong Ming, a retired journalist in Tianjin, has been compiling a dictionary of controversies concerning literature and arts. He's an old friend of mine, so I contacted him at once. According to him, there was a prize-winning picture of a young woman wearing a mandarin dress and the picture later became controversial. This is his phone number, 02-8625252."

"Thank you, Chairman Wang. That really helps."

Chen put another bill into the shining donation box at the exit and dialed Xiong's number.

After introducing himself, Chen came to the point: "Chairman Wang told me that you have some information about a controversial picture of a woman in a red mandarin dress. You have been working on a dictionary of controversies, haven't you?"

"Yes, I have," Xiong said from the other end of the line, in Tianjin. "Nowadays people hardly remember or understand the absurd controversies during those years when everything could be distorted through political interpretations. Do you remember the movie *Early Spring in February*?"

"Yes, I do. The movie was banned in the early sixties. I was still an elementary school student then, hiding a picture of that beautiful heroine in my drawer."

"It was controversial because of the so-called bourgeois elegance of the heroine," Xiong said. "The same with the picture of the woman in a mandarin dress."

"Can you tell me more about the picture?" Chen said. "Is the mandarin dress a red one?"

"It represents a beautiful woman in a stylish mandarin dress, together with her son, a Young Pioneer wearing a Red Scarf. He is pulling her hand, and pointing toward the distant horizon. The picture is entitled, 'Mother, Let's Go There.' The background is something like a private garden. It is a black and white picture so I'm not sure about the color of the dress, but it's in a graceful style."

"How could such a picture have caused a controversy?" Chen said. "It's not a movie. There is no story in it."

"Let me ask you a question, Chief Inspector Chen. What was the ideological prototype for women in Mao's time? Iron girls, masculine, militant, wearing the same shapeless Mao suits as men. No suggestion of the female form or sensuality or romantic passion. So the political climate wasn't favorable to the implicit message of the picture, particularly when it was nominated for a national prize."

"What implicit message?"

"For one thing, it represented the ideal mother as feminine, elegant, and bourgeois. In addition, the garden background is quite suggestive too."

"Can you describe the picture in greater detail?"

"Sorry, that's about all I remember. I don't have the picture in front of me. But you can easily find it. It was published in 1963 or 1964 in *China Photography*. That was the only photography magazine at the time."

"Thank you, Xiong. Your information may be very important to our work."

Chen decided to go to the library, which wasn't too far away.

At the library, with the help of Susu, he got hold of a copy of the particular issue of *China Photography* in only ten minutes. It would usually take hours to unearth a magazine published in the sixties.

It was a black and white picture, as Xiong had described. The woman wearing the mandarin dress in the picture was a stunner. Chen couldn't tell the exact color of the dress, but it was apparently not a light color.

She was in a garden, standing barefoot with a tiny brook shimmering behind her, where she might have just dabbled her feet. The boy holding her hand was about seven or eight years old, wearing the Red Scarf of a Young Pioneer. Nobody else was visible in the background.

Chen borrowed a magnifying glass from Susu and made a careful study of the mandarin dress.

It appeared identical in design to those used in the murders—short sleeves and low slits, conventional in its general effect. Even the double-fish-shaped cloth buttons looked the same.

If there was any difference at all, it was that she wore the dress gracefully, with all the buttons buttoned in a demure way. She was barefoot, but standing in the background, in the company of her son, the suggestion more of a young happy mother.

The photographer was named Kong Jianjun. In the index of the magazine Chen found that Kong was also a member of the Shanghai Artists Association.

A siren was coming from the eastern end of Nanjing Road when Chen stepped out, carrying the magazine. He was close to believing that it was Hong—her soul, or whatever it was—that had guided him.

He made a phone call to the Shanghai Artists Association.

"Kong Jianjun passed away several years ago," a young secretary said in the office. "He was mass-criticized during the Cultural Revolution, I've heard."

"Do you have his home address?"

"The one in our record is old. He had no children—left behind only his wife. She must be in her seventies. I can fax his file to your office."

"To my home. I'm on vaca—hold on, fax it to this number," he said, giving her the library fax number.

"Okay. You might also talk to the neighborhood committee if she still lives there."

"Thanks. I'll do that."

He went back to the library to pick up the fax. The pages were delivered to him by Susu, who also brought him a cup of fresh coffee and a nut cream cake.

"It's hard to owe a beauty favors," he said.

"You are quoting Daifu again," she said with a sweet smile. "Come up with something new next time."

What came to mind was, unexpectedly, a scene from years earlier, in another library, in another city. . . . *There is only the spring moon / that remains sympathetic, still shining / for a lonely visitor, reflecting / on the petals fallen / in a deserted garden.*

Time flows like water. He gulped down the strong coffee. Black and bitter, perhaps he should have declined. Susu didn't know about his recent problem.

He began studying the file. Kong had worked as a photographer at Wangkai, one of the well-known state-run studios in Shanghai. He was also a member of the Artists Association, with several awards to his credit. He passed away shortly after the Cultural Revolution. His wife was still alive, alone and living in the Yangpu district. As for Kong's trouble in connection to the picture, there was no mention of it at all. Like other "bourgeois artists," he suffered mass-criticism during the Cultural Revolution.

There wasn't any mention of the prize-winning picture of the woman in her mandarin dress, either.

Getting up from the desk, he fought down the temptation to have another cup of coffee.

TWENTY-TWO

IT WAS CLOSE TO one thirty when Chen arrived at Kong's house on Jungong Road.

From the discolored wood mailboxes at the foot of the cracked concrete staircase, he supposed that it was one of the "new homes for workers" built in the sixties. It now looked old, shabby, and overcrowded. He found her name on one of the mailboxes.

He went up and pushed open a door. It turned out to be a three-bedroom apartment shared by three families. What he saw there first was a common kitchen crammed with stoves, which supported his hypothesis. She lived in a single room of the unit.

He knocked on the door marked 203. A white-haired woman opened the door, staring out through her silver-rimmed glasses.

"Are you Mrs. Kong?"

"Everybody calls me Auntie Kong here," the old woman said, letting him in.

She wore a cotton-padded coat, cotton-padded pants, and a pair of scarlet jasmine-embroidered slippers. The room was as small as a piece of tofu, stuffed with all sorts of nondescript items. A lone chair, three-legged, leaned against the wall. At the foot of the chair was an old-fashioned rice-pot warmer made of straw, which might serve her as an ottoman. It was cold in the room, in spite of the windows' being paper-sealed.

"You may sit on the chair," she said.

"Thank you," he said, perching on the edge of the chair gingerly. "Sorry to bother you like this, Auntie Kong."

He explained the purpose of his visit, taking out his business card and the magazine.

She studied the picture in the magazine. The expression on her face was inscrutable. For two or three minutes she didn't say a word.

Chen waited, becoming aware of a smell that permeated the room. He noticed a small can boiling above the gas tank in the corner. Possibly the cat's meal. For most Shanghainese, cats were kept for the purpose of catching rats, as in the classic statement made by Comrade Deng Xiaoping: "It does not matter whether it's a black or white cat; as long as it catches rats, it's a good cat." While the young and fashionable had started introducing the concept of "pet" into the city, in such an old building, a cat still functioned above all else as a rat-catcher. For Auntie Kong, the can of leftover rice flavored with fish bones was perhaps the only cat food she could afford. But cooking in the room could be hazardous for an old woman who lived by herself. The gas tank stood by a tiny wood table with a plastic basin that contained moldering bowls and cups.

"Yes, that's a picture my old man took. In the sixties," she said in a slightly tremulous voice, "but he passed away such a long time ago. How could I remember anything about it?"

"The picture won him a national award. He must have talked to you about it. Try to recall, Auntie Kong. Anything you can think of may be important to our work."

"A national award! It brought him nothing but bad luck. That picture was a curse."

"A curse," Chen echoed. A weird word indeed. And yet a familiar word in the investigation. She must remember something about it. Something ominous. "Please tell me what kind of a curse it was."

"Who really wants to talk about those things from the Cultural Revolution?"

The memories of those years might still be too painful, he understood. Nor was it easy for her to open up to a stranger. But he was determined to be patient.

"Do you mean the people connected to the picture were cursed, Auntie Kong?"

"He was criticized because of the picture—for the crime of 'advocating the bourgeois lifestyle.' Now, after so many years, please leave him in peace."

"It's a great picture," he went on imperturbably, taking out another business card—that of the Chinese Writers Association. "I am a poet. To me, it's a masterpiece. A poem in a picture."

"A poem in a picture" had been the highest praise in traditional Chinese criticism, but Chen thought he was sincere in applying the cliché.

"It may or may not be so. But so what? Look at me. Left all alone here like a dirty, worn-out mop." She pointed to the propane gas tank. "I can't even cook in the common kitchen here. Everybody bullies me. Tell them about the so-called masterpiece. What difference will it make?"

She rose and shuffled to the stove and stirred the food boiling in the can with a chopstick. Abruptly, she turned toward the straw rice pot warmer, cooing as if there was no one else in the room.

"Black. Lunch is ready."

The lid of the warmer lifted and a cat jumped out, rubbing its head against the old woman's leg.

Chen rose to leave, reluctantly. She didn't ask him to stay.

As he pushed open the door, he cast one more look into the kitchen. There were two ramshackle tables packed in there, littered with unprepared vegetables and leftover dishes and fermented bean curd and unwashed chopsticks and spoons.

Stepping out of the building, he saw the wooden sign of the neighborhood committee across the lane. He strode over to the office. It was almost a routine practice for a cop.

In the office, he produced his business card, which, to his surprise, made little impression on a gaunt, gray-haired man surnamed Fei, the head of the committee. Chen talked to him about Auntie Kong, emphasizing that her husband had been an award-winning artist and that the committee should try to help with her living condition.

"Is Auntie Kong your relative?" Fei said curtly, combing through his hair with his frostbitten fingers.

"No. I just met her today, but she should have access to the common kitchen."

"Let me tell you something, Comrade Chief Inspector Chen. The squabbles among neighbors over the common area can be a tough issue for us. As far as I know, the resident in that room before her didn't have any space in the common kitchen—he was a Party cadre who had practically worked and lived in his factory. Besides, her neighbors still use coal briquette stoves. It's dangerous for her to move the propane gas tank into the same kitchen."

"Well," Chen said after a thoughtful pause, "can I use your phone?"

He called the head of the district police station, which functioned like the security boss for the neighborhood committee. After getting through to the director, Chen handed the phone to Fei, who listened with surprise registered on his face.

"Now I remember you, Chief Inspector Chen," Fei said in a changed tone. "You'll have to excuse a man of my age. As a proverb goes, an old man has his eyes only not to recognize Mountain Tai. Sure, I've seen you on TV, and heard stories of you, too."

"You may have heard stories of me," Chen said. "According to one of them, I always repay a debt."

"You don't have to say that, Chief Inspector Chen. It's difficult to deal with disputes among neighbors, but we should try our best. You are right about that. Let's go there."

Chen didn't bother to guess what the director had said to Fei. They went back together to Auntie Kong's building.

All the residents in the unit came out, standing in their doorways, and Fei and Chen stood in the narrow corridor. Fei announced that a decision had been made jointly by the neighborhood committee and the district police station. A small space was to be cleared for Auntie Kong in the common kitchen. Not large, but enough for a propane gas tank. Out of safety considerations, the committee would put up a partition between the gas tank and coal stoves. No one argued or protested.

After the decision was announced, Chen was about to leave when Auntie Kong sidled up and said, "Comrade Chief Inspector Chen."

"Yes, Auntie Kong?"

"May I have a word with you?"

"Of course." He turned to Fei and said, "You may go back first. Thanks for your great help."

"So you are somebody," she said, closing the door when they were back in her room. "For more than ten years, I've had to cook in this room, and you've solved the problem for me in half an hour."

"That's nothing. I admire Mr. Kong's work," he said. "The neighborhood committee office is just across the lane, so I stepped in and told them of your difficulties."

"I guess you tried to oblige me," she said, "and I am obliged. There is no free white bun falling from the blue sky, I know."

The black cat was moving back. She scooped it up and placed it on her lap, but it jumped down, ran onto the windowsill, where it curled itself against the windowpane.

"No. Don't worry about it. That's what a cop should do."

"I have just a question for you. You are not going to use the picture at the expense of other people, are you? That was my old man's worst nightmare."

"Let me tell you something, Auntie Kong," he said, putting his hand on the wall, which felt sticky—perhaps from too much cooking in the room. "Earlier this afternoon, I was in the Jin'an Temple, where

I made a pledge to Buddha: to be a good, conscientious cop. Believe it or not, shortly after making the pledge, I learned about the picture."

"I believe you, but is the picture really that important to you?"

"It may throw light onto a homicide investigation, or I wouldn't have come to you without notice."

"A picture taken almost thirty years ago is related to a murder case today?" She was incredulous.

"At this moment, it is just a possibility, but we can't afford not to check. Let me assure you: I don't believe it has anything to do with you or your husband."

"If I still remember anything about that picture at all," she started hesitantly, "it's because of his passion for it. He used up all his vacation days for the project, working like one possessed. I even suspected that he had fallen for a shameless model.' "

"A good artist has to throw himself totally into a project, I know. It takes a lot of energy to produce such a masterpiece."

"Well, she turned out to be a decent woman of a good family. And he joked about my imagination: 'Me fall for her? No, it would be like a mud-colored toad watering its mouth at an immaculate white swan. I'm so excited because no photographer has approached her yet. For a photographer, it's like discovering a gold mine.' "

"Did he tell you how he discovered her?"

"At a concert, I think. A violinist onstage. At first she refused to pose for him. It took him a couple of weeks to bring her around. She finally agreed on the condition that the picture be taken with her son. That gave him new inspiration—a mother and son instead of just a beautiful woman."

"She must have loved her son very much."

"I thought so too. Looking at the picture, people couldn't help but be touched."

"Did he tell you her name?"

"He must have, but I don't remember it now."

"Do you know anything about the process of setting up the photo? For instance, the choice of the mandarin dress?"

"Well, he raved about an oriental beauty, and about the mandarin dress bringing out the best in her, but she must have had the dress at home. He couldn't have afforded it. Sorry, I don't know whose idea it was to choose the dress."

"Where was the picture taken?"

"She lived in a mansion. So it was probably taken in its back garden. He spent a whole day there, using up five or six rolls of film, and then spent a week in the darkroom, almost like a mole. He was so carried away that he brought all the pictures back home one night, asking me to choose one for him. For the competition."

"You chose the right one for him."

"But after it won the award, he began to be worried. Initially, he didn't want to tell me why. I learned from newspaper clippings hidden in a drawer that the picture had become controversial. Some people were talking about the 'political message' in it."

"Yes, everything could be given political interpretations."

"And during the Cultural Revolution, he was mass-criticized for the picture. Chairman Mao said that some attack the Party through novels, so the Red Guards claimed that Kong had attacked the Party through the picture. Like other 'monsters,' he had to stand with a blackboard hung around his neck, and his name was crossed out on the blackboard."

"So many people suffered. My father, too, stood bent with such a blackboard."

"What's more, some others compelled him to reveal the identity of the woman in the picture, and that upset him enormously."

"Who put the pressure on him?" he said. "Did he say anything?"

"An organization of Worker Rebels, I think. It was against his professional ethic but the pressure proved too much, and he finally gave up, thinking it was no crime for someone to pose for a picture. After all, there was nothing nude or obscene in it."

"Did he know anything about what happened to her?"

"He didn't, not at first. It was only a year or so later that he heard about her death. It had nothing to do with him. So many people died in those days. And perhaps it was not too surprising for someone with a family background like hers, and herself a 'bourgeois artist.' Still, the uncertainty weighed like a rock on his mind."

"He didn't have to be so hard on himself. People could have learned her identity anyway," Chen said, thinking that the old photographer could have cared for her. Seeing no point in bringing up the possibility, he changed the subject. "Now, he used five or six rolls for this picture, you have mentioned. Did he keep those other pictures?"

"Yes, he kept them at a risk to himself, hiding them away even from me. Along with a notebook. 'The portfolio of the red mandarin dress,' he called it. After his death, I discovered them by chance. I didn't have the heart to get rid of them—they must have been so special to him."

Out of the cabinet drawer, she produced a large envelope containing a notebook and a bunch of pictures in a smaller envelope.

"Here they are, Chief Inspector Chen."

"Thank you so much, Auntie Kong," he said, rising. "I'll return them to you after looking through them."

"Don't worry. I have no use for them." She added, "But don't forget your pledge in the temple."

"No, I won't."

It was a random harvest. He started reading the notebook in a taxi outside Auntie Kong's building. It contained plenty of working notes. Kong had discovered the model at a concert, spellbound by "her sublime beauty at the soul-stirring climax of the music." Afterward, a Young Pioneer rushed onstage, holding a bouquet of flowers for her. The boy turned out to be her son, and she hugged him affectionately onstage. For a week after the concert, he spared no effort in persuading her to pose for him. It was a tough job, for she was interested neither in money nor in publicity. He finally succeeded in bringing her around by promising to photograph her together with her son. The picture was taken in the back garden of their mansion.

Chen skipped through the technical notes about light and angles to a page that contained the work address of the model—the Shanghai Music Institute—with an office telephone number beneath it. For some reason, Kong mentioned her name only once in the notebook. Mei.

Then he started examining the pictures. There were a considerable number of them, and like the old photographer, he was "spellbound."

"Sorry, I've just changed my mind," he said to the taxi driver, looking up. "Please take me to the Shanghai Music Institute."

TWENTY-THREE

HIS VISIT TO THE institute didn't begin on a promising note.

Comrade Zhao Qiguang, the current Party Secretary of the institute, showed all respect to Chen but could be of little help. Zhao had to check a registry before he was able to tell Chen anything about Mei. According to him, Mei and her husband Ming had both worked at the institute. During the Cultural Revolution, Ming committed suicide, and she died in an accident. Zhao did not know anything about the existence of the picture.

"I came to the institute five or six years ago," Zhao said, by way of explanation. "People are not so eager to talk about the Cultural Revolution."

"Yes, the government wants people to look ahead, not backward."

"You should try to talk to some old people here. They may know something, or they may know somebody who knows," Zhao said, scribbling several names on a piece of paper. "Good luck."

But the people who knew Mei had either retired or passed away.

After bumping around for quite a while, he stumbled upon Professor Liu Zhengquan of the Instrument Department.

"That's Mei!" Liu said, studying the picture. "But I've never seen the picture before."

"Can you tell me something about her?"

"The flower of the school, fallen too early to the dust."

"How did she die?"

"I don't really remember. She was in her midthirties then. Her son was about ten years old. What a tragedy!"

"What happened to her son?"

"I don't know." Liu added, "We were not in the same department. You need to talk to somebody else."

"Can you recommend someone to me?"

"Well, talk to Xiang Zilong. He's retired now and lives in Minghang district. Here's his address. He still keeps a picture of Mei in his wallet, I believe."

It was a hint about Xiang having been an admirer of Mei, a romantic who still carried a picture of her so many years later.

Chen thanked Liu, looked at his watch, and left for Minghang immediately. There was no time for him to lose.

Minghang had once been an industrial area, quite a distance from the center of the city. Fortunately, there was now a subway that stopped there. He took a taxi and hurried to the subway, and after twenty minutes, he walked out of the terminal at the other end and changed into another taxi.

Shanghai had been expanding rapidly. Minghang, too, represented a scene of numerous new apartment buildings shining and shimmering in the afternoon sunlight. It took the taxi driver quite a while to find Xiang's building.

Chen climbed up the concrete staircase and knocked at an imitation oak door on the second floor. The door opened cautiously. Chen handed over his business card to a tall, gaunt man in a cotton-padded robe and felt slippers, who examined the card with surprise on his deep-lined face.

"Yes, I am Xiang. So you are a member of Chinese Writers Association?"

The card was his from the Chinese Writers Association, Chen realized. An inexplicable slip.

"Oh, I have mixed my cards. I am Chen Cao, of the Shanghai Police Bureau, and I am also a member of the association."

"I may have heard of you, Chief Inspector Chen," Xiang said. "I don't know what wind has brought you over here today, but come on in, as a poet or as a police officer."

Xiang moved to pour Chen a cup of tea from a thermos bottle and added some water into his own cup. Xiang walked with a slight suggestion of a limp, Chen observed.

"You sprained your ankle, Professor Xiang?"

"No. Infantile paralysis at the age of three."

"Sorry for coming to see you without notice. It's because of an important case. I have to ask you some questions," Chen said, seating himself at a plastic folding chair by an apparently custom-made, extraordinary long desk, which was the main feature in a living room lined with bookshelves. "Questions about Mei. She was a colleague of yours."

"Question about Mei? She was indeed a colleague of mine, but so many years ago. Why?"

"The case didn't—and doesn't—involve her, but the information about her may throw some light on our investigation. Whatever you say will be confidential."

"You aren't going to write about her, are you?"

"Why do you ask?"

"A couple of years ago, someone approached me for information about her. I refused to tell him anything."

"Who was he?" Chen said. "Do you remember his name?"

"I forget his name, but I don't think he showed his ID to me. He said he was a writer. Anybody could have claimed to be such."

"Can you give me a detailed description of this man?"

"In his early or midthirties. Well-mannered, but rather elusive in his speech. That's about all I remember." Xing took a sip of his tea. "With this city lost in collective nostalgia, stories about once illustrious families are popular, like *The Ill-Fated Beauty of Shanghai.* Why should I let anyone exploit her memory?"

"You did the right thing, Professor Xiang. It would be horrible for a so-called writer to profit from her suffering."

"No, no one can drag her memory through the humiliating mire again."

There was a slight tremor in Xiang's voice. For an admirer of her, there was nothing too surprising about his reaction. But "humiliating mire" indicated he knew something.

"I give you my word, Professor Xiang. I'm not here for the sake of a story."

"You have mentioned a case. . . ." Xiang sounded uncertain.

"At this moment, I can't go into details. Suffice it to say that several people have died, and that more will be killed if the murderer is not stopped." Chen took out the magazine together with the other pictures. "You may have seen this magazine."

"Oh, these other pictures too," Xiang said, beginning to examine them. His face pale and earnest, he rose and strode to one of the bookshelves and took out a copy of *China Photography.* "I have kept it all these years."

There was a bookmark with a red tassel sticking out of the magazine, marking the page of the picture. The bookmark was a new one, representing the Oriental Pearl, a high-rise landmark east of the river built in the nineties.

"It was such a long time ago," Chen said. "There must be a story about it."

"Yes, a long story. How old were you at the outbreak of the Cultural Revolution?"

"Still in elementary school."

"Then you have to know something about the background."

"Of course. But please tell me from the very beginning, Professor Xiang."

"For me, it started in the early sixties. I was then just assigned to the music institute, where Mei had already worked for about two years. So beautiful, and talented too, she was the queen there. Now don't get me wrong, Chief Inspector Chen. For me, she was an inspiration more than anything else. I was frustrated at being unable to practice the classics—nothing was permitted but two or three revolutionary songs. But for her presence, which lit up the whole rehearsal room, I would have given up."

"As you have mentioned," Chen said, "she was the queen. There must have been a lot of people that admired her—and approached her, too. Have you heard or known about any such stories?"

"What do you mean?" Xiang said, literally glaring at him.

"For the investigation, I have to ask all kinds of questions. It doesn't mean anything disrespectful to her, Professor Xiang."

"No, I have not heard any story. A woman of her family background had to live with her tail tucked in, so to speak. Any peach-colored gossip could be disastrous. It was then a Communist-Puritan period—you were perhaps too young to understand. There was not a single romantic love song in the whole country."

"Chairman Mao wanted people to devote themselves to the socialist revolution. No room for romantic love—" Chen broke off, unexpectedly reminded of something similar in his paper, except that there it was Confucianism. "Her husband also worked at the institute, didn't he?"

"Her husband, Ming Deren, taught there too. Nothing so special about him. Their marriage had been—at least partially, I think—an arranged one. Before 1949, his father was a successful investment banker, and hers was only a struggling attorney. The Ming Mansion was one of the most extravagant in the city."

"Yes, I've heard of the mansion. Did they have any problems in their marriage?" Chen wondered why Xiang brought up the topic of arranged marriage.

"Not that I know of, but people thought he was no match for her."

"I see," Chen said, realizing that for Xiang, no one could have been worthy of her. "Now, how did you come to know about the picture? She must have told you or shown you the magazine."

"No. We shared an office, and I happened to overhear her phone conversation with the photographer. So I bought a copy of the magazine."

"About the mandarin dress in the picture—had you seen her wearing it?"

"No, I didn't. Neither before nor after the picture. She had several mandarin dresses, which she occasionally wore for performances, but not the one in the picture."

"So she got into trouble because of the picture?"

"I don't know. Shortly afterward, the Cultural Revolution broke out. Her father-in-law passed away and her husband committed suicide, which was condemned as a serious crime against the Party. She was turned into a 'black family member of a current counterrevolutionary' and driven out of the mansion into the attic above the garage. The mansion was taken over by a dozen 'red families.' She suffered the worst humiliating persecution."

"So she died a tragic death because of it?"

"About the circumstances of her death," Xiang said, taking a long sip at his tea, as if sipping at his memory, "my recollection may not be so reliable, you know, after all these years."

"It happened more than twenty years ago, I understand. You don't have to worry about the accuracy of the details. Whatever you tell me, I'll check and double-check," Chen said, also sipping at the tea. "Look at the picture. It's like in a proverb, a beauty's fate as thin as a piece of paper. Something really should be done for her."

That clinched it for Xiang.

"You really mean it?" Xiang said. "Yes, you cops should have done something for her."

Chen nodded, saying nothing for fear of interrupting.

"You have heard of the campaign of Mao Zedong Thought Worker Propaganda Teams and what they did at colleges and universities, haven't you?" Xiang went on without waiting for a response. "They stood for political correctness during those years in the Cultural Revolution. A team arrived at our school too, bullying in the name of reeducating the intellectuals. The head of the team soon had a nickname whispered among us—Comrade Revolutionary Activity. It was because he talked all the time about his 'revolutionary activity'—beating, criticizing, cursing us, the so-called 'class enemies.' What could we do except give him a nickname behind his back?"

"Was she the target of any of his 'revolutionary activity?' "

"Well, he kept giving 'political talks' to her. There were stories about those talks behind closed doors, but to be fair to him, I didn't notice anything really suspicious. Their talks weren't too long. Nor was the door closed—not all the time. Still, she cringed like a mouse in front of a cat. I mean, in his company, which she tried her best to avoid."

"Did you tell her about your concerns?"

"No. It would have been a crime to suspect a Mao member like that," Xiang said with a bitter smile. "Then something happened. Not at the school, but at her home. A chalk-written counterrevolutionary slogan was found on their garden wall. By that time, there were more than ten families living in the house, but the neighborhood committee saw it as an anti-Party attack by another counterrevolutionary in her family. One of her neighbors claimed to have seen her son holding a piece of chalk, and another declared that she was there behind the scenes. So the committee came to our institute. Comrade Revolutionary Activity met them, and they formed a joint investigation group and put the boy into an isolation investigation—they locked him up in the back room of the neighborhood committee until he was ready to confess his crime."

"That's too much," Chen said. "Did they torture him during the isolation investigation?"

"What exactly the joint group did there, I don't know. Comrade Revolutionary Activity spent a lot of his time in her neighborhood—every day. She wasn't put into isolation interrogation, however, like her late husband had been earlier, and like her son was then. She still came to the institute, looking deeply troubled. Then one afternoon, out of the blue, she ran out of the attic, unclothed, fell stumbling down the staircase, and died then and there. Some said she must have lost her mind. Some said she was taking a bath, jumping out upon the unexpected return of her son."

"Was her son released that day?"

"Yes, he returned that afternoon, but when he reached the door of their attic room, he turned back and rushed down the staircase. According to one of her neighbors, she fell running out after him."

"That's strange. Even if he stumbled upon her in a bath, he didn't have to run away at that, nor did she have to rush out naked."

"She was so attached to her son. She could have forgotten herself in the overwhelming joy."

"What did the Mao team member say about her death?"

"He said that her death was an accident. That's about it."

"Did anyone raise questions about the circumstances of her death?"

"No, not at the time. I was in trouble for 'poisoning the students with decadent Western classics.' Like a clay image crossing the river, I could hardly protect myself," Xiang said. "After the Cultural Revolution, I thought about approaching the factory where Comrade Revolutionary Activity had come from. He had never explained his activity in her neighborhood. As the head of the Mao team, he was supposed to stay at our school, not her neighborhood. So why was he there? But I hesitated because I didn't have anything substantial, and because it could drag her memory through the mire again. Also, I heard he had also fallen on hard times, wrecked through a series of mishaps, fired and punished."

"Hold on—Comrade Revolutionary Activity. Do you remember his name?"

"No, but I can find out," Xiang said. "Are you going to investigate him?"

"Was there anything else unusual about him?"

"Yes, there's one more thing I noticed. Usually, for one school, the Mao team was made of workers from one factory, but for ours, Comrade Revolutionary Activity, the head of the team, actually came from a different factory."

"Yes, that's something," Chen said, taking out a small notebook. "Which factory?"

"Shanghai Number Three Steel Mill."

"How old was he then?"

"In his late thirties or early forties."

"I'll check into it," Chen said. Still, whatever the Mao team member might have done, he would be in his sixties now, and according to Yu, the suspect in the tape at the Joy Gate was probably in his thirties. "Did people do anything after her death?"

"I was devastated. I thought about sending a bouquet of flowers to her grave—the least I should do. But her body had been sent to the crematory, and her ashes were disposed of overnight. There was no casket, nor a tombstone. I had done nothing for her during her life, nor after her death. How pathetic a weakling!"

"You don't have to be so hard on yourself, Professor Xiang. It was the Cultural Revolution. All are gone and past."

"Gone and past," Xiang said, taking out a record in a new cover. "I did set a classical Chinese poem to music—in memory of her."

Chen studied the cover with Yan Jidao's poem printed in the background. The foreground was a blurred figure dancing in a streaming red dress.

Waking with a hangover, I look up / to see the high balcony door / locked, the curtain / hung low. Last spring, / the sorrow of separation new, / long I stood, alone, / amidst all the falling petals: / A pair of swallows fluttered / in the drizzle. // I still remember how / Little Ping appeared the first time, / in her silken clothes embroidered / with a double character of heart,/ pouring out her passion / on the strings of a Pipa. / The bright moon illuminated her returning / like a radiant cloud.

"She would appreciate it—in the afterworld," Chen said, "if there is one."

"I would have dedicated it to her," Xiang said, with an unexpected touch of embarrassment, "but I have never told my wife about Mei."

"Don't worry. All you've told me will be confidential."

"She is coming back soon," Xiang said, putting the record back on to the shelf. "Not that she is an unreasonable woman, you know."

"Just one more question, Professor Xiang. You've mentioned her son. Have you heard anything about him?"

"Nothing was found out about the counterrevolutionary slogan. Anyway, he was left an orphan. He went to live with a relative of his. After the Cultural Revolution, he entered college, I heard."

"Do you know which college?"

"No, I don't. The last time I heard about him was a few years ago. If it's important, I can make some phone calls."

"Would you? I would really appreciate it."

"You don't have to say that, Chief Inspector Chen. At long last, a police officer is doing something for her. So I should appreciate it," Xiang said in sincerity. "I have but one request. When your investigation is over, can you give me a set of these pictures?"

"Of course, I'll have a set delivered to you tomorrow."

"*Ten years, ten years, / nothingness / between life and death.*" Xiang added, changing the subject, "You may find out something more in her neighborhood, I think."

"Do you have her address?"

"It's the celebrated old mansion on Henshan Road. Close to Baoqing Road. Everybody there can tell you. It's been turned into a restaurant. I was there and took a business card," Xiang said, rising to reach a card box. "Here it is. Old Mansion."

TWENTY-FOUR

WHEN CHEN ARRIVED AT Henshan Road, it was already past eight o'clock.

He had a hard time locating the neighborhood committee there, walking back and forth along the street. It was cold. It was crucial to find it, he told himself, fighting down a sudden suggestion of dizziness.

With the identity of the original red mandarin dress wearer established, he saw a new angle from which to approach the case.

Despite Xiang's denial, there was no ruling out the possibility of other admirers, even during the Communist-Puritan age described by Xiang. After all, the retired professor might not be a reliable narrator.

The Mao team member presented another possibility worth exploring. Comrade Revolutionary Activity could have joined the team to get near her, and that made him a possible suspect in the subsequent tragedy.

Whatever the possible scenarios, he had to first find out more about Mei through the neighborhood committee.

The neighborhood office turned out to be tucked in a shabby side street behind Henshan Road. Most of the houses on the street were identical discolored concrete two-stories, largely in disrepair, like rows of matchboxes. There was a wooden sign pointing to a farmer's market around the corner. The committee office was closed. From a cigarette peddler crouching nearby, he learned the name and address of the committee director.

"Weng Shanghan. See the window on the second floor overlooking the market?" the peddler said, shivering in the winter wind as he took a cigarette from Chen. "That's her room."

Chen walked over and climbed up the stairs to a room on the second floor. Weng, a short, spirited woman in her midforties, peered out the door with a visible frown. She must have taken him as a new neighbor seeking help. She held a hot water bottle in her hand, walking in her wool stockings across the gray concrete floor. It was a single efficiency room, which was not so convenient for hosting unexpected visitors.

As it turned out, she was busy folding afterworld money at the foot of the bed, her husband helping her smooth the silver paper. A superstitious practice, which didn't become the head of the neighborhood committee. But it was for Dongzhi night, he realized. He, too, had brought back silver afterworld money, though he burned his for Hong at the temple instead. Perhaps this explained Weng's reluctance to receive a visitor.

"Sorry to bother you so late in the evening, Comrade Weng," Chen apologized, handing over his business card as he explained the purpose of the visit, highlighting his inquiries into the Ming family.

"I'm afraid I can't tell you much," she said. "We moved into the neighborhood about five years ago. The Mings no longer lived here. In recent years, there have been a lot of changes among the residents here, especially along Henshan Road. According to the new policy, the privately owned houses have been returned to the original owners. So some moved back, and a lot moved out."

"Why didn't the Ming family move back?"

"There was a problem with the new policy. What about those residents currently living there? Sure, some of them had moved in illegally during the Cultural Revolution, but they still needed a place to stay now. So the government tried to buy the buildings from the original owners. The owners could say no, but Ming, the son of the original owner, agreed. He didn't even come back to take a look. Later the mansion was turned into a restaurant. That's another story."

"Sorry to interrupt you here," Chen said. "What is Ming's full name?"

"Let me check," she said. She took out an address book and looked through several pages. "Sorry, it's not here. He is a successful man, as I remember."

"Thank you," he said. "How much did he get from selling the mansion?"

"All the transactions were arranged by the district authorities. We weren't involved."

"Are there any records about what happened to the Ming family during the Cultural Revolution?"

"There're hardly any records left from that time in our office. For the first few years, our committee was practically paralyzed. My predecessor somehow got rid of the one and only ledger book from 1966 to 1970."

"You mean the ex-head of the neighborhood committee?"

"Yes, she passed away five or six years ago."

"It's easy not to remember," Chen said, "but I need to ask you one question. Ming's mother, Mei, died during the Cultural Revolution. Possibly in an accident. Have you heard anything about it?"

"That was so many years ago. Why?"

"It may be important to a homicide investigation."

"Really!"

"I have heard about Chief Inspector Chen before," her husband cut in for the first time, speaking to Weng. "He has worked on several important cases."

"If we heard anything about his family," Weng said, "it's because of a trick played by Pan, the owner of the Old Mansion restaurant."

"That's interesting. Please tell me about it."

"As soon as Ming sold the mansion to the government, Pan had his eyes on it. None of the residents wanted to move out. And there also might have been a number of potential buyers. So Pan started rumors about the mansion being haunted and those superstitious stories spread really fast. We had to check into it."

"You have a lot of responsibilities, Comrade Weng."

"It's ironic. We found out that those tall stories had been started much earlier, during the Cultural Revolution, by the Tong family, who lived underneath the garage attic. After Mei's death, the Tongs claimed to have heard noises in the room upstairs and footsteps on the staircase too. Even after her son moved out. Her neighbors had questions about her strange death, thought that she must have been wronged, so it was understandable for them to believe that her spirit came back to haunt the house—at least the attic. As a result, the Tongs got the 'haunted attic,' which no one else wanted—"

"Sorry to interrupt again. You said something about her strange death. Can you tell me about that?"

"I don't know any details. Her family suffered a lot during the Cultural Revolution. Both her husband and father-in-law died. She and her son were driven out of the mansion and into the attic above the garage. In the second or third year there, the boy also got into trouble. And then one day, she rushed out of the attic, stark naked, fell down the staircase, and died. It's possible that all these travails proved too much, and she collapsed. Still, the way she died was suspicious."

"Did it happen in the summer?"

"No, in the winter. There apparently was some talk about her rushing out of a bath, but that isn't true. It was out of the question for her to take a bath there, there was no heating in the attic," Weng said, shaking her head. "Pan was really effective with his ghost stories. Soon he convinced every resident, including the Tongs, that the whole mansion was haunted. Accidents happened there and people were panicky. He reached agreements and bought out all of the residents."

"Did you find out anything else about Mei's death during your investigation?"

"The superstitious part aside, one of her neighbors said that she did hear strange noises in the attic, like moaning and groaning, in the depth of night for a couple of nights before the boy's release—before, but not after. The Tongs confirmed that, adding that they also heard her weeping in the night, though they were rather evasive about the part after the boy's release."

"Did they see anybody with Mei in the room—anybody coming or going there?"

"The Tongs said they heard something that sounded like a man's grunt, but they weren't sure after so many years."

"Is there anyone in the neighborhood who knows about the Ming family, someone I can approach directly?"

"Well, most of the residents from that time have since moved away, as I've explained. But I'll check around. With luck, I may have a list for you early next week. Some are still here, I believe."

She might or might not find anybody, and it could take days. But tomorrow would be Thursday. There would be another victim before the weekend.

Still, he could see that was about all she knew. There was nothing else he could do here this evening. He rose, reluctantly, when her husband cut in again.

"There's one man you should talk to, Comrade Chief Inspector. Comrade Fan Dezong. He used to be a neighborhood cop here. Now he's retired."

"Really! Can I visit him this evening?" Chen said. Like a neighborhood cadre, a neighborhood cop usually lived in the area.

"He still has one small room here, but most of the time he stays with his son, babysitting his grandson. He comes back over in the morning and for the weekend. He patrols the food market in the morning."

"Do you have his son's address or phone number?"

"No, we don't have it here," Weng said. "But you won't miss him early tomorrow morning."

"From five to seven thirty," the husband said. "He's highly punctual for his patrolling activity, even in the cold winter. An old-fashioned cop."

"That's great. Thank you so much for your help."

Chen's cell phone rang. He made an apologetic gesture to them and pushed the talk button.

"It's me, Xiang. I haven't learned anything about her son, not yet, but I remember that Mei called him 'Xiaojia.' So his name could be Mingjia. People like to add 'xiao' or 'little' to the given name as a sort of endearment, you know. Also, I dug out a notebook. The name of Comrade Revolutionary Activity is Tian. He wasn't of the Shanghai Number Three but the Number One Steel Mill."

"That's important. I don't know how I can thank you enough, Professor Xiang."

"I'll make a couple more phone calls about her son tomorrow. I'll let you know as soon as I have learned anything."

Flipping closed the cell phone, he almost forgot he was in the company of the neighborhood committee cadre. He turned back to her, his thoughts still in turmoil.

"Thank you so much, Comrade Weng."

"It's a great honor that you have visited us here," Weng said, walking him to the door. "I'll check around first thing tomorrow morning. It's something urgent, I understand. Now, you'd better hail a taxi on Hengshan Road. It's cold outside."

TWENTY-FIVE

OUTSIDE, IT WAS A cold night.

Turning toward Henshan Road, he glanced at his watch again. Almost nine thirty.

Henshan Road stretched ahead, like an unfolded belt of neon lights glittering around the restaurants and nightclubs. Not too long ago, he had visited one of the nostalgic bars here, with White Cloud.

Where could she be tonight? In another bar, or in another's company, possibly.

He was not in a hurry to go home.

Some of the pieces he had gathered seemed to be coming together. He had to make sure that they converged into a whole before those half-formed thoughts faded into the chilly night, like in a song.

The Old Mansion was close by. It was magnificently lit at this late hour, as if still intent on stirring up memories of the nightless city, though he wondered if it could have been so flashy and flamboyant in Mei's day.

He walked in, waiting in a spacious lobby for a hostess to lead him to a table. It was evident that the restaurant enjoyed good business.

There were several old pictures on the walls. One of them presented a middle-aged man standing with several foreigners in front of the then new mansion. A picture taken in the thirties. There was a small line underneath the picture: Mr. Ming Zhengzhang, the original owner of the mansion. Chen didn't find a picture of Mei. It wasn't a good idea to evoke the memory of the Cultural Revolution; nowadays, few would be interested.

The restaurant owner had done a good job reviving the place. The dark-colored oak panels, the antique grand piano, the oil paintings on the walls, the carnation in a cut glass vase, not to mention the shining silverware on the tables, all contributed to the period atmosphere. People here could believe they were back in the thirties, instead of in the nineties.

But what about those years in between?

History is not like a soy sauce stain, easily wiped away by the pink napkin in the hand of the pretty waitress who was leading him to a table by the tall French window. He asked her a question about how the mansion became a restaurant.

She said with an apologetic smile, "Our general manager paid a large amount to the original residents, more than ten families, and then refurbished the whole house. That's about all I know."

He opened the menu, which was almost as thick as a book. Turning to the last two pages marked as "Mansion Specials," he noticed one called Live Monkey Brains, probably like what he had seen in the vacation village, and another, Live White Rats. He doubted that Mei would have served those dishes in her elegant mandarin dress.

The waitress stood beside his table, observing with an attentive smile.

"Can I have just a cup of coffee?"

"Coffee is served only after dinner. The minimum expense is two hundred Yuan here," she said. "Don't you think it's a bit late for coffee?"

She was right about that. After that scary morning, he really should be wary of coffee.

"A pot of tea, then. And a couple of cold dishes for the minimum expense—let's see, pork tongue in Shaoxin wine, lotus root stuffed with sticky rice, deboned goose feet in special house sauce, and cold tofu mixed with chopped green onion and sesame oil. Don't bring up the dishes in a hurry. Just tea for now."

"Whatever way you like," she said. "Here is the tea."

He realized he must be one of those "cheap customers" here, choosing the inexpensive dishes. He thought he detected a touch of snobbishness in her voice.

He poured himself a cup of tea. It wasn't that strong. He started chewing a tea leaf, thinking of the information he had gathered during the day.

According to Auntie Kong, the old photographer got into trouble because of the picture, so could Mei as well. Her mandarin dress in the picture appeared to be identical to those in the serial murder case. According to Professor Xiang, Comrade Revolutionary Activity, possibly responsible for her death, was none other than Tian, and his daughter Jasmine was the first victim. And according to Comrade Weng, the circumstances of her death were suspicious, with a man possibly involved.

Now he at least had a better grasp of the connection between Mei in the original mandarin dress and the victims in the red mandarin dresses. As he had discussed with Yu, Jasmine, the first victim, could have been the real target, and the rest, possibly picked for a different reason. The murderer could be someone connected with Mei, knowledgeable about her death and how it was related to Tian.

And he had partial answers to some of his other questions. The long wait between Mei's death and Jasmine's, for instance. The murderer might have taken delight in Tian's long years of suffering instead of making one fatal strike.

So meeting with the neighborhood cop could be crucial. He was probably the only one knowledgeable about the exact circumstances of her death and about the relationship between Tian's revolutionary activity and Mei's death.

Only with that established could he move forward with the scenario in his mind.

The waitress started serving the cold dishes on his table.

"We also have special Dongzhi dishes," she said. "Would you like to try some of them?"

"Oh, Dongzhi dishes," he said. "Not now, thanks."

He had no appetite, though the color combination of the white tofu and green scallion looked quite enticing. He tried a spoonful without tasting it, then he took out his notebook again.

It was too late to contact Yu at home, so he dialed Yu's cell phone. No one picked up.

He hadn't called his mother, either, since the day he had left for the vacation village. She usually went to bed late. So he dialed her number.

"I knew you would call. Your partner Yu has already contacted me," she said. "Don't worry about me, but take good care of yourself. In my eyes, you're still Little Cao."

"Little Cao" was something he hadn't heard for a long time. She, too, was sentimental on the eve of Dongzhi Festival.

And he was vaguely aware of something stirring in the recesses of his mind.

"I'll try to come over as early as possible, Mother."

"Tomorrow night is Dongzhi. If you can make it, that will be great," she said at the end of their talk, "but it doesn't matter if you can't."

He finished the tea, making a gesture for the waitress to add hot water. She came with a tray that also contained the bill.

"Can you pay the bill now, sir? It's late."

He tossed out two hundred fifty Yuan. "Keep the change."

People were not supposed to tip in the socialist China, but the restaurant was owned by a "capitalist."

He tried to make a plan for the coming day. He had only one day's time, and it had to be a plan that would work against all possible odds.

When he looked up again, he noticed the waitresses clearing away the other tables in the dining hall. He was the last diner sitting there. Because of the tip, perhaps, she did not come to hurry him up.

At the back of his mind, he seemed to hear the refrain from a poem he had read long ago. *Hurry up. Please, it's time.*

He stood up, leaving most of the dishes untouched.

"Good night, sir," a new hostess said at the gate, slightly shivering.

"Good night."

Again, he hesitated at the prospect of going back home.

He had to be here early the next morning. Hurrying back and forth like that, he wouldn't be able to get much sleep anyway. Nor was he sure that he could get a taxi at around five o'clock in the morning—for a meeting he couldn't afford to miss.

Perhaps an all-night café in the neighborhood would be an alternative, so that he could easily walk to the food market around five thirty.

The night was a deep metal blue against the neon lights. He reached for a cigarette, aware of a woman approaching him from the shadow of the restaurant.

"I'm a madam for the Henshan Nightclub," she said in a Beijing dialect. "Come with me, sir. There are hundreds of girls for you there. Only one hundred Yuan for the room fee. No minimum expense."

He was confounded, as if dragged into a movie scene of the old Shanghai red quarters. Little did he expect that it could have happened to him.

For once, he didn't instantly reject the offer.

He hadn't been unfamiliar with three-accompanying services. In the company of Big Bucks, however, Chen had never gone "all the way," feeling obliged to keep up the police officer image when with people like Gu, who made a point of paying for everything.

But it was different tonight. He wasn't going all the way, but some intimate knowledge of the profession might be helpful for the investigation.

And he could spend the rest of the night there, cozy and comfortable in the company of a young girl, instead of wandering like a homeless skunk, running about in the cold night.

"Please, Big Brother," she went on with a pleading smile. "You are a man of distinction. I wouldn't pull your leg."

His distinction probably came from the fact that he emerged from the Old Mansion, one of the most extravagant restaurants in the city. Still, he thought he had just over a thousand Yuan left in his wallet, not including the small change in his pockets. Enough for a night in the club.

"Our girls are so beautiful, and talented too. You don't have to sing if you don't want to. Some of them are highly educated, with BA or MA degrees. They talk like understanding flowers."

"Show me the way, then," he said in Shanghai dialect. He might learn something from talking to a girl there, the way he wouldn't have talked to White Cloud.

There were several tough-looking men standing at the entrance of the nightclub, yawning, turning suspicious eyes on Chen, who didn't look like a regular client.

The woman led him to a room on the second floor. Barely had he seated himself on a black leather function sofa when a bevy of girls swarmed in, wearing slips or bikinis, their bare shoulders and thighs flashing against the wall behind them, like a jade screen of female bodies.

"Choose one," the madam said with a broad grin.

He nodded toward a girl in a black mini slip, who had almond-shaped eyes and cherry lips curving into a sweet smile. Probably twenty-five or twenty-six, slightly older than the rest. She slid down beside him, her head resting against his shoulder naturally, as if they had known each other for years.

After the others moved out, a waiter came in, put a fruit platter on the coffee table, and handed over the menu to him. Too embarrassed to study the menu carefully with the girl nestling against him, he settled on a cup of tea, and she, a cup of fruit juice. Juice wouldn't be too bad, he thought, having heard stories of how these girls made a huge killing by ordering the most expensive wine.

"I'm beat tonight," he said. "Let's talk."

"That's fine. Whatever topic you like—about the cloud and rain, coming and becoming each other, about the peach blossom giggling at the spring wind, or about boring holes to steal a sight of each other. You must have seen the world. By the way, my name is Green Jade."

Cloud and rain again, so much quoted in the classical love stories, and boring holes for a sight of each other was a negative metaphor from the *Mencius*. She was clever, perhaps like in Liu Guo's poem, capable of wiping a hero's tear with a red handkerchief pulled out of her green sleeves.

Except that her slip was sleeveless, backless. She kicked off her high heels, drew her legs under her, and cuddled up closer on the sofa.

"Please tell me something about your work here," he said.

"If that's what you'd like, sir," she said, taking a gulp of her juice. "The job doesn't bring in easy money as people would like to think. Of course, I earn a tip from a generous client like you, two to three hundred Yuan. On a lucky streak, I may have two customers a night. With so many girls competing, however, it's possible to go without a client for days. The club doesn't pay me a single penny. On the contrary, I have to pay the club the 'table fee.' "

"Why? That doesn't make sense. You do the work, not the club."

"According to the club owner, he has to pay the rent, for the management, and for protection too—both to the gangsters and the police."

"What about other services apart from the karaoke part?"

"Depends what you need, where and when. You have to be specific," she said. "Let me sing a song for you first."

Perhaps his manner of questioning bothered her. She had to sing a song or two for her tip, anyway. Her choice was a surprising one—Su Dongpo's "Shuidiao Getou," about the mid-autumn festival. She started singing and dancing, her bare feet floating sensually like lotus flowers on the red carpet, flowing to the second stanza of the poem.

Moving around the vermilion mansion, /coming through the carved window, / the moon shines on the sleepless./ No cause for it to be /so spiteful as to choose / to appear full, bright,/ when we stay in separation? / As people have sorrows and joys, / meeting or parting, / as the moon waxes and wanes / in clear or cloudy skies, / things may never be perfect. / May we all live long, sharing / the same fair moon, / though thousands of miles apart. . . .

The madam came back like an apparition from the moon. "What a marvelous girl! You know what, she used to study ballet. May we all live long, sharing the fair moon. A generous tip for my introduction, please."

"You did not tell me that," he said, producing two ten Yuan bills.

"Every Shanghainese knows that," she snapped, pocketing the money as she stalked out. "So cheap! You want me to live on the howling western wind?"

His Big Buck connections might have paid more, but he didn't know.

"Don't worry about her," Green Jade said, perching herself on his lap. "She's no real madam. Just a pimp."

Perhaps he'd better ask his questions quickly, and then call it a night.

"I've heard that there's a serial murderer stalking around, going after girls in the entertainment business. Are you worried, Green Jade?"

"You bet," she said, squirming uncomfortably against him. "One of the victims worked in a nightclub like this, I've heard. Everybody is on alert. But it's useless."

"Why?"

"Why? You are a new customer here. A successful man—not simply a money-stinking upstart, but a man of learning, a successful attorney or something like that. That much I knew at first sight. But that's about all. Still, if you ask me out, I will follow you without raising any questions. Our business has suffered because of the case. Customers are worried about police raids, like at the Joy Gate. Some of them will wait until the storm blows over—"

There was a light knock on the door.

Before she said anything, the door opened and a boy of five or six came in. "Mom, Uncle Brown Bear wants you to sing the Weeping Sand for him. Madam wants me to tell you that."

"I'm sorry. He's my son. There's no one to take care of him at home tonight," she said. "Brown Bear is a regular customer. It's his favorite song. I'll come back soon."

"Brown Bear is your regular customer," Chen said. Whether it was a deliberate arrangement with the madam, he didn't know. Green Jade must have figured out he was anything but a real Big Buck.

"You are different, I know," she said, leaning over to kiss him on the forehead before she turned to her son. "Go back to the office. Don't come out again."

For a moment, Chen didn't know what to do, left alone in the room. Looking around, he saw it was not so different from other KTV rooms, except that it was more luxuriously furnished. And he was disconcerted by the light footsteps pattering outside the room. Perhaps the child's. She shouldn't have brought her boy to such a place. Fortunately he was "different," not a regular. Or the little boy could have stumbled upon a traumatizing scene. . . .

Suddenly, he shivered.

Now he had one suspect with a motive—Mei's son.

On that fatal afternoon long ago, when Mei's son returned home, what he stumbled upon was his widowed mother having sex with another man. That explained his running away in shock and her running out naked after him.

All the information gathered about him was coming back. He had the motive, he knew the dress, and he was familiar with things about her life.

That would explain a lot of things—the revenge against Tian and Jasmine, the exact duplication of the dress, the location of the first body. . . .

But what kind of a man was he now? Neither Professor Xiang nor Comrade Wong knew much. He hadn't disappeared, however. He had come back and sold the Old Mansion for understandable reasons.

All of this fit into a psychological profile Chen had discussed with Yu—a loner with a trauma in his childhood, possibly during the Cultural Revolution, and possibly with an attachment to his mother. . . .

Another waitress walked into the room, this one wearing an apron that bore an image of a bag of popcorn. She placed a small basket of popcorn on the coffee table. Chen took out a ten Yuan bill.

"It's fifty."

"Fine." He tried to behave like a good customer, taking out his wallet. For the moment, he would like to, for a new scenario had just dawned on him in this very room. He put a hundred Yuan bill on the table and motioned to her to leave.

"Thank you, sir. I used to be a model, but it's a profession of only three or four years."

It was then that Green Jade returned, staring at the popcorn girl like an intruding alien, who turned to leave in a hurry.

"Sorry," Green Jade said. "Can I have another cup of juice?"

The drink came, along with another fruit platter. Maybe it was conventional in the house. The waiter didn't even bother to ask for his approval.

That concerned him. The small fees were adding up, though he didn't have to worry about extra service, like "the rain and cloud," Green Jade had suggested. She started peeling an orange for him.

He excused himself and went out into the corridor toward a restroom in the corner. Closing the restroom door after him, he counted the money left in his wallet. He still had about nine hundred Yuan. That should do for the night. But he didn't want to go back immediately. He wanted to straighten out his thoughts, and it was difficult for him to do so with Green Jade and other waitresses coming and going all the time.

But he noticed a hot towel on a white dish being pushed in through under the door—possibly by the restroom attendant kneeling on the ground. Chen was revolted. Pushing open the door, he put a handful of change on a white bowl on the sink and left.

When he seated himself on the sofa in the private room, Green Jade leaned over to feed him a fresh tangerine with her slender fingers, the candlelight incessantly flickering from the animal-shaped container.

"Where are you going to spend the night?" she softly inquired. "It's so late. The frost thick, the road slippery. Don't leave. Really, few walk outside."

It came almost like an echo from a Song dynasty poem, he recalled, about the rendezvous between the decadent emperor and a delicate courtesan.

Seeing no response from him, she placed his hand on her bare, smooth thigh.

"Sorry, I have to leave, Green Jade," Chen said. "Please give me the bill. It's been a great night. Thanks."

"If you insist," she said. "You may pay me the tip now."

After he paid her three hundred Yuan, she had a waiter send in the bill.

A glance at the bill showed him the trouble. A cup of fruit juice cost one hundred Yuan. She had two cups. Plus his tea at one hundred twenty. The two fruit platters at two hundred fifty each. The four small dishes of dried fruits on the table came with a price too, with eighty Yuan each. And there was a twenty percent service fee. Altogether, the bill amounted to one thousand, three hundred.

It was a ripoff. But he was not in a position to protest, not as a chief inspector. As such, he might be able to get away for the night, but the stories about it would cost him much more.

"What?" she said.

"I'm so sorry, Green Jade, I don't have enough cash with me."

"Well—how much do you have?"

"About nine hundred—now six hundred after the tip."

"Don't worry. They won't kill you if you really don't have enough money," she whispered in his ear. "But you have to say you have paid me only one hundred Yuan."

That was probably why she had wanted him to pay the tip first. An experienced girl, Chen reflected, seeing a heavy-built man enter the room.

"He is Manager Zhang," she introduced.

"Sorry, it's the first time for me, Manager Zhang. I don't have enough money with me." Chen took out all his money and placed it on the coffee table.

"How much do you have?" Zhang said without counting the money.

"About six hundred," Chen said. "I'll bring seven hundred next week. I give you my word."

"Has he paid you the tip?" Zhang turned to the girl with a frown.

"Yes, he has. One hundred Yuan." She added, "He's been here for about only two or three hours. And I had to be away with Brown Bear for quite a while."

"Do you have a card?" Zhang asked.

"What card?" He wouldn't give him his business card, whether as cop or as a poet.

"Credit card."

"No, I don't have one."

To Chen's surprise, Zhang glanced at the money on the table, picked up two twenty Yuan bills, and pushed them back to Chen.

"It's the first time for you," Zhang said. "Those small dishes are on the club tonight. So are the fruit platters. You have to have your taxi money, Big Brother. It's a cold winter night outside."

It was almost anticlimactic. Perhaps it was in the best interest of the business to let a customer leave like this. It wasn't the time for Chen to find an explanation for his luck.

"Thank you so much, Manager Zhang."

"I have seen many people," Zhang said. "You are different, I know. If the hill does not turn, the water turns. If the water doesn't turn, the man turns. Who knows? We may bump into each other one day."

Zhang walked him out to the elevator. When the elevator door opened, a late customer emerged. A group of girls hurried to offer their services to the new guest with a silver ring of laughter. Chen saw Green Jade among them, running out barefoot.

She didn't look at him.

"Come again, Big Brother," Zhang said as the elevator door was closing. "It may be easier for you to get a taxi at the intersection of Henshan and Gaoan Roads."

Outside, Chen didn't get into a taxi.

It was almost four o'clock. He thought of a proverb: "Full of joy, the night is short." He wasn't sure he had enjoyed himself inside the club, but time had passed quickly there.

It was a cold night, though it was coming to its end. The exciting ideas he had while inside seemed to be somewhat chilled by the wind.

While some of the details in the case fit, others didn't.

The meeting with the retired neighborhood cop in a couple of hours would be crucial.

Afterward, Chen would check into the background of Mei's son, starting with the document concerning the sale of the Old Mansion, on which the seller, as the inheritor of the house, had to sign his name and perhaps provide some other information.

It was already Thursday, a day he couldn't afford to waste in the wrong direction.

But for the moment, he was wandering aimlessly. He had to move. It was cold. With most of the lights off, the street presented a vision he hadn't seen before. He turned into a side street, made another turn, and to his surprise, he emerged within sight of the Old Mansion again. It looked dark, deserted, desolate. A night bird flashed out of nowhere.

He thought of the poem by Su Shi, "Swallow Pavilion."

The night advanced, I awake, / no way to renew my walk / along the old garden: / a tired traveler stranded at the end of the world, / gazing homeward, heartbroken. / The Swallow Pavilion is deserted. / Where is the beauty? / Swallows alone are locked inside, for no purpose. / It is nothing but a dream, / in the past, or at present. / Whoever wakes out of the dream? / There is only a never-ending cycle / of old joy, and new grief. / Someday, someone else, / in view of the yellow tower at night, / may sigh deeply for me.

It was a sad poem. The pavilion was renowned because of Guan Panpan, a gifted Tang dynasty poet and courtesan who lived there. Guan fell in love with a poet, and after his death, she shut herself up, receiving no visitor or client for the rest of her life. Many years later, Su Shi, a Song dynasty poet, visited the pavilion and wrote the celebrated poem.

Chen imagined Mei standing in the back garden of the mansion, holding the hand of her little boy, shining like a radiant cloud in her red mandarin dress. . . .

Shivering, he made his way to the food market. Several leaves fell in the fading starlight, dropping to the hard ground with a sound like the falling of the bamboo slips used for divination at an ancient temple, darkly portentous.

There was no one visible in the market yet. Near the entrance, he was surprised to see a long line of baskets—plastic, bamboo, rattan, wood, straw—of all shapes and sizes, stretching to a concrete counter under a sign that read "yellow croaker," a fish very popular in Shanghai. Those baskets evidently stood for the wives who would soon come here, securing their positions in the line, their eyes still dreamy with their families' satisfaction on the dinner table.

He wondered whether it could be a scene that he had seen before, and he lit himself a cigarette against the wind.

Bang, bang, bang. There came a sudden clatter. He was startled by the sight of a night-shift worker cracking a gigantic frozen bar of fish with a huge hammer. Aware of Chen's approaching footsteps, the night worker turned around, appearing headless against the upturned collar of his cotton-padded imitation army overcoat. It was a ghastly image in the early morning.

Chen's nerves were still bad.

Soon, however, several middle-aged women entered the market, heading to the line to replace the baskets and bricks that marked their place. The market began to come alive.

Then a bell sounded, possibly an indication that the market was open for business, and peddlers started appearing everywhere, all at once. Some put their products on the ground, and some moved in behind stalls rented from the state-run market. It was more and more difficult to draw the line between the socialist and capitalist.

He saw an old man enter the market wearing a red armband.

TWENTY-SIX

THE OLD MAN WEARING the red armband was examining vegetables here, checking fish there, yet was carrying no basket. He must be Fan.

Not too long ago, Chen had witnessed a similar scene, that of Old Hunter patrolling another market. Fan's function here was different, however, as "private peddlers" had become the norm in "China's brand of socialism." In an age of "everybody looking forward to money," those peddlers were problematic because of their unbridled deceptive practices. It was no longer simply a matter of putting ice into fish or injecting water into chickens but of painting their product, selling spoiled meat, hawking poisonous fungus. So Fan's responsibility consisted mainly of controlling those fakes, which were sometimes fatal.

Chen walked up to the old man, who was questioning a shrimp peddler.

"You must be Uncle Fan."

"Yes. Who are you?"

"Can I talk to you—alone?" Chen handed over his business card. "It's important."

"Sure," Fan said, turning to the peddler. "Next time, I won't let you get away so easily."

"Let's have a pot of tea there," Chen said, pointing to a small eatery behind the "yellow croaker" counter. "We can sit and talk."

"They don't serve tea, but I'll ask them to make a pot for us," Fan said. "Call me Comrade Fan. It's a form of address no longer popular, but I've just gotten used to it. It reminds me of the years of the socialist revolution, when everyone was equal and working toward the same goal."

"You are right, Comrade Fan," Chen said, reminded that *comrade* was becoming a euphemism for "homosexual" among the young and fashionable in Hong Kong and Taiwan. He wondered whether Fan knew anything about the changing meaning. Linguistic evolution, like that of *thirsty illness*, was so very reflective of ideological change.

There was a couplet on both sides of the eatery door, which read vertically, "Breakfast, lunch, dinner—the same. Last year, this year, next year—like that." Above the couplet was a horizontal comment, "True in your mouth."

The taxi money left him by the nightclub manager would probably be enough, Chen calculated, for breakfast here. A waiter recommended the house special: Xi'an *mo* in mutton soup. *Mo* was a hard, baked cake, which people could break into small or large pieces as they preferred before having it boiled in the mutton soup. The waiter brought them a pot of hot tea for free.

"Comrade Fan, let me toast you with tea, though tea is not enough to show my respect."

"People don't burn incense to the Three Treasures Temple without a reason. You are a busy man, Chief Inspector Chen. I don't think you came to an old retired man like me for nothing."

"Yes, I have some questions for you. According to the neighborhood committee here, you alone can help me."

"Really! Please tell me how."

"We're engaged in a homicide investigation. I would like to ask you some questions about Mei, who used to live here. She was once the mistress of the Ming Mansion. At that time, you were the neighborhood cop."

"Mei—yes, but she died such a long time ago. How could she be involved in your investigation?"

"At the moment, all I can say is that information about her may really help our work."

"Well, I came here as a neighborhood cop two or three years before the Cultural Revolution. How old were you then? Still in elementary school, weren't you?"

"Yes," Chen nodded, raising his cup.

"The job of a neighborhood cop may be nothing in the nineties," Fan said, breaking the *mo* into smaller bits, as if they were parts of his memory, "but in the early sixties, with Chairman Mao's call for class struggle resounding all over the country, the job carried a lot of responsibilities. Everyone could be a class enemy secretly bent on sabotaging our socialist society—especially so in this neighborhood. A considerable number of residents were black in their class status. After 1949, some of the families were driven out because of their connection to the Nationalists, and working-class families moved in. Still, there were families with ties both to the old and new regimes, so they kept their mansions here. Like the Mings."

"What about the Mings?"

"They kept theirs because the old man, an influential investment banker, had denounced Chiang Kai-shek in the late forties. So the Communists declared him to be a 'patriotic democratic personage,' leaving his fortune untouched. His son was a teacher at the Shanghai Music Institute who married Mei, a violinist who also taught there. They had a son, Xiaozheng. Inside the mansion, they lived in affluence, for which their working-class neighbors grumbled a lot. As a neighborhood cop, I had to pay extra attention to them.

"Things changed dramatically with the outbreak of the Cultural Revolution. The old man died of a heart attack, which actually spared him all the humiliations. But his family was not so fortunate. Mei's husband was put into isolation interrogation as a British secret agent for the crime of having listened to the BBC. He hung himself.

"Then their house fell too. People came and took over rooms as their own. The Mings—now only Mei and her son—were pushed out into an attic room above the garage, originally the servants' quarters."

"No one did anything about it?" Chen said, but he immediately realized the ridiculousness of his question. His family, too, had been driven out of their three-bedroom apartment at the beginning of the Cultural Revolution.

"Don't you remember a popular quote from Chairman Mao? 'There are thousands of arguments for revolution, but the principal one is: it is justified to rise in rebellion.' It was considered a revolutionary activity to take away property from the rich."

"Yes, I remember. Red Guards came to my family too. Sorry for the interruption, Comrade Fan. Please go on."

"In the third year of the Cultural Revolution, there appeared on their garden wall a counterrevolutionary slogan—or something that resembled one, consisting of two short phrases. One was 'Down With,' and the other was 'Chairman Mao.' They were possibly put there by two kids, at different times. They just happened to appear close together on the wall. But something like that was enough to turn the people in the mansion into possible suspects. Because of the class struggle, focus naturally fell on the Ming family, the only one of black class status. And especially on the boy. No one could prove he did it, but no one could prove that he didn't do it, either.

"So a joint investigation group was formed, with members from the neighborhood committee and from the Mao Team at Mei's institute. The boy was locked up in the back room of the neighborhood committee—alone, in so-called isolation interrogation, which was known to be effective in breaking the resistance of a class enemy. In fact, Mei's husband had committed suicide after a week in isolation interrogation.

"She was terrified that the son would follow in the footsteps of the father. For days she was begging around like a headless fly. She even came to me. I was helpless. In those years, the local district police station was practically taken over by those rebels. So what could a neighborhood cop do?

"Then one early afternoon the boy was suddenly released. No real evidence or witness was found against him, it was said. Besides, he had caught a high fever in the back room, and the guard on duty there didn't want to keep him. So he went straight home, but upon pushing open the door, it looked as if he had seen a ghost. He turned around, fleeing and screaming. His mother rushed out after him—stark naked. She stumbled on the stairs and fell all the way down.

"He might or might not have heard her fall, but he didn't go back. He kept running like mad. Out of the house, along the street, all the way back to that back-room office—"

"That's strange," Chen said. "Did you talk to her neighbors about what happened that afternoon?"

"I did, to several of them," Fan said. "Particularly to Tofu Zhang, a neighbor in the building, who happened to be home that afternoon. He was still sleeping after working the night shift, when he heard the eerie sound. So he jumped out of bed and saw her running out naked, calling after her son. He didn't see the boy and guessed that she must have had a nightmare. But then she fell, tumbling, hitting her head against the hard ground. He thought about going out to help, but he hesitated. He was just married, and his jealous wife could have reacted like a tigress to the sight of Zhang together with a naked woman. He thought better of it and closed the door.

"No one came to her side until a couple of hours later. She died that day without regaining consciousness.

"The boy was sick for a week, delirious with a high fever. Some sympathetic neighbors managed to put him in a hospital. When he recovered, he found himself back in the empty attic room, facing his mother's picture in a black frame. It was hard for him to understand what had happened, but he understood it was useless for him to ask."

"Did the neighborhood or local police station try to look into the circumstances of her death?" Chen interrupted again.

"No, it was nothing for a woman of her black family background to die those days. An accident, the neighborhood committee concluded. I tried to talk to the boy, but he wouldn't say anything."

Comrade Fan sighed, breaking the last piece of *mo*, putting them all back into the bowl, and rubbing his hands.

It was a more detailed account about the circumstances of her death, but it didn't provide anything really new or substantial.

Chen had a feeling that Fan had something left unsaid. An old, experienced cop like Fan, however, knew what he should and shouldn't say, and there was little Chen could do about it.

Was it possible that Fan, too, had been a secret admirer? Chen made no immediate comment, finishing his part of the *mo*-breaking. The waiter took their two bowls to the kitchen. An old woman passed by their table, waving a string of beads toward them.

"I've heard that she was a stunner in her day," Chen said. "Did she have some admirer or lover?"

"It's an interesting question," Fan said. "But in those days, it was unimaginable for a woman of her black family background to have a secret lover. Even husbands and wives were divorced because of political considerations. 'A couple are like two birds; when in a disaster, one flies to the east, one to the west.' "

"It's a quote from the *Dream of the Red Chamber*," Chen said. "You have read a lot."

"Well, what can a retired old cop do? I read books while babysitting my grandson."

"Now can you tell me something about her son, Comrade Fan?"

"He moved out of the neighborhood to stay with a relative. After the Cultural Revolution, he studied at a college and got a good job, I heard. That's about all I know."

Chen hesitated to talk about the possibility he had been contemplating. He had nothing to support such a wild scenario. At least he should check some documents first.

"What a tragic story," he said. "Sometimes you can hardly believe that these things happened during the Cultural Revolution."

"How many things have happened, true or false, past or present, and you talk about them over a cup of wine," Fan said. "The tea here is not too bad."

It was like an echo from another classic novel.

Then Chen's cell phone rang. It was Detective Yu.

"Did you call me last night, Chief?"

"Yes, but it was late. So I was going to give you a call this morning."

"What's it all about, Chief? Where have you been? I looked everywhere for you. And where are you—"

"I know, and I'll explain later. Right now I'm in the company of Comrade Fan, a retired neighborhood cop of the Henshan Road Area. He is helping me."

"A neighborhood cop of Henshan Road?"

"Yes. Whatever you are doing at this moment, drop it. Go to Tian's steel mill and gather as much information as possible about him, particularly about his activity as a member of the Mao Zedong Thought Propaganda Team. Call me with anything you get—"

"Hold on, Chief. Party Secretary Li is having another emergency meeting this morning. It's Thursday morning."

"Forget about Party Secretary Li and his political meeting. If he says anything, tell him it's my order."

"I'll do that," Yu said. "Anything else?"

"Oh, ask Old Hunter to give me a call." He added, "It's important. As you have said, it's Thursday."

The waiter brought them a small dish of peeled garlic, a sort of appetizer for the *mo* in the mutton soup.

"Oh, do you know Old Hunter?" Fan asked as Chen turned off his phone.

"Yes, his son Yu Guangming is my longtime partner. Old comrades like you, like Old Hunter, are so resourceful. He is doing a great job at the traffic control committee."

"Now I remember, Chief Inspector Chen. You were the acting head of the traffic office, and you recommended him for the position. Old Hunter mentioned it to me," Fan said, putting down his chopsticks. "You also mentioned someone in a steel mill?"

"Yes, Tian of Shanghai Number One Steel Mill," Chen said. "About the investigation, let me put it this way. Mei passed away a long time ago, but the exact circumstances of her death may throw light on another case involving people still alive, including Tian."

"But what can you do about something that happened during the Cultural Revolution? It's a can of worms the government doesn't want to open up."

"Confucius says, 'You know that it is impossible to do, but as long as it is something you should do, you have to do it.' "

"It's not common for a young chief inspector to quote Confucius like that," Fan said. "Do you really mean—"

The phone rang again. This time, it was Old Hunter.

"What's up, Chief Inspector Chen?"

"I have to ask another favor of you, Uncle Yu," Chen said. "We are going to play our old trick again—like in the national model case, remember? I hate to bother you like that, but I can't rely on those people in the bureau."

"A new case?"

"I'll explain the case to you later, but any responsibility for it will be mine."

"Come on. You don't have to explain anything, Chief Inspector Chen. Whatever you want me to do, it's not something against the conscience of a retired cop, that much I know. So go ahead and tell me: when and where?"

"At this moment, I want you to hold yourself ready with a traffic violation ticket and a tow truck. Also, you'd better stay in the office for the day, so I can reach you there at any time." He changed the topic abruptly. "Oh, I am talking with someone you know: Comrade Fan. Do you want to say hi to him?"

"Hi, Old Hunter," Fan said, taking the phone. "Yes, I'm talking with Chief Inspector Chen. You have worked with him, haven't you?"

For the next two or three minutes, Fan listened carefully, barely interrupting except for saying "yes" and nodding. With the phone volume turned up to the maximum, some words in Old Hunter's excited voice were indistinctly audible, possibly telling Fan his opinion of the chief inspector. Possibly positive. But Fan remained cautious, speaking only single words or fragmented phrases instead of sentences.

Fan finally said, "I will, of course. I owe you a big one, Old Hunter."

The waiter came back to the table, carrying over two big bowls of *mo* in the steaming hot mutton soup, the *mo* golden against red soup with chopped green onion. The sight of it drove away the lingering chill of the night.

"Old Hunter and I have been cops all our lives," Fan said, raising his chopsticks. "After over thirty years on the force, we remain at the bottom. You know Old Hunter well. An able, conscientious cop. Just because he's incapable of doing things against his conscience, he's a failure professionally. I may not be as able, but I, too, have held to my principles."

"Confucius says," Chen said, " 'There are things you do, and things you do not do.' It's not easy to be a cop."

"Your father was a Confucian scholar, Old Hunter just told me. No wonder," Fan said, putting down his chopsticks. "Many years ago, I worked with Old Hunter on a homicide case. I got into big trouble, and he saved me. Suffice it to say that it was something I did on principle, which I never regretted. As a result, I was reassigned as a neighborhood cop. It was a huge setback for a young officer, but without his help, I could have ended up in one of those labor camps. Now that he's told me what kind of a man you are, I don't think I need to be concerned anymore."

"Thank you for telling me all this. But what are you concerned about, Comrade Fan?"

"About some aspects of her death. I didn't go into detail regarding them because—" Fan cleared his throat. "Because an old man's memory may not be that reliable. After all, it happened so many years ago."

Memory could always serve as a face-saving excuse. The change came from his comradeship with Old Hunter, Chen guessed.

"Also because I didn't know what you are really looking for," Fan went on. "I didn't want her memories to be dragged again through the humiliation mire for nothing."

"I understand," Chen said, recalling a similar statement by Professor Xiang.

"I think I mentioned Tofu Zhang."

"Yes, you did. Zhang hesitated and closed the door without going out to help."

"Before closing the door, he saw someone sneaking out of her room. Zhang thought it was Tian, but he wasn't absolutely sure."

"Tian—the Mao Team member from the steel mill."

"Yes, the very Tian you wanted your partner to check."

"Did anyone ask Tian about that afternoon?"

"According to Tian, he had planned to have a talk with her, but she appeared too disturbed, so he left," Fan said. "But that didn't hold water. Zhang saw him leaving after Mei's accident, not before. In those years, however, who wanted to question the word of a Mao Team member? She died in an accident anyway. It was nobody's fault."

"The district police station didn't do anything about it?"

"I was then about your age," Fan said, taking a spoon of soup instead of responding directly. "I still wanted to do something as a cop. When I heard about the tragedy, I hurried over to the scene. There I took pictures, and I talked to some of her neighbors, including Zhang. According to another neighbor, two or three nights before, he heard something weird in her room. As an old proverb goes, there are a lot of troubles before a widow's door—let alone such a black widow. No one reported it. I believed that it was worth investigating. It was no coincidence that Tian went in and out of her room. What's more, if she thought to ask me for help, she could well have turned to Tian too. The poor woman was desperate, ready to do anything for her son. And Tian, unlike me, had the power to help."

"Yes, it was unusual for Tian to join that particular Mao Team at

Mei's school in the first place," Chen said, "not to mention his then joining the investigation group in the neighborhood here."

"The release of the boy was sudden and suspicious. Also, I talked to a member of the neighborhood committee about it. It was Tian that had made the decision, though he hadn't specified the release time. The boy was sick with a high fever, so she thought she might as well let him out that afternoon."

"That explains the boy's reaction upon his return—you can imagine the scene he stumbled upon."

"Exactly. It was too much for him, and that's why she ran after him like that. She knew what a shock it must have been. She forgot her nakedness, she slipped, and she fell."

"And that also explains why the son, who loved his mother so much, ran away without even looking back," Chen said. "Indeed, all those details make sense."

"But it was a time when the police bureaus themselves were seen as a bourgeois institution. Red Guards and Worker Rebels alone had the real power. When I talked to my boss about an investigation, he brushed aside the idea."

"A question. Do you still have the pictures, Comrade Fan? The pictures of the death scene, I mean."

"Yes. I have them at home, but it may take a while to dig them out."

"I would really appreciate it if you could show them to me today."

"Wait a few minutes for me then." Fan got up and strode out of the eatery.

Chen was sitting alone at the table, waiting, when the waiter put the bill down. As he had guessed, the taxi money left in his pocket was more than enough for the meal. It cost less than seven Yuan each. For the amount spent in the nightclub last night, he could come here every morning for three months.

In *Dream of the Red Chamber*, a young girl calculates that a crab dinner in the Grand View Garden costs more than a farmer's food for a whole year. The same gap had appeared in today's society.

Chen rose to pay the bill at the counter. As he took the change, he cast another look at the couplet on the door. It was in bold calligraphy, a sharp contrast to the shabby appearance of the eatery. The horizontal comment—"True in your mouth"—seemed to be humorous, yet thought-provoking.

"It's not just about food," the restaurant owner said with a smile. "The character 'mouth' carries an association of food, but of language as well. All the words come out of the mouth, true or false."

"Yes. The couplet reminds me of another one in the *Dream of the Red Chamber,* in a celestial palace—"

"I know the one you are talking about, on the arch in the Illusion Wakening Palace, where Jia Baoyu reads the couplet and gets lost, but I can't remember the exact lines."

"The couplet reads like this," Chen said. " 'When the fictional is real, the real is fictional; where there's nothing, there's everything.' " *Jia zuo zhenshi zhen ji jia, wu wei youchu you yi wu.*

"Exactly. You must be a well-to-do scholar. A prosperous attorney or something," the owner said, glancing at the briefcase on the table.

The Italian leather briefcase was a gift from Gu, who insisted that it became Chief Inspector Chen. Ironically, it could have become him in the eyes of Green Jade too, who also took him as a prosperous "attorney or something" last night.

"The author of *Dream of the Red Chamber* was good at making puns," the restaurant owner said, "even in the names of the characters. The name Jia Baoyu, the hero of the saga, could mean 'fictional gemstone,' and there is another family in the book, Zheng, which means 'real'—"

At that word, Chen's heart skipped a beat.

Ending the conversation abruptly, he went back to the table and pulled up his briefcase. Before his departure for the vacation village, he had stuffed the files on the housing development case into the briefcase along with those on the red mandarin dress case, though he hadn't planned to study either of them there. In his hurried return to Shanghai, he hadn't had the time to look at them.

He took out the folder on the housing development case and started reading the part about Jia.

It was scanty and simplistic, focusing on Jia's possible antigovernment motive. It provided little solid information. Only a couple of sentences about his unhappy childhood during the Cultural Revolution, in which he had lost his parents. It didn't even mention his parents' names.

But that seemed to be enough for Director Zhong to conclude that Jia took the case for revenge over the Cultural Revolution.

Chen moved on to the part about Jia's personal life in the last few years.

Again, it was scanty. Perhaps because Jia kept a low profile in spite of his controversial cases. It was said that the US stocks left by his grandfather were worth millions, making Jia one of the most eligible bachelors in the city. So his continuous celibacy was noteworthy. Some even had suspicions about his sexual orientation, though there was nothing to support that. In fact, he'd had a girlfriend—a model—though they had since parted. She was surnamed Xia, about fifteen years younger than he.

On impulse, Chen snatched up his cell phone and called White Cloud.

"Do you know someone named Xia in the entertainment business? She was a model before."

"Xia—Xia Ji, possibly. I don't know her personally, but she's well-known in those circles," she said. "She no longer works as a model. She's said to have shares in a bathhouse, Gilded Age. She's a success story, which is why I've heard of her."

"A model for the bathhouse business?"

"Do you really not know?" she asked. "In a massage room there, everything is possible. But she's a partner in the business."

He recalled something about the model girlfriend of Jia's somewhere. He remembered because of her name, Xiaji, which in Chinese could also mean "summer." Chen had actually met her on a panel for a contest entitled "Three Beautiful Contest—Heart, Body, and Mind," a pageant sponsored by the New World Corporation. Chen served as a panelist out of obligation to Gu. As a published poet, he was supposed to be "capable of judging what's poetic." Xia was also there as a panelist. They didn't talk much during the contest, nor had they spoken since.

"Thank you, White Cloud. I'll talk to you later," he said, finishing up the phone call at the sight of Fan returning with an envelope in his hand.

"Comrade Fan, would you tell me the boy's name again?"

"Why? Xiaozheng, or Zheng, so that should be Ming Zheng, or Ming Xiaozheng. I don't remember which particular written character for 'zheng.' As for 'Xiao,' the character could have been added to the little boy's name as a sort of endearment, you know."

"Yes, occasionally my mother still calls me 'Xiao Cao' too."

"What's your point?"

"Chinese names are capable of meaning something. For instance, Jia Ming can mean 'fictional name.' And Ming Zheng, at least in pronunciation, can mean 'name real.' "

"What are you driving at, Chief Inspector Chen?"

"If that little boy changed his name to something like Jia Ming—false name of the descendent of the illustrious Ming Mansion, would that make sense?"

"In Chinese culture, few would change their family name, but for Mei's son, I would say it's possible. The past could have been too painful for him. And the pseudonym may have a message in itself, as if telling the world that the one with that name was 'fictional,' hiding his real identity from public scrutiny. But who is Jia Ming?"

"At this moment, it's only a guess." Chen decided not to go into detail and changed the subject. "Oh, you've brought the pictures."

Fan produced a bunch of photographs. They were black and white, not of high quality, shot from a number of perspectives. Some close-ups were blurred and out of focus.

Still, they were shocking images. Different poses of a dead woman, abandoned, lying naked on the gray concrete ground. As Chen gazed, he juxtaposed them with the photograph of Mei wearing a mandarin dress, taking her son's hand. . . .

In poetry, when two images are juxtaposed, a possible new meaning emerges. He didn't exactly grasp it yet, but he knew one was there.

"I don't know how I can ever thank you enough, Comrade Fan."

"I took the pictures as a cop," Fan said with a sudden suggestion of uneasiness, "but I soon realized there would be no investigation. Who was going to bother about such a 'black' woman? And I hated the idea of having the pictures of her naked body being passed around—not for the investigation, but for—you know what I mean."

"You are a man of principle," Chen said. "I am so glad I have met you today."

"After the Cultural Revolution, I thought about reopening the case. But the government wanted people to look ahead. So what could I do—with no evidence and no witness? Besides, Mei may have died because of Tian, but technically, it wasn't even a homicide case."

"You are right," Chen said, wondering why Fan made the speech.

"I think you may be right about her son's name change. He wants to forget about the past. That's why he sold the Old Mansion and never came back here." Fan paused shortly before he went on, "I have done nothing for her, and if what I have told you will be used against her son—"

"I have nothing but a theory at the moment. Whatever you have told me will never be used against him," Chen said, deciding that was true, to a certain extent. "A child's suffering in those years was no crime."

"Thank you for telling me that, Chief Inspector Chen."

"I have to ask you a favor. Can I borrow these pictures for a few days? I won't show them to irrelevant people. I will return them to you as soon as I finish using them."

"Of course you may."

"Thank you, Comrade Fan. You have helped a lot."

"No, you don't have to thank me for anything," Fan said. "It's what I should have done. If anything, I should thank you."

TWENTY-SEVEN

FOR THE FIRST TIME, Chen felt he was on the right track.

After leaving Fan, he made a phone call to Jia's office. A secretary answered the phone and told him that Jia was out of town until this afternoon. That might be just as well, Chen reflected. He needed time to think.

He contacted the housing office of the district government, asking for the documents concerning the sale of the Old Mansion, particularly the seller's real name and his relationship to the original owners of the mansion. The clerk promised to provide the requested information as soon as possible. For the moment, Chen decided not to reach out to Director Zhong for any more background information about Jia.

But in the meantime, he thought he should do something else. So far, what he had learned was about Jia's past, things that had happened over twenty years earlier. Now he had to learn about Jia's current life. Too much was at stake that night, and Chen couldn't afford to make a mistake.

He dialed Little Zhou and asked him to meet him in front of the Old Mansion.

He walked over to the restaurant, which looked different in the morning. With no neon lights and pretty waitresses standing outside, it looked more like a residential building.

After finishing a cigarette, he thought about calling Overseas Chinese Lu, when Little Zhou arrived in the bureau car.

"Do you know Gilded Age?" Chen asked.

"The bathhouse on Puming Road," Little Zhou said. "I've heard of it."

"Let's go there. Oh, stop by a bank on the way. I need to get some cash."

"Yes, it could be obscenely expensive," Little Zhou said, starting the car without looking over his shoulder.

Chen could see the bureau driver glancing at him in the rearview mirror. A morning trip to a bathhouse was unusual, not to mention his unexplained disappearance for the past week.

The traffic was terrible. It took them about forty-five minutes before the car arrived at the bathhouse, which looked like a splendid imperial palace. There were already a large number of cars in the parking lot.

"I may need the car for the day, Little Zhou. Can you wait here for me?"

"Of course," Little Zhou said readily. "It's important, I know."

At the bathhouse entrance, Chen made inquiries about Xia.

"Yes, Xia's here," a young girl said, looking at her watch. "In the restaurant on the third floor."

As White Cloud had thought, Xia turned out to be a partner in the bathhouse. She was responsible for public relations and entertainment, including the fashion shows during lunch and dinner.

Chen was asked to purchase an entrance ticket and to change into bathhouse pajamas and plastic slippers before going up. He complied rather than reveal his identity as a cop.

As the elevator door opened out on the third floor, he glimpsed Xia sitting at a table in front of a stage near one end of the restaurant, wearing the identical house pajamas as Chen. She was sitting in the midst of several other girls and giving orders with the air of a prosperous entrepreneur.

Naturally, not all the girls would end up being as lucky as Xia, as in a line from a Tang dynasty poem, "A successful general comes walking out of the skeletons of ten thousand soldiers." Chen thought of the victims in the serial murder case.

Instead of moving to the table, he asked a girl to send his business card to Xia, who rose at once and came over.

"I saw you coming in, like a white crane standing out among the roosters, even before I recognized you," she said amiably. She took his hand and led him to another table. "I've seen your picture in the newspapers, Chief Inspector Chen. So you have to be our special guest today."

"I've seen more of yours, and on TV too," he said. "Sorry for having come to you like this, but I need to talk to you."

"You want to talk to me, Chief Inspector Chen?" she looked surprised.

"Yes. Now."

"But now isn't a good time. I have to take care of the fashion show for our anniversary party. It starts soon."

The fashion show might have less to do with fashionable clothes than with bodies barely covered in clothes. For the anniversary party, however, Xia had to take care of special guests.

"Are you going to walk on the stage yourself?"

"No, not necessarily."

"If it wasn't important, I wouldn't have come here without calling you first," he said, glancing toward the stage. "Maybe we can talk during the show."

She looked hesitant. The girls were standing at a respectful distance, waiting for her instruction. The band had already started to tune up a light melody. It was perhaps not a good place to talk.

"You aren't here for the show, I guess," Xia said. "How about you take a break in a VIP room, and I'll join you the minute the show gets under way."

"Fine, I'll wait for you there."

A young girl led him down to the second floor into a dimly lit room with an attached bathroom. There were two couches covered with white towels and a coffee table between them. A clothes tree stood with a couple of white terrycloth robes on it. Simple, yet cozy. Leaving, the girl closed the door behind her.

The room was warm and, sitting on the couch, he felt drowsy. A shower might help, he thought, so he took off his pajamas and stepped under the showerhead.

But the shower didn't help. Stepping out, he felt weak and lightheaded. He left a message for Yu, asking him to come over to Gilded Age after he was finished at the steel mill.

Chen lay down on the couch. Some light music floated over, faint, vague, like the chant from the temple in his childhood. In spite of himself, he fell asleep.

He woke up, aware of another person moving in the room. It was Xia, wearing a white terry robe, walking barefoot on the soft carpet, her hair still wet from a shower. She perched herself on the edge of his couch, putting her hand on his shoulders.

"You look tired," she said. "Let me give your shoulders a good rub."

"Sorry. I didn't—" He did not finish the sentence. There was no point telling her that he hadn't slept last night.

"Your friend Mr. Gu talks a lot about you," she said, her fingers soft on his shoulders, "and about your valuable help to his business."

That accounted for her hospitality. He hadn't made clear the purpose of his visit, so she must have assumed it was in connection to her business. A cop could make things difficult for a bathhouse with all its private rooms and massage girls. On the other hand, he could also choose to provide "valuable help," as Gu had phrased it.

"Mr. Gu is always exaggerating," he said. "Don't take his word for it."

"Well, what about the huge difference you made to his New World Project?"

Stories about his friendship with a Big Buck would do him no good, but for the moment he might as well let her believe them. He wasn't exactly in a position to force her to cooperate.

"Thank you for the massage," he said. "It's unbearable to receive favor from a beauty—and a model entrepreneur too."

"A romantic poet in a cop's uniform," she said giggling, "but one cannot be a model forever. 'Pluck a flower while you may, / or there will be barren twigs left for you.' "

The lines came from a Tang dynasty poem. It was surprising that she would quote them like that, talking about her own beauty as something to be plucked.

But then she was rolling him over as she changed her own position, kneeling, drawing her legs under her. He thought he caught a glimpse of her breast through the opening of her robe. She started massaging his back.

"You have a lot of knots in your back," she said, focusing on his lower back, her red-painted toes appealing against the white towel.

He recalled Scholar Zhang's comment about a femme fatale in "The Story of Yingying." It was a timely reminder as he lay there, weak and exposed, but it was strange that he would think of it at this moment.

"Thank you, Xia. You really have the magic touch. I'll have to come again." He stopped her and sat up. "But today I need to talk to you about something else."

"Yes, whatever you want to talk about," she said, moving over to the other couch. She sat reclining against the headboard, crossing her legs, revealing her bare thighs. As he had suspected, she had nothing on under the robe. "No one will disturb us here. The next show won't start until six. We have the afternoon to ourselves."

"I won't beat about the bush. It's about Jia, your ex-boyfriend."

"Jia—why?" She added in haste, "I broke up with him a long time ago."

"We have reason to believe that he's involved in a serious case."

"Whatever he might be involved in," she said, sitting up, "I don't know any more than what is in the official newspapers. That housing development case must be a serious headache to some important people."

She clearly thought that Chen had come about *that* case.

"That's an anticorruption case, and he's doing a good job. A headache to corrupt officials, as you said, but it's not my concern. I know better than to side with those corrupt Red Rats. Trust me. The reason why I am talking to you today has nothing to do with that case."

"I trust you, Chief Inspector Chen, but then why?"

"It's about another case," he said. "Of course you're not involved."

"So what do you want to talk to me about?"

"Whatever you know about him. All that you tell me here will be confidential—kept within this room. I'll never use it for the housing development case, I give you my word on that."

"That's a lot to talk about," she said slowly, crisscrossing her legs again. "I think I'd better talk to my attorney first."

He had anticipated this. Xia wasn't one of those girls who would give in easily to a cop. It could take days for him to obtain her cooperation under normal circumstances.

"You know why I've come to you like this, Xia?" Chen said. "It's about the red mandarin dress case."

"What? But that's impossible. How could he have done that?"

"He's the primary suspect at this moment." He paused deliberately before going on. "The bureau will stop at nothing. Anyone connected with him will be interrogated and reinterrogated. There will be a hurricane of publicity and that won't be good for you or for your business. So I want to talk to you first. I would hate to drag you through all that unpleasantness."

"Thank you for your thoughtfulness," she said. "I appreciate it."

"If he is not guilty, your statement will serve only to help him. It has nothing to do with the housing development case." He reached out his hand, patting hers. "Mr. Gu may have exaggerated about me, but he is right about one thing: good friends help each other. You are doing me a favor, I know."

It was a hint about an exchange of favors, and perhaps something more, which she couldn't miss. Rather bogus for a cop, but justifiable in an exigency, something recommended even in the Confucian classics he had been studying.

"So where shall I start?" she said, looking up at him.

"From the beginning," he said, "from your first meeting."

"It was about three years ago," she said. "I was a college student then, in my third year, when Jia came to give a talk about career choice. I was impressed. Several months later, I had an opportunity for a modeling career, so I went to consult with him. To be fair, I was the one that took the initiative, but he sent me flowers after my first performance. So we started going out. He was a broad-minded man, caring little about the gossip concerning my profession."

"What kind of man did you find him—not just as a lover?"

"A good man: intelligent, honest, and successful too."

"Did he talk to you about his life?"

"No, not really. His parents passed away during the Cultural Revolution and his childhood was not a happy one."

"Did he ever show you pictures of his parents? Say, his mother, who was quite beautiful?"

"No. He never even talked about her, but I knew he came from an illustrious family. I brought up the subject once, and he was surprisingly upset. So I never touched on the topic again."

"Did he often lose his self-control?"

"No, nothing like that. He could occasionally lose his temper, but for a busy attorney, it's understandable."

"Did he talk to you about his pressures or problems?"

"In today's society, who isn't under pressure? No, he didn't talk about it, but I could sense it. He handled controversial cases, you know. I saw several psychology books in his office. Possibly in an effort to find ways to release stress. From time to time, he would appear absentminded, as if suddenly thinking of a case, even during our closest moments."

"Did you notice any other symptoms?"

"Symptoms—of what?" she said. "Well, he didn't sleep well, if you want to count that as a symptom of something."

"Now, in your intimate moments, did you notice anything unusual about him?"

"Can you try to be a bit more specific, Chief Inspector Chen?"

"For instance, did he ever want you to dress in a special way?"

"Not really. Off the runway, I didn't want to dress like a model, and he showed no objection to that. He bought some clothes for me. Expensive, elegant, but not too fashionable. Which is his taste, I think. Once, he wanted me to go barefoot in a park like a country girl and a small rock cut my foot. He never asked me to repeat the experience."

"What about any special dress—say, a mandarin dress?"

"Mandarin dress? Not everyone can wear one well. I'm too tall and skinny. I explained that to him, so he didn't insist on it."

"Now a more personal question, Xia. Any deviance or problem in his sex life?"

"What do you mean?" She stared at him. "Is that supposed to be the reason we broke up?"

"I'm asking you this question, Xia, because it's relevant to our investigation."

No immediate response. A shrewd businesswoman, she knew how important it was to maintain connections with a senior police officer, especially when such a case loomed in the background. She propped herself up with a couple of pillows and picked out a cigarette.

"That's something to talk about in a private room," she resumed with a wry smile. "Do you want to know how we parted?"

"Yes," he said, lighting the cigarette for her.

"People talked a lot about our relationship, but in reality, it didn't go that far. In a restaurant or a café, he would let me hold his hand, and that's about the extent of the intimacy between us. Believe it or not, he never kissed me properly, just a peck on the forehead or something like it. About a year ago, there was a fashion show at the Thousand Island Lake, close to the Yellow Mountains, where he happened to have a meeting the same week. So I arranged for us to check into the same mountain hotel. At night, I walked into his room, where we embraced and kissed like real lovers for the first time. Perhaps because of the height, about one thousand feet above sea level, you know, we felt above and beyond the earth—so lost in passion, like in the waves of white clouds outside the hotel window. But of all a sudden, he disengaged himself, saying that he couldn't. What a disaster! The next morning we left the hotel, a shadow between us. That's how we parted."

"That could be very important to our work. Thank you so much, Xia," he said. "But I still have more questions for you."

"Yes?"

"In the mountains, he couldn't, or he wouldn't?"

"He couldn't. He would have checked into the hotel without having any thoughts about it."

"I think you're right. So it's a physical problem."

"Yes, he sort of acknowledged it, but he wouldn't listen to me about seeing a doctor." She said after a pause, "He had a lot of books in his office, as I mentioned, some on sexology and pathology too. He might have tried to help himself."

"I see. Have you kept in touch with him?"

"I didn't really resent him. He couldn't help it. After we broke up, he still sent me flowers from time to time. On the opening of the bathhouse too. So when I read about the housing development case, I sneaked into his office one evening."

"Did he arrange the meeting?"

"No, I didn't even call beforehand, because he had told me that his phone line might be tapped."

"You can't be too careful," Chen said, "but he might not have been in the office, and people could have seen you going there."

"He usually works late. When we were still seeing each other, I went to his office a lot. He gave me a key to his office's side door. So it's not easy for other people to see. Neither of us was interested in publicity."

"How does it work? I mean going through the side door."

"He bought his office, a large suite for himself, when the building was still under construction. Those buildings built in the late eighties don't have a proper garage. An office unit usually gets a parking spot or two in the back of the building. As his office suite is on the corner, there's a space at the side, sort of an enclave, between the outside wall and his suite, enough for an additional car. He had a side door installed so he can walk out of his office and almost directly into his car."

"Hold on, Xia. You mean no one can see him moving out of the office into his car?"

"If his car is parked there, yes. Though he has a reserved parking space in the back as well. Occasionally he has important visitors who don't want to be seen visiting him, so instead of using the front entrance, they park by the side door. I think that's what he told me. Anyway, he gave me keys to the side door so I could get in that way. No one could really see me, especially late in the evening—"

"I see. When did you meet with him about the housing development case?"

"About a month ago."

"So you had something important to tell him."

"To be frank, I have some official connections of my own. They threw out hints about the complications of the case. About a power struggle not only in Shanghai, but in Beijing too. Whatever the result, it won't do him any good."

"Yes, I have heard that too. What did he say to you?"

"He told me not to worry. Somebody in Beijing had contacted him, assuring him of an open and fair trial for the case. He didn't go into details, but he urged me not to contact him anymore."

"Did you ask him why?"

"Yes, I did. He wasn't specific, but he said it wasn't just because of the case—the housing development case."

"Did you notice anything else unusual about him?"

"He seemed to be even more restless than before. Something heavy on his mind. When I left his office, he hugged me and recited an odd quote from a Tang dynasty poem: 'Oh, if we could have met before I was married.' "

"Yes, that's strange. He's still single—"

Their talk was interrupted by a knock on the door.

"I have told them not to interrupt," she said apologetically before rising to open the door.

The man standing in the doorway was Detective Yu, whose expression was no less startled than hers.

TWENTY-EIGHT

"CHIEF INSPECTOR CHEN!" YU made no attempt to disguise his surprise.

He had hurried all the way over to the Gilded Age, not too surprised at the urgency Chen had requested for the meeting, yet wondering why Chen wanted to meet him there, of all the places, especially after his unexplained disappearance.

Now the door opened on a scene that more than confounded Yu. There, Chen was in the company of a gorgeous woman, both of them wrapped in bathrobes, like a couple relaxing at a luxurious resort.

"Oh, Detective Yu, my partner." Chen sat up to make the introductions. "Xia, the most celebrated model in Shanghai, also a partner in this grand bathhouse."

"Detective Yu, I've heard of you. Welcome," she said, smiling. "It's time for me to go back to work. Call me if you need anything else, Chief Inspector Chen."

"Thank you so much, Xia." He added, as if in afterthought, "Oh, do you still have the key?"

"The key? Yes, I may still have it. I'll check."

She walked out gracefully, her bare feet treading soundlessly on the carpet, and closed the door after her.

Yu knew he shouldn't be surprised by anything his eccentric boss did. Still, he couldn't restrain himself from making a sarcastic comment.

"You're really enjoying your vacation here, Chief."

"I'll explain everything—in time," Chen said, "but let me make a phone call first."

Chen called someone he knew well and left a short message. "Come to the bathhouse, Gilded Age."

Chen then turned and said to Yu, "Now sit down and tell me what you've found about Tian."

"I went to the factory this morning," Yu said, perching on the couch where Xia had reclined. The couch had a long impression, still slightly wet and warm from her body. "Most of his colleagues have retired or passed away. What I learned comes from here and there, some of which you may have already learned from the interview records."

"Maybe, but I haven't had the time to grasp it as a whole. So please tell me from the beginning."

It was hot in the room. Yu took off his padded jacket, wiping sweat from his forehead. Chen poured him a cup of oolong tea.

"Thanks, Chief," Yu said. "Tian started working there in the early fifties, one of the ordinary workers. At the outbreak of the Cultural Revolution, mass organizations like Red Guards and Worker Rebels sprung up everywhere. He joined a group of Worker Rebels called Red Flag, whose members came from factories all over the city. In response to Mao's call to grab the power from the 'capitalist road officials,' Tian turned into a somebody overnight, beating and bullying 'class enemies' in the name of the proletarian dictatorship. Shortly afterward he enlisted in a Mao Zedong Thought Propaganda Team that was dispatched to the Shanghai Music Institute. There he was said to be even more swashbuckling, riding roughshod over the intellectuals."

"Was there anything unusual about his activities in the team?" Chen interrupted.

"Normally, a Mao Team was made up of the workers from one factory and dispatched to one school, but at his own request, he joined a team consisting of the workers from a different steel factory. As for his 'revolutionary activities' there, I haven't learned much. That steel factory went into bankruptcy two or three years ago. No one at Tian's steel mill really knew anything, except that he must have bullied his way around. In the late seventies, with the Cultural Revolution officially declared a well-meant mistake by Mao, Tian withdrew from the colleges, crestfallen, returning to the factory.

"Then a policy was formulated regarding the 'three evildoers' during the Cultural Revolution. Tian fell into that category, but there were many 'Rebels' like him, and nothing was really done about them. But surprisingly, letters against him were sent to a city government cadre whose father, an old professor at the music institute, had been badly beaten during those years. The letters claimed Tian was the one who broke the old man's ribs, so an investigation was carried out. Some said he beat another teacher into paralysis, some claimed that he looted gold coins, and some mentioned that he had forced a woman to have sex with him through the power of his position. Nothing was really proved, but as a result, he was fired and sentenced to three years in prison. His wife divorced him and left with his daughter—"

There was a light knock on the door. Chen opened it and in came a couple of girls wearing house pajamas and slippers.

"Do you need massage service?" one of the girls asked sweetly. "Everything's on the house, General Manager Xia has given us specific instructions."

The other girl carried in a thermos bottle and made more tea for them in new cups with fresh tea leaves and hot water.

"No, we don't, thanks. Tell Xia not to worry about us. If we need anything, I'll let her know." The girls withdrew from the room and Chen resumed. "Well, so much for his history as a Mao Team member. How about his bad luck?"

"Strange things happened to Tian and his family. His ex-wife started seeing other men, which was to be expected for a divorced woman in her early thirties, but soon pictures of her sleeping with her boyfriend got around. Some were sent to her factory and those pictures 'nailed her to the pillar of humiliation.' In the early eighties, it was still a crime for people to have sex without a marriage license. She committed suicide out of shame. The local police looked into it. They suspected the incident was a dirty trick played by one of her lovers, but the investigation yielded nothing. The daughter went back to Tian."

"That was strange," Chen said. "An ordinary worker, divorced, not too young, and with a child. The men she was seeing were perhaps ordinary workers too. How could those pictures have been taken? By a professional? I don't think an ordinary worker could have afforded to hire one for that."

"Strange things also happened to Tian's restaurant—"

"Yes, I checked into the restaurant part," Chen said. "Did you talk to his former colleagues about his rotten luck?"

"Like his neighbors, his colleagues saw all of this as retribution," Yu said. "Whatever the interpretation, he has had the worst luck imaginable, like in some folk story."

"Retribution is a common motif in our folk stories. A man who has committed wrongs in his life—or in his previous life—is punished by a supernatural force that metes out justice. But do you really believe in such?"

"Do you believe there is something behind his bad luck?" Yu said, looking up sharply. "As a paralyzed man, more dead than alive, how could Tian be involved in the case?"

"Yesterday morning, I was at the Jin'an temple, rereading your interview with Weng, Jasmine's boyfriend, when an idea occurred to me. What if it wasn't luck, but a series of mishaps caused by a man? Something you learned at Tian's factory might very well confirm my suspicions."

"Now there's an idea," Yu said, though impatient with the way

Chen talked, digressing like Old Hunter before finally coming to the point, "but I still don't see the connection to the case."

"You've just said that, as a Mao Team member, Tian forced a woman to have sex."

"Yes, somebody mentioned it, but it wasn't confirmed."

"Do you know the name of that woman?"

"No one mentioned her name but she was probably a faculty member at the institute."

"You're following a very important trail. Let me show you something," Chen said, producing a picture. "Take a look at the woman."

"The woman—" Yu said. "She's in a mandarin dress."

"Look at the style."

"Yes, the style!" Yu examined it closely. "The very style. Do you mean—"

"The woman in the picture was Mei, a violinist who taught at the institute. She was abused by Tian—to be exact, she was forced to have sex with him for the sake of her son. On the afternoon she died, Tian was seen sneaking out of her room."

"Did he kill her?"

"No, she died in an accident, technically, but he was responsible for it."

"But no one at the steel mill told me anything about that."

"Either they didn't know, or they didn't think it necessary. It was more than twenty years ago and Tian is paralyzed, more dead than alive."

"No one—I mean her family members—complained to the authorities about it? Others did, like the son of the old professor with broken ribs."

"Now take a look at the boy in the picture," Chen said.

"Yes?"

"He is Jia Ming."

"Jia Ming, the attorney for the housing development case?! You told me to—"

"Yes. The very Jia Ming. The furious luck dogging both Jasmine and Tian."

"Now, supposing Jia is the boy in the picture, the son of Mei, he has a motive," Yu said in shock, trying to grasp the full meaning of the sudden revelation. "But as an attorney, he could have taken his revenge in a different way."

"For some reason, he didn't do so. I think it could be the exact circumstances of her death. It was unbearable for him to relive the nightmare, so he adopted a different approach. He was behind others' complaints, I believe, including the letters sent to the cadre in the city government."

"Including the pictures of his ex-wife, and perhaps more," Yu said, nodding. "The pieces are coming together. The old-fashioned, custom-tailored mandarin dress. And one other thing: 'Red Flag in the Cultural Revolution' was the name of the Worker Rebel organization Tian belonged to. The ad in the newspaper was put in by someone so named. And the location of the first crime too—opposite the music institute. Still, he could have killed Jasmine a long time ago, couldn't he?"

"He could have, but for him, one quick blow might not have been as satisfying as a long series of blows."

"That may be true, but then why kill Jasmine now, all of a sudden?"

"I don't have an answer yet. Only a guess—"

"And why all the other girls?"

"Several possible explanations occur to me, but at the moment, I have only a tentative theory, not even a complete one."

"Fine, your tentative theory."

"Orphaned by his mother's death, Jia grew up with revenge as the one and only purpose in his life. He chose to settle the score in his own way."

"You killed my mother," Yu commented, "I kill your daughter."

"Also, it's more than just his mother's tragic death. Jia was too traumatized to live a normal life—"

"What do you mean?"

"A normal life as a man. He can't have sex with a woman. So Tian has been a curse to Jia and his mother as much as Jia was to Tian and

Jasmine. An attempt to exact revenge similar to the original suffering can be cathartic, but revenge takes its own toll."

"Can you specify for me here, Chief?"

"It's a long story." Chen pulled over the briefcase but didn't open it. "Suffice it to say that the scene of Tian having sex with his mother unmanned him. It was a hellish life for him, as you can imagine. He wanted his foes to suffer just like that too. In his original plan, things would eventually lead to the depraved destruction of Jasmine, but the prospect of her marrying someone and leaving for the United States triggered his killing. He had to complete his revenge. Of course, that's just a scenario. A lot of things in this case may not be accounted for rationally."

"Whatever the correct scenario is, we have to do something now," Yu said. "If it is him, he may strike again—"

There was another knock on the door. This time it was Xia, who came in carrying a covered bamboo basket.

"You and your partner haven't had lunch yet," she said.

The bamboo basket contained several dainty dishes: peeled shrimps fried with green tea leaves, squid braised with pork, cherries of frog legs, and a green vegetable Yu couldn't name. In addition, there were two small bowls of thick noodle soup.

"It's so thoughtful of you, Xia," Chen said.

"Oh, there's something for you," she said, putting a tiny envelope into his hand. "A VIP card. So you will come here again."

Yu wondered what was really in the envelope, having noticed her fingers squeeze Chen's.

"The transparent noodles are not bad, but too short. You have to use a spoon instead," Yu commented after she left the room. "How did you come to know her?"

"Well, what you call transparent noodles are shark fins. A small bowl like this costs five or six hundred Yuan, but you don't have to worry about it," Chen said, putting a spoonful into his mouth. "How did I come to know her? She is one of the last missing links in the long chain."

"What do you mean, Chief?"

"She used to be Jia's girlfriend. They parted because of his impotence."

"So it's not just a guess or scenario, but a fact," Yu said, putting the bowl down on the table. "Now that really fits. He stripped the girls without having sex with them. What are we waiting for? It's Thursday afternoon."

"The trial for the housing development case is tomorrow," Chen said. "At this moment, any rupture could be seen as sabotage against the trial."

"Hold on—tomorrow is the date for the housing development trial?"

"Yes, things are coming to a head. It's a much-publicized case. If we arrest him right now, people will jump to political interpretations, whether or not we have evidence. On the other hand, that may be to our advantage. The trial is very important to him. He, too, must be anxious for it to proceed as scheduled."

"Yes, there is too much of a coincidence in the date. People would make a martyr out of him if we failed to produce convincing evidence," Yu said. "But let me try to detain him one way or another, at least for twenty-four hours, so he won't be able to get away tonight. Officially, I don't know anything about the housing development case. If I make a blunder, it might not be a big deal."

"No. Let me trap him tonight. I have something more than simply an excuse—a trick never tried before, yet worth trying. If it doesn't work, then you can do it your way. After all, I'm not officially responsible for either case."

"What are you talking about, boss?" Yu cut him short. "Whatever you are going to do, you have to count me in."

"Well, you'll have something to do too. Remember the traffic violation trick in the national model case?"

"Yes. You want me to search his car?"

"While I keep him busy this evening, you tow away his car for a complete search. For that, you'll have help from Old Hunter. I've already contacted him."

"But what if I find nothing in the car?"

"If I am not wrong," Chen said, tearing open the small red envelope Xia had given him, "this is the key to the side door of his office. Oh, there's a drawing of the parking spot, too."

"She gave the key to you!" Yu was amazed. Peiqin might be right about Chen's problem with women, but he surely had a way with them too.

"If you don't find anything in the car, drive it to his office building. Security will recognize the car and let you in. According to the drawing, you can park in the corner spot and get in through the side door. No one will see you."

"No one will see me. I see. But what are you going to do with Jia?"

"I'll take him to a restaurant on Henshan Road. Here is the address. Have some plainclothes cops outside, but tell them not to do anything until I give the order."

"But will he agree to meet you? It's already Thursday afternoon. He must have a plan for the night, and for the trial tomorrow."

"Let's find out." Chen reached for his phone, pushing the loudspeaker button for Yu's benefit. "Hello, I want to speak Mr. Jia Ming."

"This is he." It was a voice full of assurance and confidence.

"This is Chief Inspector Chen Cao, of the Shanghai Police Bureau."

"Oh, Chief Inspector Chen. What can I do for you today?" A trace of irony seemed to come into Jia's voice. "About the housing development case, I guess. The trial date is tomorrow. You should have called me earlier."

"No, that's your case, not mine. I need your help for something totally unrelated," Chen said. "I'm writing a story that requires a lot of legal and psychological expertise, and I think you are the ideal consultant for it. So I would like to invite you out to dinner tonight."

There was a short spell of silence on the other end of the line. Jia must have been confounded by the invitation. Yu was no less surprised. It was such an unlikely move.

"I am flattered that you thought of me for your story," Jia said, "but unfortunately, it's not a good night for me. I have to prepare for the trial tomorrow. I don't think I have the time tonight."

"Come on, Mr. Jia. The trial is just a formality, as both you and I know. You don't really have to prepare for it. But for my story, I have to know whether it's a convincing one, or even publishable at all. And there's a deadline for it."

"How about tomorrow evening? My treat. To paraphrase a line from a Tang dynasty poem, 'It's worth tons of gold to meet Chief Inspector Chen.' "

"Let me tell you something, Mr. Jia. It has not been so easy for me to arrange a meeting tonight. Some people are patient, but some people are not so patient."

"A lot of things are possible tonight before such a trial, with the media paying such close attention to it, both domestic and foreign. Some people must be very busy tonight."

They had started throwing out hints at each other, Yu observed, in a context understandable only to themselves.

"Well, talking about media attention, I believe my story will get more. And I also have some wonderful pictures for the story. One of them was published in *China Photography*, entitled 'Mother, Let's Go There.' It was taken in the year of—let me think—oh, sometime in the early sixties."

There was a pause on both ends. The mention of the picture had popped out of nowhere, like a wild card pulled suddenly from under the table. Jia's failure to respond immediately bespoke itself.

"Wonderful pictures," Chen repeated, deliberately, like a card player.

"What pictures do you have? Not just the one in the magazine?"

It could be the first sign of Jia's wavering. Whatever pictures Chen had, Jia should have questioned their relevance. Yu took out a cigarette, tapping it on the coffee table, like an engrossed onlooker at the poker table.

"A professional photographer usually uses rolls of film before choosing one particular picture for publication." Chen didn't give a direct answer. "At dinner, I'll show them to you. It won't take long, and you'll definitely have time for your case tomorrow."

"So you are sure that it won't interfere with the trial tomorrow?"

"Yes, I give you my word."

"Well, where then?"

"I'm still looking for a quiet restaurant, so we can talk undisturbed. My secretary is making calls. Let's meet at Henshan Hotel around five. I have a meeting there this afternoon. There are a number of restaurants in the area."

"I'll see you at the hotel."

Putting down the phone, Chen said to Yu with unconcealed excitement in his voice, "I knew those pictures would be irresistible to him."

Yu knew nothing, except that Chen knew much more. "But why meet at the hotel first instead of the restaurant?"

"He might not come if I told him the name of the restaurant. I set it up this way for the sake of shock to Jia."

Whatever shock Chen had in mind, he started dialing again, the phone still on loudspeaker.

"I have to ask a favor of you, Overseas Chinese Lu."

"Anything you want, buddy."

"Do you know the owner of the Old Mansion on Henshan Road?"

"Yes, Big Beard Fang. I know him."

"Reserve a private room there for me tonight. Make sure that it is one that looks out into the back garden. I have to meet someone there. It's important. A matter of life and death." Chen added, "It will probably be a long talk. I'll pay for everything, overtime and any extra services."

"No problem. If necessary, the restaurant will stay open all night. I'll take care of it."

"Thank you so much. I know I can count on you, Overseas Chinese Lu."

"It is a matter of life and death after all—as you said."

"Also, as a gourmet chef, think of some cruel, slow-tormenting dishes."

"Wow—that sounds more and more exciting. You have the best man for the job, Chief. I'll come up with a banquet of them. Really cruel and cool. I'll be there too."

"I'll see you at the restaurant, then."

"Cruel dishes?" Yu said as Chen turned toward him, wiping his forehead with a towel.

"I was unnerved by a cruel course at a banquet recently. Tonight his nerves need to be rattled as well."

"You were sick?" Yu said, confused again.

"I'm fine. Don't worry about me." Chen said, as if in afterthought, "Peiqin talked to an eating girl last week."

"Yes, I included a cassette tape of it in one of the packages I sent to you."

"I listened to it. She was so clever, making the eating girl tell a story. That gave me the idea of telling a story to Jia."

Yu decided to ask no more questions, looking at the clock on the wall. The chief inspector could be annoyingly mysterious. So far he hadn't said a single word about his disappearance. But Yu had to hurry over to Jia's office and be waiting outside. Yu couldn't afford to let him out of sight from now on, not for one minute.

As Yu picked up his jacket and got ready to leave, he got another surprise. There was another knock on the door, and this time it was White Cloud who came in.

"What can I do for you, Chief?" she said to Chen while flashing a smile at Yu.

"Do you still have the red mandarin dress?" Chen said. "The one we chose at the Old City God's Market."

"Of course. You bought it for me."

"Go to the Old Mansion Restaurant this evening and carry the dress with you. Do you know where it is?"

"Yes. On Henshan Road."

"Good. Can you stay there for the entire evening—or perhaps for all night?"

"Sure, if you want me to—as your little secretary or anything else." She complied without asking questions, like a "little secretary."

"No, for a quite different role. I'll explain it to you there."

"When do you expect me there?"

"Around five. Oh, you'll have to go home for your dress first. Sorry, I just thought of the dress part. Overseas Chinese Lu will be there too."

"Great. So you are like a general in ancient times, making arrangements for a crucial battle in a bathhouse," she commented, also like a "little secretary," before she left.

What herbal pills were in Chen's medical gourd?

"I'll go to a photo studio first," Chen said. "This will be our night."

"You must have figured all this out during the last few days, boss," Yu said, apologetic for his earlier disappointment in Chen. "You got a lot of work done while you were keeping yourself out of sight."

"Well, it was done mostly last night. I didn't sleep a wink, wandering along Henshan Road like a homeless skunk."

Perhaps Yu would never really figure out his boss. But here was the bottom line: for all his eccentricities, Chen was a conscientious cop.

So it was something to be the partner of Chief Inspector Chen, Yu thought, heading out.

TWENTY-NINE

CHEN HADN'T DECIDED EXACTLY what he was going to do that evening.

Coming out of the photo studio, he walked to the restaurant, thinking in the dusk that was enveloping him.

But there was no choice left for him. He tried to reconvince himself. The best course of action would be to leave Jia untouched until after the trial. It wasn't wise to arrest him before it for people would take it as dirty political retaliation by the government. But in the meantime, he had to trap Jia for the night, and the way to do that was so unorthodox that he didn't know how to explain it to Yu. Perhaps it was just like the metaphor made by Comrade Deng Xiaoping about the reform in China: "to waddle across the river by stepping on one stone after another."

There was no delaying the showdown, however, with or without help from the bureau.

Inspector Liao would distance himself from it—not just out of self-protection, but out of long distrust for the chief inspector too.

They had had several head-on collisions. After the death of Hong, Liao hadn't so much as made a single phone call to Chen.

As for Party Secretary Li, Chen didn't want to think about him for the moment. That would be a headache for later.

And then there was Director Zhong in the background too, with all the plots and counterplots being worked out in the Forbidden City.

It was more than likely that Jia wouldn't succumb to his story. An intelligent and experienced attorney, he knew no one could convincingly prove anything against him so long as he didn't budge.

As Chen turned into West Jinling Road, he saw an old woman burning afterworld money in an aluminum basin out on the sidewalk. Shivering in her black cotton-padded clothes, she kept throwing the silver paper ingots into the fire, one by one, murmuring, in a desperate effort to communicate with the dead. It was the night of Dongzhi, he realized.

In the Chinese lunar calendar, Dongzhi comes on the longest night of the year, important in the dialectical movement of the yin and yang system. As yin moves to an extreme position, it turns into the opposite, to yang. So it was conventionally a night for the reunion of the living and the dead.

In Chen's childhood, Dongzhi meant a wonderful meal, except that the dishes on the ancestral offering table had to remain untouched until the candles burned out, a sign that the dead had already enjoyed the meal. He thought again of his mother, who must be burning afterworld money, alone, in her attic room.

But it might not be a coincidence that he was going to meet Jia on Dongzhi night. A sign that things were going to change. *The Way can be told, / but not in an ordinary way.*

He came in sight of the Old Mansion.

A hostess held the door for him respectfully. It was a different girl, one who did not recognize him.

Both Overseas Chinese Lu and White Cloud were already in the lobby. Lu was in his black three-piece suit with a florid tie and a couple of large diamond rings on his fingers, and she, in the red mandarin dress bought at the Old City God's Temple Market.

"The restaurant owner has agreed to cooperate in every way," Lu said exultantly. "He'll let me take care of your room. So I'll stay here and prepare an unbelievable feast for you."

"Thank you, Lu," he said, turning to White Cloud, handing her an envelope. "Thank you so much, White Cloud. Change into a different outfit for now, just like one of the waitresses here. You'll serve in the private room. Of course, you don't have to stay there all the time. Bring in whatever Mr. Lu prepares for the evening. At my signal, come in dressed like the woman in the picture."

"The red mandarin dress," she said, opening the envelope and examining the pictures inside. "Barefoot, the bosom buttons unbuttoned, and the side slits torn?"

"Yes, exactly like that. Go ahead and tear the side slits." Chen added, "I'll buy you another one."

"Old Heaven," Lu exclaimed, stealing a glance at the picture in her hand.

Chen then left and moved on to the hotel, which was only a two- or three-minute walk away.

Standing under the hotel arch, he didn't wait long. In less than five minutes, he saw a white Camry rolling into the driveway. Another car, possibly Yu's, pulled up behind it, at a distance.

Chen strode out and extended his hand to Jia, who was getting out of the car. He was a tall man in his late thirties, wearing a black suit, his face pale and troubled under the dancing neon light.

"Thank you for coming on such short notice, Mr. Jia. My secretary has reserved a room for us at the Old Mansion. It's very close. You have heard of the restaurant, haven't you?"

"The Old Mansion! You've spent some time choosing this restaurant for tonight, Chief Inspector Chen."

It wasn't a direct answer, but it bespoke his awareness that Chen had made a thorough study of his background.

At the gate of the restaurant, the hostess bowed to them gracefully, like a flower blossoming out of the old painting behind her. "Welcome. You'll be at home tonight."

The arrival of several beer girls in the lobby, however, served to highlight the changed times.

"At home," Jia said sarcastically, observing the sashlike streamers flung slantingly across their shoulders. "Tiger Girl, Qingdao Girl, Baiwei Girl, Sakura Girl."

The hostess led them across the hall, into an elegant room—possibly a sunroom in its original design, now converted into a private room for special customers. It overlooked the back garden, which appeared enticingly well kept, even in the depths of winter. The table was set for two, the silverware shining under the crystal chandelier like a lost dream. There was also a dainty silver bell placed on the table. Eight miniature dishes were already set on the lazy susan.

White Cloud came in and poured each of them a cup of tea, opening a menu for them. She wore a sleeveless, backless black dress.

"For our most extraordinary story, Mr. Jia," Chen said, raising the cup.

"A story," Jia said. "Do you really believe it to be more meaningful than your police work?"

"Meaning exists in your thinking. In my college years, as you may not know, poetry was the only thing meaningful for me."

"Well, I'm an attorney, one-track-minded."

"An attorney serves as a good example of this point. What is so meaningful to you in a case may be totally meaningless to others. In our age, meaning depends on an individual perspective."

"It sounds like a lecture, Chief Inspector Chen."

"For me, the story has reached a critical point, a matter of life and death," Chen said. "So I think that the view of the garden may provide a peaceful background."

"You seem to have a reason for everything." Jia's expression didn't show any change as he cast a sidelong glance out to the garden. "It's an honor to be invited by you, whether as a writer or a chief inspector."

"I'm not that hungry yet," Chen said. "Perhaps we might talk a little first."

"Fine with me."

"Great." Chen said, turning to White Cloud, "we'll go with the house specials for two. You may leave now."

"If you need me, ring the silver bell," she said. "I'll be standing outside."

"Now for the story," Chen said, looking at her retreating figure, her black hair streaming over her bare back. "Let me say this first: it is not finished. For several characters in the story, I haven't decided their names yet. In the mysteries I have translated, an unidentified person is conveniently called John Doe. For the sake of convenience, I call my protagonist J."

"Interesting! Like my name in Chinese Pinyin phonetics, it starts with a *J* too."

Jia was keeping his composure well, even beginning to display a suggestion of defiant humor. It was not the time to push through the window paper, Chen calculated. As in tai chi, an experienced player does not have to push all the way. He took the magazine out and set it on the table.

"Well, the story began with the picture," Chen said, opening the magazine with a leisurely movement, "at the moment when the picture was taken."

"Really!" Jia said, raising his voice in spite of himself.

"A story can be told from different perspectives, but it is easier to proceed from a third person, and for us, also in a mixed sense, since part of the story is still going on. What do you think?"

"Whatever you like, you are the narrator. And you majored in literature, I've heard. I wonder how you became a cop."

"Merely circumstance. In the early eighties, college graduates were assigned to their jobs by the state, which you know. Indeed, there was little we could choose for ourselves. In childhood, we all used to dream of a totally different future, didn't we?" Chen said, pointing at the picture. "It was taken in the early sixties. I was probably a couple of years younger than J, the boy in the picture. Look at him, so happy and proud. And he had every reason to be so, in the company of a beautiful mother who cares so much for him, with the Red Scarf streaming in the sunlight, full of hope for his future in the socialist China."

"You're lyrical for a chief inspector. Please go on with your story."

"It happened in a mansion much like this one, with a garden practically the same, except it's spring in the picture. Incidentally, this restaurant used to be a residential house too.

"Now, in the early sixties, the political climate was already changing. Mao started talking about the class struggle and the proletarian dictatorship in preparation for the Cultural Revolution. Still, J had a sheltered childhood. His grandfather, a successful banker before 1949, continued to receive dividends that more than ensured an affluent life for the family. The boy's parents worked at the Shanghai Music Institute, and he was their only child. He was attached to his mother, who was young, beautiful, talented, and equally devoted to him.

"Indeed, she was extraordinary. It was said that a lot of people went to a concert just for a glimpse of her. She kept a sensibly low profile. Still, a photographer discovered her. Not keen on publicity, she agreed to have the picture taken together with her son in the garden. That morning proved to be blissful for J, with her holding his hand affectionately, posing together, and with the photographer raving about the two of them making such a perfect picture. That was the happiest moment in his life. Woven with her radiant smile shining in the sunlight, the moment seemed framed in a golden frame.

"Shortly after the photo session, the Cultural Revolution broke out. J's family suffered disastrous blows—"

His narration was interrupted by the appearance of White Cloud carrying four cold dishes of the house specials on a silver tray.

"Fried sparrow tongues, wine-immersed goose feet, stewed ox eyes, ginger-steamed fish lips," she said. "They are made in accordance to a special menu left in the original mansion."

Lu must have gone out of his way to prepare these "cruel dishes," and he spared no cost. A small dish of sparrow tongues could have cost the lives of hundreds of birds. The fish lips remained slightly red, transparent, as if still alive, gasping for air.

"Incidentally, these dishes remind me of something about the story, something so cruel," Chen said. "Confucius says, 'A gentleman should stay away from killing and cooking in the kitchen.' No wonder."

Jia appeared disturbed, which was the effect expected.

"So the picture represents the happiest moment in J's life, now forever lost," Chen resumed, a crisp sparrow tongue rolling on his tongue. "His grandfather died, his father committed suicide, his mother suffered mortifying mass-criticisms, and he himself turned in a 'black puppy.' They were driven out of the mansion, into an attic room above the garage. Then something happened."

"What?" Jia said, his chopsticks trembling slightly above the ox eye.

"Now I'm coming to a crucial part of the story," Chen said, "for which your opinions will be invaluable. So I'd better read from my draft instead—it'll be more detailed, more vivid."

Chen took out his notebook, in which he had scribbled some words the previous night in the nightclub, and then again early this morning in the small eatery. Sitting across the table, however, Jia wouldn't be able to read the contents. Chen began to improvise, clearing his throat.

"It was because of a counterrevolutionary slogan found on the garden wall of the mansion. J didn't write it, nor did he know anything about it, but 'revolutionary people' suspected him. He was put into so-called isolation interrogation in a back room of the neighborhood committee. All by himself, all day long, he was denied all contact with the outside world, except for interrogations by the neighborhood committee and a stranger surnamed Tian, who came from the Mao Team stationed at the music institute. J had to stay there until he admitted his crime. What supported him through those days was the thought of his mother. He was determined that he would not get her into trouble, that he could not leave her alone. So he would not confess, nor do something in the footsteps of his father. As long as she was outside, waiting for him, the world was still theirs, as in that picture in the garden.

"But it wasn't easy for a little boy. He fell sick. One afternoon, unexpectedly, a neighborhood cadre came into the room and, without any explanation, told him that he could go home.

"He hurried back, anxious to surprise her. He climbed up the staircase soundlessly. Opening the door with his key, he was anticipating a scene of reunion, of rushing into her arms, a scene he had dreamed of hundreds of times in the dark back room.

"To his horror, he saw her kneeling on the bed, stark naked, and a naked man—none other than Tian—entering her from behind, her bare hips rising to meet each of his thrusts, groaning and grunting like animals—

"He shrieked in horror, whirling back down the staircase, lost in a nightmare. For the boy, who had worshiped his mother like the sunshine of his existence, the scene delivered a shattering blow, as if the whole earth had been snatched out from under his feet.

"She jumped up from the bed, unclothed, and ran out after him. He quickened his steps frantically. In his confusion, he might not have heard her stumbling down the staircase, or he might have mistaken it for the sound of the world tumbling behind him. He tore down the stairs, across the garden, and out of the mansion. His instinctive reaction was to run, his mind still full of the bedroom scene, so vivid with her flushed face, her hanging breasts, her body reeking of violent sex, her raven-black pubic hair still dripping wet. . . .

"He didn't look over his shoulder once, as the image of the moment had fixed and transfixed him—of a naked woman, distraught, disheveled, rushing like a demon after him—"

"You don't have to go into all these details," Jia said in a suddenly husky voice, as if reeling under the blows.

"No, those details are important for his psychological development, and for our understanding of it," Chen said. "Now, back to the story. J ran back to the back room of the neighborhood committee, where he broke down and fainted. People were puzzled at his return. In his subconscious, the room was the place where he could still believe in a wonderful world with her waiting for him there. An act of psychological significance, like trying to turn back the clock. And in that back room he wasn't aware of her death that same afternoon.

"When he finally woke up, it was to a changed world. Back in the empty attic, alone, in the company of her picture in a black frame. It was too much for him to stay there. He moved out," Chen said, putting down the notebook. "No need dwelling on that period. I don't have to read sentence by sentence. Suffice it to say that now an orphan, he went through the stages of shock, denial, depression, and anger, struggling with all the emotions twisted and embedded deep inside him. As a Chinese proverb goes, a jade is made out of all the hardships. After the Cultural Revolution, J entered a college and obtained a law degree. At that time, few were interested in such a career, but his choice was motivated by a desire to bring justice for his family, particularly for her. He managed to track down Tian, the Mao Team member.

"But there was no possibility of punishing all of Mao's followers. The government didn't encourage people to rake up their old grievances. Besides, even if he succeeded in bringing Tian to court, it wouldn't be on a homicide charge, and it would probably come at the expense of dragging her memory through the mire again. So J decided to take justice into his own hands. From his perspective, he was justified, because there was no other way. He had Tian punished in what seemed to be a series of misfortunes. He extended the revenge to people related to Tian. To his former wife and to his daughter as well. And like a cat watching a mouse making pathetic efforts to escape, he prolonged the process of their suffering, as resourcefully as the Count of Monte Cristo."

"It reads like the story of Monte Cristo," Jia cut in, "but who would take the story seriously?"

"Well, I actually read it during the Cultural Revolution. The book enjoyed an extraordinary lucky reprint at a time when all other Western novels were banned. Do you know why? Madam Mao made a positive comment about it. In fact, she herself wreaked her revenge on the people who had looked down on her. She took it seriously."

"A white-bone devil," Jia commented, like a responsive audience. "Before she married Mao, she was only a B-movie actress."

"She must have seen her actions as justified too, but let's leave Mao and Madam Mao alone," Chen said, moving his chopsticks to the ox eyes, which appeared to be staring back. "But there is one difference. For Monte Cristo still has his own life, but for J, his life was, and still is, devoid of any other meaning except revenge."

"I would like to make a comment here," Jia said, tearing the fish lips with his chopsticks, though he didn't pick them up. "In your story, he's a successful attorney, and quite well-to-do too. How could there be no life for him?"

"A couple of reasons. The first one came out of his disillusionment with his profession. Working as an attorney, he soon found himself not exactly in a position to fight for justice. As before, major cases were predetermined in the interests of the Party authorities, and then later, in the nineties, they were rigged in the interest of money as well, in a society lost in uncontrollable corruption. While his career as an attorney became a lucrative one, his idealistic passion had long ago proved impractical and irrelevant."

"How can you say that, Chief Inspector Chen? A successful cop, you must have been fighting for justice all these years. Don't tell me you, too, are so disillusioned."

"To be honest, that's the reason I am taking a literature course. The story is part of the effort."

"No wonder I haven't seen your name in the newspapers for a while."

"Oh, you have been following me, Mr. Jia?"

"Well, the newspapers have been full of the serial murder case, and full of cops too. You're a star among them," Jia said, raising his cup in mock admiration, "so I have sort of missed you of late."

"For J, the second reason may be the more important," Chen went on without responding to Jia, who, having recovered from the initial shock, seemed capable of teasing his host. "He is incapable of having sex with women—an aggravated Oedipus complex. Which is the identification of his mother as his sexual object in his unconscious, as you know. In every other aspect, he appears a healthy man, but the memory of the naked, soiled body of his mother falls like a shadow, inevitably, between the present desire and the past disaster. Whatever professional success he achieves, he can't live a normal life. Normal life was forever fixed at that moment of his grasping her hand in the picture. And it's a picture that was broken to pieces at the moment she fell down the stairs. He's worn out from all the endless effort of keeping all this secret and fighting the demon—"

"You sound like a pro, Chief Inspector Chen," Jia said sarcastically. "I didn't know that you studied psychology too."

"I have read one or two books on the subject. You surely know much more, so that's why I would really appreciate your opinion."

There was a light knock on the door again. White Cloud came in carrying a large tray that held a glass pot, a glass bowl of shrimps, and a miniature stove. The shrimps were immersed in a mixed sauce, but under the bowl lid, they still squirmed energetically. Within the stove there was a layer of pebbles, burning red above the charcoal at the bottom. She first poured the pebbles into the pot, and then the shrimps. In a hissing steam, the shrimps were jumping and turning red.

"Like his victims," Chen said, "without understanding their doom, still trying to escape."

"You've spared no pains in preparing this feast, Chief Inspector Chen."

"Now I'm coming to the climax of the story. For this part, I still need to fill in some details here and there, so the story may not read that polished yet.

"Turning, turning, turning, like a caged animal, he found himself dazed against thousands of bars. So he decided to take a most controversial case, at the possible cost of his professional career. In China, an attorney has to stay on good terms with the government; this was a case that could damage the government's image, exposing a number of Party officials who were involved in a housing development scandal, though also a case that could bring justice to a group of poor, helpless people. Whether it was a desperate effort to find some meaning in his life or an attempt at self-destruction, an end—possibly any end—to his straw-man-like existence might not be an unacceptable alternative to his subconscious. Unfortunately, the difficulties of the case added to his tension too.

"Prior to the case, he was already on the verge of breaking down. Despite how he appeared to the outside world, he was torn and tormented by a split personality—an advocator for the new legal system and a lawbreaker in the most devilish way. Not to mention the helpless mess of his personal life.

"And of all a sudden, Jasmine was killed."

"So are you saying, Chief Inspector Chen, that he turns into a killer because of his breakdown under too much stress?"

"The crisis had existed long before the breaking point. But in spite of all the abovementioned factors, there must have been something else that set him off."

"What set him off?" Jia echoed in a show of nonchalance. "Beats me."

"It was panic that his plan for revenge was falling through. He had intended to see Jasmine into depravity, supposing that her complete downfall was just a matter of time. But she then met a man who was going to marry her and take her away to the United States—out of his reach. J had reduced her to a dead-end job in the hotel, where she met the love of her life. What an irony! The prospect of her living happily with a man in the States was more than he could stand. That pushed him over the edge. So he took her out one night.

"It's difficult to say what exactly he did to her—sexually, there was no real penetration or ejaculation. But he strangled her, put her into a dress similar to the one his mother wore in the picture, and dumped her body in front of the music institute—a location symbolically important to him. It was like a sacrifice, a statement, a message to his mother, in revenge for those wronged years, but also a message he could hardly analyze for himself. So many were entangled together in his mind.

"But the story doesn't end there. As the girl breathed her last, he experienced something new and unexpected, something like total freedom. It was all he could do to hold on to the appearance of his old self. Once the demon was out, like the genie out of the bottle, it was beyond his control. Considering the repression or suppression he had suffered all those years, it's understandable to an extent why the murder provided him a release. A satisfaction previously unknown to him. A sort of mental orgasm—I doubt he attacked her sexually in an exact sense. It was a sensation so liberating that it worked like a drug, and he craved the experience."

"Now *that* reads like something from one of your mystery translations, Chief Inspector Chen," Jia commented. "In those books, a madman kills for the thrill of it, like a drug addiction. It's easy to write him off as a psycho. You don't really buy such crap, do you?"

The mahogany clock started striking, as if in echo of his question. Chen looked up. It was eleven. Jia didn't appear so eager to leave. Rather, he was talking in earnest. That didn't bode too badly for Chen.

"Let me go on with my story first, Mr. Jia," Chen said. "So he started his serial murders. It was no longer revenge, but an uncontrollable killing urge. He knew the police were on high alert, so he focused on three-accompanying girls, who were easy to pick up, and also suggestive of depravation. He was totally possessed, not caring that the women weren't related to his revenge, that they were innocent victims."

"Innocent victims," Jia echoed. "Few would so describe them. Of course, a narrator has his own perspective."

"Psychologically, it was also crucial," Chen went on without directly responding to him. "He's not delusional. Most of the time, he may be just like you and me, like ordinary people. So he still has to justify what he does, consciously or subconsciously. In his twisted mind, these girls, because of their possible sex service, deserved such a disgraceful ending."

"You don't have to launch into a lecture in the middle of a narrative. As you have said, it's an age of the individual's perspective."

"From whatever perspective, serial murder is inexcusable. And he knows that too. He's not so willing to see himself as a murderer."

"You are full of brilliantly creative imagination, Chief Inspector Chen," Jia said. "Let us say that you are going to publish the story, but what then? It's not a work of high taste, not becoming a well-known poet like you."

"A story is told for an implied audience, the audience that will be most affected by it. In the present case, that is, of course, J."

"So it's like a message to him? *I know you did it, so you'd better confess*. But what would be J's reaction?" Jia said deliberately. "I can't speak for him, but for me, as a common reader, I will say that the story doesn't hold up. It's conjecture about things that happened over twenty years ago, and all based on a psychological theory totally foreign to Chinese culture. So do you think J will turn himself in? There is no evidence or witness. It's no longer the age of proletarian dictatorship, Comrade Chief Inspector Chen."

"With four victims in the city, evidence will be found. I'm working on it."

"As a cop?"

"I am a cop, but I'm telling a story here—at the moment. Let me ask you a question. What makes a story good?"

"Credibility."

"Credibility comes from vivid and realistic details. Here, except for a couple of paragraphs, I'm only giving you something like an outline. For the final version, I'll include all the details. I don't have to use abstract terms like *Oedipus complex*. I'll simply elaborate on the boy's sexual desire for his mother."

Jia rose abruptly, poured another cup for himself, and drained it in one gulp.

"Well, if you believe your story can sell, that's great. It's none of my business. You've finished, and I think I'd better leave—to prepare for the trial tomorrow."

"No, don't leave in such a hurry, Mr. Jia. Several courses are not served yet. And I need more of your specific opinions."

"I think you are trying to tell a sensational story," Jia said, still standing there, "but people will take it as a sordid fantasy embraced by a cop without a shred of evidence. Otherwise, he wouldn't have resorted to storytelling."

"When they learn that the story is written by a cop, they will pay more attention to it."

"In China, a story from official channels would more likely than not be discredited." Jia added, "In the last analysis, your story has too many holes. No one would take it seriously."

Their talk was once again interrupted by the arrival of White Cloud. This time she was dressed like a country girl, wearing an indigo homespun top, shorts, and a white apron. Her feet were bare. She was serving them a live snake in a glass cage.

At their first meeting in the Dynasty karaoke club, Chen recalled, she had also served a snake platter, but now she was preparing the snake before their eyes.

She proved to be up to the task, swooping the snake out in a quick motion, striking it like a whip on the ground, and slicing open its belly with a sharp knife. With one pull, she took the snake's gall bladder in her hand and put it in a cup of spirits. She must have received professional training.

Still, her bare arms and feet were splashed with snake blood, and the blood spatters looked like peach blossom petals falling on her fan-shaped apron.

"This is for our honored guest," she said, handing Jia a cup that contained the greenish gall in the strong liquor.

The scene produced little effect on Jia, who swallowed the gall in the liquor in one gulp, producing a hundred Yuan bill for her.

"For your service." Jia reseated himself at the table. "He must have gone to great lengths to find you."

"Thank you." She turned to Chen. "How do you want the snake cooked?"

"Whatever way you recommend."

"In Chef Lu's usual style then. Half to fry, half to steam."

"Fine."

She withdrew, treading high-footed on the carpet.

"It's not so convenient to talk in a restaurant," Chen said to Jia. "But you were talking about holes in the story."

"Well, here is one hole," Jia said. "In your story, Jasmine must have had opportunities of getting out from under of his control, yet he managed to keep control of the situation all those years. Why not this time? He's a resourceful attorney; instead of resorting to killing, he could have thwarted her plans some other way."

"He might have tried, but for one reason or another, it didn't work out. But you have a point, Mr. Jia. A good point."

It was obvious that Jia was trying to undermine the whole basis of the story, and Chen welcomed his engagement in the exercise.

"And here is another such hole. If he were so passionately attached to his mother, then why would he strip his victims and dress them in such a way? That kind of attachment is a skeleton in the family closet, to say the least—one he would be anxious to keep hidden."

"A short, simple explanation is that things are twisted in his mind. He loves her, but he can't forgive her for what he considers to be her betrayal. But I have a more elaborate explanation for this psychological peculiarity," Chen said. "I've mentioned the Oedipus complex, in which two aspects are mixed. Secret guilt and sexual desire. For a boy in China during the sixties, the desire part could be more deeply embedded.

"Now, the memory of her most desirable moment, the afternoon when she was wearing that mandarin dress, was juxtaposed with that of another moment, the most horrible memory, that of her having sex with another man. Unforgettable and unforgivable because in his subconscious, he substitutes himself as the one and only lover. So those two moments are fused together like two sides of a coin. That's why he treated his victims as he did—the message was contradictory even to himself."

"I am no expert or critic," Jia said, "but I don't think you can apply a Western theory to China without causing confusion. For me—as a reader—the connection between his mother's death and him subsequently killing appears groundless."

"About the difficulty of applying a Western theory to China, I think you're right. In the original Oedipus story, the woman is no devil. She doesn't know, she's just doing what's commonly expected in her position. It's a tragedy of fate. J's story is different. And it happens to involve something I've been exploring in a literature paper. I've been analyzing several classical love stories in which beautiful and desirable women suddenly turn into monsters, like 'The Story of Yingying' or 'Artisan Cui and His Ghost Wife.' No matter how desirable the woman is in the romantic sense, there's always the other side—which is disastrous to the man with her. Is it something deep in Chinese culture or in the Chinese collective unconscious? It's possible, especially when we take into consideration the institution of arranged marriage. Demonization of women, especially of women involved in sexual love, is therefore understandable. So it's like a twisted Oedipus message with Chinese characteristics."

"Your lecture is profound but beyond me," Jia said. "You should write a book about it."

Chen, too, wondered at his sudden exuberance here, in the company of Jia. Perhaps that was what he had been struggling with in his paper, and it took an unexpected parallel to the case to make him see the light.

"So for J, his peculiar way of killing proved overwhelming, with the force coming not just out of his personal unconscious, but out of the collective one as well."

"I'm not interested in the theory, Chief Inspector Chen. Nor do I think your readers will ever be interested. As long as your story is full of holes, you can't make a case."

Jia evidently believed that Chen had played all his cards and was unable to touch him. In return, Jia was picking up the holes in the story to let Chen know that he thought the cop was merely bluffing in a game at psychological warfare.

Indeed, there were holes that Jia alone could fill, Chen thought, when he was struck by a new idea. Why not let Jia do the job?

Unworkable as the idea seemed, Chen instantly decided to give it a try. After all, Jia might be tempted to tell the story from his perspective—with different emphases and justifications, as long as he could maintain, psychologically, that it was nothing but a story.

"You are a good critic, Mr. Jia. Now, supposing you were the narrator, how could you improve the tale?"

"What do you mean?"

"About the holes in the narrative. Some of my explanations may not be enough to convince you. As the author, I wonder what kind of explanations you as a reader might expect, or might try to provide."

The look he gave Chen made it clear Jia knew it was a trap, and he didn't respond immediately.

"You are one of the best attorneys in the city, Mr. Jia," Chen went on. "Your legal expertise surely makes the difference."

"Which particular holes are you talking about, Chief Inspector Chen?" Jia said, still cautious.

"The red mandarin dress, to begin with. Based on the research done about the material and style, he had the dresses made in the eighties, about ten years before he started killing. Was he already planning it? No, I don't think so. Then why such a large supply of them, and in different sizes too, as if he had anticipated the need to choose for his victims?"

"That defies explanation, doesn't it? But as an audience, I think there may be a scenario more acceptable to me, and also consistent with the rest of the story." Jia paused to take a sip at the wine, as if deep in thought. "Missing his mother, he tried to have the dress in the picture reproduced. It took him quite a while to find the original material—it was long out of production—and to locate the old tailor who had made the original dress. So he decided to use up the material, having several dresses made instead of just one. One of them must be close to the original. He didn't foresee that they would be used years later."

"Excellent, Mr. Jia. He still lives in the moment of having his picture taken with her. It isn't surprising that he tried to hang on to something of it. Something tangible, so he could tell himself that the moment had existed," Chen said, nodding. "Now, about the other hole you pointed out. You were right about his capability of thwarting Jasmine's plans in some other way. Besides, Jasmine wasn't like the other victims. How could she have been willing to go out with a stranger?"

"Well," Jia said. "How can you be so sure that he had planned to kill her? Instead, he might have tried to talk her out of her passion. Then something just happened."

"How, Mr. Jia? How could he try to talk her out of love?"

"I'm not the writer, but he might have found out something about her lover—something suspicious in his business or in his marital status. So he arranged to meet her to discuss it."

"Oh yes, that explains why she would go out with him. Fantastic."

"He wanted her to stop seeing the man. She wouldn't listen. So he threatened her with the possible consequences, like disclosing their secret affair, or accusing her lover of bigamy. During their heated argument, she started shouting and screaming. He put his hand on her mouth to silence her. In a trance, all of a sudden, he saw himself turning into Tian, and doing to her what Tian had done to his mother. An uncanny experience like reincarnation. It was Tian who was attacking her—"

"Except that in the last minute," Chen cut in, "the memory of his mother still unmanned him. He strangled her instead of raping her. That explains the bruises on her legs and arms, and his washing her body afterward. He was a cautious man, worried about evidence left behind in the failed attempt."

"Well, that's your account, Chief Inspector Chen."

"Thank you, Mr. Jia, you have fixed the problem," Chen said, draining his cup. "Just one more hole. He dumped the bodies at public locations. A defiant message, I understand. But the last victim was left in the cemetery. Why? If the grave robber hadn't stumbled upon the body, it could have been left undiscovered for days."

"You aren't familiar with the cemetery, are you?"

"No, I'm not."

"In the fifties, it was the cemetery for the rich. So there is a simple explanation. His family members were buried there."

"But both his parents were cremated, with their ashes disposed of. The cemetery, too, was turned upside down. No immediate members of his family were buried there."

"Well, some families used to buy their cemetery plots far in advance. His grandfather and parents could have purchased their plots like that. So in his imagination, it was still the place where his mother lay in rest—"

Chen's cell phone started ringing at this unlikely hour. Chen picked it up in haste. The call was from Director Zhong.

"Thank God. I've finally found you, Chief Inspector Chen," Zhong said. "The Central Party Committee in Beijing has made a decision about the housing development case."

"Yes?" Chen said, turning to one side. "You mean the outcome of the trial?"

"It's a difficult case, but it's also an opportunity to show our Party's determination to fight corruption. The people see Peng as representative of it. So let's make an example of him."

"I haven't been helpful with the case. I am sorry. But I will be there tomorrow. Those corrupt officials should be punished."

Zhong had no idea that the phone conversation was going on in the presence of Jia.

"Then I'll see you in the courtroom tomorrow," Zhong said.

Turning back at the end of the phone call, Chen said, "Sorry about the interruption, Mr. Jia."

It was then that the mahogany clock started striking, sounding like the bell in the temple.

Twelve o'clock.

THIRTY

IT WAS A NEW day, technically speaking.

Chen finished his wine in a gulp, looking up at the mahogany clock. The restaurant owner had done a good job reviving the money-intoxicating and gold-glittering atmosphere of old Shanghai, paying extra attention to the details. The clock appeared to be a genuine one, having survived all those years, with its brass pendulum burnished like new.

He might have broken the cycle. It was Friday now. There was practically no possibility of Jia's trying to claim another victim before the trial.

So he picked up the silver bell from the table and rang it.

White Cloud came to the table in a floating florid dress, blossoming like a night flower. "Yes?"

"The special course for the night," Chen said. "Don't forget any details."

"All the details," she said, lighting two candles on the table before leaving.

Jia watched, making no comment about Chen's unusual instruction to her.

Chen lit a cigarette. A sudden silence wreathed the room; only the pendulum of the antique clock remained audible.

Suddenly, the lights went out in the room and there was only candlelight, shivering in the draught as the door reopened.

She returned in a red mandarin dress, with its slits badly torn, several of her bosom buttons undone, and her bare feet shining on the carpet.

Jia stood up, his face suddenly bleached of all color, as if having seen a ghost.

In a Song dynasty tale of Judge Bao that Chen had read, a criminal was shocked into confession by the apparition of a murdered woman. At that time, people were still superstitious, groveling before the fury of a ghost.

Jia was making an effort, however, to pull himself together as he slumped back in his seat. He kept his head low, wiping his forehead with a paper napkin, to avoid the sight of her.

She carried a glass pot on top of a gas stove in her hands. As she put the stove on the table, leaning over to light it, her breasts became visible through the opening of her unbuttoned dress.

There was a turtle swimming in the pot above the stove. Unaware of the water temperature that was beginning to change, it looked out at leisure. Another cruel course, that live turtle soup. With the fire turned on low, it could cook for quite a long while.

"A special soup made of chicken and scallop broth," she explained. "The turtle absorbs the essence of the soup in its struggle, so its meat, when cooked, will have an extraordinary flavor. Its movement will also make the soup more delicious."

"A strange course, an unusual restaurant," Jia said, regaining his composure, though still sweating profusely. "Even the waitress is dressed so dramatically."

"This used to be a mansion, and its mistress was a legendary beauty, especially in an elegant red mandarin dress," Chen said. "I wonder if she ever wore the dress like this. Or if she ever served such a cruel course, which is like a murder, with the young girl suffering, struggling against a sense of inevitable doom."

"You're full of associations," Jia said.

In a way, Jia had suffered a similar fate, helpless, doomed in spite of all his struggles. Looking into the glass pot, Chen had a momentary vision of the turtle turning into a boy, holding out his hand against the inevitable. He felt a sick knot churning on his stomach.

But as a cop, Chen was responsible for punishing the man for his crime against Jasmine, against the other girls, and against Hong, his colleague.

"So inhumanly cruel," he muttered in spite of himself, "but I can do the same."

"You are lost in the flight of your imagination, Chief Inspector Chen."

"No, I'm not," Chen said.

He rose, scooped up his trench coat from the clothes tree, and put it over White Cloud's shoulders. Reaching his hand out, he buttoned a breast button for her before he said, "Thank you so much for all your help. You are done here. Keep yourself warm. It's Dongzhi night, and you may want to join your family."

"No." She blushed, looking more attractive than he had ever seen before. "I'll wait outside for you."

After she left the room, he said to Jia, "No, it's not a night for stories, or special courses, you know, Mr. Jia."

"You mean it's Dongzhi night? Yes, I know."

"I want to thank you first for filling in the holes in the red mandarin dress case," Chen said, "but it's time for a showdown between us."

"What? What are you driving at? You said you wanted to tell a story. Perhaps there's something else in the story, that much I guessed, but now it is becoming the red mandarin dress case!"

"We don't need to pretend any longer. You are the protagonist in the story, Mr. Jia, and also the murderer in the red mandarin dress case."

"Now, Chief Inspector Chen. You can write any story you like. But such a fictional accusation—you don't have anything to support it. Not a single shred of evidence, or the shadow of a witness."

"Evidence and witnesses there will be, but they may not even be necessary. The murderer will talk—with or without them."

"How? Now you've crossed the line into fantasy. As a reader, I don't see how you as a cop could do anything to prosecute such a case as described in your story." Jia remained calm, hanging onto his role as a reader. "If a cop were really so confident, he would be writing a case report instead of fiction."

"You keep using the word fiction, Mr. Jia. But there is also nonfiction. Nonfiction sells better in today's market."

"What do you mean by nonfiction?"

"A real story about Mei and her son. Authentic, nostalgic, graphic, and tragic as the Old Mansion itself. A lot of people will be intrigued. For the time being, I may not even have to elaborate on the mandarin dress case aspect. Just some hints here and there. You can bet it would be a sensational bestseller."

"How could you stoop so low, Chief Inspector Chen, for the sake of making a bestseller?"

"It's about the tragedy of the Cultural Revolution, and its tragic repercussions even today. As a cop and a writer, I don't see anything low about it. If it becomes a bestseller, I'll donate the money to a private Cultural Revolution museum in Nanjing."

"A nonfiction writer has to be wary of being sued for slander, Chief Inspector Chen."

"I am a cop, and I write like a cop, basing every detail on evidence. Why should I worry about a lawsuit? It will bring in a lot of publicity, and a large number of reporters too. They are hunting for anything related to the red mandarin dress case. Don't expect them to miss the point in the book. And along with the text, I have something that will grab their interest."

"What cards have you not yet put on the table?"

"Remember the pictures I've told you about on the phone—oh, I'm so sorry. I should have shown them to you earlier," Chen said.

"The old photographer used five or six rolls of film. I'll have all of them published."

He produced the pictures from his briefcase and spread them out on the table.

It must have taken all Jia's willpower not to snatch up the pictures. Instead, he cast a casual glance at them in nonchalance.

"I don't know what pictures you are talking about, but you don't have the right to publish them."

"The photographer's widow has the right. For a poor old woman, the money from the pictures may help a little." Chen helped himself to a spoonful of the snakeskin before he took up the magazine again. "When I first looked at the picture, it reminded me of several lines from *Othello*: 'If it were now to die, / 'Twere now to be most happy; for, I fear, / My soul hath her content so absolute / That not another comfort like to this / Succeeds in unknown fate.' Absurd, you may say, but I came to understand your insistence of putting each victim in a red mandarin dress. You want to remember her at her happiest moment, your happiest as well. To do you justice, you might have wanted those victims to be happy, and beautiful too, for that moment.

"So I'll call attention to the similarities between the pictures and the murder case. In a couple of the pictures, the bosom buttons of her dress appear slightly undone. And in several of them, she walks barefoot. Not to mention the mandarin dress itself. The same material and style. The same craftsmanship too. An authority I have consulted about the mandarin dress will back me up. And what about the background of the original mandarin dress? A private garden. Now except for the last victim, the scenes where the victims were found invariably had something to do with flower and grass. The symbolic correspondence is impressive too. In fact, the flower-bed background for the first victim is only a stone's throw from the music institute."

"You are misleading people—"

"No, I don't think I have to," Chen pressed on. "The pictures of the beautiful hostess of the Ming Mansion—nowadays the celebrated Old Mansion—shall prove more than enough. There are about eighty pictures in all. Apart from using them in my story, I'll sell one or two to a newspaper or a magazine—to achieve the maximum effect. Also, let's think about a title for it. How about 'The First Red Mandarin Dress'? People will surely unearth all the details. Dirty details. Sensational details. Sexual details. It will be a feast for the reporters. And I will do my best to help them."

"We don't have to talk anymore, Chief Inspector Chen. You invited me here for a story of yours, and I listened patiently to the end. Now you are suddenly talking about a felony, accusing me of being the murderer. I don't think I need stay here any longer. As an attorney, I know my rights," Jia said, looking at Chen in the eye. "You can come to me tomorrow with a warrant, either before, during, or after the trial."

"Don't leave, Mr. Jia." Chen made a gesture for his patience. "I haven't even started telling you about another selling point. For romantic suspense, I'll include part of my interview with Xia."

"You contacted Xia!" Jia said. "Yes, to undermine the housing development case, you are capable of anything."

"No. A romantic affair between a successful attorney and a celebrated model is just another selling point for 'The First Red Mandarin Dress.' "

"You are grasping at straws. We parted such a long time ago. It has nothing to do with your fiction or nonfiction."

"People meet, people part, no one can help it. But why part? There are interpretations and interpretations. She may not say a lot, not to begin with, but I bet those paparazzi won't let her get away. Sooner or later, they will be able to dig out more intimate details about your personal life, fitting them to the psychological profile of a sex killer. They will be especially interested to learn about the source of one peculiarity of the murder case: the fact that all the victims were stripped naked but not sexually attacked. It has already riveted the attention of the reporters."

"You are making a serious mistake," Jia retorted, standing up indignantly. "Before you can lock up the attention of the reporters, there may be one or two more victims. I don't think people would be grateful to an irresponsible cop lost in his fantasy of a bestseller."

That was a threat Chen had to take seriously. Like in a Chinese proverb, a desperate dog jumps over the wall. Jia was capable of striking out again, like he did at the Joy Gate, in spite of the police surveillance.

White Cloud came into the room again, still wearing the red mandarin dress.

"Sorry, it's the time to put in the seasoning for the soup." She lifted up the lid and poured in the seasoning. She also changed the spoons and saucers for them before she turned to Jia, smiling an apologetic smile. "Please be seated."

She could have seen or heard what was going on through the frosted glass of the door. The turtle was swirling frantically in the pot, splashing out the soup.

Neither Chen nor Jia said anything in her presence. She left, lightfootedly. The room was silent except for the turtle hissing in the pot.

"It is Dongzhi night tonight. A night for family reunions, for the living and the dead," Chen resumed. "My mother wants me to be with her. But in terms of Confucian priority, a matter for one's country is more important. I have no choice. So I have to make sure there's not another victim in a red mandarin dress, and I'll take responsibility for it."

"Then it's your responsibility," Jia said, "if you hang on to your wild story at the expense of letting the real criminal slip away."

"The real criminal won't slip away. No more than the turtle in the soup. Incidentally, it is a great boost to yin and yang, fantastic ambrosia." Chen took a look into the pot. "Readers will really enjoy the part about sexual desire of the son for the mother. A taste of Oedipus complex as delicious as the soup!"

"Chinese people will not be bamboozled by your psychological terms like *Oedipus complex*."

"Exactly. Our readers will not care so much about the difference between the conscious and unconscious. They will say, 'He's so damn horny for his mother, he can't fuck any other women, and he kills them in a perverted way, achieving an orgasm in the imagined company of his mother.' "

Jia did not speak, gazing into the glass pot, in which the turtle was still moving, but much slower.

"In one of the thrillers I translated," Chen went on, "a serial killer cares little about what happens to himself, for his life is just a long tunnel without a light at the end, but he cares about the one he loves. In our case, what about her? Again, her memories will be dragged through the mire of shame and disgrace—even worse than in the Cultural Revolution—with every detail examined and exaggerated. What will those reporters really do? I have no control over that."

"Now that you have concocted such a story, you will move ahead, regardless of your responsibility as a cop," Jia said, looking up. "But there is something else you have to think about, Chief Inspector Chen. The housing development case is at a critical juncture. Any action against the plaintiff attorney could be seen as a political trick to cover up the government corruption. It is a case closely followed by media."

"I'll let you in on something too, Mr. Jia. About a month ago, somebody in the city government wanted me to look into the housing development case. I said no. Why? I, too, want to have those corrupt officials punished. However, they have kept updating me about the latest developments. A short while ago, I got a phone call about it in this room. A compromise has been reached in Beijing for the trial here, as you may know through your own channels."

"A compromise indeed! So you know how dirty all this is." After a pause Jia resumed, "In this case, not only are a number of high-ranking officials involved, but they are also interlocked in a power struggle at the top. You are no novice with politics, Chief Inspector Chen. If Beijing had really wanted to put an end to the case, I wouldn't have been allowed to move it to the present stage. So do you think they want to see a dramatic twist at this juncture?"

"Yes, I've heard of the power struggle in the Forbidden City," Chen said.

"Under normal circumstances, an attorney has to strive for the best interests of his clients. Some sort of deal is understandable. If the trial was interfered with, however, anything would be possible. Deal or no deal, the case might end up with all those official connections exposed, all the dirty details uncovered. The dogfight in the Forbidden City could come out too. What a political disaster! It is too much of a responsibility for a cop. You have to think about the consequences, Chief Inspector Chen."

"I've thought about them, Mr. Jia. Whatever the scenario, the killing of innocent people has to be stopped. When people read the story together with the pictures, they will judge."

"Some journalists are well-informed. I, too, know quite a few of them. When they learn about the politics behind the scene, do you think they will still be so enthusiastic about the story?"

"Let me assure you, Mr. Jia. I have some other pictures that will lock in their enthusiasm, in spite of all the politics."

"What pictures are you talking about?"

"The pictures taken that fatal afternoon. A neighborhood cop, Comrade Fan, came to the scene. Suspecting foul play, he took pictures—at the foot of the staircase, before the medical people came to throw a blanket over her nude body."

"You mean a picture of her lying on the ground that afternoon—"

"Yes, pictures of her lying there on the hard ground, cold, naked, as you may have imagined the scene in your mind thousands of times."

"But that's impossible—I mean those pictures—Fan never told me about them. No, it's not true. You are bluffing."

For the first time Jia didn't bother to speak like an unrelated outsider, denying his part in the story.

"Let me show you one," Chen said, taking out a picture. "A small one. I'm having all of them developed and enlarged. A number of pictures."

It was a close-up of her lying on the ground, without a shred of clothes covering her body, an image Jia hadn't looked back to see that afternoon, but which must have haunted him all these years.

Grasping the picture in his hand, Jia didn't question its authenticity.

Again the turtle started floundering frantically in the pot, in a desperate effort to climb out, yet slipping off the slippery glass surface, repeatedly. An absurd, doomed effort.

"It is horrible, isn't it?" Chen said, raising his chopsticks toward the pot.

Indeed it was, that scene under Jia's gaze, not to mention the thought of its being examined anew by millions of readers.

Unearthing a buried body was considered the most horrendous act in traditional Chinese culture, but displaying a dead naked body could be far worse. That was why Comrade Fan had withheld the pictures all these years. Still, it was likely Chen's last card.

"If the reporters were to get hold of them, together with those in the garden taken by the old photographer, and with the pictures at the crime scenes of the red mandarin dress case—"

"Stop, Chen. It's so despicably low," Jia struggled to say, his voice hissing, as if coming out of the pot too. "It's beneath you."

"To solve this case, nothing is really beneath a cop," Chen said. "Now, let me say something about 'despicably low.' Something despicably low I initially encountered while working on my literature paper, as I've told you, about the deconstructive turns in classical love stories. As I've discovered, it's at least partially because of the projection of a despicable male fantasy about women and sex—a fantasy archetypal in the unconscious of Chinese culture, or the collective unconscious, which I call the demonization of women in sexual love. It's not a moment for literary theories, I know, but I want to say that you were possessed of it."

He lifted the grass lid from the pot, ladling out the soup into a bowl for Jia, and another bowl for himself.

"When you were locked up in the back room of the neighborhood committee, your mother went to Comrade Fan. She was so worried about you. In desperation, she told him she was willing to do anything for your sake. Comrade Fan understood what she meant, but he declined, saying that Tian alone had the power to release you. To his regret, she took his advice. Not for one moment did Fan doubt that her concern for you was the cause of her being with Tian that afternoon. She did all that for you.

"You might have thought about such a possibility, but you couldn't bring yourself to accept it. In that dark back room, what sustained you was the unsullied memory of her taking your hand in the garden—'Mother, Let's Go There.' The world had collapsed around you, but she's still yours, yours alone.

"So upon your return, the scene at home was absolutely appalling, an immaculate goddess shattering into a shameless slut in the arms of your persecutor. An unforgivable betrayal of you in your mind. It pushed you over the edge.

"But you're wrong. According to my investigation, Tian had gone out of his way to assign himself to the institute. Like others, he probably watched her perform and became smitten with passion. The Cultural Revolution gave him the opportunity. He worked his way into the Mao Team to be close to her, but she tried her best to avoid his company in spite of his power. If she had succumbed to his pressure, he wouldn't have come to your neighborhood and led the joint investigation. He didn't get his opportunity until you got into trouble. She loved you more than anything else in the world. More than herself. Even under the circumstances, it was to Fan, not to Tian, that she first turned to for help.

"Now, it was only a couple of days later that you were unexpectedly released. If there was anything going on between them, it must have happened during that short period—for your sake. How desperate and painful it must have been for her to give herself to Tian, you can imagine."

"But she didn't have to. Nothing would have happened to—" Jia was unable to finish the sentence.

"Nothing would have happened to you? I doubt it. In those years, you could have been sentenced to death for such a 'political crime.' An old man was executed in the People's Square, I remember, for the crime of carrying a Mao statue on his back by wrapping a rope around its neck. *It's symbolic of hanging Chairman Mao*, the revolutionary people ruled. She knew better. She understood that Tian was capable of anything.

"But you kept imagining it from your perspective alone, never hers. The scene of her writhing and wallowing under another man crushed you. You were incapable of thinking rationally. That's how you finally stumbled on an outlet in the serial killings, an outlet for both love and hate—"

Again he was interrupted by the shrill ringing of the cell phone. This time, it was Detective Yu.

"Sorry, I have to take another phone call," Chen said, rising to move to the window. The garden outside was entirely submerged in darkness.

"Nothing in the car, Chief," Yu said. "I studied the parking spot. It's true that he could move from there and in through the side door without being seen by others. The front is hidden from view by a grove of bamboo. So I got in with the key."

"Anything in his office?"

"It's a large suite. In addition to the office, a reception room, and a study, there is also a small bedroom with a bathroom."

"That's not surprising. According to Xia, he often stays overnight there."

"But that made it possible for him to wash Jasmine's body."

"That's true."

"I haven't seen any bloodstains or anything like that there. The carpet must have been cleaned of late. It still has a detergent smell, and I saw a steam vacuum cleaner. But that's something. In those high-end offices, cleaning is usually taken care of by professional people. Why would an attorney have done the cleaning himself?"

"That's a good question."

"Then I noticed something else, Chief. The color of the carpet. It matched that of the fiber stuck on the foot of the third victim."

"Yes, he brought her in without being seen, but he failed to notice a fiber stuck between her toes."

"But any result from the fiber test won't be available until tomorrow morning. Besides, fiber evidence may not be conclusive for a homicide case."

"It will be enough to hold him for a couple of days, and to justify a full search." Chen added, "At least he can't do anything during that period."

"Should we start tonight?"

"Don't rush. Wait for my call."

When Chen moved back to the table, the turtle was turned over with its belly upward, a ghastly white belly, motionless in the pot.

"As a cop," Jia said, "you have written a compassionate story."

Chen wondered whether it was a sarcastic comment or if it indicated a subtle change on the part of Jia.

"Compassionate characterization is essential for any story," Chen said, facing Jia. "You may think no one understands you, informed by all the absurdities and atrocities you suffered during the Cultural Revolution. You are like software written by all these events, and as a result, you can operate only one way; it's beyond your own comprehension. But let me say that I tried to understand. Learning about all of your experiences, I kept saying to myself: *but for luck, what happened to Jia could have happened to me.*

"I couldn't help identifying with the boy in the picture. How happy, holding her hand like the world, how unprepared for the disaster already drawing close to the horizon. I tried to think from your perspective. I felt like I was going mad.

"In the days after her death, whenever your neighbors looked at you, you thought they were seeing her running out after you in her nakedness. It was like a demon eating you up. So you moved out, tried to leave everything behind you. Later you even changed your name. But as in a poem by Su Dongpo, you were 'trying not to think, but forgetting not.'

"Cop or not, I don't want to condemn you for taking justice into your own hands—at least in the beginning, delivering those relentless blows to Tian. What a blinding force revenge can be, I understand. I, too, was beside myself over the death of a young colleague of mine. In the Jing'an temple, I swore I would do anything to avenge her.

"But things were getting out of your control. You discovered your sexual problem, the cause of which you must have guessed. As a celebrated attorney, known for politically controversial cases, it was too much of a risk for you to go to a shrink. So you had to hang on, like you did in the black back room of the neighborhood committee, except then you still had hope, with her waiting outside for you.

"Then you collapsed with the crisis over Jasmine. Panic turned you into a killer. When you put your hand on her, the repressions or suppressions built up in you all these years erupted. As for the rest, I don't think I need to repeat any more.

"I've come here not as a judge, Mr. Jia, but I can't help being a cop. That's why I have made special arrangements, hoping we may be able to find a different way—"

"A different way? What difference will it make to a man who, as you've said, sees no light at the end of the tunnel?" Jia said slowly, deliberately. "Now what do you want?"

"What I want, as a cop, is for the killing of innocent people to stop."

"Well, if tomorrow's trial goes on as scheduled. If nothing happens to it—"

"That's what I hope. Nothing happens to it," Chen said, glancing at his watch. "Nothing out of the way."

"Oh, it's Friday already. You don't have to worry about it," Jia said, as if reading his thoughts. "And those pictures have to be destroyed."

"They will be destroyed. All the negatives too. I give you my word on it."

"Are you still going to write your story, Chief Inspector Chen?"

"No, not as long as I can help it; not that nonfiction, I mean."

"Not that nonfiction, and not that particularly or personally, but so far, there isn't a single good book written about the Cultural Revolution."

"I know," Chen said. "What a shame."

"And I have a personal request."

"A personal request?"

"Don't quit. This may sound condescending coming from me. But you are quite unusual for a cop, and you know stories are not simply black and white. Not too many cops share your understanding."

"Thank you for telling me that, Mr. Jia."

"Thank you for having told me the story, Chief Inspector Chen. Now, it's time for me to go back and prepare for the trial tomorrow—today," Jia said, rising. "After the trial, you may do whatever you want, and I'll try my best to comply."

When they walked out, they saw White Cloud still staying outside. She must have fallen asleep while waiting there, curled up on the leather sofa, her mandarin dress rumpled, and her feet bare. She wore nothing under the dress.

Jia recoiled. It was the weird hour of the night when fantasies suddenly flipped like bats, and a vision like that startled him.

THIRTY-ONE

THE TRIAL FOR THE West-Nine-Block housing development case appeared to be proceeding smoothly Friday morning.

It was in the court of Jin'an district, in which the West-Nine-Block was located. The building was a Catholic school in the twenties. In the early sixties, it was turned into a Children's Palace, Chen remembered. Only two or three stained-glass windows in the courtroom reminded people of the earlier days.

According to the inside information Chen had just received, Peng was to be sentenced to three years. An assuring message to the people in a time when the gap between rich and poor was widening like an approaching earthquake. It was in the best interest of the government to bring the case to a quick and smooth conclusion, highlighting Peng's punishment for his improper use of the state fund and for his gross negligence in the business operation.

Such a conclusion appeared to be understandable, and supposedly acceptable, to most of the public. It wouldn't touch the corrupt Party officials involved behind the scene. At the same time, it would be an opportunity for the government to show its solidarity with the ordinary people. With the state fund reassigned for residential relocation and possibly some other remedies, the residents would be satisfied, and some of them might also choose to move back into the area. As for Peng, he should know better than to protest about three years. With his connections, he would be able to get out in a couple of months.

For all Chen knew, a sort of compromise had been reached between Shanghai and Beijing, and between Jia and the city government. Such a result seemed to be the best Jia could possibly strive for on the residents' behalf.

So the trial was nothing but a formality.

Present in the courtroom was a group of residents from the West-Nine-Block. And an equally large group of journalists, including foreign ones, who must have obtained special permission from the city government to attend.

Jia sat among the residents in the front row, still in his black suit, his face taut and pale in the light of the courtroom.

Chen seated himself near the back of the room, rubbing his temples, which were throbbing like they did during acupuncture. He hadn't even had time to change his clothes after the night-long dinner in the Old Mansion. It might be just as well. Wearing a pair of amber-tinted glasses, he hoped that people wouldn't recognize him.

Yu sat beside him, also in plainclothes. He had likewise had a sleepless night. Having obtained the result of the fiber test earlier in the morning, Yu hurried through all the routine preparations for immediate action, but Chen wanted him to wait.

At Chen's suggestion, the cops stationed both inside and outside were also in plainclothes. He insisted they take no action until his order. Yu hadn't told them anything about the other case—the red mandarin dress case.

And Chen did not know what to tell Yu, either. He decided not to worry about it until after the trial was over. Even then, the practicability of immediate action was still debatable. It would be too dramatic.

A possible storm of speculation about political retaliation wouldn't be in the interest of the Party authorities.

He started wondering whether he should have come here. In spite of the horrendous crimes, he couldn't help seeing things from Jia's perspective. Justice could be a matter of perspectives, as discussed last night. Whatever wrongs Jia had suffered during the Cultural Revolution, however, the killing of the innocent today must be stopped.

Gang Hua, the defense lawyer for Peng, was standing up for closing statement.

Gang argued for leniency on the grounds of Peng's cooperation with the government, his return of the fund, and his ignorance of his employees' improper behavior. Specifically, Gang made a point about what he defined as the "historical circumstances."

"It's true that Peng got the land at a lower price and planned to sell the apartments at a higher one. But the value of real estate in Shanghai has since jumped. It didn't happen in his project alone. As for the regulation about the land use, it wasn't specified at the beginning of the development, nor was the compensation for the residents exactly formulated—there was only a range from the lower to the higher end. To ensure the timely completion of the project, Peng hired a relocation company, whose employees, perhaps too eager to do the job, pushed along without Peng's knowledge.

"We understand that some of the residents in the West-Nine-Block suffered inconvenience, even injuries, but in the long run, the housing project is in the interest of the people. How can people live any longer like in the play *Seventy-Two Families Living in a Two-Storied Shikumen House*? China has been making tremendous progress in a reform unprecedented in its history. It's new to everybody. So I am not saying that Peng shouldn't be responsible for his mistakes in the housing development project, but we have to take into consideration the historical circumstances. In a larger perspective, you have to say that Peng's business activity contributed to the prosperity of the city. If you go to the West-Nine-Block next year, you will see rows upon rows of new buildings."

It was a clever speech, saying what could be said to represent Peng as a businessman who made mistakes, some of them well-meant mistakes, because of "historical circumstances." The speech didn't say, of course, what couldn't be said: that all the corrupt practices occurred through Peng's connections with Party officials.

The audience's reaction seemed to be mixed. Some were whispering among themselves. Not all the residents were interested in anything more than the monetary compensation due them.

Then Jia rose, moving up to the front to make his closing statement.

As he took the stand, he let his glance sweep across the courtroom before acknowledging Chen in the back. Jia nodded almost imperceptibly, taking a drink from a plastic water bottle. He appeared to be full of confidence and conviction, his face taking on a strange transparency, as if another self were breaking out for the occasion.

But it could be a trick of the morning light streaming through the stained-glass windows, Chen thought.

"From my learned colleague's speech, the result of the trial seems to be already predictable," Jia started. "Peng will be punished for his business mismanagement, and the residents in the West-Nine-Block will receive compensation for their relocation. So I am visualizing the newspaper headlines, 'The City Government Upholds Justice for the People.' Or, 'Number One Shanghai Big Buck Peng Punished.' So that's the end of it. Some will be satisfied with the compensation due them, some will move into the new apartment complex, some will talk about the downfall of the upstart, and some will be pleased to hear the last of the case.

"Still, such a 'satisfactory' outcome of the trial may leave a lot of things unexplained.

"How could Peng, a dumpling peddler along Chapu Road five or six years ago, have turned into Number One Shanghai Big Buck? He's no magician, with no golden touch, but as we know, he has his connections. How could Peng have secured the land for the housing development project when there were several more qualified developers bidding for it? He has only his elementary school education, but as we know, he has his connections. How could Peng, having obtained the state approval for 'housing improvement,' have denied the original residents the right to move back? That was black and white in his business proposal, but as we know, he has his connections. How could Peng have secured government authorization to force out the residents 'by whatever means necessary'? In spite of residential relocation being new to the city, people understood 'whatever means necessary,' but as we know, he has his connections.

"And what connections?

"Perhaps I don't even have to elaborate on these here. Whatever I may say, some people will declare they are irrelevant.

"After all, anything can be explained and justified. Someone, who happens to be sitting in the courtroom, has told me that this is an age of perspectives. Things depend on the perspective, but he forgot to add that whoever is in power gains control of the perspective."

It was an unmistakable reference to him, Chen knew. He rubbed his temple again.

"Now, my learned colleague has made one specific point," Jia went on. "Historical circumstances. It is not a term invented by him. We have read and heard about it, especially with regard to the Cultural Revolution, haven't we?"

"Shall we stop him?" Yu whispered to Chen. "Where is his speech leading?"

"No, I don't think he will go too far. Let's wait just a little longer."

The trial was an unprecedented one in that a Chinese attorney was emerging triumphant, single-handedly against all the Party officials standing behind Peng. Jia deserved his moment, which might be the last cold comfort to his battered ego. Besides, Chen didn't want the trial to be affected by the red mandarin dress case. They were two separate cases, unrelated.

"We aren't here, of course, to talk about all the social and political issues involved," Jia continued. "But what about the people who have suffered loss, irrecoverable losses, in the case? Zhang Pei's parents, for instance, who died because of the horrible conditions after being driven out of their home. Or Lang Tianping, for another, who became paralyzed after being savagely beaten in the 'demolishing campaign' by the relocation company. Or Li Guoqing, whose girlfriend left him when he was detained for his skirmish with those Triad thugs hired by Peng.

"So do you think that singling out Peng for his mismanaged business operation brings justice?"

The question disturbed Chen. Where was Jia going with all this? It could be a show Jia was putting on. Anticorruption was a popular stance in the nineties. His speech would surely win him another round of applause. But would that be so important to him?

Was Jia pushing for a disastrous end for everyone? Such an option would be understandable for a man in his position. Possibly the last revenge, and the ultimate revenge too. In his mind, the Party authorities should have been held responsible for the Cultural Revolution. And for the government that was so anxious to wrap up this case with minimum political impact, having all the corrupt officials exposed, all the dirty politics examined, as Jia had threatened last night, would be disastrous.

In the interest of the Party, Chen should try to stop Jia, but it was a closing statement, saying what should be said. So what should Chief Inspector Chen do?

But Chen somehow didn't believe Jia was really going to head far down that route. It was in their tacit understanding last night that nothing too dramatic would happen at the trial. Nothing like that from either side. If Jia wanted Chen to abide by his bargain, he himself had to do so. After all, Chen had those pictures. Jia must have taken the presence of Chen as a warning. Anything out of the way on Jia's part would have its consequences. It involved her, not just him. Jia knew, Chen knew.

It was like having swallowed a fly for the chief inspector to think that he had actually helped with the housing development case.

And Chen couldn't get rid of a sense of foreboding. Something wasn't moving in the right direction. But what could that possibly be? He found his mind momentarily blank as he tried to put himself in Jia's position.

Jia must be thinking about what would happen after the trial. There was no exit for him; Jia knew that better than anybody else.

How would Jia be able to face his fall? One of the most successful attorneys in the city, talking about justice all the time, and he had to face a trial in which he himself would be tried and convicted as a criminal, with a full confession signed in his own hand. Whatever defense he might be able to put up for himself, the result would be the same. Death, plus the worst humiliation imaginable.

What's more, it could still involve her. Even without those pictures, people would eventually dig out some details, if not all of them.

But what different outcome could Jia strive for?

Chen stopped himself from thinking further along those lines. *You are no fish, so how can you know the way it thinks?* Jia's sick. That was what Chen had told Yu, and that was true.

All of a sudden, Jia started coughing, his chest heaving in a spasm, a stained pallor masking his face.

"Are you okay?" the judge said, anxious for Jia to finish his speech.

"I am fine. Just an old problem," Jia said.

The judge hesitated before asking Jia to continue. It was too important a trial to be interrupted.

"So I'm tempted to tell you a story in parallel to our case," Jia resumed with renewed strength in his voice. "A story about what happened to a little boy during the Cultural Revolution. He lost his father, lost his home, and then in a most humiliating way, lost his mother he deeply loved. The experience totally traumatized him, like a small tree so stunted that it survives only in a twisted way. As the proverb says, 'With a whole nest overturned, not a single egg will be left unbroken, though the crack may not be so visible.' He grew up with the one and only purpose of seeking justice for his family. But when the Cultural Revolution was declared a well-meant mistake by Mao, a mistake understandable in the historical circumstances—he realized that it was a hopeless mission. So finally he decided to take justice into his own hands.

"Of course, people are supposed to uphold justice not in their own hands but in a courtroom like this, we all understand. However, is there a court that prosecutes the crimes of the Cultural Revolution? Or will there ever be one?"

Chen was about to stand up when Jia was seized with another outbreak of coughing, more violent this time, his face first purple, then ghastly white. His body began reeling.

The courtroom was sunk deeply in silence.

"Don't worry. Just an old problem," Jia managed to say before collapsing to the floor.

"Is he sick?" Yu said with something more than astonishment on his face.

Chen shook his head. It was not an old problem, he suspected. Something terribly wrong. A possibility presented itself, which he might have been trying to ignore until this moment.

There could be a way out for Jia, though not that quick, not here, not like that.

Jia was already turning and making a weak gesture at Chen.

Chen stood up, taking off his glasses. He produced his badge to the court security officers who were rushing over to his side.

A reporter in the room recognized him, exclaiming, "Chief Inspector Chen Cao!"

Chen strode over and leaned down toward the fallen man. People were stunned, transfixed. The judge stepped down, hesitating for a moment before retreating into the judge's room, and the two court clerks followed suit, as if fleeing hastily from a crime scene. No one else moved. Jia started speaking with a voice audible only to the chief inspector.

"The end is coming more quickly than I expected, but it does not matter whether I finish my closing statement or not. What cannot be said has to pass over in silence," Jia said, taking an envelope out of his suit pocket. "Here are checks for those families. I have endorsed them. You have to do me the favor of giving them away."

"To their families?" Chen said, taking over the envelope.

"I have kept my word—the best I can, Chief Inspector Chen. So will you, I know."

"Yes, I will. But—"

"Thank you," Jia said with a waxy smile. "I really appreciate what you have been doing for me, believe me."

Chen believed him, who must have been sick and tired of his struggling all these years, in vain, in loneliness. Chen gave him an opportunity finally to put an end to it.

"She loves me. I know. She does all that for me," Jia said with a strange glow in his face. "You've brought back the world to me. Thank you, Chen."

Chen grasped his hand that was getting cold.

"You like poetry," Jia said again. "There's a poem in the envelope too. You may keep it as a token of my gratitude."

Closing his eyes, Jia spoke no more. After all, what else could he say?

Chen produced his cell phone to call for an ambulance. Perhaps already too late. It was nothing but a pose he had to strike, for the sake of the audience.

Like the trial, also a pose, though necessary on the part of the government.

There was something wrong with the phone. No signal. It might be just as well. Chen almost felt relieved.

But others must have called. The medical people rushed in, pushing him off the man lying on the floor.

"I have kept my word—" Chen stood up, thinking of Jia's last words as the medical people started carrying Jia out on a stretcher.

Chen didn't have to open the envelope. The checks should be more than enough as evidence, with Jia's signature, along with the fact that the checks were given to him in the presence of so many people in the courtroom.

Yu was moving over to his side, with a phone in his hand. He must have spoken to the other cops, holding them back. It was a bizarre ending. Not only to the trial of the housing development case, but for the red mandarin dress case too.

The courtroom was now like a pot of boiling water spilling all over.

Chen handed the envelope to Yu, who opened it and started examining the checks with utter disbelief on his face.

"The families of the red mandarin dress victims, including Hong's," Yu said in an awe-stricken voice. "He must have kept a record of them. With the checks signed, it's like a full confession. We will now be able to close the case."

Chen didn't speak up at once. As for how to conclude the case, he still had no idea.

"His own signature," Yu said emphatically. "It should be conclusive."

"Yes, I think so."

"Any comment, Comrade Chief Inspector Chen?" the reporter who had recognized Chen shouted at him across the crowd, trying to elbow his way through the restraining line kept by the courtroom security officers.

"Are you in charge of the case?" Another reporter joined in, pushing forward with several others.

The courtroom was now in total confusion, as if the pot of boiling water was not merely spilling all over, but the pot itself toppled upside down.

Some of the reporters followed the stretcher out. Chen and Yu were left standing alone where Jia had fallen several minutes ago. Other reporters were shifting their attention to the two cops, their cameras flashing.

Chen dragged Yu into the judge's room, which was empty, closing the door after them. Almost immediately there came loud knocking on the door, presumably by the reporters who had broken through the restraining line, but then the knocking stopped. Whoever was there at the door must have been dragged away by security.

"Did you anticipate such an ending, Chief?" Yu asked, straight to the point.

"No," Chen said, taken aback by the sharpness of the question from his longtime partner. "Not exactly. Not like that."

But it was a turn he could have foreseen. And he should have. Facing trial for the serial murder, with the skeletons of his family history exposed, with the picture of his mother's naked body unearthed, with the stories of her sex scandal examined, with the Oedipus complex exaggerated, Chen himself wouldn't have hesitated to choose the same exit Jia had.

Chen wondered about Yu's reaction. Yu might suspect Chen of having acted out of his bookish consideration, of giving in to the last appeal made by Jia last night. After all, giving a fatally wounded soldier the opportunity to kill himself was a time-honored tradition. It wasn't exactly true, but Yu didn't know everything.

"Those checks are a large sum," Yu said sarcastically, "but of course the money was meaningless to him."

Jia's last act also spoke for his contrition. Jia wasn't a delusional killer, as Chen had maintained. In his heart, Jia knew what he did was wrong. The checks made a large sum—Jia's way of offering compensation, though as he had just said in his statement, *that's no justice.*

But there was something more to it. It pleaded for leniency in a message the chief inspector alone could grasp. It was as if he was pushing the credit over to Chen, though it was a huge gamble for Jia. If Chen were not a man of his word, he could take credit for solving the murder case and still go ahead with the publication of his sensational story with all those pictures. Jia's signed checks implied his unconditional trust in Chen. As in an ancient battle, a dying soldier gave himself to his opponent whom he respected.

Chen, knowing he was trapped, broke out in a cold sweat.

"Jia didn't have to do that," Chen said finally. "He's too clever not to know the consequences. These checks sealed his crime. He did it as a way of appealing to me: he kept his word to cooperate, so now it's up to me to keep my word."

"What word?" Yu said. "So you'll start writing the case report, Chief?"

Indeed, what about the case report?

The Party authorities would push for an explanation. As a Party member police officer, he could hardly say no. And the story would have to come out.

But they might not necessarily push for the whole truth, Chen thought, if he started throwing off hints about the Cultural Revolution background of the case. If he handled it right, they probably wouldn't care too much about the mumbling vagueness of his explanation. Digging out the skeletons of history could backfire. So he might be able to trick the government into hushing up the details. Perhaps he could come up with a different story instead, acceptable to everyone. A blurred statement about the death of the serial murderer, hopefully, without even revealing his identity or the real cause. After all, whatever story he might produce, some people wouldn't believe it. As long as there were no new victims in a red mandarin dress, the storm would blow over.

"He got away too easily," Yu pushed on, obviously upset by Chen's silence. "Four victims, including Hong."

Yu hadn't yet gotten over the death of Hong. Chen understood. But again, Yu didn't know that much about Jia—or what was behind Jia's case. Chen didn't know if he would be able to explain everything to his partner.

But about the case report, he thought he had a better idea. Why not push the credit to Yu, a great partner who was standing by him, as always, in spite of the unanswered questions?

"But was there any other way out for him?" Chen said. "So, now you have to wrap up the case."

"Me?"

"Yes, it was you that checked out the background of Jasmine, discovered the name in the short list of the Joy Gate, drew my attention to the part about Tian's bad luck, and checked Tian's history as a Mao member. Not to mention Peiqin's contribution to the investigation. Her studies of the dress as an image inspired me."

"That's not true, Chief. I may have explored along those lines, but

I came up with nothing. It was on your order that I rechecked into Tian's past—"

"We don't have to argue about that. As a matter of fact, you are doing me a favor. What explanation can I possibly give to the others?"

"What do you mean?"

"Inspector Liao will be thoroughly pissed off. He must believe that I've played hide-and-seek with the bureau and worked on the case behind his back. So will Party Secretary Li. Li might well be paranoid with political suspicion."

"But the fact is," Yu said, "you brought the first serial murder case in Shanghai to conclusion."

"I gave my word to Jia. There is something in the case that I won't tell. Not just about him. Now that he's dead, having fulfilled his part of the deal, my lips are sealed. You might understand, Yu, but not the others."

He wondered whether Yu understood, but Yu wouldn't press for an explanation. Not too hard, anyway. They were friends, not just partners.

"But what can I tell them—the revenge of the Cultural Revolution? It's out of the question."

"Well, he committed the crimes in a fit of temporary insanity. Afterwards he was filled with remorse. So he signed those checks for the victims' families."

"But why should he have given the checks to you?"

"I happened to be looking into the housing development case and I met him. And that's true. Director Zhong of the Legal Reform Committee can support my statement. Even last night, Zhong called me about the housing development case, and Jia was in my presence at the time."

"Will they accept your story?"

"I don't know, but the government won't be interested in a scenario such as 'the revenge of the Cultural Revolution,' as you've just called it. Hopefully they won't push for details. In fact, the less said, the better for everyone. We may pull it off." He added, "It's possible that the

Party authorities may not even want to reveal the identity of the serial murderer. He's killed. Period."

"Aren't they anxious to punish Jia—as an example to troublemakers for the government?"

"But not punished like that, nor at the present moment. It could backfire. Of course, that's just my guess—"

The phone rang, unusually loud in the empty judge's room. It was Professor Bian, who had had an appointment with Chen that morning. The student had failed to show up.

"I know you're busy, but your paper is quite original. I would like to know how it is progressing."

"I'll turn the paper in on time," Chen said. "I'm just having some problems with the conclusion."

"It's difficult to push for a generalization in a term paper," Bian said. "Your topic is a big one. If you can succeed in finding a shared tendency among a number of stories, it should be good enough. In the future, you may try to develop that into your MA thesis."

Chen wondered if he would be able to do so. He didn't say anything immediately in response. And he was beginning to have second thoughts about his studies.

After all, it was just one more interpretation of the old texts. People would go on reading, with or without his interpretation. There might have been a sort of anti-love discourse of arranged marriage in Chinese culture, or something like an archetype of the Chinese femme fatale. But so what? Each story was different, each author was different. Like in criminal cases, a cop can hardly apply a general theory to all of them.

"Yes, I'll think about it, Professor Bian. And I've got some new ideas about 'thirsty illness.' "

So his literature project might still be something to think about in the future, he told himself. For now, he had to shelve it.

For him, there might be something more immediate, more relevant. As in the murder case: people might not feel satisfied by a partial conclusion, but at least the killing of innocent people had come to an end.

As a cop, he didn't have to worry too much about making his point, unlike a paper. What the point of the case was, he didn't even know—

"You aren't going on with your Chinese literature program, are you?" Yu queried, breaking into his thoughts.

"No, I don't think so. You don't have to worry about that," Chen said. "But I still have to finish this paper. You may not believe it, but this paper has really helped."

Yu seemed relieved and handed back the envelope. "Oh, there's a piece of paper in the envelope."

"A poem."

"For you to publish?"

Chen took out that piece of paper and started reading.

Mother, I have tried to make the far-off echo
yield a clue to what is happening to me;
in the old mansion people come and go,
seeing only what they want to see.

The recall of the red mandarin dress
wears me out, flashing in the flowers,
your bare feet, your soft hand: the stress
of memory strips me of waking hours.

But we are flattened, framed in the zoom
of one moment, click, and cloud and rain
approaching fast, a doomful gloom
scurries across the horizon again,

Oh that is all I know, all I see.
Mother, you drink the cup for me.

"There's no cup in the picture," Yu said in bewilderment.

Chen wasn't sure if the last image about the cup came from *Hamlet*, in which the queen drinks the poison for her son. In his college years, he had read a Freudian interpretation of it. He vaguely remembered.

"It's about Hamlet and his mother," Chen said, deciding not to explain any more. "There are more things in heaven and earth than in a case report."

"I'm damned," Yu said, shaking his head like a rattle drum.